ADIRONDACK
DETECTIVE
III

JOHN H. BRIANT

Chalet Publishing
P.O. Box 1154
Old Forge, New York

ADIRONDACK DETECTIVE III

Library of Congress Control Number 99-96188

ISBN 0-9648327-4-7

VOLUME III

Graphics and book design
by
John Mahaffy

Printed in the United States of America

Chalet Publishing
P.O. Box 1154
Old Forge, New York 13420-1154

Dedication

To my wife, Margaret, who has always
been there for me.

ACKNOWLEDGEMENT

I wish to extend thanks to John D. Mahaffy for his outstanding talent. He has been there since the beginning of my written words to the ADIRONDACK SERIES of Adirondack Detective, JASON BLACK.

Thank you, Lydia L. Maltzan for your computer skills and professionalism.

And, to my wife, Margaret, thank you for your patience, understanding, insight and honest opinion, and stoking the wood stove.

To my many fans and readers, I thank you for making it all possible.

FOREWORD

Residing inside the Blue Line of the great Adirondack Mountains is the answer to my boyhood dreams of long ago. My father was a logger and harvester of pulpwood during the late 1920's and early 1930's. It was during this period of time, that as a young child, I was introduced to this magnificent gift of Mother Nature.

Riding on the wood roads, experiencing the campfires and listening to the storytelling Adirondackers, ignited my curiosity. The whine of the large saws cutting up the four-foot-lengths of pulpwood and the trucking of the pulp to Lyons Falls furthered my curiosity. It was this combination of activity in my youthful years that I experienced and as the years passed the urge to reside in this beautiful place grew stronger.

It was during my years of service in the North Country that fully persuaded me to the notion of moving inside the Blue Line of the Adirondack Park. My dreams were fulfilled in 1979 when my wife and I purchased our first camp.

Although we had spent many days visiting the park and hiking the mountains, woods, and paddling the lakes, it was becoming a part of the community that made the effort worthwhile.

This is where JASON BLACK, Private Investigator, strives to ferret out the criminal element that occasionally drifts into our beloved region. In this third novel BLACK becomes involved in the investigation of such matters that tend to disrupt our mountain communities, fraught with suspense and danger.

BLACK knows the territory and he knows the people.

Other books by the Author
One Cop's Story: A Life Remembered 1995
Adirondack Detective 2000
Adirondack Detective Returns 2002

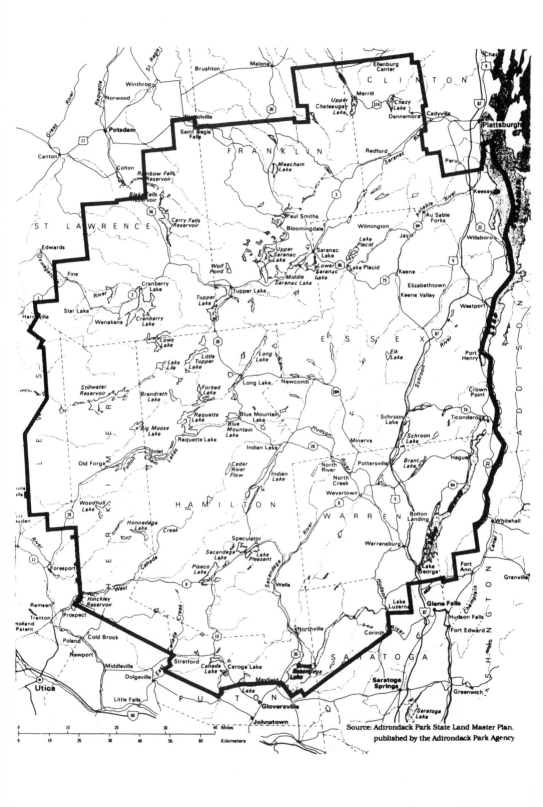

Source: Adirondack Park State Land Master Plan.
published by the Adirondack Park Agency

CHAPTER ONE

Looking out my window was like being at a museum of art. The late autumn leaves were still brilliant, displaying the yellows and browns with a smattering of reds streaking the tree line in our region. The squirrels and chippies were gathering their wares for the coming winter season. The storage areas for their booty were deep in the heart of fallen trees or the tall standing trees that formed a natural border to my property. It was quiet outside. Ruben was in his dog run looking to the edge of the forest.

Patty would be serving her customers at John's Diner. Tonight we would celebrate my fiftieth birthday on Mother Earth. Half a century of experiences, from birth to the early stages of childhood, swooping into adolescence and onward into middle age – and now I would almost be considered a senior citizen. My pecuniary riches were, you might say, almost non-existent, but I was rich in many ways. I had been blessed when Patty came into my life and my promise to myself to never marry again was broken. I looked down at my gold wedding band and thought again that my wife was an angel. I wished that my mother and father were alive so they could join us tonight. Patty's parents had lost their life in a tragic accident in Kentucky. Our hearts had both been wounded with the losses that we experienced. But we knew that both of our parents would be there in spirit for our

1

celebration.

I was going on my sixth year as a private investigator licensed by the State of New York. My main source of income in the investigation field consisted of the numerous bad-check cases that I worked on, either in collecting on them, or aiding in the pursuit of a criminal action or a civil remedy. Some of the bad-check passers that came my way were hard working folks who took that chance of writing a check when there were no funds in their accounts to cover it. The vast number of people involved in this type of activity were cordial when approached. The majority of them made the bad checks good and continued on with their lives. Some, however—the repeaters—would branch out to other regions in the Adirondack Park and pass these worthless instruments, only to be caught up with at a later date.

Working in the investigative field as a private detective, aka private investigator, especially in the Adirondack Park region, is somewhat different than pursuing the profession in a heavily populated urban area, where there is more activity. But I have enough work to keep me busy and still allow me to enjoy the beauty and the people of the region inside the Blue Line of the park. It is well instilled in my heart that the Adirondack Mountains of New York State are a very special place to pass the years of one's life.

Witnessing the interaction of the people who reside here, some born in the mountains and others moving into the region, I conclude to myself that these folks have a special love for the area, as I do. As far as I'm concerned, we're all on a level playing field, no matter what our possessions might consist of. The love of the mountains, the forests, and the animals that reside here are the common interest to the majority of us. A paradise for all who have that keen concern.

Where I challenge this notion is when people come into our region with various schemes that lean toward criminal activity against our citizenry. That, I do not like. With my past training as an investigator with the elite BCI of the State Police, it doesn't take long to evaluate the intentions of these potential scoundrels. It is my firm belief that our folks here in the mountains possess a good sense of judgment and can usually tell the difference between good and evildoers. But once in a while, like anything else, one of these types can slip by.

The recent case of one Bernard Draper, from Phoenix, Arizona, is a good example of the evildoers. Supposedly he was a man of distinction, well educated, holding a solid position in the Phoenix community, a person of financial success, supporting many organizations with substantial funds. A pillar of society with political connections in numerous levels of government. The majority of us know the type, though: under the colorful façade lies the dark side. His evil existence here in the mountains was short-lived, thanks to the efforts of my friend Lieutenant Jack Doyle of the BCI. The tentacles of the Draper organization were endeavoring to scar our region with a smuggling operation using a jewelry business as a front. Draper came here to avoid the Phoenix authorities, who were investigating him and his organization for a triple homicide of three Mexican Nationals who worked as day laborers.

It was through the diligent efforts of Major Frank Temple, Captain Roy Garrison, Lieutenant Jack Doyle of the Troopers, Chief of Police Todd Wilson of the Town of Webb PD, Captain Jay Silverstein, of the Phoenix PD, Sergeant Joseph Kelly, of the RCMP, of Cornwall, several undercover operatives, three citizens of our region, and my contributions to the case, along with others, that brought it to a successful conclusion.

The status of the case is pending as Draper is surrounded by twenty attorneys in Phoenix as they prepare for a trial in criminal court. I'm hopeful that we here in the Adirondack region will not be visited by the likes of him in the future, but we have no control over who comes and goes.

About an hour ago I let Ruben outside for his morning run into the woods at the end of our property, when a flock of Canada Geese heading south set down close by. Ruben hesitated for a moment, looked around at them, and then continued into the forest. I knew he would return shortly.

The sun was sending rays of light through the trees and the air seemed crisp. We had not had our first frost, but it wouldn't be long before we'd wake up some morning and find that the frost had humbled our plant life as we approached the winter season. I stood in the doorway enthralled by the natural beauty of these magnificent mountains known as the Adirondacks. I had made the right choice in selecting the place I wanted to live out my life. The Town of Webb region was ingrained in my heart and spirit. Again I looked down at my left hand and the gold wedding band that was recently placed there by my lovely wife, Patty.

Our wedding had taken place at the Big Moose Chapel. Patty had looked so beautiful. And our honeymoon that followed a jubilant reception at the Edge Water propelled us into the state of matrimony. This was the third ring that had been placed on my finger, and hopefully the last. Both Patty and I were aware that the path of life was filled with both positive and negative times. We had discussed many issues prior to the wedding and had agreed to work at and enjoy the years ahead of us.

I slipped on a jacket as I spotted Ruben, our retired state police K-9, coming out of the woods. I went outside and met him at the dog-run gate. I opened the gate and he bounded into the fenced-in area. I followed him and checked his food and water dishes. He came over to me and rubbed his head against my right pant leg. I petted him as he looked past me to view the skein of geese taking off into the cool air.

CHAPTER TWO

Patty pulled into the yard with her Jeep at about six o'clock. She tooted the horn and I rushed over to see what she wanted.

"Jason, help me carry in the two boxes in the back. Lila made up a special dish for us. Happy birthday, honey!" she said with open arms. We embraced and kissed. Ruben let out a bark.

I opened up the rear gate, and took out the two boxes, and carried them into the house. I wanted to ask Patty what Lila had sent in the two boxes, but refrained so as to avoid corrupting any surprise that she had in store. I set them on the counter-top.

"Honey, why don't you go outside and take Ruben for a short walk while I prepare dinner? It won't be long," she insisted.

"Okay, sweetheart, I will." I eagerly wondered what was in the two boxes.

Ruben and I took our path toward the forest. A dusting of snow lay on the level, but our worn trail made it possible for us to access the woods. There were no chippies to be found frolicking in the brush piles. Ruben's nose was close to the ground. We walked around in the woods for about ten minutes and then slowly headed back toward the log home. Ruben heeled closely behind me. I wondered what tasty surprise Patty had in store for me. I truly didn't feel fifty years old, but the numbers don't lie.

I put Ruben back into the dog run and then swept the porch off with our big broom. Patty came to the door and gaily motioned for me to come inside. I noticed that she was wearing her new apron with flowers sewn into the fabric–daisies mixed with some violets. I opened the door and removed my coat.

"Honey, wash up for dinner. It is just about ready," she shouted warmly.

"Okay, babe."

I went into the bathroom, washed my hands, and combed my hair. When I returned to our dining area I spotted four candles burning brightly and flickering. It was indeed an extra special occasion.

"Jason, sit right down. Tonight I'm going to wait on you entirely, my dear. Happy birthday, precious."

I didn't ask her what we were having. I simply unfolded my napkin, placed it on my lap and waited with pleasure as my beautiful wife served a large platter of lemon chicken filets and roasted potatoes. She then offered cabbage salad and a bowl of slivered carrots topped with butter. She had even prepared a lemon cheese sauce. The aroma of the chicken teased my taste buds. I even insisted on getting up to seat Patty, and then returned to my chair. Soft music from an FM station was playing in the background.

I looked lovingly across the table. "Patty, you didn't have to fuss so much for my birthday. But I appreciate it and I thank you for it. This chicken is a wonderful gift from Lila. I can taste the lemon, and the meat is so tender. The roasted potatoes are great, too. I sense a hint of garlic in the seasoning."

"You're a clever investigator, Sherlock," she said with a chuckle.

"I love everything, and that includes you, my darling."

After our dinner, I helped Patty clear the table. As she made some green tea she told me to go back to the table because she had a treat for me. I went back and sat down. All four candles still flickered. She then asked me to close my eyes.

It seemed like an eternity until I heard her say, "Open your eyes, Jason."

I did, and in front of me was a chocolate cake gleaming with chocolate fudge frosting. Ten candles burned brightly near the edge of the three-layer circular cake. The frosting looked irresistible. It brought back memories of my early childhood when my mother would turn the frosting bowl over to me to lick.

Patty handed me the knife to cut the cake. I served her a small piece and then cut one for myself, which just about fit the dessert plate. The steaming green tea waited in front of my plate. Two small dishes of vanilla ice cream topped off the treat. The combination tasted delicious, especially with the thick fudge frosting. This birthday celebration I would surely remember. After dinner, Patty presented me with a colorfully wrapped box. It contained a brown leather wallet that had a secret compartment. When I lifted it, I spotted two crisp new fifty-dollar bills. Immediately I took the bills out of the wallet and gave them to Patty.

"Honey, this is yours. I won't debate it for one minute. You work too hard and I want you to take this and buy yourself a new outfit," I said adamantly.

Her face playfully lost its smile. "Jason, that is for you."

"No debate, sweetheart. This is yours." She reluctantly folded the bills and placed it temporarily into her apron pocket.

"I love your apron, Patty," I said as I reached over and playfully untied it.

She smiled and put her head down admiring the colorful flowers on it and laughingly retied her apron strings.

I thanked Patty for the delicious dinner, and the brown leather wallet, but most of all for the wonderful life she had given me. We cleaned the kitchen together. She washed the dishes and I dried them. After dinner, we both retired to the living room and listened to music, while she did some knitting.

The clock was striking 10:00 when we decided to retire for the night. Ruben was curled up on his air mattress as I checked the doors. Both Patty and I were exhausted, mostly from the day's excitement. We went to bed, embraced, and fell off to sleep in each other's arms.

Patty awakened at about 5:00 a.m. She showered, dressed, kissed me goodbye, and left for John's Diner. She had to be there to open by 6:00 a.m. She didn't want to quit her job. We had talked about it. Pursuing investigation work in the Adirondacks as a private detective wasn't conducive to a large paycheck. And I knew that Patty loved her job at John's, so I wouldn't ask her to quit and stay at home.

I secured Ruben's dog run and went back inside. The geese were well on their way south to wherever they would land again. This was the time of year that geese are seen making their migratory journey south.

The cold water felt refreshing as I splashed it against my skin. I was now fully alert and ready to face the day. The clean towel felt good on my face. I went to the kitchen, scrambled a couple of eggs, made two slices of whole wheat toast, took the grape jelly from the refrigerator, and poured hot boiling water over my green-tea bag. I wished that Patty were here, but I knew she was busy at work. I peered out the window as I ate my breakfast. One cannot fully imagine or feel the peace and tranquility offered by these mountains unless you're there to experience it firsthand.

After my second cup of tea, I cleared the table and did the few dishes that were in the sink. I looked out the window as I dried the last plate and noted that Ruben's ears were straight up. He appeared to be watching an animal near the edge of the wood line. I placed the plate in the cupboard and went to the door, grabbing my binoculars from the peg inside my office. I adjusted the lens to my eyes and looked through the powerful instrument. I was amazed at the size of the raccoon as it slowly moved toward the white oak tree. I continued to keep the binoculars on this furry inhabitant of our region. His claws dug into the great oak as he ascended upward to a large limb. He was the biggest coon I had ever seen. Ruben continued his vigil. I was surprised that he did not bark. I was just about to place the binoculars back on the peg near my office door when the telephone rang.

"Hello," I said.

"Hi, honey," Patty answered.

"How is your morning going, sweetheart?" I queried.

"We've been busy, Jason. By the way, Wilt Chambers was in for breakfast and wanted me to tell you that he has some more two-man saws for your collection. I just wanted to see what my honey was up to. Did you have breakfast?"

"Yes, I scrambled a couple of eggs and toasted the last of Lila's homemade bread. Of course I covered it with grape jelly. It was delicious," I added.

"Okay, hon. I was thinking about you. Did you enjoy your birthday celebration?"

"I certainly did, dearest. Thanks again."

"Have to run now, see you tonight."

"See you, Mrs. Black," I answered, as I cradled the phone.

There had been some changes made since our wedding day. We had decided to operate on a budget, keeping separate envelopes for utilities, groceries, car repairs, and miscellaneous expenses. Patty was delegated the responsibility of placing the money in each of these envelopes. This budget program was just on a trial basis and we would decide in a month or two if we would adopt the system permanently or deposit our incomes in a joint-checking account. The private investigation account was separate from my monthly retirement check.

We also had made changes to our bedroom, adding some furniture that Patty had in storage after her divorce. With new curtains, and a matching new bedspread, my former plain bachelor bedroom had been transformed into a cozy, warm boudoir right out of a magazine.

She had been through so much with her first husband, Kenneth Olson. I knew that Town of Webb Police Chief, Todd Wilson, was very happy that Kenneth was not residing in this region. I still remembered the traumatic events that took place when Kenneth was intoxicated and how abusive he had been to Patty during their marriage.

Before I went to my office to type some bad-check case reports, I ran the vacuum cleaner and dusted throughout the log home. I noticed that Patty had placed salmon filets in the refrigerator from the freezer. We tried to have salmon at least once a week. After cleaning and dusting, I placed the cleaner in the utility room and went outside to let Ruben do a run into the woods. The retired K-9, still in good shape, bounded toward the large white oak tree. He smelled around the base of the tree and looked upward, but hesitated only a moment before disappearing into the woods. As I felt the late-autumn coolness against my face I realized that it wouldn't be long before all the leaves would be on the ground and Old Man Winter would be around the corner.

Ruben dashed from the woods directly head on toward me. I knew that he wanted to play, so I took a few minutes with him and then put him into the run. His water and food were ample for the rest of the day.

While Patty and I had spent a week on our honeymoon, the bad-check cases had built up in the mailbox. I went into my office and began the long tedious job of writing letters to the writers of these instruments known as checks, which were stamped, "Insufficient Funds." I had had good luck by corresponding with the check-writers and getting results without a criminal action. I found that diplomacy went a long way in recovering the funds, without the merchant or banking institution having to furnish witnesses to the court system.

I had just placed the last stamp on the envelopes when the telephone rang.

"Hello," I said.

"Good morning, Jason." I recognized Dale Rush's voice immediately.

"Dale, glad you called. I haven't heard from you in a couple of weeks. I did hear you overhead one day with the Stinson."

"I can explain, but not now. I just called to tell you that a group of us are getting together at the Hard Times Cafe this evening about 7:30 p.m., and I thought you and Patty might like to join us. I've got some great news to share with you both." Dale sounded excited.

"I'll check with Patty when she comes home, and if she isn't too tired we'll be there."

"That's great. I can't tell you the news, but you'll find out tonight. So long for now." I heard the click in my ear as Dale hung up the telephone.

My mind was racing. I was curious as to the surprise that Dale had in store for us. Dale was normally quite a laid-back individual, who enjoyed working on his vintage Stinson Reliant seaplane. It wasn't like him to sound excited, especially on the telephone. I considered him a good friend and we'd find out tonight what was going on in Dale's world.

I placed all my outgoing mail in my briefcase and then straightened up my cluttered desk. I was just about to leave the house when Jack Falsey pulled into the yard with his maroon work van. I looked over at Ruben in the dog run and saw his ears on alert. Jack pulled up next to my Bronco and shut his motor off. He then climbed out of the van.

"Good morning, Jason." Jack was wearing a big smile.

"Hello, Jack. It's good to see you." I reached over to shake his hand.

"The water-pump part came in and I thought before I got too busy today I would just take a minute or two and replace that old part." Jack went to the rear of the van, opened the back doors, and took out a small box containing the new part.

"Sure, Jack. I was just heading to the post office, but there's no hurry. By the way, would you care for a cup of coffee?" We entered the house.

"No, thanks. I've got to meet a customer at Big Moose. I'll take a rain check, though."

Jack Falsey was a hard worker and most efficient. He replaced the worn pump part in a few minutes. I watched him as he worked.

"I liked the old style pump better than the newer version. They were easier to work on." Jack finished the exchange of parts and washed his hands at our laundry sink.

"Yes, Jack. Some of the older appliances we've used over the years seemed to last longer than these new versions."

"Oh, yeah! I believe they call it progress," he said, nodding his head in agreement.

"Thank you for stopping. How much do I owe you?" I asked, pulling out my wallet.

"You already paid for that part the last time I was here," he said as he dried his hands.

"Thanks again, Jack. I appreciate your stopping."

"Say hello to Patty for me."

"I will. Have a good day." I watched Jack get back into his van and head for the main highway. I noted that Ruben didn't bark once while Jack was here.

I locked the log home and climbed into the Bronco. Doctor Don, our mechanic in town, had replaced the hand choke that he had installed. I hit the ignition switch and pulled the choke out just a little. My trusty Bronco started. I let it warm up before I left the driveway. The miles on the vehicle were in excess of 160,000. Someday I should consider trading it in, but not today.

The traffic into Old Forge was light. Winter would be here soon and our mountain town would be a busy place with thousands of snowmobilers. Local businesses were already starting to gear up for the forthcoming season. As soon as the first snow fell, the sport of snowmobiling would begin with the colorful array of vehicles being operated by people of all ages wearing their bright suits and donning their helmets. I continued through the Hamlet of Old Forge to our busy post office. I shut the Bronco's ignition to the off position and the engine coughed. The timing didn't seem to be right. Doctor Don would be getting a phone call from me.

When I opened my post office box, two letters slid out and onto the floor. "The Breakshire Lodge" was printed on the long white business envelope. I placed all the mail in my briefcase. As I exited the post office I held the door open for an elderly gentleman with a cane. He looked up at me and said, "thank you." I walked around to where the Bronco was parked and climbed in.

Before I started the engine, I opened up the letter from the Breakshire Lodge. It was from the owner, Tom Huston, and contained two bad checks. The letter was brief: "Jason, when you have a few minutes to spare could you look into the two enclosed insufficient fund checks and stop by to see me when you're in Lake Placid." It was signed "Sincerely, Tom Huston."

Tom Huston and I had become good friends and he had approached me on several occasions to consider employment with his lodge. He had offered Patty a position of head hostess. Patty and I had discussed it several times, weighing the pros and cons. Huston had even offered us lodging. We had told Tom that it was a generous proposition, but we had declined for now, telling him we would reconsider if we ever decided to make a move. He assured us that as long as he owned and operated the Breakshire Lodge, the offer would always be there for us to consider.

I turned the ignition switch and the Bronco's engine responded with a muffled backfire. The engine finally purred like a kitten and I headed for home. Along the way I toyed with the idea of purchasing two used snowmobiles for Patty and me. I had heard that there were two vintage Ski-Doos for sale on the South Shore Road, but I would have to discuss it with Patty before making the purchase. I had been told by Doctor Don, my mechanic, that the machines had been well cared for and that he would be willing to look them over before Patty and I transacted any deal.

When I pulled up to our log home I could see Ruben's head peering out from his doghouse. His ears went straight up, but he didn't make a move to get up from his prone position. I shut the Bronco off. There was no sputtering or cough from the engine. I grabbed the briefcase of mail and set it on the porch step, then made my way over to Ruben's dog run. When he saw me approaching he got up and came toward me. I opened the gate, the big K-9 jumped up on me, and I gave him a big hug. I could tell that he wanted to play. We wrestled around for a few minutes. This retired state police K-9 was strong and hard to handle when he played rough. I placed the mail inside the door of the log home, and Ruben and I headed for the woods.

The trail inside the forest was well known to us. Ruben sniffed under some dried wood brush piles, and one chippie took off for the nearest tree. In a way, we sort of missed seeing the huge black bear that seemed to be stalking us during the summer and part of autumn. But we were glad that the State Econ people had darted the bear and moved him to a non-residential region deep in the forest. Normally, before the closure of the landfills, the bears had frequented the Inlet and Old Forge dumps. This had been a favorite attraction for the many visitors to the region. At dusk, tourists could be seen watching the bears foraging the area for food to satisfy their hunger, which seemed to be always voracious.

Ruben and I finished our hike and I returned him to the dog run. I patted him on the head, closed the gate, and went into my log home. I couldn't help but wonder what surprise Dale Rush had in store for us that evening. I called Patty at the diner and told her about Dale's call. She was puzzled by the call and told me that she hadn't heard any rumors at the diner. She advised me that she hadn't seen Dale in about two weeks and was perplexed by his absence, as he had always stopped to have coffee at least once each day.

I had just finished filing some bad-check reports in my oak three-drawer file cabinet when I heard the Jeep pull in next to the Bronco. Ruben let out two short sharp barks and I knew that my sweet Patty had arrived home. I looked out the window and watched her as she went to the dog run to see Ruben. I went to the side door to wait for her. The minute Ruben saw me, he turned his back on us both, exhibiting his jealous streak. Patty had a big smile on her beautiful face and I quickly embraced her when she entered our home. Her lips met mine and they felt warm and inviting. She closed her eyes and we held each other closely.

"I bet you're tired, honey," I said.

"A little, dear. It was a hectic day as we had two buses pull in around noon. The last of the leaf-peepers, I guess!"

"I didn't think that we had that many leaves left on the trees with those strong winds that came in last week," I added.

"Jason, are we going to have dinner at the Hard Times?" she asked curiously. "Oh! I took the salmon out for dinner tonight."

"Honey, I don't know. Dale really didn't say." I thought a moment. "If they don't have refreshments, we can always order something from the menu. We can have the salmon tomorrow night."

I went over to the stove, put the teakettle on the burner, lit the gas, and took out two green tea bags from the canister. We did this two or three times each week when Patty came home from work. We loved to sit at the kitchen table across from each other and discuss our new marriage and the daily gossip from around town as we sipped our tea. Prior to our marriage we had been a topic of the news circuit, but now that had settled down. We felt secure and comfortable in Old Forge.

The town survives on hard work and people devoted to their vocation in life. Each business and organization, newspapers, people of the trades, plumbers, carpenters, electricians, teachers, real estate folks, restaurants, car washes, gift shops, contractors, loggers, police, fire department personnel, hardware stores, bookstores, and many more that make up our community give their all every day to welcome our visitors to the region. A tourist town of eloquence, where lasting friendships are molded, where history is remembered and researched and where new history is born. We cannot forget our wonderful library and schools and the most important medical center and devoted medical staff. It is everybody networking together all the time that keeps our town attractive and desirable.

CHAPTER THREE

Patty and I arrived at the Hard Times around 7:25 p.m. There were a number of cars and trucks in the adjacent parking areas. When we entered the bar area and started into the dining room, we noticed a head table set up and people standing together sipping their drinks. Dale Rush came over to greet us. He was wearing a blue blazer with an open-collar white-shirt and blue trousers, and he had a warm smile.

"Patty and Jason, I'm so glad you came." Dale embraced Patty and then shook my hand.

I quickly glanced around and spotted Wilt Chambers, Jack Falsey, John and Lila from John's Diner, and several others I recognized. We exchanged greetings. Patty and I found a table near the head table and sat down. Dale was welcoming other guests who had just arrived. There were several faces that I didn't recognize. I don't know why I turned around, but my sixth sense alerted me. There standing in the doorway was Tom Huston from the Breakshire Lodge in Lake Placid. Tom spotted Patty and me and rushed over to see us, giving Patty a warm embrace.

"Tom, what a pleasant surprise!" I said. I knew that Dale liked Tom Huston, as Tom had arranged flights for Dale into remote areas, taking fishermen into the backcountry.

"Patty and Jason, I'm so happy to see you both. Dale told me that you'd be here. He called me and asked me to come

17

down to Eagle Bay. Nice restaurant, my first time here," Tom remarked, pulling out a chair next to Patty and me.

"Tom, I just received your letter today with those checks."

"I could have brought them down with me, but I had mailed them a few days ago. Anyway, Jason, take your time on them, there's no hurry." Tom smiled warmly. "By the way, Jason. Have you any idea what's going on?"

"Not at all. Dale's been really quiet about this," I responded. I was just as puzzled as he was.

We continued to talk with Tom as more people crowded in. Dale kept busy greeting them and escorted people to their seats. I noticed a most attractive woman sitting near the head table. She was wearing a navy blue suit. Her auburn-colored hair was pulled back into a bun. She wore a pleasant smile. I had never seen her before. I wondered if this were Dale's surprise.

Tom and Patty were deeply engrossed in conversation. I looked around the room and noticed that Jack Falsey and Wilt were sitting together. I waved at several people who recognized Patty and me. Three waitresses were bringing drink orders to the various tables. There was a table set up with trays of sandwiches and salads, and a large punch bowl sat on another table. A few people were already helping themselves to the punch and sandwiches and returning to their tables. Lisa, the owner, was checking to see if everything were satisfactory.

The chatter and laughter of the crowd was interrupted when Dale tapped on his wineglass to get their attention. The room became quiet.

"Ladies and gentlemen. I want to thank you all for coming on such short notice. The majority of you folks have been my friends for years. We don't socialize very much, but over the years we have all at one time or another have been together as a group at various functions. Tonight is one of those functions. It has a two-fold purpose. I don't know if you've heard, but Kirby has sold his boat marina, which has a new owner. In a few minutes it will be my pleasure to introduce you to the new owner. The second purpose of this get-together is probably the most important in my life. I'm not following the proper protocol, but something has changed in my life. I'm announcing my engagement to this beautiful lady on my right."

Everybody looked surprised as Dale announced his engagement. Whistles and applause drowned out the soft music playing in the bar area.

Dale continued, "Ladies and gentlemen, I would like you to meet the new owner of Kirby's Marina, Ms. Evelyn O'Brien from Bar Harbor, Maine. Evelyn, would you kindly say a few words?"

Evelyn O'Brien stood and looked at Dale. She was visibly blushing. She appeared to be in her mid-forties, attractive and very self-assured. Everyone eagerly waited for her to speak. I was completely surprised. I'm certain that everyone else was, too.

"Hi, folks. This was completely Dale's idea of meeting here this evening. I am honored to come to this wonderful community that I've heard so much about as the new owner of Kirby's Marina. Everything has been finalized and we'll be open for business for a few more weeks, then we'll close until spring after the watercraft are placed in winter storage. I come from a Maine fishing family and worked with my father until he passed away. My older brother is now running the family business. Dale has told me so much about his friends and the area and, as I said before, I'm honored to be here in this beautiful place. I'm looking forward to meeting you individually. Thank you for coming tonight."

Everyone stood and applauded. I heard several people shout out welcomes.

Dale stood again and tapped his glass.

"Folks, I don't believe I mentioned the fact that Evelyn is a pilot and owns a Gull-winged Stinson-seaplane about the same vintage as mine. She is planning an open house at the Marina next spring at the beginning of the boating season. Some of you may be wondering how long we have known each other. All I can say is that it has been over five years. Many of you know that I'm not a public speaker and stay to myself a great deal of the time, but you all know now that those two-week vacation flights to Maine for the past few years wasn't just to go fishing in the Atlantic Ocean." Dale turned toward Evelyn and embraced her, and then placed a diamond ring on her finger.

Everyone shouted congratulations to Dale and Evelyn. Guests began rushing to the head table to meet our new member of the community. We were all happy for Dale Rush.

Although there was no mention of a wedding day, knowing Dale as I do, it probably wouldn't be too soon. We talked further with Tom Huston, introducing him to several of our locals. We congratulated Dale and Evelyn before we left for home. It had been a surprising and delightful evening. As we left the café, we complimented Lisa, the owner, for her efforts.

We went directly home after the party at the Hard Times. As we pulled into our driveway, a white tail flashed in the beam of our headlights. We just missed getting struck in the passenger side of the Bronco. The deer population was heavy, and while driving a motor vehicle one had to observe care and caution. We exited the Bronco, went to the dog run, and let Ruben out for his routine run toward the woods. Patty gave me a kiss and went inside. I waited for Ruben and he soon returned. The security lights were on and illuminated the yard. At the edge of the woods I spotted about three coons, one behind the other, making their way to a large tree. Their eyes flashed like glass reflectors as they peered toward our bright lights. I stood at the bottom of the steps. Ruben sat down near my right foot. The stars were bright this evening, and with the exception of a vehicle passing down on the highway, the stillness of this heavenly place was something to experience. It was as though the chippies had gone to bed in the nearby brush piles that were slowly returning to the forest floor. It was Mother Nature at her best. I broke the trance, and Ruben and I went inside.

We went into the living room and put some music on. Patty and I loved to listen to country music and the big bands of the past. I asked her if she'd mind if I purchased us a couple of used Ski-Doo snow sleds. She thought it was a great idea, provided they weren't too expensive. Now I would seriously pursue the purchase of the two sleds that were for sale on the South Shore Road.

At about 11:00 p.m., we prepared for bed. Patty had to be at the diner around 6:30 a.m., and I planned to take the Bronco down to Doctor Don's garage to have the timing checked. My main aim was to stop that occasional backfiring and engine cough. The old Bronco was becoming tired of turning its wheels on the roadways of the Adirondack Park, but for now it had to endure the macadam two-lane highways. I had purchased it just after I had retired from the troopers about six years ago. I had changed the tires on it several times. The four-wheel drive had come to the rescue more than once.

Since Patty and I had married, it was much cozier around what had used to be my bachelor log-home. She had bought fresh curtains for the windows, and introduced a few other changes to make our home a warmer place, adding pictures on the mantel and other improvements. Of course, Patty let me know in no uncertain terms that my office area was my responsibility.

I gave Patty a goodnight kiss, held her lovingly in my arms, and soon we both drifted off to sleep. I had given up the life of a bachelor. I can only say, yes, things here in the Black residence had definitely changed, and for the better.

CHAPTER FOUR

I heard the loud words, "Timber! Timber! Timber!" I was standing under the massive Northern Red Oak tree as it began to sway toward Mother Earth. It was falling rapidly when my eyes opened to the sun coming into the bedroom window. My heart was racing. I looked over toward Patty's side of the bed, but she had already gone to work. I lay for a while till my heart resumed its normal beat.

When I pushed the covers back to get out of bed, Ruben started to tug on the bedspread. "Settle down there, Ruben," I said sternly.

The ice cold water felt good on my face as I splashed it into my eyes. I dressed, combed my hair, and let Ruben outside. He darted off to the woods. I was thinking of calling Patty at the diner, but knew that it would be very busy. I looked at the clock: 8:10 a.m. I placed the teakettle over the hot flame and prepared to have a cup of green tea. I wasn't too hungry, so I took a bagel out of the refrigerator and put half of it into the toaster. I looked outside and saw Ruben rush into his dog run. I hastily went outside and closed the gate as I peeked over the fence to check his food and water dishes.

The bagel jumped out of the toaster into my hand. I buttered it and covered it with grape jelly. Sitting down at the table with my cup of tea and bagel, I thumbed through the *Adirondack Express*, our weekly local newspaper. I always started at the rear page and worked backward. The advertisements were of interest to me. I noted that the two Ski-Doos were still advertised. "Price negotiable" appeared at the end of the ad. I rose and placed the other half of the bagel in the trusty toaster. I couldn't understand why the toaster popped up with such force, so decided that I'd have Dr. Don take a look at it. I replenished my tea and sat back down to the table for a few minutes to enjoy the bagel. Then I glanced at my Timex and decided I'd better get busy.

Just as I cleaned off the table the telephone rang.

"Hello, honey." Patty's voice was soft and sent a shiver up my spine.

"Good morning, sweetheart. I didn't hear you leave for work this morning. Why didn't you wake me?"

"I didn't want to disturb you. I called to tell you not to start supper this evening. Lila prepared extra chicken and biscuits and I'll be bringing some home tonight. Is that okay with you, darling." She sounded rushed.

"That'll be wonderful, dear. I'll have the table set."

"Okay, sweetie. Bye."

"Bye, honey." I heard the click.

I cleaned the kitchen and ran the cleaner throughout our log home, dusting the oak furniture as I made my way from one end to the other. I had just placed the Kirby in the closet when I heard a roar. I thought the roof was coming off the house. I quickly looked out and caught a glimpse of Dale Rush's Stinson seaplane skimming the tops of the tall Blue Spruce trees at the edge of the forest. He hadn't dove over the house in quite a while. In my mind I bet a five-dollar bill Evelyn O'Brien was sitting next to Dale. I couldn't be happier. Dale needed female companionship. The war years had taken away the jovial Dale Rush, and I had been so glad to hear him laugh at the Hard Times Café the other night. The new owner of Kirby's Marina, Evelyn O'Brien, would be good for our friend.

With the log home looking in good condition internally, I decided I would write up a few bad check cases and send out a couple of letters. One of the letters dealt with Tom Huston's two insufficient-fund checks that he had mailed to me. The check-writer resided in Rhode Island. Tom didn't want to pursue criminal action at this juncture. He had known the owner of the check for a number of years and thought possibly that it was an oversight rather than a deliberate act.

While I was working in the office I turned on radio station WBRV-FM and listened to Penny Younger and his western show. Penny knew hundreds of people in the region, and listening to his program was not only entertaining, but most interesting.

My intention to write only two letters expanded into five more letters, with two large envelopes to my good buddy, Private Detective Jack Flynn, in Phoenix, Arizona. They contained the final reports concerning the Bernie Draper organization as it concerned the New York State operation. After the apprehension of Draper, I had had to submit several depositions concerning my participation as a private investigator. I already had received numerous letters of appreciation from several department heads, including the New York State Troopers.

If Draper had gotten a foothold in our State of New York, no telling how far it could have spread. The diligent work of Lieutenant Jack Doyle and his able staff of investigators and undercover operatives had smothered the criminal activities, and his holdings in this jurisdiction are under the control of the government until the cases are cleared. I was pleased that Chief Todd Wilson and his department had received recognition and letters of appreciation from high-level commanders. I had seen the chief recently and we had discussed the case in its entirety over coffee and donuts. He had informed me that with growth coming into the Adirondack region from all walks of life, it was wise to keep one's eyes open and ears to the ground for possible information pertaining to any criminal activities. Many of our cities throughout the nation have high crime zones and we don't need them spreading to our mountains. There's no doubt about it: along with the good coming to live here, there's bound to be a lemon or two.

Of course there will always be the get-rich-quick schemes being created each day like the viruses on computers. Hopefully the law enforcement community will identify these potential criminal cases and deal with them in a court of law. For me, a former law enforcement officer, I continue to wait for the phone calls or letters requesting my services as a private investigator aka private detective.

I pulled myself away from my desk and covered the typewriter with a clear plastic cover. I grabbed the mail in the outgoing basket and went to the post office. The Bronco seemed to skip a little as I made my way through Old Forge. It coughed with a thud when I shut the engine off in the north-side parking area. I went inside and checked my mailbox. More bad-check cases had arrived. Ellen and her staff were busy sorting the afternoon mail. I placed my letters through the slot and handed the two larger envelopes to a smiling clerk.

On the way back I stopped at Charlie Kiefer's and picked up the *New York Times* and the *Syracuse Post-Standard*. Charlie was well known for his postcard collection and I had attended many of his postcard programs over the years. The cards were historic and showed what the architecture was like in years gone by. It was educational to view them.

When I arrived at the log home I let Ruben out of his dog run and he took off for the forest that he was so familiar with. I was certain that the "chippies" were glad to see him. Ruben would come back shortly and go directly to his fenced-in run. I went inside, washed my hands, and splashed cold water on my face. I felt fully refreshed. I set the table with plates, silverware, and napkins. While I was waiting for Patty, I filled the teakettle and heated some water.

As I was filling the kettle I heard the water pump start up. It purred like a kitten. Jack Falsey kept our pump and furnace in good running condition. We were fortunate to have a person like Jack with his keen knowledge about pumps, plumbing, and a host of other things. I was still waiting for Jack to take me out fishing. Jack and his fishing buddy Rick knew where the fish were, as they had fished the Fulton Chain of Lakes for years.

Ruben let out a loud bark when Patty pulled in with her red Jeep. The first thing she did was rush over to the big K-9. I saw Patty give Ruben a dog biscuit. She petted him and returned to the Jeep. I went outside and Patty handed me a warm dish covered with aluminum foil: chicken and biscuits! I took them from her as she leaned over and kissed me on the cheek. We walked in together, and I placed the dish on the kitchen cabinet.

"How was your day, my dearest?" I asked, looking into her eyes.

"Honey, it was busy. We had some of the girls in from the card club around 3:00 and I believe they were conducting their meeting for the month. My arms are sore from pouring tea and coffee for over an hour." She looked tired.

"I bet that was interesting," I said sympathetically.

"It was. I heard some talk about Dale and Evelyn O'Brien. Folks are so glad that Dale has a lady friend."

"I'm happy for Dale, Patty."

"I am, too, honey. The talk was all positive." Patty was smiling.

"The table is set and I've turned on the oven. It should be hot by now."

Patty opened the oven door and I slid the covered baking dish into the hot oven. I looked over at Patty, who had already started shredding cabbage for coleslaw. All the ingredients were lined up on the counter. I heard the steady beat of the French knife as it hit the cutting board, changing the firm head of cabbage to thin shreds that make up the slaw. Before Patty had been married to the wild man, Kenneth, she had been the salad chef at a fashionable restaurant near her Kentucky home. Little had she known then that she'd be a waitress in the great Adirondacks, married to a private detective.

The aroma of the chicken and biscuits teased our taste buds as Patty removed the aluminum foil. She had opened up a can of sliced beets and arranged a small glass plate of mixed sweet pickles. She also surprised me with my favorite, a dish of cranberry sauce.

The two lit candles in the middle of the table added an aura of romance, and as I was placing the succulent tender chicken on her plate I looked into her eyes for an instant. It was a look of happiness and contentment. I felt her love and I'm certain she sensed mine. I reached over to caress her hand. Then we said grace, returning to our dinner. We both agreed the chicken and biscuits were very delicious.

I told Patty to go into the living room and rest, while I cleared the table, put things away, and did the dishes. She insisted that she would help me, but I told her to relax, as morning would come soon enough and she would be facing another long day of work at John's Diner. She sat down in our rocking chair and rocked back and forth, while she glanced at the daily paper.

I finished my chores and went into the living room. Patty had dozed off with the newspaper on her lap. I placed a lightweight afghan over her. The house was cooler than usual even with the oven on. I probably should have kept it on for a while, but I had turned it off to conserve fuel. It was getting a little too late to light up the fireplace. There was no doubt about it: we'd be having a frost soon.

While Patty napped in our favorite oak rocking chair, I slipped out the rear door to check on the big K-9. I could tell that the temperatures were dropping as Ruben's nose was sending out a visible cloud from his nostrils. I went over to him and petted his head. He pressed his big head against my pant leg and looked up at me. "Good boy!" I said.

I let him run to the woods by himself. I didn't want to leave Patty alone. I watched the big shepherd as he ran toward me. I put him back into his run and closed the gate.

When I entered the log home I could hear Patty stirring in the living room.

"Jason, where are you?" she asked in a low voice.

"Right here, honey. I just took care of Ruben."

I went into the living room as Patty was folding up the afghan. She placed it on the top of our oak chest near the fireplace. I took three long strides to her side and embraced her slender petite body, holding her closely. Her warm soft lips met mine as she stood up on her toes. I held her for several seconds and we smothered each other with kisses of admiration. After my last divorce, I had been sure that I could never fully love again. I had been wrong in thinking that way. Patty had awakened my inner self, and I truly loved her.

She asked me if I had gone over to see the Ski-Doos that were for sale on the South Shore Road. We mutually decided to look at them together over the weekend.

I put some music on and we sat on the couch listening to a mixture of the old-time waltzes, polkas, and country. We both loved music from all eras. Once in a while we'd play some classical music and big band music from the past.

Morning would be here before we knew it. Patty would be at the diner, and I had planned to get some exercise by chopping wood for the fireplace. Investigative work was slow except for my check cases, but I had a sixth sense that the telephone would be ringing soon. I went outside and let Ruben out to make his final run for the night. When he returned we both went inside. At about 10:30, Patty and I retired. Ruben had journeyed off to dog-slumber-land on his air mattress.

I heard the alarm clock go off at 5:15. Patty reached over and silenced the noisy clock with the push of a button. I heard her get out of bed and go to the bathroom. The last thing I heard was the shower and our water pump running as it drew up the water from our deep well. I awoke for a minute again when Patty started her red Jeep. She let it run for a few minutes, which told me that it had to be cold outside. I fell back to sleep.

I woke up when the telephone rang. It jangled three times before I lifted the receiver.

"Hello, hello" I mumbled.

"Honey, it's 9:15. Are you up?" Patty's voice was concerned.

"I am now, sweetheart," I said.

"Be careful if you chop wood today," she exclaimed

caringly.

"I will, babe. Have a good day. I'll make a ham salad sandwich for lunch. See you tonight, dear."

"See you, lover." I heard the click.

I pushed the covers back and got out of bed. My legs were stiff and sore. I wondered if I had a strain. I shaved and showered and dressed in some work clothes. I let Ruben out for a run. While he was chasing the chippies I put the teakettle on and decided to have a cup of decaf and a couple of scrambled eggs with some whole wheat toast.

I went to the refrigerator, took out two medium eggs, cracked them against the edge of a small bowl, and whipped them up. The thick iron frying pan was heated and I poured the eggs slowly over some melted butter. I turned the burner down and cooked the eggs slowly. I liked soft scrambled eggs.

Before I sat down to enjoy breakfast, I looked out. Ruben was sitting in his dog run. I sat down and covered my whole wheat toast with grape jelly. I took the pepper mill and turned it a couple times over the eggs. They were delicious. I cleaned up the kitchen. With winter rapidly approaching, the wood blocks piled north of the house wouldn't chop themselves. I went into my storage area and took out a ten-pound sledgehammer, a couple of wedges, and my trusty double-bladed axe. After closing Ruben's gate I walked over to where Charlie Perkins had dropped a load of wooden blocks ready for chopping.

I took the biggest wedge and tapped it into the center of the first block of maple. I was used to the ten-pound sledgehammer, but it had been a while since I had used it. For the forty-degree temperature I had on a wool shirt and heavy wool trousers.

The first swing connected squarely on top of the wedge, and I heard the block give off a weak cracking sound as I connected with its top. I went for the second swing with all the power I could muster, and when the sledge hit the wedge, the block gave way into two halves. After about twenty minutes of swinging the hammer, I had split several blocks of wood. I then took a fifteen-minute rest. I surmised that some of the more experienced woodchoppers in the Adirondacks would probably chide me. But I was tenacious, and I'd stick with this wood chopping until I was dead tired or had all the wood chopped. I surprised myself. By mid-afternoon I had two cords of wood piled just west of our log home. Every muscle in my body was aching, but I knew the soreness would pass with continued chopping. It was great exercise. I was hoping that Patty would be impressed. She enjoyed the fireplace blazing on cold winter nights.

I was so engrossed in my work that I kept putting off having any lunch. Finally I stopped chopping and put the tools away. I went over to Ruben and we wrestled for a while. He liked that. I then went inside and took a fast shower. I was tired, but I felt refreshed. I had exercised, and that was important, as it's important for everyone. After my shower I put on a faded pair of blue jeans and a blue denim shirt. Not only had I missed lunch, but I had missed the Penny Younger show on WBRV. Many times when I'm working in the office I listen to Penny's great mix of excellent country music and the interesting conversation that goes with it.

The telephone rang just as I was getting ready to run downtown for the newspapers. I went into my office and answered it.

"Hello, Jason. Tom Huston here."

"Hello, Tom. Good to hear from you. I did receive your letter with the checks. I thought I told you at Dale's get-together," I said.

"Jason, I'm not calling about the checks. I have a problem that you may be able to help me with." My curiosity was fully engaged.

"What is it, Tom?"

"I'd like to meet with you tomorrow, if possible, Jason. Would you be able to come to the Breakshire?" he asked.

"Certainly, Tom. I'll drive up tomorrow morning. Is there any special time?" I was curious.

"Could you be in my office by 10:00 a.m.? I'd rather not

discuss this on the telephone." He seemed relieved. Apparently he was very anxious to meet with me.

"Tom, I'll be there by ten." Knowing Tom as I did I knew that he must have a good reason to ask me to drive to the Breakshire Lodge in Lake Placid.

I called Patty at the diner and asked her to bring a paper home and to pick up the mail.

"I'll stop at the post office after I get out of work. Honey, would you mind preparing pancakes for supper this evening?" she asked.

"Sure, sweetheart. Sounds like a good idea. Would you like Canadian bacon or sausage with them?"

"Canadian bacon will be fine," she added.

"Okay, babe. See you in a little while."

I heard the click as she hung up the telephone. I immediately went to the refrigerator and took the Canadian bacon out of the freezer. Pancakes were always a favorite with Patty and me. It didn't matter if it was for breakfast, lunch, or supper. Another item we loved was the amber-colored syrup that we always purchased from a farmer on Route 12 between Boonville and Lowville. We were regular customers. Not only did the syrup taste good on pancakes, it also went well over vanilla ice cream. I placed the griddle over the low flame and proceeded to set the table. Patty would be pulling into the yard in about twenty-five minutes.

As Patty's Jeep entered our driveway, I placed four slices of Canadian bacon on the heated griddle. The pancake batter followed, in six medium-sized circular hotcakes. When Patty came through the door I told her to prepare for some of the best pancakes in the Town of Webb. She smiled and rushed toward me, giving me a warm kiss on the cheek. But she looked weary.

"How did your day go, Patty?" I asked concerned.

"It was busy as usual. Wilt Chambers and Charlie Perkins pulled their big rigs into the rear parking lot and spent an hour or two at the diner. They both wondered where you've been keeping yourself. I told them that you were busy at home."

"That was nice they stopped in. I know I should have come down for lunch, but I've been puttering out back chopping wood all day for our fireplace. Oh! By the way, Tom Huston called and would like me to stop at the Breakshire Lodge tomorrow."

"Is there anything wrong, Jason?" She looked concerned.

"I don't think so, honey. He sounded okay on the telephone. It's probably something to do with the business."

"Tom Huston really likes you, Jason. And he really respects you. I can tell by the way he looks at you," she added, admiringly.

"I believe he is fond of us both. You know how much he would like us to move to Lake Placid and work at the lodge for him."

"I know he does, but I feel this is where we belong, Jason."

"I love you, honey, and I love Old Forge. And we can't forget Ruben. We both love him, too."

The pancakes were golden brown as I removed them from the griddle. The bacon sizzled. We both sat down at the table and enjoyed our pancake and bacon supper. The coffee was hot and the heated maple syrup poured over the pancakes truly teased the taste buds. I returned to the griddle to pour more batter. While I was up, I refilled Patty's cup. My one cup was sufficient. With the coolness in the air and winter just around the corner, we'd be enjoying the pancake suppers frequently.

Patty and I cleaned up the kitchen and did the dishes together. We talked as we worked. One subject we spent some time on was our friend Dale and his new friend, Evelyn. We both agreed she was a beautiful lady. We had wondered why Dale flew to Maine every so often, and now we knew.

"Patty, doesn't it seem strange that Tom Huston didn't mention any problems to me when we were at the Hard Times Café?"

"I was thinking the same thing. Maybe he didn't want to mention anything on Dale's joyous occasion."

"That's probably the reason. Well, anyway, I'll be seeing him tomorrow." I smiled again. "I certainly wish Dale the very best in his future."

"Yes, we both want the best for him. I noticed the other night how happy he appeared."

"Oh, before I forget: let's be sure we do go over and look at those two Ski-Doos Saturday or Sunday. Is that okay with you?" I asked.

"Yes, honey, it's all right with me." She smiled. "I'm looking forward to it."

We both discussed the idea of having our own sleds and the snowmobile trips that would possibly come up in the future. In this part of the country snow could fall any time during October. We would look forward to those adventures. With our work schedules we both were aware that it might be difficult to find the time to ride the sleds, but we'd work that into our schedule.

It was almost 10:00 p.m. when we crawled into bed. The bedroom was cool. We embraced each other warmly. My life was now complete with Patty at my side. Contentedly, after making love, we fell off into a deep slumber in our cozy Adirondack log home.

CHAPTER FIVE

I came out of a deep sleep to see Ruben standing in our bedroom. Glancing at the clock, I saw the hands read two-thirty. I heard Patty's steady breathing as she slept soundly. I noticed that Ruben was at full alert. Then I heard the scratching on the roof. I knew it must be the pesky coon that comes around every so often to let us know he is still in the region.

"It's okay, Ruben. Go back and lay down. Go on now!" He slowly moved toward the door and into the other room to his air mattress.

I lay on my back listening, and soon the noise stopped. It was difficult to get back to sleep. My mind was active and I thought about the many personal moments that Patty and I had experienced since our wedding day. Those times are sacred to us. Our intimate times together had been fulfilling to our marriage. I loved her dearly and I felt sure she loved me.

We were in the right place, the great Adirondacks of northern New York State, where peace and tranquility still prevailed. Where previous generations worked and lived in good and difficult times enduring the hardships of stormy weather conditions, lack of work, and sickness long before modern-day medicines became available. The footprints on the trails of the past generations may have worn away, but the historical significance will live on forever in the history books of the era. The vast amount of literature that had been and is being written about this place on earth has enriched the present generation and will enrich generations to come, and hopefully humankind will see fit to maintain this model of lifestyle. Our former leaders had vision in the late 1800's when they designated the "forever wild" clause for the Adirondacks.

The residents and the people who visit this glorious park should never forget what they see or what they feel as the various aspects of Mother Nature bring to our vision the greenery before us. Autumn gives us numerous colors that radiate from every branch and bush standing toward the heavens above. In the winter season, the blanket of snow and ice presents a different scene. Hopefully the fast-moving snowmobiler will make time in their haste to take in the true offering of the winter season and absorb what they see.

I must have fallen off to sleep, as the alarm sounded, awakening me. Patty was already in the bathroom readying herself for another day at John's busy diner. I pushed the covers back and met Patty coming out of the bathroom. I shaved and took a shower, while Patty had a cup of coffee and a bran muffin. By the time I reached the kitchen she was outside putting Ruben into the run. As I opened the door, she ran over to me for a quick kiss.

"Have a good day, honey," I said to her. "I have no idea when I'll get back from Lake Placid. I'll call you."

"Say hello to Mr. Huston for me. Take care, honey."

"Be careful driving," I cautioned her. "I love you, baby."

I watched Patty climb into the Jeep and start the engine. I waved at her as she turned around and headed for the main highway. After closing the door I made myself a cup of green tea and warmed the last of the bran muffins. I removed the grape jelly jar lid and covered my muffin. I sipped the hot tea. After this light breakfast, I went outside and let Ruben out of the dog run. We headed for the woods. The temperature dipped to a low forty degrees overnight and it appeared we were approaching the time for a light frost.

It was good to walk in the woods without the huge black bear on the prowl. Ruben heeled close to me as we walked the path through the wooded area. I looked over at the two large oak trees and remembered what Wilt had said: "If you'd like to turn them into some money, let me know." Wilt had observed the trees when he had taken a walk into the forest while waiting for me to return home. I remembered the day well, as he had delivered some two-man saws for my collection.

I'd have to look up Wilt and Charlie Perkins soon. I hadn't seen them for a while. Patty frequently saw them at the diner. I had heard that Wilt was carving a couple of black bears for some customers. We soon headed back to the dog run, and I put Ruben inside and closed the gate.

I entered my log home, checked the doors, and made certain that the stove was shut off. I took the notebook from the top of the desk, placing it in my leather briefcase. My jacket was already in the Bronco.

When I locked the door, Ruben let out a low resounding bark. "Sorry—I can't take you with me on this trip, big boy." I went over and petted his handsome head, then turned and walked to the Bronco. As I backed around, I could see that Ruben was already pouting. His back was toward me.

I climbed into the Bronco, started the engine, backed up and turned around, and headed toward Route 28.

The Bronco purred like a kitten as I followed winding Route 28 north to Route 30. When I drove through Long Lake, I looked over at Gertie's Diner. The parking lot was full. I wanted to stop, but thought it would be a good idea to proceed directly to Lake Placid and the Berkshire Lodge. I looked down at the fuel gauge and noticed that the needle was riding on the quarter-of-a-tank level, so just north of the bridge in Long Lake I pulled into a filling station to gas up. On trips, I usually got nineteen to twenty-one miles to the gallon. While the pump was running, I checked the oil and cleaned the windshield. The attendant was polite and thanked me for stopping by. I glanced at my wristwatch and climbed into the Bronco. The entire trip was approximately two hours, therefore it would take me about an hour to reach my destination. The journey to the Breakshire was uneventful. There were a few northbound cars and trucks headed toward Tupper Lake, but from Tupper to Lake Placid traffic was light. I pulled into the parking lot nearest the entrance to the lodge. I noticed several workers installing storm windows on the quaint lodge. It wouldn't be long before the wind would be whipping the cold snow against them. Here it was late October, and we had been fortunate not to have had any snowstorms. I shivered just thinking of the onslaught of winter and the potential driving hazards. I turned off the Bronco's ignition switch, exiting the vehicle. I locked the door, as my best camera was lying on the rear seat covered with my jacket.

The entrance was picturesque, with full shrubbery lining the adjacent wall that surrounded that part of the lodge. The ivy on the walls had been thinned out and it appeared well-manicured. The two workmen gave me a wave as I ascended the stone steps to the main entrance. The windows glistened; apparently they had been recently cleaned. Tom Huston was a smart businessman. He demanded that everything around the lodge should be neat and clean.

Opening the large heavy wooden entrance door, I entered, immediately observing the large black bear and the two cubs that Wilt Chambers and I had presented to Tom. I knew that many photos had been taken next to the three bears. They were popular with Tom Huston, and his customers fell in love with them. They looked so real. I went over to the two clerks on the desk, who recognized me immediately.

"Mr. Black, it has been a long time since we've seen you," said Helen Schmid, the desk clerk, with a smile.

"Hi, Helen. Yes, it has been a while. Is Mr. Huston in?" I asked.

"He has been awaiting your arrival. I'll buzz him for you." She sounded her usual efficient self, immediately hitting his office button.

"Thank you, Helen."

I went over to the large leather davenport and seated myself. I had just started to look at the most current *Adirondack Life*, when Tom Huston came out of his office and approached me. He wore a big smile. He had on a blue blazer, grey slacks, and a white shirt and tie. His grey hair added to his distinguished appearance. He extended his right hand and clasped mine.

"Jason, it is so good to see you. How was your trip from Old Forge?" He appeared to be genuinely pleased I was there.

"It was a good drive, Tom. Say, the lodge looks great. I observed your men installing the large storm windows. Are you expecting foul weather?"

"We want to be ready, Jason. You know how Mother Nature can surprise us at times."

"Indeed I do, Tom."

"Come into my office I'd like to introduce you to my two nephews, whom I haven't seen in several years. They are just about to leave for Portland, Maine."

I followed Tom into his office. I noticed the waxed surface of his hallway floor. You could almost see your face when you looked down at the highly polished tile.

"After you, Jason." Tom held open the office door and I entered his elaborate office. I noticed that two young men were seated near his desk in two comfortable leather chairs. They arose from their sitting position and turned toward Tom and me. Both appeared to be over six feet. They were wearing business suits and appeared to be in their mid-to-late twenties.

"Jason, I'd like you to meet my two nephews, Brenton and Matthew Powers, from Long Island. Gentlemen, this is Jason Black, private investigator and a close friend of mine." Tom seemed very proud of his nephews.

"It is a pleasure to meet you, Mr. Black," Brenton said.

"We've heard a lot about you from our uncle," Matthew chimed in.

"It is my pleasure, gentlemen. Your uncle and I have known each other for some time," I added.

We sat around Tom's desk. He had ordered some coffee and Danish pastries. They were located on a small serving table close to our chairs. The young men—both bachelors— were ruggedly handsome and well mannered. Matthew preferred to be addressed as Matt. A graduate of LeMoyne College in Syracuse, he was associated with a large pharmaceutical corporation. His older brother, Brenton, graduated from Hofstra University on Long Island and was self-employed. I also learned that they had been trained in the martial arts and that Matt was a proficient boxer. As I sat there in Tom's office listening to them speak, I felt they would have made outstanding law enforcement officers.

Brenton and Matt appeared to be well-adjusted to this fast-moving, highly competitive society. I could tell that these two fellows would do very well in their endeavors. We sipped coffee, ate pastries, and talked. We discussed some of their college life, their sailing adventures off Long Island, and the many cultural interests available in New York City. They enjoyed going to the professional ball games in the Big Apple. I was pleased that Tom had brought me in to meet these two inspiring young men; however, I was anxious to ascertain the reason for Tom's request for my presence. Evidently he did not want to discuss the matter in front of his nephews.

It was about 11:30 when Tom and I bid farewell to Matt and Brenton. They were driving on to Boston to meet their parents, who were about to sail to England, and later the two young men would continue on to Portland, Maine. I shook their hands and bid them farewell. They told me if I were ever on Long Island to look them up. Before they departed, Tom proudly showed them the picture of his late son. Tom's eyes filled with tears as it stirred his emotions. Again, Tom quickly recovered with that ever-winning smile. I waited in Tom's office while he walked them to their car. While he was gone, I picked up his copy of *Adirondack Life* and thumbed through the pages.

Tom returned to the office in about fifteen minutes. He wore a big smile when he came through the door.

"Jason, how did you like those two big fellows?" he asked proudly.

"Tom, I was very impressed. They are quite the gentlemen. It makes one feel confident about the future of our great country just to know that there are young men out there of their caliber. I can envision both of them wearing the grey uniform of the New York State Troopers."

"I believe that Brenton did consider that career field at one time. However, I believe he is pursuing business and, of course, Matt is very comfortable in his present position. He has the credentials to be an excellent writer. Both of them are smart, and I know one thing: no shyster ever wants to confront them, for the shyster will get the short end," he said with pride.

"They seem like genuine fellows."

"That they are. I'm only sorry to have held you up. They dropped in unexpectedly." Now his face changed. "Jason, I believe I have a serious dilemma. I didn't consult with you sooner, because it was a police matter and the police have been doing everything possible to find the person or persons responsible." His concern was obvious.

"What is it, Tom?" I asked, curious.

"Since I've been here in the Lake Placid region I have experienced considerable success, and as a result I have invested in several pieces of real estate. I own several older homes and three small buildings. The properties are located in various areas throughout the park. I've had one of my employees check these properties at least once a month. Last week he was checking one of them in the Newcomb area, an older Victorian house. He found the rear door damaged and open. He checked the interior and found considerable damage to the contents. When I purchased the house it contained some valuable antiques, furniture, dishes and turn-of-the-century pitcher and bowl sets.

"My man, Cedric Dimmler, called me on his cell phone and told me what he had discovered. We called the troopers and they came and took a report. We haven't been able to determine what may have been stolen, without taking an inventory, which he is doing as we speak. Jason, Cedric found a can half full of gas. The troopers secured it and are processing it for fingerprints. The can wasn't ours and had to be brought onto the property. What their intention was we don't know, but it is suspicious. Maybe they were going to set the house on fire."

"Tom, that doesn't sound good. I'm certain that Lieutenant Jack Doyle and his BCI people will look into the case and attempt to identify the perpetrator." I had complete confidence in Jack's ability.

"Yes, that is all well and good, but I have experienced some difficulty in acquiring two or three pieces of property where family members of the sellers weren't happy about the sales of the properties. Family dynamics apparently flared up and threats were made."

"Did you mention that to the troopers?" I asked.

"Yes, I told the trooper who came to see me."

"I assume you gave him all the sellers' names, those families that seem to dispute the transactions?"

"Yes, Jason. I gave them all the information I had. I'd like to have you do some checking for me on a couple of questionable people who could be involved in this matter. Would you consider that?" he inquired, almost pleading.

"I'll be glad to look into the case, Tom, but keep in mind that my investigation will be a little different in scope than the troopers'. They probably won't appreciate my intervening; however, I'll look into the matter and see what develops. If I come up with any good leads, I'll let you and Jack Doyle know about my findings."

"Jason, I appreciate that. Don't worry, I'll pay you for your services plus your mileage. I wish you good luck. Owning property in this day and age isn't conducive to steady nerves. And the insurance on my properties is very costly to begin with."

"I know what you're saying. Tom, when your man finishes with the inventory, let the troopers know what is missing and also give me a list. I will check out some shops that might deal in things of that nature. I will need a good description of any missing items."

"I'll see that you get it."

"When you have the information, call me. If I'm out, leave

a message and I'll call you back." I really did not want to get involved with an ongoing police investigation again, but I could sense Tom's uneasiness. This problem had really disturbed him.

Breathing a sigh of relief, Tom said, "Okay, I'll do that. Now how about some lunch?" he asked.

"Good idea, Tom." I was beginning to feel hungry.

I checked my watch. It was about 1:00, and the coffee and pastry we had had when visiting with Tom's nephews had worn off. Tom and I went to the dining room and we took a table in the far-end corner of the room. He indicated that they had fresh salmon flown in from Washington State and thought that would be a good choice.

I soon found out that he was correct. We each enjoyed salmon steaks with creamed potatoes. Prior to the main entrée, we enjoyed a crisp fresh salad with honey mustard dressing. The lunch was followed with a slice of caramel-covered pecan pie and fresh coffee. It was an outstanding lunch. We talked about Patty and our mutual friends, Wilt, Dale and Charlie Perkins. Tom informed me that he was lining up his fishermen friends for their annual spring fishing trips and that he had Dale Rush in mind for the transportation of the men back into the remote lakes. I assured Tom that when I saw Dale I would mention that plan to him. I knew that Dale would appreciate the lucrative trips into the backcountry.

It was well past 3:00 before I left the Breakshire. The trip back to Old Forge was a good one. Traffic was light. The temperatures were cooling down. Winter would soon be arriving.

Ruben was standing at attention when I pulled into the yard. Patty arrived a few minutes later. She was bubbling over with laughter.

"What are you so happy about, honey?" I asked, surprised to see her in such a joyous state.

"Jason, you wouldn't believe it. I was so busy today. We had two buses of leaf-peepers pull into the parking lot at about 2:00 p.m. Evidently it was a group of senior citizens from the southern tier. They had called this morning to make reservations—you know so many of the restaurants have scaled back their hours. They fell in love with the Old Forge region. John called in an extra waitress. They were a fun group, and did they tip!" she exclaimed.

"You say they were leaf-peepers. I really don't get it, honey."

"Well, if you had been in the diner you would understand why I'm so happy. After they left I found over fifty dollars they had left on the table for my gratuity."

"Yes, I can understand the joy of that. Wonderful, honey! I'm really happy for you."

"Some of those people were in their seventies, and boy they had spirit. It made me so happy to meet people like that, just down to earth people with the lust for life. They were all wonderful. There was a lady with one arm. Jason, she had a positive attitude that I've never seen before."

"You're right, honey. There are many fine people in our society, and thank God for that."

"How was your trip to Lake Placid, and how is Mr. Huston?" she asked cheerfully.

"He sends his best to you, Patty. He was fine, and I met his two nephews today. They're from Long Island."

"How old are they?"

"I'd say they're in their late twenties. Fine gentlemen. I didn't know he even had any nephews. It was a surprise! They seem to be happy doing what they do. One is in business for himself and the other works for a drug company."

"That's nice. I hope I can meet them sometime," she added. "By the way, are you hungry?" she asked.

I thought for a minute. "Have we got any hot dogs?"

"Sure have, sweetie. How about some beans and franks?"

"That will be fine. I'm not too hungry, as Tom and I had a late lunch."

I pitched in to help Patty, chopping some cabbage for coleslaw. In about forty minutes we sat down at the kitchen table. Our menu tonight consisted of franks, coleslaw, and beans, along with warmed hot dog rolls. Patty had mixed some lemonade. Everything was tasty for such a hastily prepared dinner.

After supper, we washed the dishes, cleaned the kitchen, and decided to take Ruben for a romp in the woods. We placed the big K-9 on a leash. We walked for about an hour. It felt good to get some exercise after my trip to Lake Placid. We returned home, went inside, and discussed our impending purchase of two snowmobiles. Patty would be working till noon on Saturday, but we planned to look into the two sleds for sale when she was through.

Winter would be howling into our region anytime now. Monday I would proceed to the Newcomb area to see what I could find out, if anything, about Tom Huston's dilemma. It bothered me deeply to hear about criminal activity in this region. If the deviants would put their energies into worthwhile projects, they could possibly be successful in lawful ventures.

Many times in my law enforcement career during interviews with criminals I would attempt to ascertain why they pursued the criminal path as opposed to a path of honesty and hard work. They often came from dysfunctional families, where alcohol, child abuse, and lack of parental supervision prevailed. These issues prompted me into taking courses about childhood development. My studies indicated that they received no loving or cuddling from their parents during the early development years. Authorities in the field cite that the constant viewing of violent programming on television tends to desensitize them to the reality of their actions. Associating with the wrong element has an impact, too. Society somehow must endeavor to recognize the problems to prevent the escalation of criminal behavior.

What would I discover concerning the criminal attack on Tom Huston's property? I knew one thing: I would attempt to identify the perpetrator(s). If I did develop any useful information I would contact Lieutenant Jack Doyle at Troop S, second in command of the BCI.

It was almost 10:30 when we went to bed. The reading

lights were turned on and we read till our eyes tired. Patty fell off to sleep first. I took her book and placed it on the shelf at the head of the bed. I reached over, gave her a warm embrace, and a soft gentle kiss on her cheek, not wanting to waken her. She stirred, rolled over toward me, and said sleepily, "I love you, dear." I followed her soon afterwards into a deep sleep after I turned both lights off. Ruben was sleeping on his air mattress.

CHAPTER SIX

I was trying to pull over a speeding caterpillar tractor going down a straight steep grade. The sirens were wailing as I pulled alongside of a steel-helmeted construction worker. He wouldn't look over. It was then that I heard the bell on the alarm clock go off. Patty was next to me, and she reached over and put her arms around me, smothering me with a warm passionate kiss. I reciprocated. After a brief moment, I realized the caterpillar tractor was only a vision in my dream.

"Honey, I wish we didn't have to get out of bed," she said, as the alarm clock wound down.

"I wish we didn't have to either, dearest," I said, holding her close to my body as our lips met again.

Patty reluctantly pushed me away, and jumped out of bed, resolutely realizing she had to get ready for work.

I pushed the covers back. Patty was first in the bathroom. I went to the door and let the dog out. I watched him as he ran to the edge of the forest. I had noticed that Ruben didn't come into the bedroom as much since Patty and I had married. He never pulled on the bedspread any more, either. He was certainly a highly sensitive dog.

"Okay, honey. The bathroom is all yours!" Patty shouted as she hurried back to the bedroom. She was already dressed. I went into the bathroom and splashed ice cold Adirondack water on my face and, after patting my skin dry with a towel, went to the stove in the kitchen and put the teakettle over the flame. It was just a short time before we were sipping our coffee. I was wearing the new navy blue bathrobe that Patty had bought me while on our honeymoon. It was warm and comfortable. I poured Patty a second cup and warmed mine. Patty would have some breakfast when she got to the diner. She loved a good cheese and egg sandwich on a toasted bun.

"Jason, I've got to leave for work! I don't mean to rush off, honey, but it's getting late. You know how Lila wants me to open the diner at 6:30 a.m. sharp." Patty liked to be prompt. Many of her customers would be waiting for her. Since she had been abducted, and then rescued so dramatically, her popularity had grown with the locals. They knew what she had gone through with the two escaped Ohio killers.

I walked her to the door. Ruben was in his run. I put my arms around my wife and kissed her on the cheek, not wanting to smudge her lipstick. She went outside, closed Ruben's gate, and then got into her Jeep. I stayed in the doorway until she got it started. We waved as she backed around and headed toward Route 28. She would work till noon, stop at the post office to see if we had any mail, and then head home.

I went into the bathroom and shaved and showered, then moved to the kitchen to prepare two slices of French toast. The teakettle was still half full of hot water. I brought it to a boil and made a cup of green tea, adding a spoon of honey. The griddle was hot. I dipped the two slices in the egg batter and placed them on the griddle along with two strips of bacon. I heated my plate and placed the two slices on it with the bacon, which was crisp to the bite. The toast was tasty, too, especially covered with Grade A maple syrup. I avoided thinking about calories all through breakfast, deciding to enjoy my meal without any guilt.

After breakfast, I did the dishes, then went through the log home with a dust cloth and the trusty vacuum cleaner. It didn't take long to shape up the house. Outside I swept the walk and Ruben's dog run, and hosed down and scrubbed the run. Ruben watched me from the porch, then focused on a couple of chippies that came close to his immediate territory. He growled, barking at them as they hightailed it back into the woods.

I went into the office, straightened up the desk, and placed some papers in the filing cabinet. I sat at the desk for a while meditating and thinking about the strategy I would use in checking out Tom Huston's request of my services. I'd hold off on calling Lieutenant Jack Doyle until I developed useful information. I wanted to make my inquiries without people looking over my shoulder. Jack Doyle would understand. There were a lot of advantages in being a private eye that a person doesn't enjoy in a government setting. I had had excellent training in the state police academy and that I'd always be thankful for, but along the job path with the state I had developed my own individual methods that aided me in my investigations. My father, who possessed many talents, had spent several years as a private eye and shared with me some of his ideologies that a trainee does not receive in a structured academy setting.

Patty pulled into the yard at about 12:45, and after exiting the Jeep she ran over to pet Ruben. I met her at the door and we embraced.

"Were you busy this morning, honey?" I asked as I held her.

"Yes, we were! The customers kept coming through the door. Lila had to make extra pancake batter. With the cooler temperatures, everyone was ordering pancakes, some with sausage, others with eggs. Oh! By the way, Wilt and Charlie stopped in for coffee and told me to tell you that they'll be looking you up soon."

"Honey, stop talking about food, you're making me hungry," I chided playfully. "I know I've got to see Wilt and Charlie soon, but it looks as though I'm going to be busy looking into a case for Tom." Patty diplomatically didn't ask me what the case involved.

I turned the burner on and heated some water. It was green-tea time at the Blacks'. We sat at the table sipping tea and nibbling on oatmeal cookies. We discussed whether or not we should buy the two Ski-Doos that were still for sale on the South Shore Road. We decided we would, so within an hour we headed the Bronco to Dick Smith's house. I had known Dick for a couple of years. He had moved to Old Forge from the Rochester area and loved the region, especially for the winter season, as he snowmobiled and was an avid cross-country skier. We pulled into his driveway. The two yellow Ski-Doos looked in excellent condition. Dick was in his garage and came over to greet us.

"Hello, Patty and Jason. How have you been?" Dick Smith was a friendly person who possessed a good sense of humor.

"Do these sleds run?" I asked.

"They sure do." Dick went over to the first sled, turned the ignition switch on, and started the sled.

Patty and I listened as he applied the throttle. He had the rear of the sled on a block of wood and the track moved freely. After turning the first sled off, he moved to the second one. It started right up. The engine purred.

"Jason, I installed new tracks on both of these sleds. They are like new," he said proudly.

"I see that your sign indicates the price of eight hundred dollars apiece. Is that firm?" I queried.

"Jason, you and Patty can have these sleds for twelve hundred. I can't come down any further. If you have any problems with them, bring them back and I'll take care of it. Within reason, of course." I knew that Dick Smith was an honorable man and his word was golden.

"Dick, could you bring them over to our place?" I asked.

"Yes, Jason. No problem. I have an extra trailer—which, by the way, you can have for a hundred. It's in good shape. The new ones are rather expensive and this used one will give you good service. I see you have a hitch on your Bronco."

"That's nice of you, Dick. Could you bring the sleds and the trailer over to our place?"

"I certainly can."

Patty pulled out our checkbook and wrote out a check for

the total amount, handing it to Dick.

We made arrangements to meet Dick at our place at about three. We shook hands and left his yard. We drove down to Doctor Don's, picking up a two-inch ball for the hitch. Patty wanted to do some food shopping, so I dropped her off at the grocery store.

I continued on down to the Old Forge Hardware Store to pick up a few things: a couple of files for sharpening my chain saw and some bar oil. I added some steel wool to my list. While I was at the store I chatted with Mike, the manager, and nodded to Linda and Sarah, who were busy conducting a staff meeting. Danielle was engaged in accepting an incoming order of new arrivals for her well-stocked book department. It was a busy place. I thanked the cashier and went outside to the Bronco.

The air was getting cooler every day and I noticed that many of the townspeople were wearing heavier sweaters or medium-weight jackets. It wouldn't be long before the sounds of the snowmobiles would be cutting the crisp cold air of Old Forge in the wintertime. And now Patty and I would be joining the throngs of people out riding the trail system in our township of Webb. The motels and restaurants would soon be enjoying full capacity comparable to that of their summer season, often referred to as the snowmobile capital of the East.

When I turned around I spotted Marty coming out of his True Value store. I tooted the horn and he gave me a wave. He had a nicely stocked store. I can only speak well of the businesspeople of our community. They are all dedicated workers and strive to serve the visiting tourists in the highest tradition of commercial enterprise. Old Forge has a little something to offer everybody. That seems to be the trend in all the Adirondack communities. Hopefully, present leaders and future planners will help keep these wonderful places for this generation and generations to come.

The parking lot at the grocery store was crowded, and Patty was standing by the exit ramp holding onto a cart full of groceries. She waved as I pulled up to her. I applied the emergency brake and got out to assist her in unloading.

"Have you been waiting long, honey?" I asked, concerned.

"No, dear. I just walked out." We were happy to see each other.

I helped her into the Bronco, then pushed the grocery cart back into the store. On the way home we stopped at the post office and picked up the mail. Several letters from check passers had arrived. This was good, as several of my outstanding-check cases would be closed.

When we pulled into the driveway, Ruben was waiting at full attention. He ran back and forth excitedly along the fence of his dog run. We both got out of the car, walking over to pet him. Patty rubbed his back and looked up at me.

"Honey, I believe it's about time to take Ruben to Lynn's kennel for grooming." She patted his head. Ruben loved Patty and was very protective of her.

Patty went inside and I brought the groceries in, making two trips. After Patty put the groceries away, we sat down and enjoyed a cup of green tea. We had just finished when Dick Smith arrived with our two Ski-Doos and trailer.

Patty and I went outside to meet him. He parked his pickup and joined us.

"Hello, Patty and Jason. I'm a little earlier than planned, but my wife has some chores for me to do, so I decided to drop the sleds and trailer off. I'm glad you're here," he added.

"There's no problem, Dick. I'll help you unhook the trailer. Just a minute. I'll get a piece of wood to block the wheels." I was pleased with the sleds. And the trailer appeared to be in excellent condition.

Dick and I unhooked the trailer and set its tongue on the wood, blocking the trailer's wheels. He handed me the registrations, which he had signed over to me, along with a bill of sale.

"We're pleased with the sleds and trailer. Patty and I are looking forward to using them," I said.

Dick smiled and thanked us for purchasing them.

"If you have any trouble with either of these machines, I

want you to call me. Oh! I almost forgot: I have a couple of good used snowmobile suits and helmets. We're about the same size, so my wife and I thought you could use these until you purchase your own gear." He walked over to his truck and opened the passenger side door, taking the suits and helmets out of the back and handing them to me.

"That's so very nice of you, Dick," I said. "But can't I pay you for these?"

"No, you can't. We were about to give them to the Salvation Army, but thought you might be able to use them."

"That's very kind of you, but I want you to take this twenty dollar bill." I urged Dick to take it. He reluctantly accepted the money, but I felt better that he did.

"Now all we need is some snow, Jason. I think you'll enjoy the sleds."

"I'm sure we will. Give our best to your family, and thank your wife for us."

"Stop by sometime, you two. We always have the coffeepot on," he offered.

We told him we would. Dick left the yard. I took a tarp and placed it over the sleds. As a matter of security, I chained the sleds and trailer to a sturdy post.

Patty told me that she was going to catch up on a few things before preparing dinner. Tonight she planned to have Maryland fried chicken, mashed potatoes, chicken gravy, beet greens, stuffing, and a salad, with apple crisp for dessert.

While she was busy cooking, I went outdoors to spend some time with the dog. I took him out of the dog run and we walked into the woods. I had to agree with Patty: Ruben was due for a grooming. I would make an appointment at Lynn's kennel next week. The leaf-bearing trees had shed and were prepared for the onslaught of winter and the strong winds of the North Country. I could feel it in the air and in my bones. Ruben ferreted out a couple of chippies and was in a close race with them. I could hear a crow cawing. Crows were plentiful around our log home, and many of the other birds stayed out of their way when they appeared.

We finished our walk and I returned Ruben to his dog run. It would be a while before dinner, so I decided I'd work up an appetite by splitting some more fireplace wood. Some of the blocks had knots and it was a difficult task to drive the wedge in far enough for the split. I set aside a couple of the difficult ones. I decided that a fifteen-pound sledge might be the way to go, as the ten-pound didn't seem to have the impact of the fifteen-pounder. The wood was accumulating, so I piled it into face cords.

I looked up when I heard a vehicle approaching. It was the big white Dodge. Wilt pulled up close to my woodpile and got out. He was looking good with his weight loss. We shook hands.

"Jason, I was passing by. I thought I'd take a chance finding you at home. I've got a couple of two-man saws for your collection." Wilt moved to the rear of his truck and removed the two saws.

"Let me help you, buddy. Boy! They look in very good condition. Where did you find those?"

"I was checking out a wood lot way up on Rondaxe Road on the Jasper Willis property. Jasper is going on eighty-eight years of age and told me I could have them for ten dollars apiece. So, Jason, I picked them up for you. Even though he's up in age and doesn't use the saws any more, he sharpened them once a week whether they needed it or not." A big grin came over Wilt's face.

"Wilt, they're fine saws and the teeth look sharp as a razor." I felt the point with my thumb.

"You want to be careful how you handle those saws. They can come up and nick you. Let's try one on that wood block." Wilt took one of the saws and handed me one end. I noticed that the handles were in good shape and that Wilt wanted to show me how a real lumberjack pulls a saw. We began pulling the two-man saw back and forth. First to Wilt and then back to me. The sawdust fell from the block of wood with every rip of the sharp antiquated saw blade. Wilt looked at me with a determined look on his rugged face.

"Well, Jason, this is the way to saw wood." He wore a devilish grin.

"Guess you're right on that, but it is easier with a chainsaw. You know, Wilt, my dad had me on the end of a two-man saw when I was six years old. I know a little bit about two-man saws," I retorted.

"I know you do, Jason. I'm just kidding with you a little." He laughed.

Wilt and I both agreed that Jasper kept his saws sharp. He had pulled on these saws until eighty-six, and that was a long career for a lumberman. My collection was becoming larger. Not only did I have saws, but many old axes. If they could talk, they could tell about the sweat that soaked their handles from the rugged lumberjacks of yesteryear and how each night the axes would be sharpened to a fine edge. Exercise clubs weren't needed in the forests of the past, because the art of the lumberjack was the felling of trees and the roll of the log as they were sent downstream. Men like Jasper Willis knew only too well the toil of laboring and the danger they faced each day as the words "Timber, timber!" echoed through the forest.

"Jason, let me take your sledgehammer and that wedge. While I'm here I'm going to split some of these blocks." I handed the hammer and a wedge to him. I didn't say anything because I knew how proud this lumberman was. In his mind, no one could chop wood like Wilt.

Wilt set up a dozen blocks, then went to each one and placed the wedge on top, tapping it into a crack in the wood. Then with a mighty blow of the sledgehammer the block gave way to two pieces. He repeated this and soon the split wood was beginning to pile up at his feet. Patty came to the door and joined me in watching in awe as Wilt transformed the blocks to cord wood. Even in the cooler temperatures, the perspiration rolled down his cheeks. After he had finished, Patty came outside with a fluffy towel and Wilt wiped away the sweat from his brow.

"You're staying for supper, Wilt Chambers. Jason and I won't take no for an answer," she informed him.

Wilt looked up and smiled. "I was hoping you'd ask."

We followed Patty into the log home and both washed up before dinner.

The aroma of the Maryland fried chicken had taken over, permeating the room.

Wilt spoke up. "Thank you for inviting me. I never had Maryland fried chicken before. This is going to be a treat," he said, rubbing his hands in anticipation.

"We're happy to have you here. Jason really appreciates all the help you gave him with the wood," Patty said.

I helped Patty place everything on the table. We sat down. Patty asked Wilt to say grace. We bowed our heads.

"Dear God, we thank you for the gifts we're about to receive. And, Dear God, always keep Patty and Jason safe from harm and watch over all of us. Amen."

Patty started passing the dishes around, first to Wilt and from Wilt to me. Dinner conversation was rather light as we all enjoyed the wonderful meal Patty had prepared. The chicken was tender and the stuffing delicious, all complemented by the gravy. Wilt and I had seconds of everything.

While we had been chopping wood, Patty had made some apple crisp, knowing that it was one of my favorite desserts. She topped each serving off with a small dip of vanilla ice cream. I poured steaming hot coffee into our cups. After we finished eating, we sat at the table and engaged in a long conversation about the area.

Wilt talked about events going on in Boonville and we mentioned some of the planned winter activities going on in Old Forge and the general region. I wanted to tell Wilt about the new case I was about to look into for Tom Huston, but at this juncture, I didn't feel that it was the thing to do. Patty seemed so happy that Wilt had stayed for supper. He had always been so kind to both of us.

"How is Charlie Perkins and his family, Wilt?" I asked. "I haven't seen him around lately."

"They're doing good, Jason. Charlie keeps busy. He's toying with the idea of taking some fireplace wood down to

Florida. You know the economy isn't doing well these days, and some of the smaller loggers have had to sell their equipment and seek other employment."

"I know what you mean. There are certain fields that are laying off employees. Let's hope the economy will pick up a little."

We all agreed that the economy needed a boost, especially for the people on the lower pay scales. Whether it would come to be a reality we'd have to wait and see. Wilt and I thanked Patty for the wonderful supper, sending her into the living room to rest while we did the dishes and cleaned up the kitchen. She rejected our proposal at first, but then, deciding she was outnumbered, removed her apron and gratefully went into the other room.

Wilt washed and I dried the dishes and put them away. He asked if I'd seen Tom Huston lately. I told him that I had recently taken a drive to the lodge. Wilt had grown fond of Tom. And he knew that the three black bears that he had carved for Tom were still standing in the lobby. The owner of the Breakshire Lodge had sent Wilt many potential customers who were interested in purchasing carved bears.

The dishes were placed in the cupboard and our chores in the kitchen were completed. We moved into the living room where Patty was knitting a sweater. She continued working on her project while she joined in our conversation. Wilt again thanked her for dinner, exclaiming how much he had enjoyed the chicken dinner.

We shared with him the news of our recent purchase of the sleds and the trailer. He told us that it was a good deal. Wilt thanked us both and left about 9:00 for home. We walked him to his pickup and watched him drive away.

We took Ruben out of the dog run and walked him for a short distance before going in for the night. He was a good fellow. We both loved him dearly.

Patty went back to her knitting and I went into my office to check some reports, write a couple of letters, and seal some outgoing envelopes.

I had not yet devised a strategy that I would follow in response to Tom's request for my assistance. It was true the state troopers had the ongoing burglary investigation, however, Tom, being a friend, wanted me to look into the matter to see if I could develop any useful information and come up with the identity of the perpetrator.

After completing my office work I joined Patty in the living room. She continued to work on her knitting. We turned the television on and watched the late news. It was 11:30 by the time we decided to retire for the night. I checked the doors. My ninety-pound burglar alarm was on his air mattress and his eyes followed my every move. After brushing my teeth I climbed into bed. Patty joined me in a few minutes. We chatted about our day and decided that tomorrow would be a day of rest. We embraced, kissed, and happily drifted off to sleep. Happiness is being with the one you love.

The remainder of the weekend passed by quickly. After a hearty breakfast, Patty took up her knitting needles to work on her project. I went into my office and spent a big share of the day researching the Brady Book on checks. The Brady Book is the bible to the world of checks and the transactional crimes that take place.

Many of the large-scale check schemes were intricate and interesting, but in their haste for the almighty dollar the greed sometimes tripped the perpetrators up. Before I had retired from the troopers, as a member of the elite BCI, I had been involved in the investigation involving multiple check cases in New York State. The scheme was initiated in the Chicago area and flowed eastward into Ohio and into the Buffalo region. Several jurisdictions had worked their sectors concerning the case. In my area of responsibility, I had discovered that five checks totaling thousands of dollars had been passed. The final results had been the indictments of several codefendants, who I understand had plea-bargained. The losses had been tremendous and the recovery of funds minimal. Millions of dollars had been literally stolen in this manner. Unfortunately, these losses in the long run had been covered by the consumers. Beware of this type of criminal. They are smart, cunning, and would drain checking and savings accounts indiscriminately, if they get the opportunity.

Patty happily continued to work on her sweater, and my day was divided by a hike in the forest with Ruben. In the afternoon I put some silicone compound around the edges of our windows. I had had it done by a local handyman the year before, but by doing it myself we would save about thirty dollars. Very few windows needed the application. I used three tubes and challenged any amount of water to leak into the interior walls. I was quite satisfied with my endeavors.

While Patty prepared a tasty stew for supper, I went into my office and finished typing some bad-check letters to my clients. I had let Ruben in, and he was sprawled out between the living room and the office, lying on his right side. When I glanced over at him his right ear was twitching. I surmised he was dreaming of those feisty scampering chippies that had a way of challenging him when he was in the woods.

I had just placed the cover over my antiquated typewriter when the telephone rang. Patty answered it in the kitchen and called in to me, "Jason! Telephone! It's Gary Leach."

"Thanks, honey," I answered, picking up the office phone. "Hello, Gary. How are you?" I asked.

"Jason, I just received a cell phone call from a motorist passing by your driveway who claims to have spotted what appeared to him to be a sick coyote. It may be rabid. I called the Town of Webb Police and the State, but they're down south near Otter Lake handling a bad head-on personal-injury accident. Could I impose on you to check it out and call me back at home?"

"I'll check it out right away, Gary," I replied with concern.

"Don't take any chances. If you see the animal and it appears to be sickly, destroy it, but try not to shoot it in the head. We'll want to send the head to Cornell for examination," he cautioned.

"I'll call you if I encounter it," I assured him.

"Thanks, Jason." I heard Gary hang up.

I told Patty about Gary's call and removed my .41 Caliber Smith & Wesson revolver from the gun safe. Ruben was on full alert. I opened the cylinder and inserted six hollow-point cartridges, closing it firmly.

"Jason, what are you doing?" Patty came toward me, obviously anxious.

"I'm going outside to check for a possible rabid coyote."

"Honey! Be careful! Don't get bit!" Patty looked very frightened.

"No, Ruben, stay! You can't go with me," I said sternly.

I went out the side door and walked along the hedgerow toward Route 28. I had the revolver in my left hand. I remembered when I'd been on the job with the state, I usually shot as an expert. Now, however, I'd have to settle for being a sharpshooter in my retirement years, without having to participate in a test of my skills at a pistol range three times a year. I also understood that Gary must be busy or he would have taken care of the matter. I hadn't asked him about the other E-Con personnel in the region; I was glad to assist Gary any time. He was a good man. I had no complaints about him unless it was that he walked too fast on hikes. He was in good shape and kept himself that way. I knew one thing: in the past it had been Gary who had walked into the backcountry on many occasions to locate missing hunters or lost kids. I remembered how I had gotten turned around in back of Long Lake on a hunting trip with some fellows from Syracuse. I had had to fire my rifle three times until I was finally located by my hunting partners. Talk about a feeling of panic!

My boots felt good, especially with the cooler temperatures. I moved slowly, looking in every direction for a possible sign of the coyote. I was about fifteen minutes into my search when I spotted him near a brushy area just off Route 28, north of our driveway entrance. He wasn't moving, but I noticed he was shaking and looked sickly. It was clear he wasn't well enough to charge me, and I made the decision he needed to be killed. I crept as close as I possibly could without arousing him. I carefully took aim, placing the red dot in the location of the heart, and squeezed a round off. The slug made contact and tore into his diseased body.

Before I had left the log home I had picked up a pair of Patty's rubber gloves from the kitchen and a large plastic bag. I placed the revolver into the holster on my side and put the rubber gloves on. With a stick I prodded the still form of the coyote and ascertained that he was dead. I slid him into the bag with the stick. I don't think he weighed more than thirty pounds. I secured the bag with a plastic tie.

As I returned to the house, a partridge took off from a brush pile directly in front of me. Usually it was a wild turkey that would fly down from a tree. The turkeys must have moved farther north, as I hadn't seen many of them on or near our property lately.

Ruben was in the window with Patty as I slowly approached the log home. I was certain that Patty knew that I had been successful in locating the sick animal. Ruben's ears were straight up and I could hear him making squealing sounds from inside the house. I heard Patty pleading with him to quiet down. I placed the plastic bag containing the sickly coyote near the rear of the Bronco and went inside to call Gary back. He advised me that he would stop by and pick it up after supper. He thanked me for taking care of the matter and indicated that he would bring a 'destruction of animal form' with him for me to sign.

I went to the bathroom and thoroughly washed my hands after discarding the rubber gloves wrapped in a plastic bag. I then joined Patty in the kitchen where she had the table set for supper. I noticed two candles glowing in the center of the oak table. She smiled and came over to me and kissed me on the cheek.

"You must have gotten the coyote. I heard the shot." She furrowed her brow in sympathy.

"Yes, honey. I hit him in the heart area. It is too bad that he had to be destroyed, however, but I'm pretty sure he does have rabies. I placed him in the plastic bag and put it out by the Bronco. I imagine Gary will be stopping by soon." Very purposely I changed the subject. "Honey, your beef stew smells wonderful! Boy, am I hungry!" I exclaimed.

Patty had the table set with our finest china. Two candles were lit and shadows pranced. The aroma of the stew with its dark brown gravy teased my taste buds. The carrots, peas, potatoes, and celery would go well over the fresh hot biscuits. A cabbage salad, garnished with a tomato shaped in the form of a flower, was situated on the table near the center. I pulled Patty's chair out from the table and seated her. The flickering candlelight added a romantic aura to our modest dining area. Before I seated myself, I served Patty with a large spoon.

"Honey, I hope you like my stew," she said modestly.

"I know I will, sweetheart."

Each of us had two sizable helpings of the stew, which was delicious. The cabbage salad contained small chunks of pineapple, adding to the flavor, just the way we like it. I looked at Patty and grinned.

"Darling, the supper was perfect. You're quite the chef," I praised her.

"You're always saying that, Jason. You never complain." She blushed. "But thanks for the compliment."

We talked about the coyote, wondering if there could possibly be a rabies epidemic in our area. We both knew the dangers of the disease and the possible fatal outcome if bitten. Luckily, Ruben's shots were up to date.

"Patty, those biscuits you made were out of this world. Was that your recipe?"

"Yes, honey. Actually it was my mom's and I've held onto that recipe for years."

Ruben let out a loud bark as Forest Ranger Gary Leach pulled in with his red state truck. I went outside to meet him.

"Hello, Gary. How have you been?" I said, reaching over to shake his extended hand.

"Good, Jason. We're busy getting ready for winter. They say it's going to be a tough one this year. I see you've bought a couple of sleds. I looked at them over on the South Shore Road. They told me that you purchased them," he added.

"Yes, we thought we'd try some snowmobiling this winter."

"They look like good sleds. Have fun with them, but be careful. They can be dangerous." Gary was safety-conscious.

"I agree with you. I've seen some of these younger folks have some close calls and even a few have lost their lives. It's tragic."

"Yeah! You can say that again. All it takes is a little care and caution. By the way, I appreciate what you did, getting rid of that coyote. I'll take it off your hands and make arrangements to get the head to Cornell for examination."

"Glad to assist you, Gary. We don't need any sick critters around."

We chatted for a few more minutes and he had me sign the 'destruction of animal' form for the record. He told me he appreciated the way I had put the dead coyote in the plastic garbage bag. He asked me how Ruben was doing and we both walked over to the run. Gary had met Ruben before and knew the dog. He told me that if I ever wanted to sell him he would love to own him. I didn't want to turn Gary down, but after I explained the bond that the K-9 and I had, he seemed to understand that I'd never sell him as long as I was alive. We shook hands and he left my yard.

I have always been one of Gary Leach's greatest admirers. His knowledge of the area is unsurpassed. He knows every trail, lake, and mountain in the region.

After Gary left, I paused for a few moments. The air was crisp and I wouldn't be surprised if a frost would be visiting us soon. Then I went inside and helped Patty with the dishes and the cleaning of the kitchen. I had just finished wiping the last of the dishes when the telephone rang. Patty answered it.

"Jason, Mr. Huston is on the line." Patty handed me the phone.

"Hello, Tom. How are you?"

"Jason, I've been fine, but I do have a dilemma. Have you been able to develop any information regarding my property at Newcomb? I called the troopers and they informed me that they are working on the case. I told them that the only items definitely missing are an antique brass bell and some expensive fishing equipment." Tom's voice sounded troubled.

"No, I haven't. I plan to go to Newcomb on Monday and meet with a friend of mine who resides near your property."

"That's fine. What I'm mostly worried about is that gas can the troopers found in the house during their initial investigation. I think that someone was scared off. I fear they planned to burn the house down."

"It certainly is a possibility, Tom. I can understand why you're concerned. I know I would be." I wished I could have a better answer for him.

"Jason, I'll appreciate any information that you may obtain. I've told my insurance agent that the troopers are working on the case. And, that I have hired you as a private investigator to work in conjunction with their investigation," he added.

"Tom, my friend in Newcomb is Bob Bearor, an historian and an author, as well as a former member of the famed 101st Airborne of the US Army. He has his thumb on the pulse of the community and is well-liked. I'm going to see him as I have said and see what develops. Don't worry, Tom, Newcomb is a small town and we may be able to identify or find a lead over there. Even though the troopers are diligent in the performance of their duties, I might be able to learn something from the back streets. The main objective is to make an identification of the possible perpetrator."

"Jason, I don't know if I told you, but since I've been here at Lake Placid operating the Breakshire I have made many friends, but also an enemy or two. Among my real estate investments in this part of the Adirondack Park, some of my properties are old and quaint and worth a lot of money. If there is a person out there who wants to do me wrong, I want to know who it is?" Tom's voice rose to a high pitch. I could tell he was upset. I would do everything in my power to assist my friend. I knew that district well, and somewhere out there was the person or persons who had a dark side or an imagined grievance against him.

Tom asked how Patty was. I gave the phone to my wife and she chatted with him for a few minutes. After she was finished, I told Tom that I would contact him soon, hopefully with some useful information. We bid farewell and I hung up the phone.

I immediately called my friend Bob Bearor in Newcomb. I hoped to find him at home, as he was also involved in historical reenactments and presented programs throughout the Adirondack Park and other regions, which sometimes resulted in his absence for a period of time.

"Good evening, Bob. This is Jason Black from Old Forge."

"I thought it was you, Jason. How have you been?" he asked in a friendly tone.

"Good, Bob. Say, I'm working on a case for a gentleman from Lake Placid and I was wondering if I could meet with you tomorrow—providing you have some free time, of course."

"Jason, I'm free tomorrow. Certainly, stop by the house. What time do you think you'll be here?"

"Is 10:30 in the morning all right with you?" I queried.

"That'll be fine. I'm looking forward to seeing you. It has been a while."

"Yes, it has. See you tomorrow, Bob."

We hung up. I knew that if anything were going on in the Newcomb area, Bob would have an idea that could prove to be helpful.

Just before dark, Patty and I took Ruben for a stroll to the forest. Again I noted that our property did contain some sizable trees and thought of how Wilt Chambers, whenever he visited us, kept his eye on a couple of white oaks. Numerous times he'd reminded me, "Jason, those trees are worth a lot of money." I always acknowledged Wilt's statement with my own: "It's like money in a savings account, Wilt." He would roar with laughter and then slap me on the back with his large hand.

Patty and I both commented on how we felt more secure since the gigantic black bear had been darted and moved to another location. At the time the state biologist had indicated that the big bear would be less bothersome in the deep woods

of the park. Of course we had agreed with him. Residents and
visitors alike had the best intentions when they feed the bear
and the deer, but it wasn't the thing to do. The problem became
dangerously widespread when visitors to the area impeded
traffic along the South Shore Road by improperly parking their
cars, creating a traffic hazard. A law was enacted making it
illegal to feed the deer. This cut down considerably on the
number of violators, but there remained those few who still fed
the deer—directly under the warning violation sign.

Ruben sniffed near a small brush pile and a partridge took
off, catching us off guard. Ruben appeared startled with the
hasty flight of the fowl. I remembered when I had checked out
a property in the vicinity of Handsome Pond in the Long Lake
region, and a Broad Winged Hawk had circled overhead. He
had moved in a circular pattern and landed in a clearing
nearby. I couldn't help but wonder what the hawk had targeted.

When we returned to the log home we went inside. The
dark of night was upon us. Ruben headed for his air mattress. I
nodded at Patty.

"Honey, Ruben knows what side his bread is buttered on,"
she said, jokingly.

"Yep, he certainly does." I agreed, nodding.

We listened to some big band music, including the Glenn
Miller, Benny Goodman, and some of Tommy Dorsey's great
numbers. I respected all of the talented musicians, who
probably started playing when they were children. A little
music was good for everybody, soothing and relaxing.

We retired about 10:20, turning on our reading lamps. Patty
fell off to sleep first. I took the book she was reading and
placed it on the shelf at the head of our bed. I reached over,
kissing her softly on her cheek. I followed her soon to
dreamland.

CHAPTER SEVEN

The early morning air was crisp and our first noticeable frost covered the ground. I locked up and headed to the Bronco. Patty had already been at work for two hours when I called to say good-bye, advising her that I was leaving. I toyed with the idea of taking Ruben to Newcomb with me, but decided against it, putting him in his dog run instead. He immediately went inside his doghouse and didn't look too happy when I climbed into the vehicle. I looked over at him and rolled the window down.

"I'll see you later, Ruben." He put his head down between his paws, pouting.

I had to wait for a log truck coming down the hill toward Old Forge before I went out onto Route 28. He had just kicked it down into a lower gear and I could hear the air whiz as he applied his airbrakes. He looked as though he were hauling a heavy load. Some of the logs had frost on them. I wasn't familiar with the outfit, but assumed he was an independent logger, probably with a skidder, a bulldozer, and a loader. The tractor looked like a Brockway. The rig appeared to be in good condition. Probably my logger friends, Wilt Chambers and Charlie Perkins, knew him. The binders over the load looked tight and well placed.

Memories flowed when I spotted log trucks. My thoughts returned to Pulaski, when my senior man, Al Secor, had had me climb up on the top of the logs with the measuring tape, only to find the driver had met the legal height limit. I missed Al, who had passed on. I had had a good many meals at the home of Al and Grace Secor. I was certain they were still looking down on me from heaven above.

Route 28 had very little traffic. I picked up Route 30 at Blue Mountain and continued on north. I had planned on stopping at Gertie's in Long Lake, but decided to proceed directly to Newcomb to meet Bob Bearor. It was late morning when I pulled into Bob's driveway. I exited the Bronco and made my way toward his quaint home. The cobblestone walkway was an excellent addition to his property, and the surrounding grounds were well manicured in this attractive Adirondack setting. I knocked on the door. It was only a matter of seconds before he answered.

"Good morning, Bob," I said.

"Jason, it has been a while since I've seen you. Come in." Bob opened the storm door, letting me through.

"Yes, it's been a while," I agreed.

"How would you like a cup of coffee? I just brewed a pot," he offered.

"I'd love a cup," I replied.

I followed Bob into the spacious kitchen. I noticed the oak cabinets and the Corian countertops. A wagon wheel with six lamps was suspended from the cathedral ceiling. The windows were adorned with brightly colored curtains, which went well with the light beige wallpaper, giving the room its own unique quality. Bob and his wife had done all of the work.

The aroma of the coffee reached my nostrils.

"Where did you get those beautiful oak cabinets, Bob?" I asked with a touch of envy.

"You're looking at him, Jason. You know my wife has a great deal of patience. I built the cabinets myself right here in our kitchen. She kept the coffeepot full and I kept the saw busy. How do you like them?"

"They're beautiful, Bob. I love oak, too, and so does my wife. I wish I had the talent to create something like that."

"Listen, Jason. Anyone can do it, but you've got to create a diagram with the proper dimensions, laying it all out. Once you have it on paper, like a blueprint, visualized in your mind you can proceed with the project. You want to start out slow and take your time sawing the wood. Oh, yes. We could have purchased the cabinets already built, but we wanted the real thing, not just a thin oak coating."

"You can be proud of your accomplishment," I said with admiration.

Bob poured the coffee and complemented it with a plate of apple and cheese Danish. I had known Bob for a long time. He was a veteran of the famed 101st Airborne Division and had about seventy jumps to his credit. He was ruggedly handsome and kept himself in excellent physical condition. He was a great family man.

"What can I do for you, Jason? You mentioned something about a case you're working on." Bob showed his curiosity.

I explained to Bob about the entry to the Huston property, located diagonally across the road from him. I shared the information about the bell and the fishing equipment that was missing. I was careful to tell him about the half-filled gasoline can that was found at the scene by the troopers.

"Jason, I saw the activity over there. I had no idea who had purchased the property until just now. It appeared the troopers were doing their job. They took pictures and affixed a crime scene tape on trees around the house." Bob was descriptive.

"The troopers are checking the can for prints and making comparisons against those of known arsonists. If a fire ever started here in this community, several homes could be involved."

"That's true, Jason. Do they have any idea who may have committed this crime?" he asked, showing concern.

"If they have any suspect in mind, I don't know about it. I would appreciate it if you would contact me if you observe anything suspicious. It's a wonder the BCI—you know, the Bureau of Criminal Investigation—hasn't interviewed you," I stated.

"They may have stopped over, but we've been away for a few days, doing some research on a new book I'm starting. I'm not happy writing non-fiction material unless I go out into the field or the woods to experience the conditions I write about."

"Yes, I can understand that," I said, nodding my head in acknowledgement.

"If I see anything suspicious, I'll give you a call. I've been trying to think of anyone around here who could be a possible suspect, but at the moment, no one comes to mind. Folks around here are too busy working to make ends meet instead of getting involved in something like that."

"I can appreciate that, Bob. That is one thing that is peculiar to most of us, the work ethic. It is a continuous struggle to survive. If anything should develop on my end, I will call you."

"Jason, I'll keep a watchful eye on the property. Thank you for filling me in on the case. Don't be a stranger; you and the wife can stop by any time. Just call first to make certain we're home." Bob appeared anxious to assist me.

"Thank you for the coffee and the delicious Danish, and say hello to your wife."

Bob walked me to the door and out to the Bronco. He remarked about the Bronco and told me that it looked in good shape for an older model. I had to agree with him, gratefully; being a private detective, money was not too plentiful for me. I waved at Bob as I backed out of the driveway onto the road. I drove down the street a short way to the Huston property, an older Victorian home which needed painting. I got out of the Bronco and walked around the massive structure. The entrance door that the perpetrator had used was boarded up with half-inch plywood.

I didn't have a key to look inside. I noticed that the troopers must have dusted for fingerprints, as smudges of fingerprint powder clung to the wood and glass panes of several windows. A couple of spent flashbulbs lay on the ground. I mused to myself, remembering the many times when I'd been a member of the BCI and on those numerous crime scenes with the old-fashioned box camera.

There had always been some spectator that rushed to retrieve the spent flashbulbs as they plopped to the ground. I'd never forget the teary eyes of family members as they identified the deceased at scenes or in the morgues of my districts. I'd observed many tragedies during my career and knew that was one reason why a person has to maintain a sense of humor in order to survive the continuous barrage of unpleasant cases dealing with homicides and other matters dealing with loss of life. Yes, a barrier had to be maintained for self-preservation.

I looked around this stately home. I had had no idea that my friend Tom Huston owned so much property in the Adirondacks. I could understand now why Tom had been able to offer Patty and me lucrative positions at the Breakshire. I walked a considerable distance to the rear of the Victorian. A fence lined the Huston property in the rear of the home. There were numerous trees and several hedgerows. I paced off the distance from the back of the house to the rear fence line. It was approximately two hundred and ten paces, approximately six hundred feet. I looked closely for any sighting of evidentiary value, and found a small piece of blue denim, possibly from a pair of blue jeans. It was rectangular and measured about one inch across. It was sitting nicely on a sharp part of the barbed wire fence. I noted also that the wire was the middle strand of the three-wire fence and it had been stretched, possibly by someone climbing over. I looked closely for a shoe or boot print, but observed nothing.

I continued to walk further away from the fence into a slightly wooded area. I was just about to turn around, when I came upon a one-lane wooded road, which appeared to be well-traveled. There were some damp areas on the dirt road, apparently caused by a nearby spring, which ran off a slight hill. On closer observation, I spotted tire tracks that could have been made by a small pickup or a smaller SUV. I looked further, but didn't see anything that would enrich my search. I surmised that this area was possibly used as a lovers' lane, as I did see evidence of such activity thrown into the weeds.

I sauntered back to the Huston property and continued looking for anything that might identify the perp. I unfastened the piece of blue denim and placed it in my wallet. It was hard to believe that the troopers hadn't found the piece of cloth; perhaps they had just missed it. There had been the speculation that the burglar had been frightened off. My guess was that he had made his way in the dark to the fence, getting a pant leg caught on the barb during a hasty retreat. Had he cased the house, he would have been able to locate the wooded road easily. When he decided to hit the house, he would have been able to make his way from the vehicle without being detected. Anyone on the lovers' lane would just think it was another couple enjoying the autumn night.

I made a complete check around the property to ascertain that the doors and windows were all secured. My watch indicated it was 1:10. I left Newcomb via Route 28N heading toward Long Lake. I decided to stop at the Interpretive Center and make a telephone call to Tom Huston. I couldn't use my cell phone in this isolated region of the Adirondacks. There were a few cars parked in the upper parking area and the late autumn hikers were getting in their exercise on the three trail systems before Mother Nature sent us that fluffy white stuff we know as snow. Walking with hiking boots was easier than plodding along on Bear Cat snowshoes in deep snow.

After using the restroom facilities, I made the telephone call to Tom. He asked me if I'd mind coming to the Breakshire as soon as possible, as some further developments had occurred. I advised Tom that I would be on my way. I then called Patty at the diner to tell her of my plans. I hung up the telephone and thanked the employee on the desk.

Patty and I had visited the center in the past. It was a great place to enjoy nature and relate to the wilds of the Adirondack region. It was another place that solidified my continuous love for these old mountains.

Due to the light traffic on the highway, I decided to clean out the engine of the Bronco by hitting the gas pedal a little more than usual for about five miles. A trooper patrolling the region probably would have stopped me; however, I had it up to sixty miles per hour only for the short run.

I wanted to stop at Gertie's, but I had to get to Lake Placid in a hurry. I decided if they were open when I came back through I'd stop and say hello. It had been a long time since I'd seen Bob and his wife.

Tupper Lake was busy when I passed through. Route 3 had several log trucks carrying their heavy loads. I wouldn't have been surprised to learn that the harvested logs were heading to Japan as they do from Newport, Oregon. It had been a few years since I had visited Newport, that busy coastal town with great fishing, tourism, and log preparation. I had spent two days in the area where the logs were placed in the water and then loaded onto Japanese ships where they were processed and sold back to the United States. Prize timber!

I also recalled two young ladies wearing rubberized aprons and wielding thin-bladed long knives, creating filets for members of fishing parties upon their return trip from a successful day of fishing. The art of cutting the fish into filets had been something to watch. The two knife wielders, with precise motions, had cut the large fish into filets in a matter of seconds. The fishermen would drop dollar bills into their glass jar as a tribute for the women's speed and precision. I remembered how I had shouted down to them, "Good work!" They looked up from the dock, smiling. One had hollered up.

"Our knives are sharp—come on down!"

"No thanks, we're not fishing today," I had replied.

When I arrived at the Breakshire, I went inside and hurried past the two clerks on duty. One of them recognized me and said, "Mr. Huston is waiting for you in his office."

I responded, "Thank you."

I went down the short hallway and knocked on his door. When I heard, "Come in," I opened the door and found Tom just getting up from his desk.

"Boy, Jason, am I glad to see you." I had never seen Tom Huston look so pale.

"Tom, I got here just as fast I could. What is the matter?" I quickly asked.

I listened while Tom informed me of the two telephone calls he had received at the lodge. One had come in at 9:00 a.m. and the other shortly after at 9:30. He told me he had not recognized the voice. "It sounded like a male trying to disguise his voice by speaking in a low, garbled tone. As best I could make it out, it sounded like he said, 'We're going to ruin you and your business, Tom Huston.' Tom was visibly shaken.

"Did they say anything else, Tom? Did you hear any background noise, anything at all?" I asked. I noticed Tom's hands were trembling. It wasn't like him. He was always upbeat and strong-willed, no matter what event transpired.

"I've been wracking my brain trying to think of any possibilities whereby something like this might arise. I've always tried to conduct my business in a gentlemanly and ethical manner. You know, Jason, I'll walk across the street to avoid any confrontation with anyone." He spoke rapidly, placing his right hand to his forehead, perplexed.

"Tom, I've known you now for several years. You have an outstanding position here in the community and you're very highly respected. I want you to think, Tom. Is there a slight possibility of any one in your family, or any former business associates, that may have a deep hidden grievance against you? What about the brass ship's bell that was taken from your house in Newcomb? Is there any connection?"

"I have no idea, Jason. I'll have to think about it." He shook his head in despair.

"Do you mind, Tom, if I call Lieutenant Jack Doyle and advise him of this?"

"No, I don't, but I would be unhappy if this information got around town. This is my livelihood, Jason."

"I know exactly what you mean. I trust Doyle. He will be discreet in his investigation. And he's in a position to hear about things better than we can. But if you really don't want me to involve him, tell me now and I'll not mention it."

"Jason, I trust your judgment. I don't mind if you share the information with Jack Doyle," he agreed.

"Good. I'll pass it by him and get his opinion. In the meantime, keep track of any more of those calls. At this point, whoever this creep is, he is harassing you. We'll get to the bottom of it, but it may take a while. Please be sure to make a list of your properties and the addresses and get them to me," I requested.

I advised Tom of my trip to his Newcomb property and how I had contacted my friend, Bob Bearor. Bob would keep his eye on the property and report any suspicious activity to me. The small piece of blue denim that I had retrieved from his barbed wire fence was of interest to Tom. We talked for another half-hour. He asked me if I would like to dine with him that evening. I thanked him for his offer, but said that Patty would be worried if I didn't head for Old Forge. He told me to give her his regards, with an apology for holding me up.

Tom walked me to the Bronco. He seemed more relaxed. I assured him that I would do everything in my power to identify the telephone caller. He stood by the curb as I backed the Bronco from the parking space. I tooted the horn and he waved. I observed him as he walked back to the lodge. I knew that Tom was worried. He had had his life wrapped up in his lodge and his property ever since the tragic loss of his son, his only heir.

I drove southwesterly on Route 3, pulling into Troop S headquarters. I hadn't planned on contacting Lieutenant Jack Doyle of the BCI at this juncture of my investigation, but with the two telephone calls to Tom, I felt it necessary to notify him. I exited the Bronco and went into the station and requested to see Lieutenant Doyle. I was told by the receptionist to have a seat and that he would be right with me.

The magazine I removed from the rack looked interesting. I had just started to read an article on acid rain, when I was told that the lieutenant would see me. I walked down the hallway to the BCI offices. Jack Doyle came to the door and ushered me in.

"Good to see you, Jason. What's up?" He wore his big Irish

grin.

"I have something I would like to discuss with you."

"Have a seat."

I took the comfortable leather chair next to his desk. I told him that it concerned our mutual friend, Tom Huston, of the Breakshire Lodge. I referred him to the burglary case of Tom's Newcomb house and about the threatening telephone calls that Tom had received. The lieutenant was already aware of the ongoing burglary investigation and that a can half full of gasoline had been found at the Newcomb scene.

"Jason, I'll have the investigator that's working on the burglary case contact Tom. Maybe we can have a locking device installed to determine the origin of the call. I am cognizant to the fact that a brass ship's bell was stolen from the house, as well as some expensive fishing equipment."

I was pleased but not surprised to learn that Jack was aware of the criminal activity in his jurisdiction. He was one of the sharpest and hardworking lieutenants in the division.

"I appreciate that, Jack."

I removed my wallet and took out the piece of blue denim that I had found on the rear fence of the Huston property. I told the lieutenant how I had walked into the wooded area and found an old road that the perpetrator could have used. Jack seemed pleased to have the piece of blue denim. He placed it in a plastic evidence bag, then took a short statement from me as to my finding it. I indicated to him that Tom Huston had me in his employ and that I was going to be conducting my own investigation of his properties scattered throughout the Adirondack Park. I would be on the case until it was brought to a successful conclusion. It was evident that the caller was intent on causing some type of harm to Tom Huston, either to harm him financially or the destruction of his reputation.

The lieutenant assured me that his personnel would be alerted to the case and would keep in contact with Huston. I thanked him and left.

The highway into Tupper Lake was not crowded. The leaf-peepers in this beautiful north country, who had been driving along Route 30 for several weeks taking pictures with their cameras, were now gone. Winter was just around the corner.

When I reached Long Lake I wheeled into the parking lot of Gertie's Restaurant, parked the Bronco, and went inside. I would have a quick cup of tea. Gertie was cleaning the grill with a stone and looked up.

"Jason, where have you been? We've missed you. How's Patty?" She wore a big grin, happy to see me.

"Gertie, I've been busy. But you folks might see me more frequently. I'm working on a case in the Lake Placid area," I explained.

She carefully didn't ask me what kind of a case.

"Would you like a cup of green tea? We purchased it just for you, Jason."

"You bet I would. Where's Bob." I asked, looking around.

"He's gone home to take a nap. He opened early." She placed a tea bag in a cup. "You know, it won't be long before the hunters will be chasing the white-tailed deer."

"The time sure flies. I bet you get tired, Gertie." She looked exhausted.

"Time waits for no one, Jason. And yes, I'm bushed today," she said, as she poured the hot water into my cup.

The tea was hot, tasted good, and warmed me up. I placed two dollars on the counter, thanked Gertie, and told her to say hello to Bob. I left the restaurant and headed south on Route 30 for home and Patty.

The journey to Blue Mountain was uneventful, with no traffic until I pulled into Blue Mountain. I slowed the Bronco down to a crawl as I drove through the hamlet. The lake on my right looked cold and uninviting. Soon the snow would form a border around it when the mercury started to drop below freezing. Then the lake would take on another aura. Each had its very own special beauty. Oh, the wonders of nature.

As I drove by Drew's Inn, I observed several cars parked in the lot. I imagined Chef Mike cooking up a storm to please his loyal clientele with one of his daily specials. I wondered what the offering would be for this evening. My mouth began to water thinking about his delicious chicken and biscuits.

Inlet, Eagle Bay, and the entire Central Adirondack area were presently between seasons. Soon the red coats of the hunters would be seen invading the woods in their search for sport or food. The deer and the bear would be headed for the deep forest as soon as the retorts of a few rifle shots from the hunters' rifles resounded. I recalled the days when I had joined the avid group of hunters who loved this region to pursue their sport. But now it was my home, and I let the deer and the bear roam free. The hunting rifle had been retired to my gun vault.

Ruben was in his dog run at full attention when I pulled into the yard. Patty's Jeep was already turned around and ready for her departure in the morning for John's Diner, and her loyal customers. I had no sooner shut my engine off than Patty ran out of the door towards me. She had her arms ready to give me a big hug. I caught her as she flew into my arms.

"Oh, honey! I've missed you so much today." She placed her warm lips on mine and held me close. I didn't object. We hugged for a minute. Ruben let out a bark. We went over to the run and let him out.

"Did your day go well, honey?" I asked.

"We're always busy. But, most importantly, how did your day go?" she inquired.

"Tom's very upset with whoever is targeting him. He wants me to be available to look into it for him. The state police are involved, but they have other cases that they are working on," I explained.

Patty furrowed her brow sympathetically.

"I know how much faith Tom has in you, Jason." Then, changing the subject, she asked, "Do you mind franks and beans for supper, sweetheart? They will be quick and easy."

"That will be fine. Oh! On the way on the way home I stopped at Gertie's for a cup of tea. She told me to give you her best. Bob was home resting," I added.

Patty returned to the house and I took Ruben for a short walk. He ran ahead seeking out a chippie to chase. There were none. With the crisp temperatures the chippies were thinking about keeping warm and probably knew that Ruben was on the prowl.

I returned Ruben to the run and went inside to clean up for dinner. When I turned the faucet on in the bathroom, I heard a loud noise. Our water pump was going to need a visit from the plumber. It didn't make the noise all the time, but tonight it got my attention.

Patty had the candles lit when I went back into the dining area. They flickered, creating shadows on the walls. I sat down as she was serving the hot dogs with sweetened coleslaw, baked beans, sliced beets with onions, and corn bread. Assorted pickles filled a cut-glass dish that was one of our wedding presents. We drank ice-cold glasses of fresh lemonade.

"Patty, you didn't have to fuss. Everything looks elegant," I said, as I walked to the table.

"A dinner fit for a king and his queen," she shot back, flushing.

The candles continued to flicker and Patty's eyes sparkled in their glow as the light cast shadows on the walls.

During supper Patty talked about the goings on at John's Diner and the customers that were loyal not only to John and Lila, but to her also. She mentioned the people who made the diner the height of their social activity and the seniors who took their walk each day who would stop by for a cup of tea or coffee and maybe a sandwich or a dish of rice pudding. The culture of the diner atmosphere was friendly and comfortable for all who entered. Patty told me about some of the lasting friendships that had begun over a plate of sunny-side eggs and hash browns.

Like barbershops and beauty salons, the diner was not only a place to go to eat, but a meeting ground where local bits and pieces of news were discussed and even, on occasion, rumors were spawned. Strangers often invaded the locals' domain, raising their curiosity and inciting questions about why they were in the area. Were they here to purchase real estate, perhaps? Or were they here for a genuine love of the mountains? Or were they merely passing through admiring the scenery.

The hot dogs covered with the sweetened coleslaw and a dash of pickle relish tasted good. We each had two apiece. We sat around the dinner table, relaxing, enjoying each other's company, as I poured us each another glass of lemonade.

After supper, I cleared the table and washed the dishes in order to give Patty a break from the routine of the kitchen duties. She went outside and checked on Ruben, taking him out of the run and for a walk in the woods. I was putting the last dish away when the telephone rang. It was Bob Bearor calling from Newcomb.

"Hello, Jason. Sorry to bother you at dinnertime, but just wanted you to know that I made an interesting observation near the Huston property. I was out walking our yellow lab when an older car went by very slowly. There was a male driving it. The car was a rusty brown Chrysler four-door sedan, about a 1986, I believe. I couldn't get the plate number as both of the plates were covered with mud. It turned around in my driveway and slowly drove to the front of the Huston house and stopped. He was only there for a couple of minutes and then took off. I was thinking about going over to him and asking what he wanted, but thought it might interfere with the investigation." Bob seemed eager to assist.

"Were you able to see his face?" I asked.

"No, I wasn't. He was wearing large dark glasses, the type that fit over a pair of regular eyeglasses. I'll say one thing, I've been around Newcomb a long time and know who the locals are, but I've never seen this car before. It didn't appear legitimate, Jason. That's why I called you."

"I appreciate the call and I've jotted down all of the information. Let me know anything you notice, regardless of how insignificant it appears, Bob."

"Wish I could give you more information, but I'll keep a lookout, and if he shows again I'll try to get the plate number. Wearing those large sunglasses made it impossible to give a good description of his face," he went on.

"Thanks again for all your efforts."

"Take care, Jason. I'll call if anything further develops."

"Take it easy." I really appreciated Bob's call.

It was too late to contact Jack Doyle, so I decided I'd give him a call in the morning. I went into the office, and as I passed the window I could see Patty and Ruben outside by the dog run. The K-9 was very protective of us and the property. We were fortunate to have this highly trained dog and considered him an important part of our family.

We both retired to the bedroom at 10:30. Ruben retired to his favorite area of the log home, stretching out on his air mattress. Patty was reading a book from the library, and I was reading a history of World War II. At 11:00 the reading lamps were turned off. Patty snuggled close to me and we fell off to sleep in each other's arms.

CHAPTER EIGHT

I slept through Patty's alarm, not hearing her rise and get ready for work. I did feel a tug on the bedspread as Ruben apparently felt I had had enough sleep. It was time for his early morning run. I pushed the covers back and sleepily made my way to the door. It didn't take Ruben long to bound off into the woods. In a matter of minutes, he came out and made a beeline to his dog run. I was amazed that I hadn't heard Patty leave for work. The trip to Newcomb and Lake Placid must have taken more out of me than I realized.

With Ruben squared away and safely in the dog run, I shaved and took a fast shower. I then prepared myself a scrambled egg and two slices of whole wheat toast. Instead of decaf, I made a cup of green tea. I sat down at the table. It was lonesome without Patty, and I looked forward to when she'd be home later in the afternoon. I glanced at yesterday's *Post-Standard*. I always enjoyed looking through the classified section of the paper. I noticed there seemed to be many used cars on the market. I knew that one day the Bronco would give out and I'd have to replace it. For the time being, with the help of Doctor Don, my mechanic, the Bronco would get by for a while. Doctor Don kept Patty's Jeep in top running condition. In the Adirondacks it is important to keep vehicles in good shape.

After breakfast I called Lieutenant Jack Doyle and related

to him the information about the person operating the older model Chrysler that was allegedly looking over the Huston property. He informed me that he would have one of his investigators do a sweep through the area. I told him that I'd contact him if there were any new developments.

The next call was to Tom Huston at the Breakshire Lodge. I told him about the person in the old Chrysler and urged him to check his personnel files for any past employee who might be disgruntled over some imagined grievance.

"Jason, I'll check the files and let you know. I haven't had many employee problems here. The only incident I recollect is one involving our chef who had difficulty with a kitchen worker a few years ago. All I remember is that the chef went out into the parking lot to get into his car and found all his tires flattened. I'll look into it. But I was never directly involved." He added, "And, on rare occasions, I have had to discharge an employee."

"Tom, it may not have any connection at all, but it's worth looking into. I called Jack Doyle before I called you. He is alerting one of his investigators to check out Newcomb and the area for any possible sighting of the vehicle. He'll probably check garages, gas stations, and any junk yard or car dealers around Tupper Lake. There was a time, Tom, when you knew who was traveling our highways, but today they could be from anyplace."

"True. While I think of it, hope you and Patty are enjoying your married life. Jason, I miss my wife so very much." I could hear the change in Tom's voice, to great sadness. His wife had died of cancer several years before. "Well, I'll let you go. Let me know what you find out. Jason, today I'm going to send you a list of my properties here in the Adirondack Park. I'm also sending a copy of it to the lieutenant for his files."

"That's a good idea. I'll talk with you later, Tom."

"Goodbye for now."

I heard the click as Tom hung up his telephone. I made some notes about our conversation on a pad and typed up a file card and a short preliminary report concerning Tom Huston's property and the telephone threats. I realized I should have inquired if he had received any more calls, but then decided he certainly would have informed me if he had.

When I finished in the office I looked out at Ruben. He appeared alert. I could understand why, as a fat woodchuck was slowly moving across our property, only to disappear into a hole at the edge of the woods. Patty and I had seen the woodchuck before, but he or she wasn't bothering us and certainly had the right to be in his or her space. I never worried too much about the animals. They were here before us. My only concern was getting between a mother bear and her cubs. You could be in trouble then. And, of course, a possibly rabid animal posed an added worry.

I went to the post office and picked up our mail. There were several bad checks and a note from a local attorney, as well as two national magazines in the box. I placed the mail in my briefcase and stopped by to say hello to the postmaster. Many of us take the post office folks for granted, but all it takes is to observe a busy post office with dozens of customers and all kinds of outgoing and incoming mail in order to understand that the work ethic is very much alive. A busy place.

The parking lot was full and I had to wait my turn before backing up. I headed toward home, first stopping at the Old Forge Hardware and Furniture Store to pick up some art supplies.

As one of my main hobbies, I have always enjoyed sketching. I had some old sketch drawings of log cabins, trees and mountains, and a fire tower or two. Patty recently had shown an interest in this type of activity. Creativity wasn't that costly. We could always find paper and pencils, and I had a box of oil paint in tubes on the top shelf of the closet. You could say that we could be as busy as we wanted to be. Now we even had a couple of snow sleds to ride on the Town of Webb trail system when the snow arrived.

I had mentioned to Patty that on the cold winter nights we could do some watercolors or make an attempt to paint in oil.

When I arrived at the store I spoke with the present manager, Michael, who was in conversation with his predecessor, Henry Kashiwa. They looked up as I approached, and included me in their discussion. After a brief exchange, I asked Mike if he could please direct me to the art supplies.

Henry spoke up. "Are you taking up painting, Jason?"

"Yes, Henry. Patty and I thought we'd try it. Both of us have limited experience, but thought it would be interesting and help pass the long winter days."

Henry broke out in a big smile.

"Hopefully, someday we'll be entering one of our paintings at the annual show at the Arts Center."

"Good luck painting, Jason," Mike added.

The three of us chatted for a while and talked about the forthcoming winter. We predicted it would be a tough one ahead. I asked Henry if he were enjoying his much deserved retirement and he indicated that he was, but Mirnie, his lovely wife, kept him busy around the house and the yard. Henry also mentioned that they'd been doing some traveling to visit members of their family.

I thanked both of them and proceeded to the art department. I picked out brushes, and an assortment of oil paints and watercolors, along with several canvases. In addition, I purchased two easels and cleaning solution. In all likelihood, neither Patty nor I would become a master artist, but the activity would foster creativity and definitely would fill some of the void on winter nights as the great north wind swirled the snow down from the heavens. Along with plans for snow-sledding we needed more as we geared up to prepare for a cold, snowy winter. Besides our jobs, snowmobiling and creating works of art would help pass the time away.

As I was checking out, Mike stopped by the cash register and asked if I had found everything that I needed in the art department. I told him yes, and he helped me carry the purchases to the Bronco.

I arrived home in a few minutes and put everything away. I was just making a cup of green tea when the telephone rang. It was Dale Rush. I hadn't heard from him since the party at the Hard Times Café.

"Hello, Jason." He sounded excited.

"Dale, where in the heck have you been? How's your new friend, Evelyn?"

"Great, Jason. I've been helping her around the marina. We tore Kirby's sign down and burned it. The wood was decayed from termites. We put up a new one, which reads "O'Brien's Marina.""

"Good. I won't have to see Kirby's name anymore. Did Evelyn mount lights by her new sign?" I enjoyed knowing it would frost Kirby to see a new sign in place.

"Yes, I put them up for her. She has hired a fellow from Long Island to act as her manager. His name is Jim Jenny, about 46 years old. He knows the boat business, and has experience in an executive position with a national trucking firm. And he's a pilot with about seventy-five hundred hours of flying experience. He's got quite a sense of humor, too. You'll get a chance to meet him soon, I hope."

It had been a long time since I'd heard Dale so talkative. He sounded more like the Dale Rush people had known before his war experiences.

"Could I ask you a personal question?"

"Sure, go ahead."

"When's the big day?"

"Not until next year, but in the meantime we'll enjoy ourselves here in Old Forge and maybe go to Florida or Arizona for a few weeks this winter. One of the main reasons for me calling today was to ask you and Patty to join us on a flight to Maine. Evelyn has some business she has to attend to. She wants me to fly her plane to her brother's and leave it there for the winter in storage until she enlarges the marina here to accommodate both our planes. I'm not planning on installing the skis this winter." He waited for my response.

A trip to Maine sounded like a good idea, but I now had to consider Patty's feelings.

"Sounds great to me. I'll check with Patty to see if she can get the time off. How long would we be up there?" I asked.

"Three days at the most. I thought we could sample some of that Maine lobster while we're there." He knew how much I enjoyed that delicacy.

"I'll check with Patty and let you know. Thanks for thinking of us, Dale. It sounds great to me," I reiterated.

"We'd like to take off on Friday afternoon about 1:00 p.m. I checked with the national weather bureau and it looks good for Friday. By the way, we'll be returning in Evelyn's SUV," he added.

"I'll let you know by tonight. I assume you'll still be at the marina."

"Yes, I'll be here. Talk with you later."

After we hung up I glanced at my watch. I pondered with the idea of calling Patty at work, but decided to wait until she arrived home. We had talked for twenty minutes. I continued working in my office till Patty came home from John's Diner.

When the Jeep pulled in, Ruben let out a series of short barks. He raced back and forth in his run, and when Patty went over to him his tail was wagging. Patty reached into her jacket pocket and gave Ruben a dog biscuit, then petted his head. I watched them from the doorway. As I gazed at my beautiful wife I couldn't help but congratulate myself for having her in my life. Patty looked up and waved.

In a few minutes Patty was inside the doorway. I held her close and gave her a warm gentle kiss. She held me tight to her chest.

"Jason Black, I love you more than you'll ever know."

"Patty Black, I love you, too. How was your day, my sweetheart? I was going to stop in for lunch, but I ended up not having any at all. I did some shopping today for our cold winter nights. I picked up some art supplies."

"That's wonderful, darling. You know that I did some drawing in high school and started to do some painting in watercolors, but didn't follow through with it. We should have some fun. We both like mountain scenes." Her eyes lit up along with her magical smile.

I excitedly told Patty about the call from Dale asking us to join Evelyn and him for a flight to Maine for a few days. She told me that she had never flown in a small plane before. "I've only been in the commercial airline planes. The big ones. Do you think that it will be safe?" she asked with a concerned look.

I tried to reassure her. "It is probably safer than riding in an automobile, especially with all the traffic on the highway today."

We discussed it for a few minutes and we both agreed that it would be a wonderful little break from our routine schedule. "Patty, do you think John and Lila will give you a few days off?" I asked.

"Honey, there won't be any problem. In fact, just the other day Lila mentioned to me that I should have some time to rest as the diner has been somewhat stressful lately," she said, crinkling her brow.

"Well, see what she says."

"I will talk with her in the morning."

I called Dale and told him that we'd be happy to join them for the flight to Maine. We were both looking forward to the plane trip and the lobster.

For supper we had pancakes with maple syrup accompanied by some sausages we took out of the freezer. We added some chunky applesauce from the refrigerator, warming it up to put on the golden brown cakes. We accompanied the food with cups of hot tea.

After doing the dishes and cleaning the kitchen, we took Ruben for his daily walk down to the woods. We both wore heavier jackets. The air was crisp and cold. The walk was refreshing, and even Ruben seemed to move a little faster. We could see our breath. I held Patty's hand as we walked along. There were no chippies tonight, and I could tell that Ruben was disappointed.

The evening passed by swiftly, and soon Ruben was joining us inside on his place on the air mattress. Patty and I read for a while and went to bed around 10:00.

It seemed that we no sooner fell off to slumber than the Big

Ben alarm clock sounded. Patty must have shut it off, as the bell stopped ringing. I fell back to sleep and woke again when Ruben tugged on the bedspread. My dream of pulling in a lake trout was interrupted, and I'd never know if I were able to bring it to shore.

I pushed the covers back and got up, went to the bathroom, and splashed some cold Adirondack well water into my eyes. I felt refreshed and fully awake. I then let Ruben out for his daily trek to the woods. While he was checking out the brush piles along the edge of our property line, I realized that Patty had been at the diner for nearly two hours. I quickly made the bed and straightened up the room, thinking with contentment about how my wife and I worked together to keep our log home neat and livable.

It wasn't long before Ruben was sitting just inside his dog run gate waiting for me to come out and close it. He always scanned the area, and if he noticed anything he would bark. We hadn't seen many squirrels recently because at this time of the year the varmints were readying for a long winter.

After some toast and green tea I called Lieutenant Jack Doyle at Troop S Headquarters to see if there were any new developments that he would care to share with me. Tom Huston was a close friend, and I was determined to assist in this investigation any way I could. Someone apparently had a beef with Huston. I knew that Tom's work ethics were unquestionable, but now apparently someone wanted to harm him professionally and possibly personally.

"Good morning, Jason. You're calling early," he said in his non-business voice.

"Yes, I am. My concern is that someone is out to destroy Tom Huston and his business."

"You may be right, Jason. My investigators are hearing a few rumors about a young white male, unknown to us at this time, who was critically discussing Huston in one of the taverns in Saranac Lake. We are in the process of trying to identify the person, who we hope may have the fingerprint match to the set our evidence people found on the half-filled can of gasoline. That's all I can tell you. I know that you're close to Huston, and I understand the concern you have over this matter."

"Jack, I appreciate your comment. When I talked with Tom, I asked him to reflect on the past to determine who might have a grievance with him. And he is preparing a list of his Adirondack properties for my case file."

"Would you share a copy of those properties with me?"

"I'd be glad to, Jack, but Tom has already informed me that he would mail you a copy. By the way, a friend of mine has asked Patty and I to join him on a flight to Maine to stay for a few days, starting this Friday. I thought I'd let you know just in case you were trying to contact me. When we get back, I'll check out a few of the places in the Lake Placid area to see what I can hear. I do have some contacts that your people wouldn't be aware of. I hesitate to leave at this time, but it would only be a three-day stay. "

"Yes, Jason. Listen, don't worry. I'll have a patrol make a special effort to cover the lodge in your absence. And you don't have to tell me about your contacts, I'm very much aware of the unique way you ferret out information. I believe that Ed Wortley once indicated at a Chamber of Commerce meeting that you possess the 'all-seeing-eye.' How's that for a memory, Jason?" he asked.

"All I can say to you is that we try."

The lieutenant and I talked about the memories we shared about the Division and some of the former members who had gone on their final patrols: members who had dedicated their lives to the troopers and several who had made the supreme sacrifice for the people they served, never to be forgotten. The painful memory of Jack's own brother, Bill, who was killed by a ruthless maniac many years before, was deeply ingrained in our hearts and souls. After our reminiscing, the lieutenant assured me that in the event of any new developments in the Huston matter, he would contact me personally.

He said goodbye, wishing us a safe flight to Maine.

I called Tom Huston at the Breakshire Lodge. Fortunately

he was in his office. I told him about my telephone call to the lieutenant, who had informed me that some unknown person was shooting their mouth off in one of the local taverns speaking very disrespectfully about the Breakshire and Tom Huston.

"Jason, I've been mulling over in my mind possible people I might have agitated in the past. I haven't been able to come up with the name of any individual that I personally had a problem with. I have always tried to keep my standards highly professional in all the avenues of business that I conduct with others." His voice again revealed deep concern.

"Tom, it could be a mentally deranged individual with an imagined grievance. Maybe even someone you never met before."

"You could be right on that. I'm going to be extremely cautious on this matter. I have too much at stake. By the way, I dropped that list of properties in the mail to you at Old Forge and a copy to the Lieutenant. You should have yours soon."

I advised Tom that Patty and I were joining Dale and his new friend, Evelyn O'Brien on a flight to Maine. I assured him that Lt. Doyle had been informed, and would provide a special patrol to check the lodge. Tom asked me to say hello to Dale. As I was about to say good-bye, I told Tom I would give him a call upon our return, and that the four of us would drive up to the Breakshire for dinner in the near future. He indicated that he'd look forward to seeing us.

From the conversation with Tom Huston I sensed that the burglary of his Newcomb Victorian home and the finding of a gasoline can half full of fuel was taking a toll on him. It would anybody. Not knowing the identity of the perpetrator was painfully disturbing to him. This was a man who cared deeply for the Lake Placid region, a man who treated everyone with kindness and affection. I dearly hoped that through the untiring efforts of the troopers and the small part I would play, a suspect would be developed. Only time would tell.

CHAPTER NINE

Friday morning came rapidly. After securing the house, double-checking the locks on the windows and doors, Ruben was taken to one of his favorite places, Lynn's Eagle Bay Kennel, where he would prance around as king of the dogs. We told Ruben to be good. Before Patty and I left the kennel, he had already turned his back to us, his unmistakable way of pouting. We both loved him, but couldn't help smiling a bit.

Evelyn O'Brien and Dale were standing by a dark green Stinson Reliant with white floats on it. The plane appeared in excellent condition. For some reason it looked larger than Dale's red and white plane. They were putting their bags aboard. Dale had told us not to bring more clothes than we needed for three days. Both were dressed casually and were wearing flier's sunglasses. When they spotted us, they broke out in smiles and greeted us like royalty. I recognized another plane tied up at the dock, with its pilot, Supervisor for the Town of Inlet, John R. Risley (aka J.R.) and his lovely wife, Chris.

Patty and I walked over to where J.R. and Chris were preparing to take off. We chatted for a few minutes and told them to have a good flight. I had known J.R.'s father for several years. He was the late Bruce Risley, an excellent pilot and a member of the elite BCI of the state troopers. I watched as J.R. started the engine on his Cessna seaplane, and I waved at them as he taxied toward the middle of Fourth Lake.

Dale had already stowed our bags away onboard the Stinson, and he was making a last-minute cursory check of the aircraft. Patty and Evelyn were deeply engrossed in conversation. In about twenty more minutes we boarded Evelyn's Stinson, with Dale at the controls. Evelyn and Patty were seated behind us. I was next to Dale, who was busy checking the instrument panel. It was 10:55 a.m. when we lifted off for Bar Harbor, Maine. I looked around at Patty to see how she was doing, as this was her first flight in a small plane. She appeared a little nervous, but managed an apprehensive smile.

"Patty will do fine." Evelyn said, reaching over for my wife's hand.

Dale headed northeast across the Adirondacks into Vermont and across part of New Hampshire. Evidently, he had flown this way many weekends to meet Evelyn in Bar Harbor. I chuckled to myself again over how it had come as a complete surprise to me when Dale had revealed his best-kept secret at the Hard Times Café and placed a diamond ring on her finger that evening.

"Dale, where will we be landing?" I was curious.

"We'll be landing at Prospect Harbor. We've made reservations at the Ocean Side Meadows Inn. It's a nice place to stay. Evelyn called her brother last week. He had to fly to England on a business matter or we would be staying with him, but we thought this would be a treat. The Ocean Side is top shelf with outstanding accommodations." Dale seemed happy, and even more like his old self.

I had visited Bar Harbor once several years before. As Dale started to cross the Acadia National Park, Evelyn told us that most of Acadia is on an island named Mt. Desert Island, consisting of private land as well as park land, and containing seaside villages, which are generally filled in the summer. Other park properties are scattered on some islands and a peninsula.

She went on to tell us that Mt. Desert at one time was a

continental mainland, with a mountainous granite ridge on the edge of the Atlantic Ocean. She explained that Samuel de Champlain, who had explored the coast in 1604, named the island L'Isle des Monts Deserts. The original name of the park, Lafayette National Park, which covered about 35,000 acres, was changed in 1929. Dale brought the plane down to take a look around the park's visitor center. I noticed that there was very little turbulence.

I admit that it was nice to look over the Acadia National Park, but as a fan of the great Adirondack Park I could view other places only as a tourist. I asked the ladies if they were enjoying the flight. They nodded their heads, indicating their approval.

Dale brought the Stinson in for a perfect landing on the waters of Prospect Harbor. There was a little choppiness to the surface, but it didn't cause a problem. This was not the first time Dale had landed there. He had secured permission to do so from the Bangor International Airport. I noticed that two other seaplanes were secured at dockside. The temperature seemed comparable to what it had been in the Adirondacks, with highs in the forties.

The Ocean Side Meadows Inn had transportation waiting for us. I assumed that Evelyn had made all the arrangements. Dale secured her seaplane.

The four of us, along with our luggage, entered the limousine. The chauffeur was courteous and wheeled the long white limo toward the inn with the efficiency of an expert. When we arrived we exited the vehicle and went into the lobby, while our luggage was removed and taken to our rooms. Dale gave the chauffeur, Melvin, a sizable gratuity. He graciously thanked us and went out to his limo, which was parked by the entrance.

Dale and Evelyn had adjoining rooms, and Patty and I were down the hall a short distance. The rooms were breathtaking. The furniture appeared to be colonial and matched the elaborate wallpaper. On the table of each room was a bottle of champagne in a large receptacle of chopped ice. Each had a corkscrew and two glasses sitting on a tray. The tray was hand-painted with images of starfish and lobster traps. They were unique. I couldn't help but wonder who the clever artist was, and then I noticed in one of the starfish was the name, C. J. Leeson.

After we had all freshened up, Evelyn knocked on our door and suggested that we all go to her family's marina known as O'Brien's Cruise Lines. She wanted to pick up some important papers that had to be filed with the IRS.

She had already made arrangements for a large-size rental car that would accommodate the four of us, a four-door black Lincoln sedan, which was waiting in the parking area near the front entrance.

Once we were in the car, Evelyn said, "Dale, after we leave our offices I want to take everyone to the Seaside Lobster Bin for some of the best lobster on the East Coast. Perhaps Patty and Jason would enjoy some fresh lobster drenched in melted butter." She smiled, looking over at Patty and me.

"We'd love some," Patty responded. "We both love lobster."

"Jason, when Dale flew here on weekends, that is the first place we'd head for. I won't be but a minute in the office and then we'll have Dale chauffeur us to the restaurant. I told Dale that we should have a place in Old Forge that specializes in just lobster and lobster bisque, especially in the summer time."

I could tell that Evelyn was a fellow lobster fan. We all agreed with her. It would be unique to have that type of establishment, even though lobster is available at some of our Old Forge restaurants. I could see Evelyn's point, especially for the people who love seafood.

Evelyn explained the origin of their family business, and related how her brother had purchased her share of the Bar Harbor-based cruise lines in order to enable her to acquire Kirby's in the Old Forge area. She would operate her own marina—of course, with the help of Dale Rush. She would miss the coast, but was looking forward to her new life and challenges.

We pulled up in front of a massive ocean side structure. Evelyn exited the vehicle, informing us she would be right back. She entered through a door marked with a small sign indicating it was the office. A large sign caught Patty's and my immediate attention: The O'Brien's Cruise Lines, painted in large black letters on a white background. The corner of the large sign displayed two antiquated sailing ships from the 18th century. Large white-capped ocean waves were painted on the background, along with two diving pelicans looking for their meal. A white fish hung from one of the pelican's mouths. Patty quickly took the camera from her pocketbook, jumped out of the car, and snapped a picture of the sign.

Dale got out, opened the hood on the Lincoln, and checked the oil, after mentioning that the oil light flickered on for an instant. He wiped the oil stick with a tissue and placed it in the round-long tube and hollered back to me the oil was on the full line on the stick. Everything appeared orderly. It was only a matter of five minutes before Evelyn returned carrying a large brown manila envelope. She was wearing a big smile.

"That didn't take too long, did it?" she asked.

"I'd wait for you forever," Dale answered, with a chuckle.

I looked at Patty and gave her a wink. It was clear that our friend Dale had been hit hard by Cupid's arrow, and we were happy for him.

Evelyn pointed out interesting sights as we proceeded to the Seaside Lobster Bin. The restaurant was located on Newport Drive. There were other eating establishments in the area, but the Seaside Lobster Bin was unique. The large sign in front displayed a large trap full of the creatures. My taste buds had become stimulated in anticipation of the feast that would be forthcoming.

Dale pulled the Lincoln into a parking space a short distance from the entrance. He got out and opened the car doors for Evelyn and Patty. I opened my door and stepped out. I looked around at the grounds, which were well-manicured. Two large anchors painted black, and appropriately spaced were situated by the front entrance. Decorative lobster traps draped with fishing nets were placed along the walkways. Lights on black iron posts adorned the perimeter of the property.

People were standing in line to be seated as we entered. There were waitresses and waiters rushing to and fro, some with large trays being supported by one arm loaded with steaming whole lobsters and plates containing just the harvested lobster meat garnished with dark green parsley. I eagerly noted all the cut glass bowls containing melted butter. Large pitchers of light and dark ice-cold beer were served to the customers, along with frosted glasses and roasted peanuts. I looked down on the floor and saw the thousands of peanut shells crunching under people's feet.

As I followed Dale, Patty, and Evelyn, I gazed around at the booths and tables. Customers were cracking the lobster shells and then dipping large strips of white meat into the bowls of melted butter. One senior citizen was wiping melted butter from his chin with a large linen napkin. He looked up at me with his aged face and large bushy brows with a twinkle in his eye and muttered, "Mighty good, lad." I smiled at him and walked on.

Our table for four was by the window overlooking the grounds of the Seaside Lobster Bin. Some of the bushes had been covered to protect them from the frost that was due to hit soon. The table of cherry wood was covered with a white linen tablecloth. Two candles flickered in the center. Dale seated Evelyn, and I pulled the captain's chair out for Patty.

A server bearing a nametag approached the table. "I'm Felix. I will be your waiter today." He was a tall, sandy-haired man, probably in his twenties. He wore a pink shirt, which displayed a small whole lobster above the left pocket, opposite his nameplate. His slacks were gray. A small pearl earring adorned his left ear lobe.

"What can I get you for drinks, folks?" he asked cordially, then took our order: beer to be served with our meal, all deciding on the whole-lobster dinners. While we were waiting, the girls engaged in conversation, as Dale and I commented on

Old Forge and the continuing growth that the south central Adirondacks was experiencing. We discussed the influx of snowmobilers and their acquisition of property in our region.

Dale felt there was a strong need for tighter controls on sleds going over private property. He himself had sustained damage to his shrubs and small-planted trees on his land. I agreed with him that the operators of the individual sleds should respect posted areas and adopt a more respectful attitude toward the rights of property owners. I myself had been the owner of four sleds in the past, and had enjoyed the winter adventures of snowmobiling, but I always respected private property. After all, the trail system provided ample territory for the snowmobile enthusiast.

Prior to the serving of our lobsters, our waiter arrived at the table with four hot steaming bowls of lobster bisque. Oyster crackers accompanied the bisque, which was an added offering to all the patrons. It was delicious, with tender chunks of meat floating near the top. We all enjoyed this added treat.

Felix, assisted by another waiter, brought our large platters of lobster, and melted butter, accompanied by salt potatoes. Two pitchers of cold beer were poured into our fat frosted beer glasses. The shells of steaming lobsters cracked easily with the tongs provided. Greedily we dipped generous portions of lobster into the depths of the butter bowls, savoring the delicacy, until only empty shells occupied our platters. During this culinary delight very little conversation took place. As we sipped the rest of our beer, Evelyn turned to Patty and me. "So, you two, did you enjoy that Maine lobster?" she asked, smiling warmly.

Dale was busily wiping the remaining melted butter from his chin.

"I sure did!" Patty exclaimed, and I nodded my head in agreement.

"The restaurant has been here for years and is one of the finest in the area. The cook's from a family of chefs who all graduated from the Culinary Institute of America. My brothers and I have come to this restaurant for years, and the food is always delicious. I'm so happy that you liked it. Dale and I kind of think of it as our special place to come to when we're in Maine.

Dale's eyes met hers "Yup, it sure is a wonderful place for lobster," he chimed in, teasingly.

None of us could even think about having dessert. When Felix brought the check, Evelyn hastily took it from his hand, insisting it was her treat, but did consent to our leaving the gratuity. Felix thanked us for our patronage, as well as the gratuity we left him. Before we left the restaurant we learned that he would soon be off to Oxford, England for some special studies in history. We wished him well.

Before we returned to the inn we did some sightseeing at Acadia National Park. It was breathtaking. Evelyn shared some historical background, relating that almost 20,000 years ago, thick sheets of ice flowed over the mountains, rounding their tops, cutting passes, gouging out lake beds, and making the valleys wider. The melting of the glaciers made the sea rise, flooding the valleys and drenching the coast. The land transformed to today's lake-studded mountain island, which branches out from the Atlantic similar to the claw of a lobster. We listened closely to Evelyn as she described this unique region.

It was dark when Dale pulled the Lincoln into the parking space at the inn. Four tired people exited the big car. Dale locked it and we made our way to our rooms.

Our room was elegant. We agreed that the accommodations were first class, but we both missed the comfort of our bed in our log home. We wondered how Ruben was faring at the kennel. One thing we both agreed on, we sure missed him.

The next two days were filled with more sightseeing, including a tour of the coastline and a drive from one end of Bar Harbor to the other. Our only regret was that we couldn't meet Evelyn's brothers, as they were both in England on business.

She did give us a tour of O'Brien's Marina. We were impressed as she explained the history going back several generations, when her great-great-grandfather drove the first nail into a wooden building where he went on to labor over his creation of sailboats and fishing boats. She shared with us the story of his demise, as taken from family history: he was whaling and his leg became tangled in the line and the harpooned whale took him from the whaling ship to the depths of the Atlantic, never to be seen again. I noticed tears forming in her eyes as she ended her account. I shuddered, realizing how terrifying it must have been to feel the tightening of the rope on his leg as he was pulled by such a powerful force. What a horrible drowning! I couldn't help imagining his agony, with no control over his last moments of life....

The end of our time in Maine was in sight. It was decided that we would depart early in the morning from the inn. Evelyn would stop at O'Brien's Marina once more, and then Dale would drive the rental to Old Forge and then drop it off at the Syracuse airport. Evelyn would follow Dale with his SUV.

We told Dale and Evelyn we were staying in for the evening as I had to do some work on my case. This choice had a two-fold purpose: Dale and Evelyn could have some time alone, and I would be able to make my calls. Patty curled up on the davenport while I was on the phone. We both decided that we would stay in the room, order some sandwiches, and watch some television later. We both missed our Ruben.

Dale let us off at the inn and they continued on their way. We went to our room and watched the national news, and then I placed several calls to Lake Placid and Raybrook. It was rather late to make calls, but luckily Jack Doyle was still in his office at Troop S Headquarters. He told me about another burglary at a Huston property located in North Creek. There had been no arson attempt or gas cans found at the scene. The only item taken was a grandfather clock. After we had finished our call, I phoned Tom Huston on his private number.

"Tom, Jason here. I just talked to the lieutenant and he informed me of the North Creek burglary."

"Good to hear from you, Jason. Did he mention anything about the threatening call I received? Some male called last night at 5:00 p.m. and told me he was going to ruin me and my business." Tom sounded truly troubled.

"No! He didn't. Maybe he didn't want to worry me." I felt even more concerned for Tom now.

"When will you return to Old Forge?" he asked.

"We're leaving early in the morning."

"Call me when you get back. I might have an idea or two. I've been doing some serious thinking about my past dealings with people."

"Tom, try not to worry. We'll find out who this bird is. When we do let's hope the justice system will deal with him. I assume your list of properties will be waiting for me in the mail box, which will be helpful."

"You're right. Okay then. I'll see you when you get back. Say hello to Patty, Dale, and his lady friend for me."

"I will. Take care, Tom" Although I'd tried to be encouraging to him, I was worried about the growing developments in this case. Who was this person who was instilling fear into the heart of my friend, Tom Huston?

Patty and I shared a tuna-fish sandwich and some ice tea. We watched a television movie, a love story without violence. We succumbed to some love-making of our own. I kissed Patty goodnight. It was a long kiss! We drifted off to sleep in each other's arms.

The telephone sounded at 3:30 a.m. with two short rings. I reached over and picked up the receiver.

"Good morning, Mr. Black. I hope you slept well, sir," the night clerk said.

"Thank you for calling."

Patty had rolled over toward me and reached out to embrace me. We held each other for a short while and then pushed the covers back. The telephone rang again. This time it was Dale making certain that we were awake and getting ready to travel.

At 4:15 a.m. we placed our luggage in the rear of the Lincoln. Dale and I checked out, while Evelyn and Patty made a visit to the powder room. The four of us had made coffee in our rooms before we left. The plan was to stop along the way for breakfast. Before leaving the grounds of the Ocean Side Meadows Inn, Dale checked over everything. He was a stickler for detail. The windshield, mirrors, and back window were glistening. He had even wiped off the tail lamps.

The four of us agreed that the inn had been an excellent place to stay. This was the third day of our journey and we were headed back to the Adirondacks. On the way to Ellsworth, Evelyn told us that even though she would miss Bar Harbor she was looking forward to spending the remainder of her life in the Adirondack region.

"What led you to become a pilot, Evelyn?" I asked.

"My dad had been a bush pilot long before he entered the marina business, and as a small child I spent many hours in the air with him. So, when I became old enough, he taught me how to fly, and I entered a flight school. The rest is history. I became a partner with my brothers in the family business after dad passed away. My mother died two years before dad." There was a tone of sadness in her voice.

Dale spoke up, "Jason, I never told you this, but a couple years ago when I took a couple of Maine fishermen back to Bangor and then flew to the coast, I noticed my fuel gauge acting up. I set down at the O'Brien Marina and this young lady greeted me at the aviation fuel pump. I knew right away that I had to get to know her."

Patty and I were happy for Dale and Evelyn. I knew personally how lonesome life could be. The twists and turns of life's journey is a mixed bag. To be able to share a thought with another person is important to everyone. It's important to be a good listener, too, and not to draw hasty conclusions. Patty and I were careful to discuss all issues that might arise, a policy that makes for a stronger union. A healthy couple shares each other's thoughts and then decides which avenue to pursue.

Dale wasn't only a good pilot; he could drive the big Lincoln like a professional chauffeur. Daylight was beginning to break as the sun started to rise from the east. As we entered I-95 at Bangor, Dale pulled into the parking lot of a quaint

New England diner. It appeared that they had just opened for the day. Dale and I opened the doors for Evelyn and Patty. Several cars had just pulled into the parking lot.

We entered the diner, which consisted of a long row of stools, large booths, and several tables. We opted for a booth. We had just sat down when a waitress appeared and took our order. We started out with four glasses of orange juice, and three cups of coffee, and I ordered a pot of black tea. We decided that the special posted on the menu would be our choice: scrambled eggs with bacon and toast.

While the short order cook prepared our food, we chatted about our trip. I asked Evelyn if she had ever gone to the L.L. Bean store at Freeport, Maine, a place I had always wanted to visit.

"Jason, I've been there many times. It carries a good line of sporting goods and is popular with hunters and fishermen and tourists."

"One time, a couple of fishermen I flew into the Adirondacks presented me with a five-cell flashlight from L.L. Bean. I still have it at home," Dale interjected.

Our breakfast soon arrived with assorted jams and jellies for our toast. Everyone agreed the chef knew his business. The eggs were scrambled just right, without becoming dry. The bacon was straight and crisp. The waitress kept our cups full and brought me a second pot of black tea. When she returned with the check, I intercepted it as she was handing it to Dale. But he insisted that he leave the gratuity.

Before we left the diner, we all made a trip to the rest room prior to the long drive ahead.

Traffic was light on Interstate 95 that morning. We spotted a Maine State Police cruiser situated near the entrance ramp, probably watching for speeders. Dale tooted the horn as we passed him.

When I observed the Maine Trooper sitting in his cruiser I remembered my days with the New York State Troopers and the many times that I had observed passing cars and trucks, knowing that good and evil rode those highways. The invention of the wheel and the motor car had been important to the development of our country, but as years passed and criminal activity crept into the fiber of our society, the good and evil would sometimes come in contact with each other. My memories consisted of numerous cases that I personally came in contact with. That was in the past, and now as a private investigator I couldn't help but wonder, why evil was entering the life of Tom Huston, owner of the Breakshire Lodge in Lake Placid.

In a few hours we found ourselves on I-89 headed toward White River Junction and Rutland, Vermont. A few weeks earlier we would have been in long lines of leaf-peepers, but now they were preparing for the onslaught of the winter ahead, along with the rest of us. I could hear the girls chatting in the rear seat. They obviously got along with each other very well. Dale was keeping his eyes on the highway and wasn't saying much.

We stopped at Whitehall near the New York and Vermont border for lunch. The diner was well known. Booths lined one side and there was a row of stools at the counter. The stainless steel behind the grill and counter sparkled. We seated ourselves in a booth. The waitress appeared and informed us that the lunch special was stuffed green peppers with homemade bread. The four of us opted for cheeseburgers, with iced tea to drink. In a few minutes our cheeseburgers were placed before us. Each plate was complemented by a slice of dill pickle. The burgers were delicious. We then treated ourselves to dishes of rice pudding topped with real whipped cream.

When we arrived in Glen Falls, Dale pulled into a service station for gas. Route I-87 was heavy with traffic both north and southbound. We headed north on I-87 to Warrensburg and on to Route 28.

I looked over at Dale and asked him if he'd like me to relieve him at the wheel.

"No, Jason. I'm okay." He sounded sleepy.

The remainder of the trip took about an hour and fifteen minutes. Dale and Evelyn dropped Patty and me off at the marina. They wanted us to come into the office for coffee. We declined, as we were both tired from the long drive home. We thanked Evelyn and Dale for the wonderful time we had had on the trip and, after transferring our luggage to the Bronco, we drove home.

As we pulled into our driveway we could see that our security light had come on. When I stopped the Bronco the brakes made a slight grinding noise. We got out and Patty helped me with the luggage. I checked the log home and found everything to be in order. In the morning I would go to the kennel and pick up Ruben. I knew he missed us and we missed him.

Upon entering, the house seemed cool. I turned the thermostat up, and the furnace started immediately, quickly warming the interior. We unpacked our luggage, hanging clothes in the closet, clean socks and underwear in their proper drawers, and soiled laundry in the hamper.

We decided on a light snack, cream of tomato soup, and grilled cheese sandwiches. Patty washed the dishes, while I dried them and put them away. What a team! With the two of us working together, our chores seemed effortless. We retired to the living room for the couch and a short night of television. But we were exhausted from our long drive, and decided to call it an evening early.

We got ready for bed and talked about our three-day trip to Maine. We both agreed that it was a good time and someday we'd return to Bar Harbor and explore the region more fully. The northeastern coast was scenic and offered many sights for the tourists; however, the one place I adore is the Adirondack Park. When I was a child riding with my late father in his log truck, the environment of the wooded forest became imbedded in my heart and soul and it will remain that way until my final day on earth.

Sleep arrived instantly for Patty, while I read for a while. My eyelids finally succumbed to drowsiness. I believe I heard the raccoon on the back roof as I surrendered to sleep. The next sound was the Big Ben alarm. Patty must have pushed the button down, as I fell off again into the state of slumber.

CHAPTER TEN

Patty had been at work for two and one half hours before I pushed the covers back. I didn't want to oversleep, especially this morning when I had to go to Eagle Bay to pick up the K-9. A hasty shower and shave, followed by a cup of green tea, snapped me awake and somewhat alert as I answered the ringing telephone at 9:45.

"Good morning, private sleuth! Jack Doyle here. It's about time you got back. Didn't you check your answering machine? I've been trying to call you." The lieutenant sounded a bit tense.

"Jack! Hold it!" I quickly checked my answering machine only to find that the tape had broken. "Lieutenant, I'm sorry, but the tape broke, apparently from old age. I'll replace it today. What's up?" I asked.

"Have you talked with Tom Huston in the last day or so? He contacted me this morning to tell me that he had to fire a groundskeeper about two years ago. There is a possibility that the groundskeeper's son could possibly be a suspect in his two burglaries. It seems that Huston, just by accident, came upon the gardener, Scott Harris, in the act of stealing a Briggs and Stratton engine. Further investigation by Huston revealed several other items had gone missing from time to time. Huston gave Harris the chance to tell all or to talk to a trooper. Harris spilled his guts, admitting the thefts, but Huston didn't want to pursue criminal action, giving him the option to resign."

"I called him from Maine before we left. Maybe that was before he had come across that information," I mused.

"Oh! I see. Well, he indicated he had just recollected the firing and wanted me to know about it. The son's name is Morey Harris, about 28 years old. He doesn't have a criminal record, but apparently is a druggie. The father and son may be revengeful against Huston. It could be an unpleasant situation."

"You're right. It could get nasty."

"Jason, I have an investigator checking this out. If you come up with any information during your investigation, please let us know right away. I know that Mr. Huston thinks a great deal of you."

"He's a fine person, Jack. Did you receive a copy of his list of Adirondack properties? I haven't checked my mailbox yet. I hope to receive them today. I'm certain he was sending you a copy of the list."

"He mentioned it over the telephone. My copy hasn't arrived yet."

"I can't get up to Placid today, but maybe tomorrow I'll do some checking around. I have a couple of ideas. Jack, I've heard of Morey Harris and what I heard isn't favorable. You'd better tell your investigator to use caution in the event he comes across him."

"I'll mention that to him. By the way, the investigator's name is Bill Timmer, in case you come in contact with him. He's a good cop."

The lieutenant and I talked a few minutes longer and then hung up. I mulled over the information Doyle had shared with me. I remembered Scott Harris when he had worked at the Breakshire. I had never talked to him, but did encounter him several times as I walked around the grounds of the lodge. He didn't appear to be a friendly fellow, but was obviously capable in maintaining the rolling lawns and shrubbery. I had even mentioned to Tom on several occasions how well-groomed his grounds appeared. His only remark at the time was: "Scott gets the credit for that." It always amazed me why certain employees take advantage of their employers, especially when they receive adequate pay for their services plus fringe benefits, such as their meals during the workday. Scott Harris, according to Tom, had the full run of the lodge and the grounds. That privilege ended when Tom caught him placing the Briggs and Stratton engine into his vehicle.

After my conversation with Doyle, I thought I had better call Tom. I had promised to call him on my return, and I would like to find out more about the discharge of Scott Harris. I dialed the phone and the desk clerk at the Breakshire Lodge answered.

"Tom Huston, please. Jason Black calling."

"I'm sorry, Mr. Black, Mr. Huston is attending a meeting downtown this morning. I'll have him call you when he returns."

"Thank you. I may be out myself. I'll call back later."

Disappointed that I was unable to reach Tom, I hung up.

I made a few notes in my spiral notebook and then decided to pick up Ruben at Lynn's Eagle Bay Kennel. I locked up the house and went outside. The raw cold hit my face. It was a good thing that I had put on a heavier jacket. I climbed into the Bronco and started it. I didn't leave the yard until the engine had warmed up. I noticed that the needle on the temperature gauge didn't move very far toward the center. I'd have to have my mechanic check that out. Before I headed toward Eagle Bay I proceeded to the post office to pick up the mail. When I opened up the box, several letters fell to the floor. I glanced at them: the electric bill, a bill from the propane supplier, a couple of magazines, and possibly some bad checks, but to my disappointment, no envelope from Tom. Perhaps it would arrive tomorrow. While I was there I went into the office and said hello to the staff. Everybody was hard at work. The postmaster waved and gave me a big smile.

I longed to stop at John's for a mid-morning coffee or green tea, but motored on by toward Eagle Bay and Ruben. Traffic was light. When I arrived at the kennel I found Lynn in her office doing bookwork. She looked up as I entered the lobby.

"Well, I see you're back. How was the trip?" She laid her pen down.

"Lynn, the four of us had a most enjoyable time. We checked out Bar Harbor and the Acadia National Park. The lobster was tasty, especially when you dunked it in melted hot butter. How is Ruben?" I asked.

"Glad you had a good time. When you mention lobster, I'm ready to head to Maine myself. Ruben has been a good dog. Some of the staff spent some time with him. What a joy that animal is!"

Lynn got up from her desk and left the office for a few minutes. I heard a loud bark as she brought Ruben down the hall toward the lobby. Like so many times before, Ruben pulled hard on the leash and rushed toward me. Lynn let the leash drop to the floor. The big K-9 came to me and rubbed his big head against my pant leg. He was glad to see his master. I talked with Lynn for a few minutes. She thanked me again for locating and returning Brian of Widmere to her. She told me that Mrs. Rose had lost her battle with the dreaded cancer and had passed away.

"Lynn, I'm sorry to hear that. But Mrs. Rose won't have to suffer anymore," I added.

"I attended the funeral. It was sad." Lynn's eyes were filled with tears.

In a few minutes she had composed herself and managed to smile. I knew that she had thought a great deal of Mrs. Rose and couldn't bring charges against her at the time Mrs. Rose had taken Brian, Lynn's Malamute. I bid farewell to Lynn and left her kennel, putting Ruben into the rear of the Bronco. He was glad to be headed home.

I drove the Bronco south on Route 28. The state highway department was adding to their huge sand pile for the forthcoming winter. The snowmobile dealers were preparing their new sleds for display. I wondered how our two sleds that we had purchased from the gentle man on South Shore road would perform. I hadn't been on a snowmobile for a long time and Patty had never ridden one.

And, to add to my thoughts I worried about my friend, Tom Huston. It agitated me to think that anyone would target a kind person like Tom. When he came to the Lake Placid region he was welcomed with open arms and is still very popular with everyone. Now he is facing threats to his business, and two of his Adirondack properties have been burglarized, with the suspicion that one of them was going to be set on fire. I wondered about the possible suspect, Morey Harris, the son of Scott Harris, the former groundskeeper at the Breakshire Lodge. There was the possibility that the father, Scott, could be implicated as well. I knew that Lieutenant Doyle had assigned an investigator to their case. I would attempt to develop useful information to help bring one or both of them to justice. With winter soon upon us, the task wouldn't be an easy one.

When I pulled into my driveway I was surprised to see a pickup truck parked near the dog run. Ruben let out a bark. I told him to settle down. It was a new Chevrolet ¾ ton. On the door was painted O'Brien's Marina. I didn't recognize the man who got out of the truck. I surmised it might be Jim Jenny, the newly appointed manager for the marina. He wore a friendly smile as he approached.

"I assume you are Jason Black, private eye," he said humorously. "I'm Jim Jenny, manager of O'Brien's Marina."

"It's a pleasure to meet you, Jim. Yes, I'm Jason Black. How can I help you?" I noticed a brown manila envelope in his left hand. He extended his right hand and we shook hands. He had a good grip.

"Jason, Evelyn asked me to drop some checks off to you. They are marked 'insufficient funds.' She wants to start out with a clean sweep. A couple of these may have been received by the former owner, a Mr. Kirby, I believe."

"Yes, Jim, Kirby was the former owner. You would have thought that he would have taken care of them before the sale of the property. However, I will be most happy to see what I can do to retrieve Evelyn's funds."

"I understand you're a good friend of Dale Rush, the pilot Evelyn's fiance. He speaks well of you, Jason."

"Dale and I go back several years. I understand you're a pilot as well." I could tell that Jim Jenny was a friendly chap.

"Well, I'd better be going. I had quite a time finding this place. You have a nice log home," he said, as he looked over my domain.

"It's a pleasure to meet you, Jim," I said.

"Likewise, Jason. Stop over to the marina sometime. We're going to be working on snowmobiles over the winter. And speaking of winter, it is getting colder."

"We'll be getting snow soon. I observed a skein of geese heading south yesterday."

We bid farewell and Jim pulled out of the yard. I was glad that he had a sense of humor, which is an important asset in handling the people business. He'd do well. Evelyn O'Brien had been fortunate to find him. I knew one thing for sure: he was much different than the former head of the marina operations. With the change of ownership I'd consider buying a boat from them next summer. Of course, that would have to be with Patty's approval.

I hadn't been in the house for more than fifteen minutes before a big white Dodge pulled in. Wilt Chambers got out of the truck and went over to Ruben. I looked out the window and saw Ruben's tail in motion. I put my jacket on and went outside to greet my friend.

"Hello, Wilt! How have you been?" I asked. I was happy to see my logger buddy.

"Jason, I heard you and Patty went to Maine." Patty must have told him at the diner.

"Yes, we had a good time looking the Bar Harbor region over and tasting some very good lobster."

"You're not thinking of moving, are you, Jason?" His expression showed concern.

"No, Wilt. I'd never move away from Old Forge. You know that, ya big rascal. Who would I get to collect the two-man saws?" I said jokingly.

"I'm only kidding you a little. I saw Patty for a second this morning. She looks so happy, Jason."

"Yes, we're both happy. We picked up a couple of snowmobiles for winter, and if we find some time we'll hit a few trails. I haven't been on a sled in a long time."

"Well, you be careful on them. They can be dangerous," Wilt said, watching out for us, as usual.

"Yes, I know. I remember a few spills I took up in the Santa Clara region and one over in Dewittville, Quebec. On that one I had to visit a doctor and have my elbow drained of fluid. But, Wilt, getting into the backcountry of the Adirondacks is a trip that envelops you into the depths of Mother Nature. The most beautiful scenes of the trees and mountains meeting at the skyline, the wind rustling through the spruce and pine as your face feels the cold of winter. There's nothing like it!"

"I'm in the woods just about every day. I have to agree with you. Just being out there, under the trees, humbles a person."

"Wilt, seeing the different families enjoying their time together, with the parenting of the child that takes place on the snowmobile trail—it's so beneficial, because they will be the snowmobilers of tomorrow. The cycle of life keeps turning from one generation to another. I remember how my father taught me how to swing an axe when he was trimming a downed tree. It's all a continued learning process. By the way, how would you like to join me for a hot of cup of tea?" Wilt nodded his head approvingly.

"Yeah, I could use a cup of that green tea you're always boasting about."

In a few minutes Wilt and I were sipping our tea. I had poured it into two of John's Diner cups to make Wilt feel at home, as he visited the diner frequently.

"I stopped by, Jason, to bring you four two-man saws from the Higgins' auction. They had cars and pickups lined up for a mile. Their farm is over near the West Road out of Turin. They had some antiques that caught my eye. I picked up a spinning wheel for my aged Aunt Tilda. She always wanted one, and by golly I found a beauty." I could tell that Wilt was happy in locating the spinning wheel. He was always doing things for people, and not just his relatives. He was a good friend.

We finished our tea and went outside to the big white Dodge. The saws lay next to each other on the rubberized mat in the rear. I noticed right away that they were razor-sharp. The teeth were not worn down as on many of the saws I have in my collection. The wooden handles were in good condition. There was no rust on the blades.

"These saws are in very good condition, Wilt. How much did you have to pay for them?"

"They were eight dollars apiece." Wilt pulled out a receipt from the auction for the amount of thirty-two dollars. "Jason, give me thirty dollars and you buy the coffee next time we meet at the diner."

"Fair enough, and I'll treat you to one of those super cheeseburgers that Lila creates."

Wilt smiled. "Well, thanks for the tea, but I must be going. I have to meet Charlie Perkins this afternoon in North Creek." We shook hands.

I watched Wilt as he left the driveway for Route 28. My saw collection was getting bigger. Now I had fifty-six two-man saws. I liked to visualize them in operation at the same time. It would take one hundred and twelve lumberjacks to make it happen. That would be a lot of timber plummeting to earth. Oh, how I longed for the days of that era. Progress and modernization were great for our nation, but also created dilemmas along the way. To peek back in time to those working logging camps deep in the woods would certainly be revealing and interesting. The aroma of the food at day's end must have pleased many hardworking lumberjacks.

Ruben was making a fuss in the dog run. He probably was ready for a romp into the woods. I went over and opened the gate. The big dog bolted out, running off toward the woods.

While Ruben checked the woods for the chippies, I put the saws away. When I finished I headed toward the woods and spotted the K-9 in hot pursuit. The chippie apparently won, for Ruben bounded toward me at a fast clip. After I put him into his dog run, I went into the office and made some telephone calls. The first one was to Lieutenant Doyle at Troop S headquarters.

"Jason, I'm glad you called. My investigator developed some information yesterday concerning the location of Morey Harris, our possible suspect in the Huston burglary. We had to call the investigator away for another important case, which will keep him tied up indefinitely. I can't go into it with you, Jason, due to the sensitivity of the matter. I will share this with you. Harris and his father are living off Route 28N between Newcomb and Minerva. Are you familiar with that area?" he asked.

"Yes, I know it well, but haven't been over there lately."

"You won't be able to see the ramshackle house from the highway. Supposedly it's in the vicinity of Hewitt Pond. If you're in that area, you want to be careful. The investigator reported that Harris has a couple of mean pit bulls. We're short of personnel, with vacations and people on sick leave—but keep in mind, Jason, you're not on the job anymore." He never failed to remind me.

"Yeah, Jack, I know."

"Whatever you do is your business. I'm your friend and I'm telling you to be careful. If you do come up with some good information, please let me know. I've talked on the telephone with your friend, Tom Huston, and he's worried. I did receive his list of properties. He told me when I was talking with him that he isn't a believer in the stock market anymore and puts his money into real estate as a better investment."

"Yes, I received the list, too, and I'm impressed."

The lieutenant and I talked together for a few minutes longer about the many changes that had taken place in the New York State Troopers, some for the better and some for the worse. It was a constantly changing environment. We bid each other goodbye.

I checked the clock and noted that the afternoon had passed

rapidly. I went to the bathroom and threw some cold water on my face. It was refreshing. I called Patty and told her that I'd start dinner. We decided on pork chops, mashed potatoes, acorn squash, and applesauce. As soon as I hung up I cut up the apples and took the chops out of the freezer, thawing them in the microwave. I peeled the potatoes, placed them in a pot, and covered them with water. I then set the table.

While I was waiting for Patty to get home, I went into the office and called several people, including Wilt, Charlie Perkins, Jack Falsey, and Dale Rush. I had heard that Penny Younger and his band was going to be playing at the Fiddlers' Hall near Osceola the next week and wondered if they'd like to join Patty and me at the event. I was pleased when they all agreed to meet us there. Charlie Perkins told me that every so often he picked up his banjo and played for his kids. We talked for a while and Charlie indicated that he had to get going. We both said goodbye and hung up.

I looked out the window and was surprised to see that it was snowing lightly, with small flakes lazily falling to the warm ground. Ruben was trying to catch a few of them. It was a good thing that I had installed the storm windows, I realized. I had thought the snow would be coming over the mountain, and here it was. It probably would be a week or two before the heavy stuff would come. Anyway, the snowmobiles were ready. All we'd have to do is find the time to ride. It wouldn't be for a while. Patty was busy, and I'd be in the Newcomb and North Creek region snooping around.

Patty's Jeep pulled into the yard at about 5:10. I had everything ready for my sweetheart and me. When she got out of the vehicle she made a beeline to Ruben and gave him a big hug. He always looked forward to Patty's attention and would bark if she missed stopping by the run to see him. A spoiled K-9, that's for certain. When she came through the door I was there to greet her. I picked her up in my arms and kissed her passionately.

"Supper's ready, honey," I said, as I set her down.

"It smells good, my darling. I'm famished." I helped her

off with her jacket and again took advantage of her with another kiss.

"I bet you're tired, Patty."

"Yes, I'm tired tonight, Jason. We had a busy day at the diner. Say, you'll be interested to hear that Lila had to order some green tea. Many of our customers are requesting it."

"Is that so?" I was amused.

"That's right, honey."

Patty went to the bathroom to wash up for dinner. As soon as she was ready I seated her. I lit the two candles. They flickered, causing some shadows on the walls and tablecloth. I sat down to join her. After saying grace, I filled our plates, and we began our dinner. Her eyes sparkled, as always, from the light of the candles.

She commented on how wonderful everything tasted. She asked for seconds and I placed another pork chop on her plate.

"I love you, Jason. You sure know how to spoil a girl," she said.

"I love you, too, darling."

"What are you up to, Jason?"

"Nothing, dear, but I know you're tired and I know that you'd do it for me if I had just arrived home from work."

"You know I would, Jason," she responded, seriously.

We talked about her day's activities and she told me that several people had asked her to say hello to me. A couple of troopers had stopped for lunch and wanted to be remembered to me. I was happy to be remembered by my former coworkers.

Patty insisted that she would do the dishes. I took care of Ruben's meal and told Patty that it wouldn't be long before we'd be starting up the two Ski-Doos. We both agreed that we'd wait until the appropriate amount of snow fell.

The evening passed rapidly and we went to bed about 10:30. We turned on the radio to soft, relaxing music, fell into each other's arms, intimately expressed our love for each other, and eventually fell off to sleep.

CHAPTER ELEVEN

When I woke up, Patty had already left for work, and Ruben was standing in the doorway waiting to be let outside. I got up reluctantly and let the big dog out the side door. For some reason I was tired and dragged out. At fifty years of age I knew that more exercise was important. Just lifting a few weights didn't account for a full regimen of activity that would maintain one's physical capability. Walking was an important key to keep the circulation moving.

After shaving and a hurried shower, I dressed. I consulted my schedule and decided that I'd check out the area where Morey Harris lived, between Newcomb and Winebrook Hills in the Minerva area.

Knowing there were two mean pit bulls at the Harris house, I wasn't going to take a chance of being mauled to death. I decided that my .41 caliber revolver would equalize any potential threat of bodily harm. We had had pit bulls in the family over the years. They were good pets, gentle like any other canine. Apparently the dogs owned by Harris had been trained to be mean. From Jack Doyle's description they were on the vicious side. I secured Ruben in his dog run, locked the log home, and left for Drew's Restaurant just north of Inlet.

Traffic was light on Route 28, and as I peered out the windshield I observed clouds forming. The air was cold and crisp, and my down-lined jacket felt good—supplemented, of course, by the Bronco's heater. My thoughts drifted to Patty and what she was doing at that moment in time. She was probably pouring coffee into a customer's coffee cup. I was wishing that she were here with me, but that was out of the question. I loved her dearly. I pulled into the parking lot of Drew's next to a class C camper. I noted that it was covered with dried mud on the wheels. I got out of the Bronco and went inside.

I seated myself in a booth just as Lance, the waiter, approached me with a menu.

"Good morning, Lance. I won't need the menu. Just give me Number 2 and a cup of tea."

"How do you want your eggs?" he asked politely.

"I'll have them over medium, please." Lance turned on his heel and headed for the kitchen, where Chef Michael was tending the grill. Number 2 consisted of eggs, home fries, and toast.

While I was waiting for my order I glanced at the *Adirondack Express*. This fine publication had a wide distribution in the south central Adirondack region and the reader could glean local news and important events that had been scheduled. It was the newspaper of record. I was just glancing at the advertisements when Lance appeared with my order. He was a friendly young man and a capable waiter.

The home-fried potatoes were prepared to perfection and the eggs were also perfect. I applied catsup to the potatoes. Chef Michael stuck his head out of the kitchen to say hello.

"What are you up to today, Jason?" he inquired.

"Right now, chef, I'm enjoying a wonderful breakfast. I'm headed to the Newcomb area this morning. By the way, Mike, your red roof has held up well. Do you remember the day when Dale Rush buzzed you when you were painting it?"

"Do I! You and Dale came out of nowhere. I almost spilled the can of red paint. Have a good trip, Jason. Tell that hot shot pilot when you see him that I said hello. I heard that he is engaged or getting engaged to Evelyn O'Brien, the owner of O'Brien's Marina." Mike wore a big smile.

"That's right. I'm happy for both of them. Dale's a good man, one fine pilot."

"I know he is, and we here at Drew's wish him the very best. However, if I had spilled that red paint on my clothes, I would have sent him the cleaning bill." He laughed and returned to his culinary duties in the kitchen.

Lance appeared with my check and I paid him. We talked a few minutes and then I left Drew's for the Bronco and the Newcomb region. Traffic continued to be light. The wind came up and I could feel the power of Mother Nature against my old Bronco. By the time I arrived in the Newcomb area my knuckles were white from gripping the steering wheel so tightly. I felt in my bones that winter was closing in slowly, destined to cover our wonderful mountains with snow soon.

I couldn't help but think of Tom Huston and the pressure brought on his shoulders by the two burglaries of his properties, the half-filled gas can, and the threatening telephone calls. These were criminal acts and the predator was running amuck in the region. What would he plan next? Would he bring harm to Huston? A person who dedicated his life to serving people. Not if I had anything to do about it.

Route 28N is a two-lane macadam road, which is pretty well-maintained. It turns south from Newcomb into the Vanderwhacker Mountain region toward Minerva. I took a secondary road to the east toward Hewitt Pond. It had been a while since I had visited this particular region. I noticed that there were changes, which included some building of camps.

I had gone approximately two miles when I came upon a ramshackle house. It probably had worn a coat of white paint in the 1940's, but now it had given way to vast divisions of wood-chewing termites, as evidenced by sagging roofs and decayed timbers. It appeared that the wooden window frames had been eaten away. No one seemed to be at home. An old Studebaker was sitting on wooden blocks in the overgrown side yard. Some of the weeds touched the edge of the twisted metal fenders. I stopped near the driveway and pretended to scan a road map, in the event people were inside. A mailbox hung off a wooden post and a faded letter "H" was on the side of the box. I took my binoculars from their case to get a closer look. Two dirty white pit bulls were barking and pulling on small chains near the entrance of the house. I could see saliva dripping from their lower jaws. Apparently the state police investigator had made a similar observation, according to Lieutenant Doyle. I put my binoculars back in their leather case.

Placing the map on the dashboard, I exited the Bronco, then went to the front and opened the hood—a guise to make one believe that I might have a problem with the vehicle. As I was standing by the raised hood I snapped four pictures with my camera of the leaning house and grounds with the two grease-coated pit bulls churning up a ruckus near the broken-down doorsteps. The barking and the gurgling growls sent a chill up my spine that I will never forget and will probably dream about some nights. I imagined that the mail carrier in the area never entered the yard, which these two dogs claimed as their territory. Probably at one time innocent, loving pups, they had unfortunately found themselves under the control and ownership of a trainer who must have abused them into the syndrome of meanness. Standing by the Bronco I felt their ferociousness even though they were several yards from me. They were grunting, barking, and growling as they pulled against the chains. It was cruel of the owner to maintain the two dogs in this manner. I was surprised that the state police investigator had not contacted the S.P.C.A., but he probably did not want to interfere with the ongoing investigation.

It was difficult for me to understand that Scott Harris, once a trusted employee of Tom Huston, had a dark side that led him to thievery, which was the reason that Tom had discharged him from his employ. It was Tom who had not pressed charges against Harris. And now Scott's son, Morey Harris, might be seeking revenge for his father's dismissal. Along with the investigation being conducted by the state troopers, I was continuing my own inquiry into the matter. Tom wanted me to look into every aspect of the case in my position as a private investigator.

I took out my binoculars for a second time and scanned the yard. Three mangy-looking cats came out from beneath the heaved-in porch. They were black and white. The pit bulls had exhausted themselves, though one of them was still looking in my direction. The other one was lying on the porch. I looked closely to see if I could locate a brass ship's bell, but didn't see one. I did see three or four five-gallon gasoline cans sitting by a small steam engine. I completed my observations, climbed back into the Bronco, drove to Hewitt Pond, and turned around.

When I reached Route 28N I turned right and headed back toward Newcomb. I stopped by to see my friend, Bob Bearor, the author and historian. We had a cup of tea together. There had been no more unusual activity at the Huston Victorian house. He did indicate that troop cars stopped by there periodically to check the property. I thanked Bob, left, and headed toward Long Lake.

Snowflakes were lazily falling from the sky. There was no accumulation, but they were enough to signal that winter was about to make its grand entrance on Mother Nature's stage, the Adirondack Park, six million acres of public and privately owned land, with over a million of those acres to remain forever wild.

I was about five miles from Long Lake when I spotted an older-model Chrysler. It was headed east on Route 28N toward Newcomb. It appeared rusty. Smoke was billowing from the exhaust pipe. It appeared to be a 1986 four-door. The reason I decided to turn around and follow must have been initiated by my former training as an active law enforcement officer. I waited till I came to a curve and then I made a reverse Y turn, also part of my trooper training. Another eastbound vehicle passed me just prior to my turn. It afforded cover for the Bronco in the event the Chrysler operator was checking his rear-view mirror. It didn't take me long to catch up to the two eastbound vehicles. There were sufficient curves on the highway that prevented the car ahead of me from passing the rusty Chrysler.

When we arrived in Newcomb, the car just ahead of me pulled into a driveway and the Chrysler continued on toward Minerva. My thought immediately was that Morey Harris was behind the wheel of the rusty Chrysler. I continued to follow him at a distance. I looked down at my speedometer; the needle was at about 45 m.p.h. I noted that he was wavering, which was possibly a steering deficiency as opposed to driving while under the influence of alcohol. The smell of oil poured in from the heavy layer of smoke that flowed out of his tail-pipe. The snowflakes that had been falling had not accumulated but had completely dissipated. Of course, the winter's falling snow here in the Adirondacks can sometimes be regional, just like the falling rain.

My hunch that Morey Harris was driving the rusty Chrysler became reality as he made a wide left-hand turn onto the road to Hewitt Pond. I was able to see the long scar on the left side of his face. He didn't glance toward me, but kept looking straight ahead. He had to pull to the right on the narrow road as a black pickup truck was approaching Route 28N. I continued on toward Minerva until I found a place to turn around. I made my way back to the Hewitt Pond area. I should have continued to Newcomb, but my curiosity was building, so I decided to drive past the Harris's ramshackle dwelling. I drove by slowly. The rusty Chrysler was driven in close to the side porch. The two pit bulls were lying at the bottom of the porch stairs. Morey had already exited the vehicle and was in the house. I caught a movement at the front window, which appeared to be covered by burlap potato bags sewed together. My previous visit had given me time to look closely at the leaning house with my powerful binoculars. The burlap in the windows prevented any outsider from peering in. I made the assumption that when I approached the house, Morey must have looked out, because a face appeared in the window for an instant and then it was gone.

My watch indicated that mid-afternoon had passed. I drove near Hewitt Pond, pulled into a lane, and shut the Bronco off. I waited there for about twenty minutes, and then I turned around and went back by the Harris place. The rusty Chrysler was not in sight. I headed toward Newcomb on Route 28N.

CHAPTER TWELVE

The Breakshire Lodge was receiving guests for their night stay. Tom Huston, looking pale and tired after spending an afternoon with his accountant, was sitting at his elaborate desk. He had the radio on and National Public Radio was playing some classical music. Tom was sipping on a cup of green tea. He was paying close attention to the program when the telephone rang. He picked up the receiver.

"Good afternoon. This is Tom Huston. Can I help you?" he asked.

"No, you can't help me, Huston, but I'm going to ruin you and put you out of business!" A voice whispered angrily over the phone.

"Who is this?" Tom asked, but all he heard was the click on the phone.

Tom Huston had been apprised of the fact that his phone line was being monitored by the telephone company security, so he immediately dialed the number to lock in the incoming call. He waited for a few minutes, then contacted the telephone company and the state troopers. It was soon ascertained that the incoming call had been made from a telephone booth in the Long Lake region. This was the third threatening phone call targeting the well-established and popular lodge and its owner, Tom Huston.

When Tom called Lieutenant Jack Doyle about the call,

the lieutenant asked him if there were any distinct phrase or phrases or words spoken. Tom related the exact conversation to Doyle.

"Lieutenant, the caller seemed to be speaking with a lisp. His speech seemed to be faltering. I wish I could tell you more, but he wasn't on the telephone that long."

"Our people are working with telephone security. Tom, do you think you've heard that voice before?" Jack questioned.

"I believe it is the same person who has made all the threatening calls to my office. This person sounds vindictive and I sense that this could be connected with the discharging of one of my grounds personnel, Scott Harris. At first I thought it could have been the kitchen worker that I discharged, but I believe it's connected with Harris and possibly his son, Morey." Tom offered dejectedly.

"Did the son ever work in your employ?"

"No, he never did," he answered, shaking his head.

CHAPTER THIRTEEN

I was upset that I hadn't seen the Chrysler leave the Harris residence. When I got back on Route 28N I headed to Newcomb and then on to Long Lake. It was very late in the afternoon. I made a quick stop at Gertie's Diner for a hot cup of tea. I talked with Bob and Gertie for a few minutes and then headed for Old Forge. I knew that Patty would be getting home from John's Diner and would be waiting.

It was almost 7:00 when I pulled the Bronco into the yard next to Patty's red Jeep. I looked for Ruben, but he wasn't in sight. I exited the Bronco and had just locked the door when I heard Patty.

"Honey! Here we are."

I looked toward the edge of the woods. Patty and Ruben were running toward me. Ruben won the race. When Patty caught up, I went over and embraced her. She kissed me passionately. The three of us walked over to the run and Ruben went inside. I closed the gate.

"When you weren't here, dearest, I decided to take Ruben for a run to the woods. We did spot a small bear near the Bald Mountain trail. We looked around for the mother, but didn't see her."

"Honey, never get between the mother and a cub bear because that could possibly spell trouble. How did Ruben act when you saw the small bear?" I asked with concern.

"You would have been proud of him, Jason. He stayed right beside me. His ears went up at attention. He was definitely on guard. How'd your day go, hon?"

"I was up in the Newcomb region most of the day and stopped by to see Bob Bearor—you know, the author. He is working on another book. Oh! I stopped at Gertie's for a minute and of course they both asked for you. Even Bob was there."

"I hope you told them I said hello."

"Sure did, sweetheart."

I went over to Patty and kissed her again. I told her that I had run into a few snowflakes in the Newcomb area and indicated to her that it wouldn't be long before we'd be trying out our sleds. She smiled in anticipation.

"I have a surprise for you for our late dinner. We're having salmon patties, mashed potatoes, broccoli, home-made tartar sauce, and apple crisp for dessert."

"Wonderful!" I was getting hunger pangs.

"Lila made some salmon patties for the employees and gave me a couple extra. Wasn't that nice of her?" she asked.

"It certainly was thoughtful of her," I agreed.

I went to the bathroom and washed my hands, while Patty set the table and checked everything on the stove.

"Jason, will you light the candles?" Patty asked.

"Yes, honey, I'll be happy to," I answered, reaching for a match.

The first match didn't ignite, but the second one did. I lit both of the candles and, as always, the shadows danced on the walls of our dining area. I assisted Patty with the condiments and the hot food. I pulled her chair out and seated her. She said grace, thanking the good Lord for the gifts. We always took turns saying the blessing.

The salmon patties were delicious. We both had seconds. Patty had made a pot of green tea. She served it with the heated apple crisp, topped with a dollop of whipped cream—just a tad on each, for we know how the calories built up. Needless to say, the combination was delicious.

Patty told me about her day and about the many customers who had come into the diner, while we cleaned off the table, snuffing out the candles. She mentioned that an older retired trooper and a retired forest ranger had had lunch together. Both had asked about me. Patty had told them that I was busy working.

"They were both genuinely sincere," she said.

It didn't take long to do the dishes and bring the kitchen back to a spit-and-polish condition. We worked well together as a team, and above all we enjoyed our time together, including our walks and rides in the Bronco or the Jeep with our big K-9. That's when Ruben seemed the happiest.

We then went outside and took Ruben for a brisk walk into the woods. The temperatures were dipping lower with each day approaching winter. Our heavier jackets felt good. When we returned to the log home, snowflakes were falling from the sky. I hadn't heard what tomorrow's weather was going to be. Both of us agreed that if this kept up all night we'd have an accumulation in the morning.

It was a couple of hours to bedtime. Since Patty had the next day off, we decided to take out our easels. We placed a quantity of oil paint on our palettes and prepared a container for our brushes. With white paint we covered each canvas. This was the beginning of a hobby to help pass the long winter. Our goal was to paint scenes of mountains, woods, and cabins. Both of us loved Old Forge and the entire region inside the Blue Line. This is where we lived and worked, and our desire was to capture its aura in our art.

The picture that we were using for the scene was that of a small log cabin adjacent to a brook running into Third Lake. Behind the cabin was a small mountain range. An assortment of pines and maples grew behind the rustic cabin and extended to the top of the mountain just before the tree-line.

"Jason, can you help me with this brush?" Patty asked. "I don't know what I've done wrong."

Observing that her brush contained too much paint, I took it from her and cleaned it. I dipped into the light blue with the cleaned brush, put a small amount of paint on it, and handed it back to her. She held the brush in her right hand and lightly stroked the brush from left to right. The strokes left a colorful skyline. I watched her closely and soon I saw her dimples as her beautiful face broke into a smile. She looked up into my eyes and moved her head close to mine. I could see she was enjoying herself.

I leaned over and gave her a warm, tender kiss. She laid her brush down and placed her arms around me, drawing me close to her. My heart skipped a beat and our lips met again with warmth and love. I had truly found happiness.

I squeezed her hand, and softly said, "We better return to our task at hand and continue our humble efforts to create a mountain scene on canvas."

Patty nodded her head in agreement, picking up her paintbrush.

The two hours to bedtime extended to another two hours. We cleaned our brushes, straightened the area, and finally retired to our bedroom well past midnight.

Our attempts at a mountain scene were probably elementary to a master artist, but to us they looked great, providing no one inspected them too closely. Although we had used the same picture as our guide, our paintings had come out differently with contrasting shades of brown for the cabins. However, the trees stood out in variations of green shading, with specks of yellow reflecting the sunlight shining through. We both understood that shading is one of the most important elements to the artist.

Patty was in bed before me. I checked the doors and looked in on Ruben, who must have been in doggie heaven, as his paw moved several times. He was sound asleep and his usually pointed ears were flopped over the side of his head. After I brushed my teeth, I looked out at the falling snow, then climbed into bed. We fell off to sleep wrapped up in each other's arms.

CHAPTER FOURTEEN

My first awareness of another day was the aroma of sizzling Canadian bacon and the odor of freshly perked coffee. I reached over to hug Patty, but realized that she was out in the kitchen preparing an Adirondack breakfast. I pushed the covers back and hurried to the bathroom. The cold water felt good as I rubbed it into my eyes and face. I quickly looked outside and was delighted by what I viewed. Mother Nature had brought us several inches of fluffy snow. The Jeep and the Bronco each had white caps on the roofs and hood. It looked like a foot had fallen.

I dressed quickly and went to the kitchen. Patty was in the midst of setting the table.

"We're having scrambled eggs with Canadian bacon, home fries, and homemade bread for toast," she said with a satisfied smile.

I noticed that the orange juice was already placed by our plates.

"Do you want to try snowmobiling today, Patty?" I waited hopefully for her response.

"I'd love to, honey!" she answered. "But do you have anything on your agenda?"

"All I have to do this morning is call Jack Doyle at Troop S Headquarters and Tom Huston at Lake Placid after breakfast," I assured her.

I said the blessing and then Patty and I enjoyed the wonderful breakfast she had prepared for us. Usually she would have already left for work. This was a real treat, having my wife home for breakfast. Fellows from the diner, like Wilt, Jim from the real estate office, Charlie, Jack Falsey, and Doctor Don saw Patty at breakfast more than I did. Oh! There had been Dale, too, but now Dale was busy having breakfast with Ms. O'Brien at the marina. It was a true pleasure having Patty do the honors at the stove in our kitchen.

The Canadian bacon was wonderful, along with the scrambled eggs and home fries. We sat chatting with refills of hot coffee.

I helped Patty with the dishes after breakfast and swept up the kitchen. Ruben was already out in his doghouse. The snow that had covered the ground was just spitting small flakes. The sun in the east was readying itself to come over the mountain shortly. While Patty got our snowmobile suits I went into my office and made my two telephone calls.

The first was to Lieutenant Jack Doyle, who informed me that two more of Tom Huston's properties had been burglarized, one in Keene and another in Wilmington, both places being inside the Blue Line of the Adirondack Park. The dwellings were older homes that Tom had purchased for the purpose of restoring them, possibly to become rental properties. Like all of Huston's properties, they were investments. Both entries were made through the rear of the houses and apparently had been perpetrated before any snow fell in that particular region. We discussed Tom's dilemma in detail. I shared with Jack my observations of Morey Harris and that I had viewed the ramshackle house at Hewitt Pond.

"Jason, Harris probably had some of the stolen goods in his car when you saw him," he commented.

"I wouldn't doubt it, Jack. When do you think you might move on him for an arrest?" I was more than curious, as Tom was a good person and a good friend.

"We want to right now, but we want a good case, so we'll need a little more than mere suspicion. You know how the justice system works, Jason," he added.

"Indeed I do, sir," I said, in agreement.

We talked a few minutes longer. I assured the lieutenant that I would pass on any useful information concerning Harris or anything else I uncovered as a private investigator looking into the Huston case.

My next call was to my friend and employer, Tom Huston. He sounded distraught. He told me what he knew about the case and that people in the area had observed a rusty old Chrysler near the scene of each of the alleged crimes. I asked him if the BCI in Raybrook were aware of the rusty old Chrysler and he assured me that they had all the facts.

I wondered for a moment why Jack hadn't shared that information with me about the Chrysler. Then I surmised that we both had had Morey Harris pegged as a possible suspect. It was just probably an oversight.

"Tom, do you know what was taken?"

"My carpenter had dropped off brand-new tools at each place, getting ready for his two crews to begin the remodeling. There were a total of two new saws, along with two kegs of nails and eight new hammers. The police have all that information." Tom's voice sounded strained.

I assured Tom that the troopers would do a good job handling that end of the case. I shared with him my observations of Morey Harris. I told him that I didn't see the father around. Tom then informed me that the father used to drive an old green GMC pickup with an amber light on top. However, he didn't know what he would be driving now. I made a note of the pickup. We chatted a few minutes longer and ended our call.

I was worried about Tom. I knew how it was, for I had been through similar circumstances, only mine had been hang-up calls from some unknown whack. I assured Tom that Lieutenant Doyle and his investigators would eventually bring the case to a successful conclusion. I did some filing on my bad-check cases and returned to Patty in the kitchen.

Looking out the window I could make out Ruben's ears as

he lay on the mat in his doghouse. Patty was just beginning to don her snowmobile suit. She had mine laid out on our bed.

In about twenty minutes both of us were dressed and outside with our Ski-Doos. I had previously fueled them. My machine started up without hesitation, while Patty's machine needed a new spark plug, which I replaced. We had planned to enter the trail system, but decided instead to stay around our own property. I wanted Patty to get the feel of the machine as I gave her some counseling on the do's and don'ts of snowmobiling before attempting the trails.

"Honey, as you know, I have never been on a snowmobile in my life. I'm anxious to learn how to operate one." She looked stunning in her snowmobile suit. It fit her perfectly.

"You'll do fine. I'll show you everything I know about it," I reassured her.

We shut my sled off and I told her to sit in front of me on her sled. Our helmets fit well and both of us had our goggles pulled down over our eyes. The glare from the snow prompted us to use them. I took the position on the rear of the seat and we started out slowly. I placed my arms around her and onto the controls. The throttle responded to my right hand and the machine surged ahead. We went down to the edge of the woods and turned north along the edge of the forest. On the third time around I let Patty take the controls. The sled jerked a couple of times, but soon she got the feel. It wasn't long before she became an able operator. When I thought it was all right for her to be on her sled alone, I got off her sled and stood by watching her make several maneuvers in the field. After executing several turns and circles, she ran a straight line near the edge of the woods and increased her speed.

I climbed on my Ski-Doo and followed her for a while. She seemed able to operate the machine just fine. We then rode side by side. With her helmet and goggles pulled down over her eyes, I would have sworn that we had a visitor from outer space. When I told her about it later, she broke out in laughter. I surprised her when we stopped to rest: I took out my flask and asked her if she would like to sip some peach brandy for warmth.

"Just a little taste, my darling," she said, pushing up her goggles and removing her helmet. She took the flask and pressed it against her lips.

"How is it?" I asked. I watched her wrinkle her nose.

"Tastes just like peaches," she said with a giggle.

I took the flask from her and had a sip, then put the top back on. I told her that many snowmobilers carry brandy with them, especially in the frigid cold of winter. We stayed out for another hour and decided we had had enough for the day.

Ruben had come out of his doghouse and had watched the entire event.

We drove the machines onto the trailer and covered them. Inside, after removing the heavy snowmobile suits, we donned dungarees and sweatshirts, for a trek down to DiOrio's store to purchase some groceries for the week.

I pushed the cart while Patty selected the various groceries, keeping in mind that we were both diet-conscious. We ran into Dale Rush and Evelyn O'Brien. They were at the deli picking up ham and Swiss cheese. The four of us chatted about the trip to Bar Harbor. They told us that the boats were put away for the winter at the marina, along with Dale's Stinson.

Evelyn shared the news that she and Dale were going to Florida for a few days in about a week and that Jim Jenny would be left in charge at the marina store. I was surprised to learn that they were opening one of their buildings for the purpose of working on snowmobiles over the winter. She had hired a mechanic, whom Jenny would supervise.

"Dale, you be careful in Florida, especially if you rent one of the planes. There's a great deal of air traffic over the State of Florida, and landing at their airports is much different than landing on Fourth Lake," I offered as a word of caution.

Evelyn looked at Dale, waiting for his response.

"Jason, I think I'll be able to handle it. Remember I landed on several aircraft carriers in the Pacific," he said, rather sharply.

"I'm kidding you, ace. Don't get upset," I said, trying to

placate him.

We all broke out in laughter.

"Before we leave for Florida, why don't the four of us get together for dinner?" Dale suggested.

Patty spoke up. "That'll be wonderful. Shall we have it at our place?" she asked.

"I've got an idea, folks," I interjected. "We'll go over to Charlie Brown's Bistro in Boonville."

Everyone agreed, and we set the date for the following Wednesday. I was elected to drive to Charlie's in the Bronco. Evelyn had never been there. It would be a way of showing her the Moose River Road and where the famous furniture factory was located in Boonville.

We bid farewell to Evelyn and Dale and finished our shopping. I noticed that Patty's face looked a little wind-burned from our ride on the snowmobiles.

"Are you okay, Patty?" I asked, concerned. "Your face appears a little red. Probably just from our ride this morning."

"I'm fine, darling. How about yourself?" she responded.

We paid for our groceries and left the store. The wind was whipping up as we loaded our bags into the rear of the Bronco. I closed the rear door and we both climbed in. As I let the Bronco idle for a few minutes, I took out a couple of sticks of gum, giving one to Patty. The spearmint was fresh.

"You know, Patty, Dale and Evelyn seem to hit it off quite well. I truly believe that Dale has found his true love."

"Honey, I think they make a wonderful couple. They're both educated, love flying, and even have the same type of airplanes. I wouldn't be surprised if we went to a wedding in the near future." We both smiled knowingly, remembering our wonderful wedding the year before. I reached over and gently stroked her cheek.

We left the parking lot and headed toward home. A large truck was depositing additional sand to the large pile near the town highway department. Casey Crofut was assisting his driver as he backed the large dump truck. Casey was an energetic young man and had a great deal of responsibility as superintendent of the highway department. We commented that he and his staff would have their work cut out for them over this winter, which looked to be a tough one. I knew Casey's father, the former Town of Webb Chief of Police, Robert Crofut, who had served in that capacity for many years. Chief Crofut had always been dedicated to the citizens of the region and had performed his duties in an outstanding manner.

When we pulled into our driveway, a snowshoe rabbit made a beeline across our property. It was impossible to miss seeing the big fellow as he hopped into a bushy area of the lot.

As I drove up close to our side entrance I glanced over at Ruben who was snuggled up in his doghouse. I had added a slanted roof to the opening of the structure, which kept the blowing snow from sifting in. I told Patty to go inside and turn up the furnace and that I would bring in the groceries.

In about half an hour the groceries were all put away. We decided that we'd eat a light supper of hot cakes and Canadian bacon. It was fast and didn't require a great deal of preparation. After the national news, we both went to the kitchen. I mixed up the batter, as she made a fresh pot of coffee. Patty placed the pancake griddle over two of the burners on the kitchen stove, while I sliced four medium pieces of the bacon. The aroma of the bacon and the coffee permeated the kitchen and dining area and toyed with our taste buds. Our breakfast-food supper was taking shape. Patty decided that I could take my turn at the griddle. We didn't use the box of ready-mixed pancake flour. Occasionally I made them from scratch, and tonight was the night. I used regular flour, baking powder, oil, a pinch of salt, sugar, and two eggs. I mixed those ingredients and added sour milk and beat the batter with a wooden spoon. It took a while for the proper blend to take shape. I didn't want the batter to be too thick nor too thin. When I thought the consistency was just right, I stopped and poured the batter into a pitcher.

Patty was about to take over pouring the batter onto the griddle, but I decided that I would continue with the cooking chores. I poured the first six pancakes onto the griddle and placed the bacon at one end. I reached into the refrigerator for the maple syrup. I removed the cap, poured some into a small pitcher, and heated it in the microwave. As Patty came out of the bathroom after washing her hands, I told her that everything was ready.

"You never cease to amaze me, Jason!" she exclaimed.

"What do you mean by that, my precious one?" I waited happily for her response.

"Oh! That you're just too good to me." She blushed.

"Honey, I love you and you're on your feet all the time at the diner. I feel that I have to relieve you once in a while. Anyway, you know how I love to experiment with pancakes. I'm always looking for just the right taste and color when they are taken off the griddle."

The pancakes came out golden brown. I stacked them on a medium-size platter, along with the four slices of Canadian bacon. Everything looked great. I quickly placed the steaming pancakes on the table and seated Patty. I rushed to pour the coffee, shut the burner down under the griddle, and return to the table. Patty had lit the two candles and I said the blessing.

We didn't speak while we prepared our plates. I looked over at my blond-haired wife and she smiled as she lifted the first fork of pancake to her lips. I followed her with my fork, only I had added a small piece of bacon to the helping. The sour milk had really enhanced the taste. When we finished three pancakes, Patty asked me to put a couple more on the griddle for her.

Instead of two, I raised the flame under the griddle and poured four more. In about three minutes the two of us enjoyed the four additional pancakes in short order. I told Patty about the time in the U.S. Marine Corps at breakfast when a particular batch of pancakes was served. The marines in the mess hall had jumped up in amazement at how sickening sweet the pancakes were. The cook on duty had added what he thought to be melted shortening to the batter, but instead it was a sugary substance. All the fellows had been upset, except for two marines from Beckley, West Virginia. Both of them had gone up to the cook after completing their breakfast and asked, "Cookie, can we have that recipe for those hot cakes? They were delicious!" The cook had blushed and said; "Are you fellas kidding?" The result of that moment had been that the two marines from West Virginia had left the mess hall, happily each with a copy of the recipe.

"Is that what really happened, Jason, or are you kidding?" Patty asked skeptically.

"Honey, that is the truth, so help me God!" I insisted.

I told Patty to take care of Ruben while I did up the dishes. After our great supper, the kitchen was back in good condition in forty-five minutes. It was getting cold out. Patty came in from tending Ruben, and we decided to bundle up in warm jackets and take a short walk with the K-9.

After our walk we came inside and hung up our jackets. To supplement our furnace I started a fire in the fireplace. Some of the dry wood from the year before crackled as it burned brightly. A few sparks jumped from the burning pieces of wood, but were stopped by the fine fireplace screen. Patty selected a disk of country western music.

It was about 10:00 p.m. when we decided to retire to the bedroom. The reading lamps were on and we read until we rolled over into each other's arms. Our passions grew strong for each other, enveloping us into a complete expression of our mutual desire. It was late before we fell off to sleep. The alarm went off at five-thirty in the morning. Patty had to be at the diner by 6:00. I rolled over and fell back to sleep. I faintly remember Patty giving me a kiss on the cheek before she left for work.

I was still in bed when the telephone rang. I glanced over at the Big Ben alarm clock. It was 8:30. I pushed the bed covers back and got out of bed, slipping on my bathrobe. I answered the phone on the fourth ring.

"Hello," I said sleepily.

"Jason, this is Tom Huston. Sorry to call you so early, but I wanted to let you know that we have additional problems. I got up early this morning to get ready for a meeting to be held in

Plattsburgh at noon today. I went to the garage to put my briefcase and other documents in my car. I noticed that the garage door was ajar. When I entered the garage I couldn't believe what I saw. Every window in my new Lincoln had been smashed. And that's not all: the two rear tires were flat." His voice was shaky.

"Did you call the police right away?" I felt so bad for my friend, realizing how upset he was.

"They're here investigating as we speak." He was trying to regain his composure.

"Jason, this situation is preying on my nerves and I'm getting terribly stressed out."

"You must be, Tom."

"Jason, would you mind coming up to my office? I'm not going to the meeting. Something has to be done to alleviate this continuous crime spree against me." I could hear the anger building in the normally placid Tom Huston.

"I agree with you fully, Tom. I'll leave shortly," I assured him.

"I will appreciate it more than you'll ever know," he said as he hung up.

I quickly got dressed, downed a lukewarm cup of coffee with a bran muffin, and called Patty at the diner. I told her that I had no idea when I'd be getting home.

"Be careful driving, Jason," she pleaded.

"I will, darling. I'll check Ruben before I leave. Are the roads slippery?"

"Route 28 has been sanded."

"Take care, sweetheart. I'll keep in touch."

I went to the closet for my heavy jacket, a cap, and a pair of deerskin gloves. After checking the house, turning down the thermostat, and filling Ruben's dishes, I left for Lake Placid. I brought along my 9mm semi-automatic pistol and ammo. Although I probably would never have to use it, I also realized a person couldn't be certain in a society where violence could erupt at any time.

Snowflakes lazily spiraled to the ground and disappeared as

they struck my windshield. The defroster on the Bronco always functioned like a hot-air furnace, and sometimes during the winter season I had to shut it off so the interior would cool down.

The trip to the Breakshire Lodge was uneventful, except for gassing up in Tupper Lake. There was a logger parked in the parking lot of the gas station, sipping on a cup of coffee. I sauntered over to his truck. He had a black beard and was wearing steel-rimmed glasses. He looked down from his cab as I approached.

"Can I help you, mister?" he asked politely.

"No, not really. I just wanted to take a look at your rig. You certainly keep it in good shape."

"Thank you," he said. "This rig is my bread and butter. I've been logging for twenty years, and it seems to be more difficult each year to make ends meet. I've got three kids and all of them are looking forward to a college education. I sure hope the logging business improves," he added.

"My name is Jason Black. What's yours?" I asked.

"Vance Timmerman. Nice to meet you, Jason."

"Likewise." Vance proceeded to climb down from the cab of his Brockway tractor and extend his right hand. I shook it. He was a tall fellow with a powerful grip.

"Yep! My wife and kids are the most important people in my life."

"I can appreciate that, Vance."

"What do you do, Jason?"

I told Vance that I was a retired member of the New York State Troopers and that I was now doing some private investigation work in the area.

"Boy! I wouldn't want that job, with all the danger and things going on today. I've always been treated fairly by the fellas. I remember a couple of years ago, one of my chains gave way and several logs came off the trailer. Two troopers came to the scene and directed traffic while I reloaded the logs. I always carry some extra chains with me. I was lucky that no one was following close to the rig."

"Yes, you were fortunate," I said, nodding.

As we talked for a few minutes longer, I asked him if he knew Charlie Perkins and Wilt Chambers. "I sure do. They're fine fellas," he replied.

We both agreed to that. I wished Vance Timmerman well and went back to the Bronco to continue on with my trip to Lake Placid.

As I drove I thought about the struggling loggers who work throughout the Adirondacks and in the adjacent forests inside and outside the Blue Line. The work was difficult and dangerous—although, with the modern machinery available to them, all it would take would be a log to move the wrong way to end their life or cause serious injury. I thought of my father and how hard he had worked years ago in the logging and pulp operation he had been involved in. I understood why I always respected people in that line of work.

I pulled into a parking space near the entrance to the Breakshire Lodge. There were a few cars in the parking area. I didn't observe any police vehicles. I exited the Bronco and went into the lodge. I noticed Tom Huston in a conversation with one of his two desk clerks. He appeared distraught and pale. He turned and motioned to me to proceed into his office. When I passed him he managed to smile, but I could tell he was severely disturbed. I went down the hallway and into his office, sat down in one of his comfortable leather chairs, and waited for him.

Ten minutes went by before Tom came in. I got up to greet him and shook his hand. It was painful for me to see this self-assured executive looking so distressed.

"You just missed the troopers. There were two of them here on the investigation of my damaged car. This is really getting to me. Do you think it is Harris or his son who is involved in this? Everything seems to point in that direction. But why aren't they being arrested or questioned? I cannot comprehend the delay. These attacks are burglaries and criminal mischief cases. What's your honest opinion, Jason?" His voice was shaking as he spoke.

"I couldn't swear to it in a court of law, but my gut feeling is that Morey Harris is behind this. Rumor has it that his father may have moved to Florida, but Morey is still living near Hewitt Pond, between North Creek and Newcomb. In all fairness to the troopers, they have to build a solid case. They're probably gathering evidence as we speak," I said, trying to reassure him.

"One of the troopers conveyed that fact about the father. No one offered any information about Morey Harris. Jason, can you possibly stay here at the lodge a few days? I've got a feeling that something else will happen. The troopers do as good a job as they can patrolling the area, but last night they had to go to another part of the county on an accident call. If you could stay here for a few days maybe you could learn something," he said, almost pleading.

"Yes, I'll stay here, Tom, but I'll need some clothes and my shaving kit. I'll call Patty and maybe she can start north with the items."

"I hope you don't mind, Jason, but I don't know how much more I can take. Someone has a vendetta towards me and I want to know why!" he exclaimed.

I called Patty at John's Diner. As things were slow at the diner, she said she would speak to Lila and leave right away. She would pick up what I needed and meet me at Gertie's Diner in Long Lake to drop the items off.

When I told him I would leave for Long Lake and then return to the lodge for a few days, Tom said, "Jason, I appreciate this more than you'll ever know. Before you leave I want you to have a cup of coffee with me and a sandwich."

I agreed and we proceeded to the dining room. A table was ready for us and a waitress was already pouring two cups of coffee. We sat down and soon the waitress returned with what Tom had ordered: two tunafish sandwiches with crisp lettuce on homemade wheat bread.

We talked about several possibilities as to the tightening of security at the lodge. Although five of his fifteen properties had been burglarized, thankfully there had been only one arson attempt. He assured me that the troopers had gone out of their way in keeping an eye out for any intrusions toward his properties. Frighteningly, it was just as though the person or persons doing this were watching the patrols.

"Tom, I know the Troop S territory very well, and even though we reside in one of the finest places on earth, there are still bound to be those folks who don't care about the work ethic and who will go out and steal and rob and burglarize at their whim. That's why cameras and alarm systems are beneficial. Any of us can become a victim at any time." I tried to explain my view to Tom in the best way I could.

"I see your point, Jason. I understand, and I'll appreciate any help you can give me with this crisis."

I understood how Tom felt. No one wants their property violated. He gave me a key for room #108 in the event I returned late. I thanked him and departed for Long Lake to get my clothes from Patty.

The trip was uneventful. I gassed the Bronco at a station just before I crossed the bridge into Long Lake. I must have been running on fumes, for it took eighteen gallons. I went in, paid the attendant, and purchased a pack of gum. Outside I climbed into the Bronco and headed toward Gertie's Diner, where I spotted Patty's red Jeep right away. She had backed it in facing the lake near the two seaplanes that were tied to the docking area. Traffic was light, so I pulled in and backed around next to the Jeep, leaving ample room for Patty to get out from behind the wheel. As always, I noticed the alluring smile she displayed and the way her blond hair draped onto her shoulders. My heart just about skipped a beat.

She immediately exited the Jeep, opened the rear passenger door, and took out the leather clothing bag, a small suitcase, and my shaving kit. I started to get out to assist her.

"I've got it, honey," she called over to me.

I proceeded to open the rear door of the Bronco. She reached in and hung the clothing bag on the hook, then closed the door. We embraced, happy to see each other. We finally pulled apart and entered Gertie's.

There were no other customers. Gertie, in the process of cleaning the grill with a stone, looked up when we entered.

"Patty and Jason Black, how are you?" Gertie was wearing her usual welcoming, warm smile. She immediately stopped what she was doing, rushed around the counter, and embraced Patty. Then she gave me a big hug.

"You just missed Bob. He's gone home for the day to rest. We were busy all day. It slowed down, so I sent him on home," she explained. "What can I get for you two?"

"If you're getting ready to close, we don't want to be a bother," Patty said.

"Oh, hush. You're no bother. I have some ham and scalloped potatoes left. All I have to do is warm it a little. Is that all right? I know Jason loves it."

"That sounds good to me, Gertie," Patty responded.

"It sure does," I added.

There was just one waitress on duty, and she had been busy counting her gratuities at a table. She finished putting the money into her purse and immediately came over to seat us. Gertie went to the kitchen to prepare our meal. The waitress brought us two glasses of ice water and two cups of coffee.

While we waited for our meal, Patty and I discussed the probability that I would be away for a few days. I didn't go into the facts about the case, but I knew she knew it concerned Tom Huston's recent burglaries and other crimes against his business and himself. I assured Patty that I would call her in the morning and evenings while I was gone.

"Sweetheart, I have no fear, especially with Ruben with me," she said confidently.

"I know you'll be okay. If you weren't working, I'd have you join me. You know that." I reached over to hold her hand.

"I know, honey. I'll be fine." I could tell she knew I needed my worry assuaged.

The coffee was delicious, as usual. In a few minutes the waitress brought us our ham and scalloped potatoes. Both plates were steaming hot. We declined a salad, but opted for some of Gertie's homemade bread. We were hungry and the food was delicious. Just the right seasoning. When we had finished the main entrée, Gertie came over to the table personally, carrying two peach shortcakes topped with real whipped cream. She wore a big grin. Patty and I were always treated like royalty by Gertie.

"The dessert is on the house, Jason. I do not want to hear any arguments from you," she admonished.

"You know how I feel about paying for the entire meal, Gertie," I protested.

"I know how you are, Jason. But this one time, I want to do it for you and Patty. After all, you're like family to Bob and me," she added with sincerity.

"Okay, Gertie. Just this one time." I knew it would break Gerie's heart if I forced the issue. I'd make it up somehow, when she least suspected it.

We finished our wonderful dessert, paid our bill, and left a sizable tip for the waitress. With a big hug to Gertie, we left the diner.

After Patty and I went for a short walk to help digest our dinner, she left for Old Forge and I left for the Breakshire. I knew we both had sadness in our hearts as we drove in opposite directions. We loved each other so very much, that was undeniable.

It was difficult not to worry about her being alone. I couldn't forget that horrible night prior to our marriage, when she had been abducted by the two escaped killers from Ohio. But life must go on. She assured me she would call as soon as she arrived home. I continued my drive to Lake Placid, but my thoughts kept returning to my wife.

Patty had many friends in the region—not only the locals, but some she had made from the customer base at the diner. Each year the visiting tourists would stop by to have a meal at John's and to say hello to Patty and all the diner staff. It wasn't only in the summer, but all the seasons, each with its own individual beauty, a draw for return trips to the area.

There was so much to do in this beautiful area and so much to see. As familiar as I was with the region inside the Blue

Line, I still feel humbled whether I'm tramping through the woods and forest lands, boating, paddling my canoe, or driving through the mountains. It will always be breathtaking to me, maybe because of my early childhood and being with my father as he pursued logging and pulping inside and outside the Blue Line.

Then there were the forest rangers, the game protectors, police and the many people that make up the e-con service, as well as people from all branches and organizations. Many of these folks loved the Adirondacks and the region. My thoughts traveled to all the people who worked in the region and the millions who visited this six-million-acre park, where a lot of good takes place, but where evil lurks in the hearts of some.

It was this evil that had brought me where I was going in the capacity of a private detective, at the request of a dear friend.

The highway to Lake Placid was bare, but the cold crisp air assured me that winter was in place and that the winter sports and activities would soon be in full swing. When I reached the Breakshire I pulled into the rear of the parking area, took out my clothes and gear, locked the Bronco, and went inside to #108, a spacious room with two king-size beds, a desk, two chairs, a small refrigerator, and cable television. My eye caught the note and a bottle of chilled white wine in a container of ice. Next to it rested a covered tray of crackers, with Swiss cheese cut perfectly to fit them. A small jar of mustard and several napkins were on the tray. I knew that this gift was the work of Tom Huston.

I had been in the room for only a few minutes when the telephone rang. I picked up the receiver.

"Hello," I answered, hoping it was Patty.

"Jason, Tom here. Is everything okay?"

"Fine. You didn't have to fuss for me, Tom. But that was thoughtful of you to furnish me the wine, crackers, and cheese," I said. Tom was always the perfect host.

"No problem, Jason. Will you please stop at my office in the morning around nine tomorrow?" he asked.

"I'll be there."

"Thank you. It means so much to me to have you here at the lodge. Maybe we can finally get to the bottom of this nightmare."

"I hope we can. We'll certainly try. By the way, you haven't any ghosts here in the lodge, have you?" I said, jokingly, trying to brighten his spirit.

There was a silence.

"Jason, I hope not. No, I don't believe we have any ghosts." He chuckled. "Goodnight, Jason."

"Goodnight."

I quickly glanced at my watch. It wasn't too late to call Patty. I dialed the number, and she answered after the first ring.

"Hello, sweetheart! Is everything okay?" I was concerned, being away from home.

"Darling, everything is fine. I just let Ruben in from his little trip to the woods. I'm just about ready for bed. I miss you, Jason." Her voice was sincere.

"I miss you, too, honey. Make certain that the doors are locked."

"Jason, I don't want to make you upset, but about half an hour ago an older model car pulled in right up to the dog run. It idled there for about five minutes. No one got out. Ruben went wild and barked fiercely. I had the shades pulled down, but I peeked outside and watched it. It backed around and left the yard."

"Who in the heck do you think it was?"

"I have no idea. The car, an older model, looked beat up, and the muffler was loud. When it was near the dog run the driver must have lit a cigarette, as I saw a lighted match that was then put out. I don't know, Jason—I didn't call the police, for I thought it might have been lovers looking for an inconspicuous place."

"Maybe it was or maybe it wasn't. I don't like that, Patty. I'm concerned. The suspect in the case the troopers are working drives an older Chrysler sedan, rusty and beat up. But I don't see how this suspect could know where we live or why he'd drive there. It probably isn't connected at all." Her news only added to my worry.

"Honey, don't worry. I've already loaded the shotgun with double-aught buck. Remember, Jason, I'm originally a Kentucky girl, and we don't cotton to trespassers or burglars. And I want you to know that Ruben's ears stood straight up when that car was by the dog run. After all, that's Ruben's territory."

I could feel my muscles tightening at Patty's words. I should be home, but I was there at the Breakshire for the purpose of assisting my friend and employer. I tried to calm myself with the reminder that if anybody tried to break in, Ruben would react to the intrusion and, besides, Patty would know how to defend herself. Unfortunately she had had to learn how to do so during her first marriage, when her husband, Kenneth had assaulted her more than once while in an intoxicated condition.

"Sweetheart, you'll be okay. Try to get some sleep. Call me right away if anyone should come around. Let's hope it really was just lovers trying to find a place! You've got the number for the Breakshire. I'm at extension 108. Goodnight, darling."

"I'm not concerned, Jason. I just wanted to let you know. Call me tomorrow," she said.

"I will, babe. Sleep tight."

I heard Patty's click as she hung up the receiver. It bothered me quite a bit to think that someone would drive up to our side door and sit there for five minutes in the dark, especially when there was no legitimacy to do so. I was aware of our deteriorating society; it is in the newspapers daily and on the news twenty-four hours a day over the radio and television. I was also aware that readers of the news and listeners to the news broadcasts have to be able to separate the true facts from the falsehoods.

The small glass of wine just before I went to bed tasted good. I read for a few minutes and drifted off to sleep, worrying about Patty.

CHAPTER FIFTEEN

It was about 3:00 a.m. when an old, rusted Chrysler sedan pulled into the driveway of the Harris residence near Hewitt Pond, south of Newcomb just off Route 28N. Morey Harris pulled his car close to his father's ramshackle house. The porch drooped toward the ground. Two ferocious dogs met their master at the broken-down doorstep. An owl could be heard off in the distance, hooting an eerie sound. Morey pushed the side door open. It creaked as the hinges thirsted for lubrication. They hadn't been oiled in years.

Morey's father had been discharged by Tom Huston. He had had a good position as groundskeeper at the Breakshire Lodge, but Tom had been forced to let him go when he caught the man in the act of stealing property. Morey had been getting a small allowance from his father, but the allowance had stopped, and his father had sought employment in another area, leaving Morey to shift for himself. Without the presence of his father, Morey was consumed by anger and had adopted a revengeful attitude toward Huston, blaming him for the absence of his weekly allowance, not truly acknowledging his father was at fault, not Huston. Living alone near Hewitt Pond, Morey had had time to formulate a plan to take his imagined grievance out on Huston by burglarizing several of the lodge owner's properties. He had already attempted to burn down the stately Victorian home in Newcomb, but had failed in his efforts. However, in burglarizing other properties of Huston, to his great satisfaction he had acquired expensive items consisting of tools, saws, a ship's bell, and construction equipment.

Traveling to other areas of the State of New York, he easily sold some of the stolen property at flea markets. Morey used the money from these sales to put gas in his car. His next move toward Huston had not yet been formulated by him. He had been clever in his criminally inclined mind to avoid contact with the troopers directly. He had hidden several times when trooper patrols had come close to him at the crime scenes. Also, on the edge of his mind, was of the possibility of a private detective friend of Huston, who might be looking into his revengeful crime spree. His father had mentioned a particular man of this profession who had come to the Breakshire periodically to have lunch. Morey had scoffed at his father when he had talked about this man, yet part of him was aware of the danger.

Morey was headstrong, not wrapped too tightly. His capacity to function as a good citizen was hampered by the fact that his parents hadn't shown him the love that takes place with normal parenting. In a way, he was to be pitied for his lack of proper training. Morey Harris had one goal in his mind, and that was to harass and hurt Tom Huston, a gentle man who cared about people.

CHAPTER SIXTEEN

I woke up and went into the bathroom. I missed Patty so very much, even though I had been away from her just overnight. Room 108, like the other rooms at the Breakshire Lodge, provided a small coffeepot. I proceeded to plug it in and make myself a fresh cup prior to my shave and shower. I had ample time before my nine o'clock meeting with Tom.

Finished with the shower and getting dressed, I poured myself another cup of coffee and added a half-spoon of sugar. The coffee tasted good. But when I went to check my clothing bag, a box of green-tea bags fell into my hand. My sweetheart had put them in without telling me. I decided that a cup of green tea, my favorite, could wait till later in the day. I tidied up the room, then called Patty at John's Diner in Old Forge. I could tell she had missed me, too. We talked a few minutes about the car that had pulled into the yard, but dismissed it as possible lovers looking for a secluded place to spend some time.

"I love you, Patty. Take good care of yourself and Ruben. You two are my family," I said to her sincerely.

"I will, dearest. You be careful. And please say hello to Mr. Huston for me. Call me tonight, if you get a chance." She sounded so very lonely. I could hear the customers in the background and the music that Lila and John played for them.

We finished talking and I placed the phone on the cradle. I

157

had no sooner hung up when the telephone sounded two short rings.

"Good morning, Jason. Did you sleep well?" Tom's voice sounded almost cheerful.

"Yes, I slept very well." Of course, I said silently to myself, *I would have rather been at home with Patty during the night.*

"I've ordered our breakfast and we'll eat in the office, if you don't mind, Jason."

"That's fine. I'll be right down," I responded.

I could only surmise what benefit I'd be to Tom at this juncture. Lieutenant Jack Doyle was personally supervising his staff on this case involving the attempted arson and the burglaries. Though it was true he did not have ample personnel to cover all of Huston's properties at the same time, his people were periodically checking them, especially after dark. Jack had uniformed troopers passing in and out of the Breakshire when they were available to do so. Captain Roy Garrison had been promoted to major, after Frank Temple had decided to retire to enjoy a life with less pressure and to do some of the salmon fishing he enjoyed so much. I knew both of these men very well; they were dedicated to the state troopers.

When I left the room for Tom's office I removed the "Do Not Disturb" sign and proceeded down the hall. I went directly to his office and knocked on the door.

"Come in," he said.

I entered. Tom arose from his desk, grasped my hand, and gave me a handshake. He indicated that breakfast would be forthcoming. I noticed that his spirits seemed somewhat better, but that he appeared to be a man carrying a heavy load.

We talked for a few minutes, then paused when a knock came to the door. I noticed that a small table had been set up for our breakfast. Tom got up from his desk, went over to the door, and opened it. One of the waitresses came into the office, pushing a cart carrying several covered dishes. She carefully placed them on the table, poured our coffee, and asked Mr. Huston if there were anything else.

"Not at the present. Everything seems just fine," he replied. "Thank you."

The waitress hurriedly left the office. She smiled at us as she went out the door.

Tom had ordered ham and eggs, home fries, and whole wheat toast, with assorted jellies. After we removed the covers, we sat down at the table to enjoy a wonderful breakfast. As we ate, Tom asked me if I would check out his Newcomb Victorian during the day. He had paid a good price for the house and it was his favorite possession, as far as real property went. I knew he was worried about it. I assured him that I had someone who lived nearby keeping an eye out for anything suspicious, a fact which pleased Tom. I told him that it was Bob Bearor, an area author and an historical scholar.

"I've met this man at one of his programs, Jason. He is a fine chap," Tom said hopefully. "His wife, too. A great couple."

"Yes, Tom. They are wonderful people," I agreed.

I reassured my friend that while I was staying at the Breakshire I would be watchful for any suspicious activity. That day I would be checking the Hewitt Pond region for Morey Harris.

After breakfast I thanked Tom, returned to my room, picked up my semi-automatic pistol (leaving it unloaded,) and my notebook. The chambermaids were nearing my room. I asked them to leave an extra bar of soap, and they said they would. I then proceeded out the side entrance door, walked around the lodge twice, and approached the Bronco.

I went to the Bronco, unlocked it, and secured my pistol in a safe place. I didn't take it on every case, for sure, but on this one I thought I might need it. The alleged suspect was believed to be a dangerous person, and I wasn't going to take any chances. Anyone who would attempt to commit arson wasn't dealing with a full deck, in my estimation. I had investigated several arsons as a member of the troopers.

I thought about one case that I had worked on with a sheriff's investigator, in the northern Adirondack region, where the suspect would set the fire usually in the kitchen of houses that were empty. He had used torn pages from a national magazine that displayed nudity. One day a uniformed trooper had contacted me over his car radio, wanting to meet me. He had a fellow he was talking to. Prior to my arrival, he had spotted this fellow peddling a bicycle in the vicinity of an arson attempt. The man had admitted that he had tried to set the house on fire, but it had gone out. Going to the scene, we found the torn-out pages partially burned. He had attempted to set the fire in the middle of the kitchen, on the floor. Further grilling of the suspect had revealed that he had caused several fires in the region.

A sheriff's detective had also been working on some cases involving suspicious fires. When we had gotten together with the suspect and informed him of his rights, the suspect had orally admitted to setting the fires with the torn pages which revealed nudity. After some time in a correctional facility, the perpetrator had been released and told to seek help from a mental health professional. Fortunately, no one had been injured in those fires—however, they can and do occur across our country every day, somewhere!

As my mind traversed such important thoughts, I was glad the traffic was light and, even though some fresh new snow had fallen overnight, the highways were just wet. As always, the pristine beauty of the region and the snow of winter clinging to the trees of the forest created an unforgettable scene, especially with fresh falling snow. I thought of how much Patty and I loved the Adirondacks, and of how we had opted for the beauty of Old Forge and the Fulton Chain of Lakes.

As I drove to Newcomb on 28N, I passed the Adirondack Visitors' Interpretive Center located to the left. I recalled how I had attended an area meeting discussing the creation of this project. The director had informed his audience that he had visited sites throughout the country prior to selecting and building in this very special location. It now stands to inform visitors of the fauna and flora peculiar to the Adirondack Park.

I never had visited the center without taking one of the serene nature walks provided there.

Newcomb was quiet as I came into town. The first thing I saw was Tom's stately-looking Victorian house. It had an elegant aura about it. Just a short way down the street resided my friend, Bob Bearor, a former member of the famed 101st Airborne Division. As I drove by I didn't see his vehicle.

One of these days, I told myself, Patty and I would have to take him up on his offer to accompany him and his wife on a tour of the Santanoni Preserve. The preserve consisted of the Great Camp Santanoni, now owned by the State of New York, and 12,500 acres, the largest tract of land donated to the Adirondack Preserve in the last decade. During the summer months, visitors can walk or bicycle the nearly five miles into the camp, or take advantage of the wagon ride. Some of the buildings are currently under preservation to help restore them because of their historical value. Santanoni is one of the remaining great camps scattered throughout the Adirondacks.

I turned around and parked a short distance from Tom's Victorian home. The snow on the ground was about four inches. Before I checked the property I donned my overshoes and buttoned my jacket, as it was chilly, especially with the strong breeze that was blowing. The neighborhood appeared to be quiet and peaceful. I walked down the driveway to the side door, opened the storm door, and tried the knob. It was a solid door and I found it locked and secure. The next security check was to the back of the house, which consisted of an enclosed screen porch with four steps leading to the rear entrance. I noticed the new construction work that Tom had done. The new addition to the porch matched perfectly. I knew that Tom liked a large porch. The combination screens and storm windows caught my eye. Tom was more or less conservative, but when it came to new construction he selected the best materials on the market or if not accessible, the best available product.

My thoughts drifted to Morey Harris. If he had been successful in setting fire to this lovely home it could have taken the whole neighborhood out, especially if there had been a strong wind. And a grim possibility was that the suspect would make another attempt. I hoped the troopers would soon end the suspect's crime spree with an arrest, but I knew that Lieutenant Doyle wanted to build a solid case in this matter.

Feeling that my security check was complete, I took another walk around the property and headed to the Bronco. When I started the Bronco I noticed that the fuel gauge read half-full. I'd have enough until I returned to Long Lake.

Before I made my turn to the south to the Vanderwhacker Mountain region and Hewitt Pond, I pulled off the road by Harris Lake. The campground there was always busy in the summertime, but now the white snow covered the area. It was my love for lakes that drew me to this one. I got out of the Bronco and walked toward the lake. I hadn't gone fifty feet when a red fox appeared ahead of me. It was moving slowly, coming in my direction from my right. Knowing that any animal could have rabies, I was cautious. As it neared the fox didn't look sickly, though. He hesitated and looked in my direction. I stopped walking. The fox continued to move on toward a brushy area and disappeared. The camera that I kept in the Bronco came in handy at times. I wasn't able to take a picture of the fox, but when I returned to the Bronco I got out the camera and took two pictures of Lake Harris. Patty and I had started an album of Adirondack photos and now we would have more to add to it. We had excellent luck with single-use cameras. They were inexpensive and the photos taken by them were of good quality.

A town truck from Newcomb passed by as I climbed back into the Bronco. I noticed that he had on a load of sand, probably taking it to the sand-pile. The fellows who work for the towns inside the Blue Line become our heroes many times over the winter months. Having been rescued from snowdrifts by state, county, and town employees over the years had left me with a great deal of respect for their efforts to keep the roads safe for all motorists. It takes efforts from all walks of life to keep our society functioning. And I believe that the majority of people in this great country work hard and do their best to do the right thing. We would be in trouble if the deviants of our society became the majority.

I looked over toward Vanderwhacker Mountain as I drove in a southerly direction toward Hewitt Pond. I knew the mountain had a fire tower and someday Patty and I would climb it. We could carry our lunch with us and take some photos. Essex County was a great place to visit.

The rest area on Route 28N near the road to Hewitt Pond was empty. My plan was to go by Harris's house and conduct a surveillance. I made a left-hand turn onto the road to Harris's. When I was about five hundred feet from the house I noticed an older model car sitting in the middle of the highway with the hood up. I stopped the Bronco immediately. The older model car was Morey Harris's rusty Chrysler. It appeared to me that he was having engine trouble. I had to make a quick decision. Should I turn around by making a trooper reverse Y turn, or should I proceed toward him and offer assistance?

I decided to take the risk. I felt that Morey wouldn't recognize me, as we'd never seen each other before. I quickly checked the Bronco for any telltale signs of my present occupation as a private detective and proceeded toward the Chrysler. There he was, a pudgy white male wearing grease-stained clothes and a coonskin hat. He was bent over the hood, peering into the engine compartment. It was Morey Harris himself. I pulled the Bronco as far off the narrow road as possible and climbed out. The pudgy Harris didn't even look in my direction.

"Can I assist you, mister?" I asked.

"Huh?" He appeared startled.

"Can I be of assistance? I see that you are having some difficulty." I offered.

"Huh! Huh! I got trouble." He finally straightened up and looked in my direction. His face was covered with grease and his hands were the same way. He was about five-feet eight inches tall and must have weighed two hundred and fifty pounds. His bare belly bulged out from under his dirty shirt.

He apparently was chewing tobacco, as he spat out a brown juice, which ran down his chin.

"What's your name?" I asked politely.

"What's yours?" he shot back.

"My name is Jay," I half-lied.

"Well now, my name is Morey Harris. I live in that house over there," he answered sharply while pointing in the direction of that ramshackle house with the drooping porch.

"What seems to be your trouble, Morey?" I asked.

"I don't know. The dang engine just quit working." He acted nervous.

"I'll be glad to assist you, if I can."

"Well, maybe you can give me a little push into my driveway. I'll have to call somebody," he said, hesitantly.

I wanted to look into the rusty Chrysler, so I walked around it and told him the best place for me to push the car. I peeked into the dirty windows and observed several boxes of what appeared to be new tools of some kind. Of course, I didn't ask him where he had obtained them or what they were for. I didn't want to blow my cover. I'd just push him into the driveway and see what happened.

"Okay, Morey. You get behind your steering wheel and I'll see what my old car can do," I volunteered.

He climbed into the Chrysler.

I put the Bronco into four-wheel drive and got around behind the car.

"Are you all set, Morey?" I asked.

"Yep," he hollered back.

I slowly drove to the rear bumper of his car and got out to see if they matched. They did. I then got back into the Bronco and slowly pushed against the rust bucket. It was about a hundred feet to the entrance of the driveway. Morey turned into the driveway and I followed slowly, continually pushing against the rear bumper of his car. Instead of stopping just inside the driveway, I decided I'd push him right up to the house. That way I could take a look around the place that Morey called home. In a way I felt sorry for this guy. He was to be pitied. Morey hit the brake on the clunker and I held off.

I turned the Bronco off and exited the vehicle.

"Do you live here alone, Morey?" I asked.

"Yeah, all alone. My dad went to Florida to try and find work," he responded sadly.

"Is that so. What kind of work does your dad do?" I asked.

"He's a darn good gardener, oh yeah! He retired from the Breakshire Lodge up in Lake Placid. You heard of that place?" He waited for my response.

"Yes, I've heard of the Breakshire Lodge. How long did your dad work there?" I tried to engage him in conversation to see if I could get some information.

"He worked there a few years, until he retired."

I could see that Morey was getting nervous again.

"Well, that's nice that he retired."

"Yeah, but I miss him. He used to give me an allowance and now he's gone and left me to shift for myself." Morey's eyes seemed to be tearing up.

"I'm sure your dad cares—most dads do—and maybe he'll start sending you an allowance from Florida. Where did he go to in Florida?" I pressed him.

"I don't know for certain, maybe a place called Bradenton."

I knew that town was on the West Coast of Florida.

"Is your mom with your dad?" I asked.

"My mom passed away a while ago," he replied, tearing up.

"Have you gotten a job?" I thought maybe he'd give me a story about the tools in the rear seat of his car. He became silent, apparently seeking the right words to say. His eyes squinted up to the left.

"Well, I guess you could say that I go to flea markets, but with winter being here it's hard to find one. You might say I'm a salesman who sells tools."

"That's interesting. Do you have a store of some kind?" I asked nonchalantly.

"No, I sell them out of my car, wherever I can. Sometimes

I go into beer joints. Usually there's someone interested in buying some tools." I noticed that he was beginning to shake. I didn't want to push him any further. Suddenly he looked at me speculatively. "In fact, I have tools in my car right now, if you're interested." I was certain they were some of the ones taken from Huston's burglaries.

I knew that I could purchase one of the tools and show it to Huston for possible identification and possibly use it as evidence, but I feared they would be too generic to distinguish them.

"Well, Morey, I don't have any need for tools at the moment. But I do have a friend that may be interested," I replied. "He's always looking for tools."

"Gee! Do you really think he'd be interested?" His face lit up.

"I think he would be. I'll contact him. If he is, I'll bring him down to take a look at them. Just give me your phone number."

"Sure you can have it, but it doesn't work." He added resentfully, "The telephone company just shut it off yesterday, because I don't have any money to pay the bill."

"Oh! I see! That does present a problem."

"Well, I'll probably be here working on the Chrysler anyway."

"It could be something going on with the computer. I had a friend that had a 1986 and he was in the garage all the time with it. Yours is a 1986, isn't it?"

"Yeah, it is." He paused. "Say, I want to thank you for pushing me into the driveway, Jay. By the way, where do you live? Not around here, I'll bet, because I never saw you before."

I had to think fast.

"Down near Utica. I'm up here looking for old barns. I like to buy them and remove the old wood," I answered.

It wasn't the truth, of course, but I did love old barn wood.

"I don't think there are any old barns down this way, but you might find some up near Newcomb," he offered.

"Well, thanks for the information, Morey." I had to be careful on my next question to him. I paused for a moment and then asked him, "Oh! By the way, do you know a fellow by the name of Tom Huston?"

His reaction was immediate. His face turned crimson and his mouth twisted into several contortions. His eyes went wild. It appeared that Morey Harris was about to blow a gasket. The simple question I had asked him had ignited his rage. His mouth flew open and shut several times without uttering a word. In all my life I had never witnessed such a reaction to a question. I asked him another one.

"Are you all right, Morey?" I was concerned.

His eyes now began to roll around. It appeared that he was trying to regain control of his emotions. His face was still reddish in color; his blood pressure must have skyrocketed. Was it his hatred toward Huston? Or his guilty conscience? Or was it both?

I didn't want to leave him in this emotional state. So I tried to temper the situation by asking him a non-related question.

"Morey, do you like to fish?"

He slowly adjusted his attitude and replied. "I love to fish, Jay." He seemed to relax and appeared to have returned to reality. After a moment, he looked directly at me suspiciously. "Why did you ask me about Tom Huston?"

"The only reason was that we had talked about your dad having been employed at the Breakshire Lodge. And somewhere I had heard that a Mr. Tom Huston was the owner. That's all." He seemed to accept my response.

We talked about fishing and the locations of good fishing places. He mentioned that he loved to ice fish and that his dad had taken him to Oneida Lake years before to catch jack-perch. After a couple more minutes I told him that I had to leave and that I'd be in touch with him about the tools. For some reason, he seemed to believe in me and I had indicated to him that I had a mechanic friend near North River who had been known to work on Chryslers. I went one step further and told him that we might go fishing the following spring. I didn't say any more about the tools, nor did I again mention Tom Huston. I told him that I'd be back in a few days. We bid farewell and I entered the Bronco.

As I turned my head to view the driveway while backing down it, I thought, *There's a guy destined to ruination, a person living somewhere below poverty level who will never get a break to live an average life with his dad.* His mother had passed away. My mind mulled over his explosive reaction to the mere mention of Tom's name, one of the kindest people on this earth, just because Huston had fired Morey's father, shutting off his monthly allowance. His emotional instability was unbelievable. I now knew that Morey Harris needed to be monitored closely, before something drastic occurred to Huston or himself. This young criminal was a menace.

Once out on the road I looked over at the Harris house. Morey had the hood up, peering at the engine. Even though I felt sorry for this pathetic individual, I still had my job to do. It was clear that Morey's attitude toward Tom Huston was dangerous and explosive. From my evaluation of the situation, I found it hard to believe that Morey Harris was employable. I could not understand how his father could have moved from the area, leaving his son to fend for himself. He was a sad case who could become violent. I decided that I would call Lieutenant Jack Doyle from the Breakshire Lodge. There was no telling what action he might take against Tom Huston while carrying an imagined grievance around in his mind. One fortunate factor, however, was that with his car disabled, he would be grounded for a day or two at least.

I stopped in another parking area after I got onto Route 28N so I could view Vanderwhacker Mountain. It measured 3,386 feet and, out of almost twenty peaks in the region, still has a fire tower. I had been told by friends that a foot trail does go to the summit and that a hiker can obtain the best view of the high peaks from the south looking north. A person could even locate the course of the Hudson River from this peak. As I sat in the Bronco entering notes of my encounter with Morey Harris into my notebook, I couldn't help but feel the presence of what the Adirondack Park is all about. I shuddered to think of what would happen to this beautiful part of New York State if the caretakers reneged on their responsibility to this magnificent place.

I knew that I would have to bring Patty here, maybe not that winter, but possibly the next summer, to climb the foot trail to the top to view the high peaks. Patty would love to view the Boreas River, one of the most beautiful in the Adirondacks.

When I finished entering the events in my notebook, I got out of the Bronco for a few minutes to stretch my legs. During my half-century on earth I had learned a long time ago the danger of sitting too long without moving about. Keeping blood circulation on the move is most important for a longer life. Of course, I knew, too, that many physically fit people meet their maker in all kinds of accidents. None of us can predict what's coming around the corner on the path of life. All we can do is face each day to the best of our ability, following the rules and the practice of good ethics in dealing with all humankind.

The air was crisp and the wind was picking up. Knowing that Morey Harris was temporarily without wheels, I surmised that I could probably go to Old Forge to be with Patty for the night, but I also knew I had promised Tom that I would stay a few days. I could not deter from the mission. After all, I wasn't positive that Morey Harris was the sole perpetrator of these crimes. So, reluctantly, I headed the Bronco toward Newcomb.

CHAPTER SEVENTEEN

Morey Harris was still looking at his engine underneath the hood of the rusty Chrysler. With a screwdriver he had removed a resistor on the firewall that might be the culprit. Morey did not possess mechanical skills himself. A neighbor had stopped by to say hello after Jay had left. He, too, had observed Morey bent over the fender, still covered with grease on his face and hands. Morey told his neighbor of his dilemma and then the neighbor looked under the hood. After a few minutes he found a wire that had come disconnected near the resistor mount on the firewall, which was needed for the car to run.

"Morey, I believe this is the problem!" he exclaimed.

"What is it, Luther?" Morey looked confused.

"This dang wire came unfastened and the screw is missing. Do you have any?"

Morey disappeared into the ramshackle house with the drooping roof. After a few minutes he reappeared, holding a quart glass jar containing a mixture of nails, bolts, screws, and thumbtacks.

"Here, Luther. My old man had this setting in the cupboard. Take a look."

Morey handed Luther the quart jar of bits and pieces. Luther tipped the jar's contents onto a piece of newspaper. He rummaged through the collection of screws and nails

171

accidentally pushing his forefinger into a sharp thumbtack.

"Ow! Ooooowww!! What the heck do you have in this jar?" Blood was trickling down his finger. He reached into his pocket for a rag.

"Blame it on my old man, he's the one who put those in there." Morey looked at Luther, his neighbor, disgruntled.

"Well, anyways, help me wrap this rag around my finger, so we can get your rusty wreck started." Morey took the dirty piece of cloth and wrapped it around Luther's finger.

"Morey, I think this is the problem." He took the screwdriver and turned the small metal screw into the firewall. He then removed the air cleaner and told Morey to get behind the steering wheel.

"Hit the switch!" Luther said, holding his hand flat over the carburetor.

Morey pumped the gas pedal once and the rusty bucket started with a sputter and a gasp. A smile came over his face.

"Luther, you got it to run!" Morey didn't know what the words "thank you" meant.

Luther grabbed a dirty cloth and wiped his hands.

"Morey, are you doing any deer jacking? I'm out of venison. All that deer meat you gave me tasted so good. When do ya think you'll be getting some more?" Luther pointedly waited for the answer.

"I'm busy doing something else right now, but I'll get us some more soon." Morey was known for deer jacking in the region, and the E-Con game protectors were always on the alert for him. He liked the Sacandaga Lake region the best. If a deer came into his sights in season or out of season, Harris would shoot it.

"Morey, tell me, where are you getting all those tools you have in your car? They look expensive." Morey's face turned crimson and he seemed agitated, but surprisingly replied, "Yeah, I'll sell you some."

"No, I don't need any tools. My father left me his in his will. I sold some that I didn't need. Well, Morey, I'm glad we got your car running. I've got to go home now. When you get *some more venison, give me a call."*

"When I get some, I'll call you. I'll let you skin it for me and cut it up," he said.

"That's a deal, as long as I get the tenderloin. Nothing like it when you fry it in butter and garlic. Well, I'd better get home. So long!" he said, shuffling off.

"I'll see you later, Luther," Morey called gruffly.

CHAPTER EIGHTEEN

I slowed down when I went by Bob Bearor's house. Bob's vehicle still wasn't in the driveway. Most likely, he and his wife were doing some research somewhere. I'd catch him later.

The Bronco performed well. Some snowflakes were lazily floating to the ground. The air was crisp. I was glad that I had my heavier jacket on. As I drove toward Long Lake I thought of my beautiful wife and wondered what she was doing.

The case was escalating in intensity. Now I knew firsthand that it involved a revengeful young man with a dull intellect and little or no social skills. His only mind-set at the present time was to cause Tom Huston misery, and almost certainly it was he who had made an arson attempt and committed several burglaries. It was a stroke of luck for me that Morey Harris's old car had stopped running where it did. I had been able to meet him as a citizen helping him get off the highway and into his driveway. The meeting had not been hostile. Instead, it had offered me the opportunity to meet him casually, without him becoming suspicious that I was some kind of authority figure investigating him.

The suspect's childhood development probably lacked the required love of the parents. In his late twenties, now on his own, Morey Harris was on a self-destructive journey, and where it would end was a wide-open question.

When I arrived in Long Lake I located a public

telephone and called Lieutenant Jack Doyle. I gave Jack an update on their suspect.

"Jack, I hope that this information will be useful in your investigation."

"It certainly answers some of our questions. Our investigators have been working twenty-four hours a day on some cases near the border. We have a lot of problems, Jason," he explained.

"I know that the present world situation isn't helping our society. The loss of jobs country-wide has raised the crime rate. It's reflected in the rise of burglaries and thefts. In other words, Jack, we're in a quandary."

"You can say that again. Listen, Jason, we want to put this Harris suspect in jail. The property, including the ship's bell, the antique clock, tools, saws, hammers, and nails, amounts to a great deal of money. We want to make certain that when we do, we have an airtight case. Our uniformed night patrols have observed the old Chrysler in all sections of the Adirondack Park. When they've checked him out they've found nothing that was a violation. Partly thanks to you, we have good intelligence that Morey Harris has a vendetta against Mr. Huston, but so far we haven't got quite enough to have a warrant issued. Keep us informed if you come up with any new leads," he requested.

"I'll keep you posted. You'd better think of a search warrant in the future. He'll probably sell all those tools in the back seat of his car. I feel somewhat secure tonight as his car was not running when I left him earlier," I said.

"Okay. Thanks for all your help. Take care, Jason."

After I hung up the receiver I called Patty. She had just gotten home from the diner. She told me that everything was okay at home. Ruben had been watching over her, and she indicated that she felt secure, but missed me.

Oh, how I missed her, too! "I love you, Patty."

"I love you, too, my dear. Please be careful."

I hung up the telephone and wished that I could head for Old Forge. But I was committed to my work. I got back into the Bronco and headed to Gertie's for some dinner. When I pulled into the parking area I discovered that they were closed. I hoped they were both all right.

Continuing on toward Tupper Lake, I decided that I would stop at the Hotel Saranac. The snow was coming down with more intensity. However, the accumulation on the highway wasn't a problem for this four-wheel-drive vehicle. When I arrived in Saranac Lake I went directly to the hotel. The dining room had several customers. The hostess took me to a table near the window looking out onto the street. The waitress appeared shortly and I placed my order.

"Waitress, I'll start off with a cup of hot tea, and I believe I'll have your fried shrimp and scallops, and a baked potato with sour cream and chives."

"Would you prefer bread or dinner rolls, sir?" she asked.

"I'll take the dinner rolls," I replied.

"Thank you, sir."

The waitress hurried to place the order. I tasted the glass of ice water. It was refreshing. The dining room presented a very homey atmosphere with its wooden chairs and tables covered with red-and-white checkered cloths.

My dinner was served in about ten minutes. It looked wonderful, steaming hot and garnished with parsley. The tartar sauce was just the way I liked it. Many of the chefs in the area were from the culinary program at Paul Smiths College, which is associated with the Hotel Saranac. I recalled many dining visits I had made to this excellent restaurant while I was a member of the BCI of the state troopers, and more recently during Patty's hospitalization while she lay comatose at the Saranac Hospital after her accident. Some memories were not so pleasant.

The waitress, Arlene, brought me another pot of tea. She was pleasant and efficient. I had learned in my conversation with her that she was working her way through college. Before giving me my check, she recited the desserts available.

"Arlene, I guess I'll have to pass this time. It's difficult to resist apple pie, but my wife feels that I should refrain from desserts for a while. Thank you anyway. Dinner was excellent. My compliments to the chef. I hope to bring my wife, Patty, here for dinner sometime."

"You do that, and please ask for me." She was very courteous.

I paid my check by credit card and added her tip to the slip. As I left the dining room I encountered an elderly gentleman and his wife attempting to get his walker through the double doors. I stood aside, held the door, and let them pass.

"Thank you, young man," the wife said.

"You're welcome, ma'am," I answered.

The hostess came to assist them. It made me feel good to know that people in our society are willing to take a moment to assist those who have difficulty in getting around. I knew it could be me in a few years.

I nodded to the registry clerk as I passed the main desk and left the hotel. I had had to park a considerable distance away. About two inches of fresh snow had accumulated since I had parked the Bronco. It covered the windshield. I took the brush that I had in the back of the vehicle and cleaned the snow off all of the windows. I missed Patty so very much and I hoped she was okay.

I climbed in and started the engine. For an older model, the Bronco sounded pretty good. My mechanic, Dr. Don, knew the secret of tuning up an engine. He had placed new tires on the Bronco several times, and installed complete muffling systems, headlamps, windshield wipers, and brakes. My income as a private detective had not provided enough funds to buy a new vehicle. I calculated that as long as the wheels went around and the body didn't deteriorate to a rusty heap, I would continue to maintain this four-wheel drive Bronco.

Once again a direct life experience sharply reminded me that extreme caution should always be used when pulling away from the curb. After checking for traffic, I began to pull out into the street. All of a sudden I heard an air horn blowing behind me. I slammed on the brakes. It was a good thing, for a maroon Peterbilt log truck flashed by me. Where in the heck did he come from, I asked myself. Whew! That was close. I carefully continued to pull away from the curb. I was amazed at what had just happened. I would have loved to talk to that gentleman about safe driving. He had definitely been exceeding the speed limit.

I finally reached Route 3 and then Route 86, and headed toward Raybrook, Lake Placid, and the Breakshire Lodge.

CHAPTER NINETEEN

Jason Black was wrongly confident that Morey Harris would be out of action for a few days. He had no way of knowing that the Chrysler was back in operation after one little metal screw had brought the car back to life.

Morey didn't have a bed in the old ramshackle house. He slept on an old couch, with his two drooling pit bull dogs next to him. Morey never locked up at night, trusting his two pit bull dogs to scare anyone coming close to the house.

Morey was in a deep sleep. He always snored loudly. This night the raucous sound was even keeping his two pit bulls from sleeping, and both of them were fully awake.

A curious black bear, weighing about six hundred pounds, perhaps even attracted by the sounds of the snoring, roamed around Morey's ramshackle house with the drooping roof. The bear wasn't new to the neighborhood. In fact, Morey had slightly wounded the animal the year before, prior to the start of bear season. The bear had snarled and given off an ungodly growl that would have scared a ghost, if one had been in the area. Bleeding, it had taken off into the heavy brush. Some people say that bears don't forget. This one hadn't.

The large bear was also lured by the smell of bacon through the partially open door. The aroma had lingered long after Morey had consumed the fried strips for supper. Why the two pit bulls didn't react protectively enough when the bear first approached will probably never be known. The big bear charged in through the door. The snoring stopped as Morey, with his mouth wide open and his brown eyes bulging out of his eye sockets, awoke on the worn couch, terrified.

The bear's eyes were red with rage. One pit bull locked onto the animal's right rear leg. The bear lashed out at him with its left front paw. Then it moved its gigantic head down to the remaining pit bull and locked its large jaw on the back of the dog. In agony, he sent out a yelping screech that could be heard for miles.

Morey finally gathered his senses together and sprang over the top of the couch. On his belly, he crawled into the nearby room where he kept his shotgun, which was fully loaded with deer slugs. The black bear was busy shaking one pit bull while trying to loosen the locked jaw of the other pit bull on its right rear leg.

Morey aimed for the neck of the bear with his 12-gauge semi-automatic. The shots were deafening in the small living room of the ramshackle house near Hewitt Pond. Morey may have been lacking in social skills, but he was an expert when it came to shooting a gun. His father had taken him out in the woods beginning at the age of five to train him to shoot a .22 caliber rifle. He fired five shots one after the other, and all the slugs found their target. The big black bear swung its head toward Morey, releasing the dog from its mouth. When it did, the pit bull went flying through the air. The dog on the right rear leg was still locked on. The bear went wild, lashing out with its two front legs, knocking over the depression-era furniture in the living room. Then there was one last howling groan from the bear. It stood up, striking its head against the ceiling, looked wildly at Morey and, with its life draining away, crumpled to the floor with a crash onto the locked-on pit bull. The pit bull that had been flying through the air lay unconscious next to the big iron wood stove, which had ended his flight.

Morey, the color drained out of him and full of rage, attempted to free the other pit bull, but to no avail. The bear was dead weight. Its massive remains covered the pit bull completely. Tears poured out of Morey's eyes. He loved his dogs, but no one else. Morey didn't care for anyone, except his two beloved dogs. He went over to the remaining dog and cradled him up in his arms. The dog's back was injured badly. His heart had stopped beating. Morey sobbed and sobbed. He carried the pit bull's corpse outside and disposed of it. Then stopped crying, went into an old shed, and brought out a long log chain.

He backed the rusty old Chrysler over to the side door of the house, got out, and took the chain inside. After wrapping the chain around the front left leg of the dead bear, he went outside and hooked the other end of the chain to the rusty trailer hitch on the car. He went back inside the house to check the clearance. He knew he had to pull the bear from the living room through the kitchen and out the side door.

His plan was to pull the bear out of the house, rescue the dog under the bear, then pull the bear out of his driveway and down the road. He knew of a clearing in the forest where he could take it. In his confused state of mind, he had even toyed with the idea of calling a conservation officer, just to protect himself from a violation of law.

The task at hand went smoothly until he got the bear to the side door. It wouldn't pull through because of its massive size. Morey might have been lacking in intellectual skills, but he did possess a certain amount of cunning. With the ferocity of the imminent winter storms, he knew better than to chop a hole in his house. He went inside to reassess the situation. He then refastened the chain to both the bear's rear legs, went back outside, and jumped into his car.

The Chrysler strained and the rear wheels spun on the light snow. He rocked the car by shifting into drive and then reverse, and then on the third time he gassed the car, giving the engine a boost in power, and successfully dragged the bear out of the house. Morey sprung out of the car and rushed back into the house, only to find his beloved dog flattened beyond recognition. The tears reappeared in Morey's eyes. He carefully picked up the dead dog and laid it next to the other one. He dried his eyes on his greasy shirtsleeve, went outdoors, and reentered the Chrysler. He still had to dispose of the bear's body.

The power of the Chrysler was sufficient enough to pull the corpse. Of course, the snow made the tow easier. Morey jockeyed the bear out of his driveway and down the road to a small clearing which had access from the roadway.

He considered cutting off part of the bear for meat, but the sadness of losing his two dogs was too much, even for Morey Harris. He dragged the big bear to the edge of the forest and stopped the Chrysler. He didn't have a flashlight with him, so he had to disconnect the chain from the bear and the rear of the car mostly by feel. The coy dogs would have a feast, he thought. With the chain detached, he wound it loosely and placed it in the trunk.

He returned to his house and with a shovel dug a large hole behind the ramshackle house to bury the only objects of his love, his two pit bulls. He sobbed and sobbed, and when he had completed the task he walked back into his house. He would wait until morning before he cleaned up the mess in the living room. And he knew he would have to get another guard dog, because he didn't dare live alone.

His resentment towards Tom Huston had grown to hate. Now in his own mind he blamed Huston not only for his financial predicament, but also for the situation that had allowed the bear to attack. Although it was a figment of his imagination, there would only be a short period of time before Morey would pursue a path of further revenge.

CHAPTER TWENTY

I pulled into the Breakshire Lodge parking area and secured the Bronco for the evening. I was especially tired tonight. I entered through the front entrance and went to the desk clerk on duty.

"Good evening, Mr. Black." The clerk peered over his steel-rimmed glasses.

"Good evening, James. Did I have any telephone calls?" I asked.

"No, sir. There were no calls for you," he answered politely.

I thanked James and proceeded through the door and down the hall to my room. The room was in excellent condition. I smiled when I observed the extra shampoo and soap on top of the bathroom cabinet. I noticed that several green-tea bags lay on the tray, along with coffee for the making.

I walked over to the phone to call Patty before it got any later. She was her usual cheerful self. I gave her a short recap of my day and asked her how her day had gone. She said it was just a normal one at the diner, rather uneventful. "Good night, my love. I sure do miss you. Sweet dreams," I said. We hung up, both professing our love for each other again.

Then, I called Tom and gave him an update. He was pleased to hear from me.

I decided to lie down on the bed for a while to rest. I'd go outside to check the grounds around midnight. I didn't have a great deal of concern, because I knew that the suspect was at Hewitt Pond without a car that would run. I turned up the thermostat and then removed my shoes. I hung up my trousers, shirt, and heavy jacket.

The firm mattress felt good. I lay on my back and looked up at the spirals on the ceiling. The entire room was decorated in the Adirondack décor of these beautiful mountains. I could hear the late arrivals passing by in the hallway and the sound of doors opening and closing. I felt relaxed and closed my eyes.

It was 11:30 when I awoke. The hallway was quiet. In the distance I heard the muffled sounds of a television news announcer finishing up his commentary, and then there was complete silence. I went into the bathroom to splash some cold water onto my face and combed my hair. I then drank a glass of water.

Tom Huston had given me full authority at the lodge for the security of the grounds and buildings during my stay. Tom had his own suite of rooms at the lodge and was easily accessible to me in the event of a problem. During our meetings, Tom had suggested that if I should desire any assistance with my operation, I should use my own discretion in hiring someone with a security background.

I had taken Tom's advice and had placed a call to a longtime associate of mine in Plattsburgh. Wayne Beyea, a retired Senior Investigator of the New York State Police, operated his own investigative agency. I asked him if he would be available to assist me with an investigation at the Breakshire Lodge in Lake Placid. Beyea advised me that he was involved with an out-of-state investigation and wouldn't be able to, but suggested that I contact Gordon Whigham, whom I had worked with in the past. I thanked the private investigator and after further conversation we concluded our call.

I called Gordon Whigham, who was receptive to my request for assistance. He indicated that he would be in Lake Placid tomorrow and would meet Tom and me at the Breakshire Lodge. Gordon was licensed by the State of

New York and was an expert in industrial security. When I had been with the troopers, he had assisted me in several of my investigations. Intelligent, trustworthy, and mild-mannered, he was more than capable of handling any type of security breech that could take place at the lodge.

I removed my heavy jacket from the hanger and put it on. Its three-quarter length was appropriate for the cold nights in the Adirondacks. I removed my firearm from the briefcase and slipped it into my shoulder holster. I probably would have no need for it tonight, but just in case, I'd be prepared. I also carried a flashlight.

As residents of the Adirondacks, we must realize that occasionally our magnificent mountains are visited by criminals or people who have dishonest deeds on their mind. Our businesspeople are here to serve the visiting public from the world over, but they frown on dishonesty and are constantly alert to the deviance of a few that take advantage of our mountain hospitality.

I quietly left the room and proceeded to the main lobby. During staff meetings, Tom had alerted some of the key staff at the lodge to my presence. I noticed that James was just about to go off duty and was being relieved by Oscar Vinton, a well-known skier from Colorado, who had recently been hired to cover the desk from midnight till 7:30 a.m. He was the son of a close friend of Tom Huston. I approached the desk.

"Good evening, Mr. Black." He was tall, handsome, and well-mannered.

"Hello, Oscar. Did you do any skiing today?" I was curious. His face appeared to be wind-burned.

"No, but maybe tomorrow afternoon. Oh! By the way, Mr. Black. Mr. Huston left this for you." He handed me a beeper. "It's fully charged, sir."

"Thank you, Oscar. For your information, I'll be prowling the grounds for a couple of hours. I assume that all the entrances are locked except the main one here off the lobby."

"Yes, I checked them before I relieved James." His fellow clerk was leaving and gave us a wave as he walked toward the front entrance.

"By the way, Oscar, how is college going?" I asked.

"I have my BS from Arizona State and I'm taking the winter off. I'll start my master's program in education at Northern Arizona University next fall," he replied.

"I'm happy for you. I don't have to tell you that education is important in this challenging society today." It would appear that this young man was eager to achieve in life.

"You be careful out there tonight," he cautioned.

"I will, Oscar. I'll stop back later for a cup of coffee," I responded.

I liked this young man. I was certain that he would do well out there in the academic world. Before I went outside I checked several of the banquet rooms, kitchen and dining rooms, and the inside pool area. Some of the chefs would arrive around 3:00 a.m. I went out through the lobby. I noticed that Oscar was on the telephone. I nodded to him as I passed.

The cold air bit into my face. Fortunately I had brought along a cap, tucked into my deep jacket pocket. I reached into the pocket and removed the hat, placing it on my head. I had to be careful because I suffered from sinus periodically, especially in a cold breeze.

On the grounds of the stately-looking Breakshire Lodge, Tom had had outside security lights installed. It was almost like daylight outdoors.

The white snow that blanketed these palatial grounds added to the beauty of the lodge. The trees that rimmed the property each stood like a tall sentry guard around a castle. I walked down a row of parked vehicles, the majority of them expensive-looking cars, with a few four-wheel drive pickups scattered among them. One large MCI coach with Alaska registration plates was located to the rear of parking area one. I estimated it must have cost nearly 300k. One of the cars in the lot had its inside dome light on. I jotted the license number down to give to the desk clerk to notify the party so they would not arise to a dead battery. I noticed that many of the cars supported empty ski racks. The skis apparently had been taken into the owners' rooms to avoid any possible theft that could occur even in a secured lot.

Many of the plants had been covered for the winter season. All the tools used by the groundskeepers were secured in a locked building, along with the tractors and mowers. The lodge owned two large heavy-duty pickups equipped with plows for snow removal. For the walks, there were two smaller snow blowers. Tom Huston was particular about the lodge and the surrounding grounds. And he treated all of his employees well. All he expected from his personnel was loyalty and a good day's work.

I made several walking patrols around the lodge and through the snow-covered garden. All the white lawn furniture had been secured for the winter. I had just rounded the corner of a shed looking out onto parking lot 2 when I noticed an old car circling the lot. From where I was standing, I was unable to identify the vehicle, but I had a sinking feeling that somehow it was Morey Harris's old, rusty Chrysler. I glanced at my watch: two thirty-five. *What in the hell is this Morey Harris up to?* I thought. *Somehow he must have gotten his car running. He must have had help from someone. He certainly did not seem to possess any mechanical knowledge himself.*

I continued to stand in the shadows of the gazebo. He circled again and then he went out of my view for a few minutes. I decided I should try to get to the Bronco and follow him. It was as though he were looking for one of the tool sheds on the grounds. By the time I reached the Bronco it was too late. I saw him leave the grounds and disappear down a side street. I was amazed that he had been resourceful enough to get his car running. Why would Morey Harris drive all the way up here from Hewitt Pond to drive around the Breakshire Lodge a couple of times and leave? He had to be up to something, and whatever it was had to be something to do with the anger he felt towards Tom Huston. I would have challenged him on the Breakshire property, but my authority was nil off the property. If he had committed a crime in my presence on the property or even off the property, I could have exercised my right as a citizen and made a citizen's arrest and turned him over to a police agency. But he had done nothing but drive around.

More questions teased my curiosity. Was he carrying a firearm? A gas can? I had no way of answering that question. Morey Harris continued to be an enigma! Whatever he was up to would have to remain a mystery for now. At about 3:00 a.m. I went into the main lobby and joined the night desk clerk for a hot cup of coffee and a sweet roll, a specialty of the pastry chef. I gave him the license number from the vehicle that had left the dome light on. In our conversation, Oscar mentioned to me he had seen an old car drive up near the front entrance steps and then leave hurriedly. I was sure it had been Harris, but not wanting to alarm Oscar, I didn't go into any details about the incident. It must have been the same old Chrysler that I had observed. I thanked Oscar for the coffee and rolls, then advised him that I would make one more tour of the grounds before going to my room for some shut-eye.

I wanted to call Patty, but certainly did not want to disturb her sleep. She'd have to be on her feet all the next day at the diner. I knew that Gordy, my counterpart from Plattsburgh, would be arriving at about 10:00 a.m. Maybe between Gordy and me, we could come up with some ideas about our uninvited guest. Only time would tell.

CHAPTER TWENTY-ONE

Morey Harris could hardly see over the hood of his Chrysler as he made his way into Long Lake. The falling snow was pelting against his cracked windshield. Taking a left-hand turn onto Route 28N, he headed toward Newcomb. Hoping to figure out how to do some damage, he had driven to the Breakshire Lodge, circled around the parking area twice, and pulled up in front. He had left when he observed the night clerk look out at him from his desk inside. Harris feared the clerk would call the troopers or the Lake Placid Police Department. Crazed with anger about his imagined grievance against Tom Huston, it had been his intention to harm the lodge. On the rear seat of the Chrysler was his shotgun loaded with deer slugs. Harris was walking on a tightrope and his mental capacity was being challenged to the limit. The shotgun was not the only object in the rear seat. Sitting between the seat and the rear of the front passenger seat was a half-full gas can. Its fumes permeated the interior of the car. Harris had the window down partway in order to let the cold crisp air enter to combat the smell. Large snowflakes found their way into the driver's side.

Morey hated Huston for firing his father from the lodge, and therefore cutting off the monthly allowance that his father had always given him. He wouldn't have lost his two beloved dogs to a bear either, he figured, if his situation were

191

different. It was beyond his comprehension that his father had been fired for being a dishonest employee. But word of his father's dismissal from the Breakshire had circulated through the region, making it difficult for the man to obtain employment. Morey was deeply resentful that his father had left the area, moving to Florida where he had connections, leaving his son to fend for himself.

For revenge, and in order to sustain himself, Morey had started breaking into properties owned by Huston. He had stolen tools and anything else of value that he could get his hands on. Morey missed his father terribly and couldn't understand why he had left him. Why didn't his father take him along? As he struggled with the steering wheel of the Chrysler, driving through the rapidly accumulating falling snow toward Hewitt Pond and his ramshackle house, he burned with vindictiveness toward a man he really didn't know, a kind and generous man, Tom Huston.

CHAPTER TWENTY-TWO

I awoke at about 9:30 in the morning, realizing that I was in Room 108 of the lodge instead of my log home in Old Forge. I decided to make a quick call to Patty to see how she was, and to let her know that I was all right. I reached over for the phone next to my bed. Lila answered on the seventh ring and explained that Patty was busy taking an order for a large group. I assured her I wouldn't mind calling later.

I had known Patty would probably be very busy at the diner with all the snowmobilers who would be coming into Old Forge by the dozens with the snowfall. The motels would be filling up with people who loved this activity. Many of them, bundled in their snowmobile attire, would be stopping at John's Diner for a bite to eat before they hit the trail system.

It was this sport that brought many to the region during the winter season. For the most part the participants cooperated with the area law enforcement people and obeyed the rules and regulations. On rare occasions mishaps would occur and injuries and even death would result, usually due to carelessness on the part of the sled operator. We were most fortunate to have Police Chief Todd Wilson and his efficient staff to monitor their activities. The state troopers were often called upon to assist in these matters.

I pushed the covers back and went into the bathroom. Shaving and showering was a continuing ritual each day of my life and had been since I was sixteen years old. This morning was no different than the many times before. I took the shaving cream out of my shaving kit and pressed the top. The white foam felt good on my face as I placed a hot steaming washcloth on it. As I drew the razor down each side of my face and under my chin, I felt the sting of a nick. I quickly applied a small piece of tissue, which stopped the bleeding, and completed the shave.

Finishing up with a hot shower, I turned the handle to the cold water, and cold it was. After feeling the chill from the icy water I grabbed the large bath towel. I dried my hair with the blower provided by the lodge. In a few minutes I was fully dressed.

I tidied up the room and then went down to the lobby. The big clock over Wilt Chambers' carved black bear indicated that it was 10:20 a.m. Gordon Whigham was sitting in the lobby reading *Albany Times Union.* I walked over to him. He looked up.

"Jason Black, how are you?" he asked with a grin on his face.

"Gordy, I've been good. How about yourself?" I flashed back.

Gordy and I were friends from my Troop S days in the North Country. We chatted about numerous people we knew and the good times that we had shared with Gordy and his wife while we were together on Lake Champlain.

"How long do you think you'll be needing my services, Jason?" he inquired.

"Oh, just a few days, Gordy, I hope. I'll explain it over some breakfast. Okay?" I asked. I was famished.

"That's okay with me. I could use some vittles," he said agreeably.

"Sit here for a few minutes. I've got to call my wife and check with Mr. Huston. I believe he'd like to join us in the dining room."

Gordy agreed and went back to reading the paper. I went to the telephone booth and called Patty at John's Diner. She was so glad to hear from me, apologizing for being busy when I had called earlier. I was happy to hear her voice. I missed her so very much. She asked me if I had any idea when I would be returning home. I told her it would probably be a few days more.

"Honey, I'll call you as soon as I know," I assured her.

"Jason, by the way, I took Ruben to the Eagle Bay Kennels for grooming. He looks beautiful, all spruced up. He misses you, too, sweetheart," she added.

"Take care and be safe, Patty. Love ya, babe. Pat the dog for me."

"I will, hon. Love you, too. Bye!"

I went down the hallway and knocked on Tom's office door. I heard his voice.

"Come in."

"Good morning, Tom. Would you like to join Gordon Whigham and me for a coffee?" I knew that Tom must have already eaten. "We're going for breakfast."

"Yes, I'd love to."

Tom closed a file cabinet behind his desk and put on his blue blazer. He didn't like to go into the dining room without proper attire. As we came down the hallway into the lobby, Gordy was turning the pages of the latest *Adirondack Life* magazine. Seeing us approach, he rose to join us.

"Gordy, I would like you to meet Tom Huston, the owner of the Breakshire."

Tom broke into a smile and extended his right hand to shake. "It is indeed a pleasure to meet you, Mr. Whigham."

"Likewise, sir."

With the formalities over, we entered the dining room. Tom motioned a waitress to come to our table. We seated ourselves. The waitress, Geraldine, approached. She appeared to be in her mid-forties and spoke with a Scottish accent. She was very polite. Gordy and I ordered scrambled eggs with bacon, wheat toast, and coffee. Tom opted for a cup of coffee, explaining that indeed he had already had breakfast earlier.

I acquainted Tom with Gordy's background in the

investigative and security area. I thanked Gordy for giving us a few days from the other projects that he was working on in the Malone area.

"Jason, according to my night clerk we had an uninvited person driving through our parking area early this morning." Tom was obviously curious about the old car driving around his property.

"Yes, Tom. I was walking close to the lodge in the north parking lot and made the observation myself. I believe it was the son of your former groundskeeper. The troopers are aware of Morey Harris and have expended a great deal of time on the case. However, Harris is cunning and has been able to avoid the patrols. There is no doubt about it: Morey Harris has an imagined grievance against you, Tom, and the Breakshire Lodge."

Tom looked worried. He nodded his head gravely.

"Jason, have the troopers confronted Harris about his actions?" he queried.

"I don't think so. Lieutenant Doyle wants all his ducks in a row before he has his investigators interview Morey Harris," I explained.

Gordy was listening closely to what Tom and I were discussing. We finished our breakfast and the waitress refilled our coffee cups.

"Jason, I have all the confidence in the world in you. This situation has practically drained me emotionally. It seems certain now that my act of discharging a dishonest employee has unleashed a series of events that include the attempted burning of my property in Newcomb and several entries to my properties in other hamlets and towns. Harris must have gotten a list from his father as to the locations of my properties. You know when his dad was head groundskeeper, he had had the responsibility for the maintenance of all the lawns. I'm afraid that Morey Harris is going to try to cause me physical harm," he said dejectedly.

"You're correct. I believe that if he finds an opportunity, he will do just that."

I related to Tom and Gordy how I had gone to Hewitt Pond and had an encounter with Morey Harris. I told about pushing the old Chrysler into Harris's driveway and how I was not only able to get close to the house but managed to look into his car and see how it was loaded with various tools, probably ones from Tom's properties.

"Jason, I appreciate your efforts. And Gordy, I want to thank you for coming down to lend Jason a hand on this matter."

"Mr. Huston, I've known Jason Black for a long time, and if there is anyone who can bring this case to a successful conclusion, it is this man. I'll do everything I can to assist him. Hopefully we'll soon have some positive results."

Tom listened closely to Gordy and a slight smile came over his face.

"Listen, fellows, I appreciate you both being here. If you develop information relative to this situation, let me know right away. I don't care if it's two o'clock in the morning—give my suite a call."

"We certainly will," I acknowledged.

Tom shook Gordy's hand again and thanked us. We both assured him that we would develop a plan for the lodge's security and for his own personal security for the next few days. Tom took care of the check and left the dining room for his office. I asked Gordy to accompany me to my room to discuss our plan in private.

CHAPTER TWENTY-THREE

Morey Harris had arrived at the ramshackle house in the wee hours of the morning. He was tired and full of rage. His plan for the night had utterly failed. He had wanted to inflict damage on the Breakshire Lodge, but he had caught a glimpse of a person lurking on the grounds at the rear when he circled the parking lot. This scared him off. He then had gone to the front entrance and observed the desk clerk peering out the door, so he had decided to leave.

He lay on the couch with an old quilt wrapped around his shoulders. The wood stove was completely out. He missed his two pit bull dogs. Morey pushed the quilt off onto the floor, rolled off the couch, and prepared to take a standing position.

A beady-eyed rat hustled across the kitchen cabinet, apparently looking for something to eat. Morey lit the match under the rear burner of his four-burner gas stove. He filled the enamel coffeepot and boiled some water for a cup of instant coffee. He then removed a box of stale graham crackers from the top shelf of the metal cabinet. The only vision that Morey possessed at the present time was to bring harm to Tom Huston and his lodge. While he drank his coffee and nibbled on his graham crackers he looked outside. His old rusty Chrysler was covered with snow. He thought about the tools in the back seat. He had to get rid of them in the event the troopers stopped him on the road. He decided that he would take them

199

to Utica to see if he could sell them. His money was getting low and he hadn't heard from his father since he had left for Florida.

Morey didn't worry about his food supply. He was fond of venison, rabbit, and partridge. Any time he wanted a deer, he just went out the back door and he could take his pick. Morey did on occasion share his venison, which was generally out of season, with his neighbor, Luther.

Before Morey left for Utica he locked up the house. He removed the slugs from his shotgun and placed it into his trunk.

CHAPTER TWENTY-FOUR

I brought Gordy up to date on the case and informed him that the troopers had the initial investigation of the arson attempt and the burglaries of the Huston properties. I also informed him that periodically I called Lieutenant Jack Doyle to update any information I had developed. I stressed to him that our mission was to keep an eye on Huston's Breakshire Lodge and on the buildings and houses that he owned.

We understood that we'd be putting in many hours in the next few days. Even though the trooper patrols were checking Huston's properties in various towns and hamlets throughout the Adirondacks, Gordy and I decided that we'd check out a few of them ourselves.

The Bronco was filled with gasoline. Of course I preferred to drive. Gordy and I climbed into the Bronco and headed to St. Regis Falls and Santa Clara to check on houses, one in each location.

The highways from Lake Placid to Santa Clara were wet and there was a good accumulation of snow in the adjacent forests along our journey. We arrived in Santa Clara at about 1:30 p.m. The Huston property was located on one of the side streets. It was a solidly built wood frame home with an attached garage. The old Collins Hotel could be viewed from the front yard of the house.

Memories of Patty's nightmare flashed into my mind

whenever I returned to the Santa Clara area. I told Gordy about the kidnapping of Patty, now my wife. I was surprised that he had not heard of the ordeal because of the widespread manhunt and the media coverage, and my involvement in apprehending the dangerous killer after he stepped out of the woods near my location. Gordy asked several questions.

I summed it up quickly. "I fortunately apprehended him without incident."

"Jason, you never cease to amaze me," was Gordy's only comment.

We exited the Bronco and proceeded to walk around the house. It was easy to see that new construction on the property had taken place. The windows and doors, including the garage doors, were secure. While we were walking around the property, a neighbor approached us. She was wearing a parka attached to a heavy winter jacket.

"Can I help you gentlemen?" she asked honestly inquiring.

We identified ourselves as private investigators hired by the owner of the home, explaining to her our purpose for being on the property. She indicated to us that she had observed the troopers checking the property periodically.

"Aren't you Jason Black?" she questioned, looking directly at me.

"Yes, I am, ma'am," I replied, startled that she had recognized me.

"Jason, I'm Shirley Collins. My mother-in-law, Fannie, used to operate the Santa Clara Hotel. You knew me and my husband. But that was years ago," she added.

"Yes, I did, Shirley." Now I remembered her. "It's so nice to see you. It's been a long time."

I introduced Gordy to Shirley.

"Would you two like some coffee or a cup of hot chocolate?" she asked. "It would warm you up."

She evidently was as hospitable as Fannie. We thanked her for the offer and suggested that we'd take a rain check.

I gave Shirley a business card in the event she observed any activity around the Huston property that might be of value in our investigation.

Thanking Shirley again, we climbed into the Bronco and drove on to St. Regis Falls. The next Huston property was a larger, stately, three-story home situated behind a row of large blue spruce trees. The garage was actually a small barn. The window shades in the home were drawn. All the doors were secured. There were no close neighbors. The house was set back off the street about one hundred yards. I didn't recognize the type of architecture, although it appeared to be Victorian.

"Jason, I can't believe that this Morey Harris has made such an issue out of his father's firing from the Breakshire. My God, man, the father brought it upon himself to begin with." Gordy spoke harshly.

"You're right, but according to Tom Huston, Morey was babied by his dad, and now that dad is no longer around, this twenty-nine year old son is in a state of crisis. It's a sad state of affairs. There is no telling what he will do next. You should have seen his face when I happened to mention Tom Huston to him at the time I pushed his car into his driveway. You wouldn't believe the reaction I observed." I still got chills just thinking of his response.

I informed Gordy that we'd work as a team instead of going in separate directions. Both of us would carry small arms. Gordy had a carry permit for a .32 caliber semi-automatic and I had my 9 mm semi-automatic. Neither one of us cared that much for firearms, but when dealing with a potentially dangerous person, one cannot foresee what behavior a person will exhibit in a tense situation. To predict what action Morey would take against us or the regular police if cornered could only be a guess, but at least we would be ready to respond with the appropriate action.

We already knew that the troopers couldn't put a tail on Harris full-time, because of pending matters and manpower obligations in other regions. The danger with this case was that the suspect possessed such a hostile attitude toward Tom and could be capable of doing harm to him. Gordy and I had to exercise caution and, of course, common sense. We had no idea when we would wrap this case up: today, tomorrow, next week, or later. It was open-ended.

We returned to the Breakshire Lodge at about 5:00 p.m., after finding nothing unusual when we checked the remaining properties owned by Huston. One of the properties in the Jay area was unreachable because a bridge was blocked off due to structural problems. The building was about five miles from the bridge and the narrow roadway was covered with snow. There appeared to be no tracks of any kind on the snow-covered roadway. I made an entry in my notebook to check the property when the bridge repairs were completed.

After securing the Bronco in the lodge parking area, Gordy and I went to our rooms. Tom had arranged for Gordy to occupy room 109, located across the hall from 108. I told Gordy that I would meet him in the dining room about 6:30 p.m. for dinner.

I unlocked my door and entered. Tiredness had overtaken me, so I lay down on the bed to rest. My thoughts were of Patty, but then they drifted to Morey Harris. It was difficult to predict his next move, to harm Tom Huston or Tom's properties. He knew all their locations as, according to Tom, the father had taken Morey with him at different times to assist him with the trimming of hedges and the mowing of lawns. For sure it was just a matter of time before Morey would strike again.

CHAPTER TWENTY-FIVE

Jason Black would not have to wait much longer for Morey Harris's next move. Morey had driven to Utica and had gone to several west-side bars. There he encountered several people who jumped at the chance of buying some tools at a large discounted price. Morey explained to his potential customers that he had sickness in his family and needed to raise some funds immediately. Some of the bar patrons believed this plea and shelled out money for saws, hammers, nails, extension cords, levels, assorted wrenches, and two plumb lines. In addition, there were almost-new battery-operated screwdrivers and expensive lights, plus some copper piping, and two expensive water pumps. At the last bar, one of the patrons whispered in Morey's ear.

"Hey bud, you'd better get out of here. An off-duty detective just sat down at the bar."

Morey's eyes flashed to the left and then to the right. He couldn't stand cops. He immediately left the bar. But the detective, yearning for a cold beer, took a quick look at Morey as he passed by headed for the door. He wondered why the suspicious-looking pudgy guy was leaving the bar in such a hurry, but he was off duty and about to sip his frosted glass of beer.

In his haste to start his rusty Chrysler, Morey flooded it. He held the gas pedal to the floor and tried again. The backfire that sounded was enough to alarm any neighborhood. Several patrons of the bar rushed out onto the street only to see a rusty old Chrysler make a right-hand turn and disappear.

Beads of sweat were sliding down Morey's forehead as he wheeled onto Route 12 and headed north. He realized that he had had a close call. Pretty soon he thought, the large off-duty detective seated at the bar would have pieced together the facts as the bar patrons explained to him how they had come to be in possession of numerous new or barely used tools. As it happened, the detective did not inquire into the identity of the pudgy fellow. And the bar patrons kept their mouth shut about the tools they had purchased at such an unbelievable discount.

North of Utica, Morey took a left-hand turn toward Poland, where he picked up Route 8. He then drove through Coldbrook, and Ohio, and on to Indian Lake and before turning right toward North River and North Creek. At North Creek he turned onto Route 28N. The highway to Hewitt Pond was snow-covered and the rusty Chrysler swayed to the left and to the right. Morey's tires had very little tread, making it difficult for him to stay on the road. He was gleeful, however, to have over three hundred dollars in his pocket. He had no guilt as to how he had obtained it.

Morey missed his two pit bulls and thought of them often. He shuddered at the memory of the large bear charging into his ramshackle house. He teared up when the images came into his mind of the bear holding one of the dogs between his crushing jaws, shaking his pet to death. And, how when he shot the bear with his shotgun, the bear fell onto his floor, pinning and killing his remaining dog.

He missed his father, who had left him alone. Although Morey was twenty-nine years old, his mind-set was much younger. He lacked development, as he had dropped out of school at sixteen, while still in sixth grade. Morey's dark side came to the forefront after his father left for Florida. He did remember his father's parting words. "You're on your own now, Morey." Just that short statement had shocked Morey. This is when he started to blame that wealthy man who owned the Breakshire Lodge in Lake Placid for all his problems.

Morey climbed out of the car and went into his ramshackle house. It was bitter cold. He went out to the makeshift woodshed and brought in some kindling and larger pieces of wood. He started a fire in the wood stove. He had just shut the door on the stove and opened the damper, when he spotted a movement to his right. A sickly looking red squirrel had gained entrance into the house and was clutching a burlap curtain hanging on one of the windows. Morey threw a stick of wood at him. The squirrel scampered to the open door and out onto the porch. Morey quickly closed the door.

Tom Huston was on Morey's mind and it had become an obsession. Morey's deduction process wasn't honed to reality. He planned to play out his imagined grievance against Huston.

CHAPTER TWENTY-SIX

I must have fallen off to sleep immediately. The lodge offered a firm but comfortable mattress, very conducive to sleep. When I awoke I glanced at my wristwatch. It was 5:50 p.m. I dialed Gordy's room. He answered on the third ring.

"Hope I didn't wake you up, Gordy."

"No, Jason. I was just shaving. Something about this mountain air that makes my whiskers grow rapidly," he replied.

"I've got to call Patty. What time would you like to have dinner?" I asked.

"Is six-thirty still all right with you?" he queried.

"Fine! I'll be ready. Just knock on the door," I said.

"Okay."

I heard the click when Gordy hung up. I immediately called Patty.

"Hello, sweetheart. I sure do miss you, Patty."

"I miss you too, darling." She sounded so sweet.

"Gordy and I are going to have dinner at 6:30. Wish you were here, baby."

"Is Gordy your detective friend from Plattsburgh?" she inquired.

"Yes, he is. You'll have to meet him sometime. You'll like Gordy and his wife. We'll take a drive there some time in the summer," I advised her. "By the way, how is work? And how

209

is Ruben doing?" I wanted to hear all the details.

"Work is busy and the tips are good. Ruben is being a good dog. He sleeps at the foot of the bed every night. When do you think this case will be wrapped up? Everybody knows you're out of town. But don't worry, honey, Ruben is on guard and I've loaded the 12 gauge automatic with buckshot. You know I know how to shoot. Just like Annie Oakley!" she said reassuring me.

"Patty, I hope you never have to, but if you do, make certain you're right. In this day and age, it's the law-abiding citizen that's in trouble," I cautioned.

"I learned well from you, teacher. Don't fret. You taught me all the laws of self-defense."

"I'm not worried. I know that Wilt and Dale keep an eye out for you when I'm out of town. Well, listen, honey, I have to go now. I'll be glad when the troopers catch this bird. You can count on it: I'll come home as soon as I can. Tom asked me again if you'd like to come to the lodge and stay here with me. I thanked him and told him that you felt obligated to John and Lila."

"I'd be there in a heartbeat, but you're right. I owe John and Lila a great deal and I can't let them down."

"I know, sweetheart, I know. I have to go, sweetie." I missed her so very much.

"I love you, Jason."

I could hear her tearing up.

"I love you, too, babe. Don't worry. I'll be home soon."

It was now 6:15. I shaved rapidly and dressed. At 6:30, Gordy knocked at the door.

We walked down the corridor to the dining room. As we entered we noticed that the area was only about half-filled. The hostess seated us and left us menus. It was only minutes before Mildred, our waitress, appeared, wearing a pleasant smile. She took our drink orders first. Gordy ordered a glass of white wine, and I ordered a glass of premium draft beer. I wasn't much of a drinker and had learned early on when I was a member of the U.S. Marine Corps that drinking can cause you difficulty. My days at Camp Pendleton and TDY to San Diego are imbedded in my mind. I remember well the time when I was playing pool and beat a sore loser. The jarhead tried to hit me with a pool cue, but I ducked, and a visiting first sergeant took the blow, which knocked out his two front teeth. I learned firmly that moderation is always the best policy when it comes to alcohol.

"What looks good to you, Jason?" Gordy asked as he perused the extensive menu.

"Everything, Gordy." I had acquired quite an appetite.

It was such a cold evening outside that we both decided on roast pork with all the trimmings. Tom Huston was a stickler in many of his operations at the lodge, but he paid particular attention to the chefs he employed. He trusted his kitchen staff and purchased the best quality of food that money could buy. Not only that, he worked hard with his head chef to accommodate his customers with fair prices for his meals. Tom made routine checks himself three or four times a week to insure that the chefs were putting their best skills forward.

Gordy and I had just finished our conversation relative to the Morey Harris issue when our meal was served. Mildred carried the tray high in the air. She placed it on a small serving table and politely presented the dinner plates to Gordy and then to me. Everything looked super. She refilled our water glasses and inquired if we would like another drink. We both declined, beginning to consume our food. The roast pork was tender and flavored just right. Neither Gordy nor I had wanted a green salad, opting instead for only the main course.

The mashed potatoes, gravy, squash, and chunky applesauce went very well with the pork. We took our time enjoying every morsel of our dinner. The hint of garlic teased my taste buds. Gordy proclaimed that dinner was indeed a treat. After the main meal, we selected bread pudding with lemon sauce topped by real whipped cream. We accompanied the dessert with steaming cups of coffee and cream.

We had eaten so much, we had to loosen our belts. It had certainly been a satisfying culinary experience. We were just getting ready to take the check to the cashier, when Tom Huston, dressed in a gray pin-stripe suit, blue shirt, and a gray and blue tie, approached our table to join us.

"Gentlemen, how was the roast pork?" he asked.

"Delicious, delicious!" I exclaimed.

Gordy echoed his approval.

"I'm glad to hear that," he responded. Then his tone changed markedly. "I don't want to alarm you, but I just received a threatening phone call. I can't swear to it, but I'd be willing to bet it was the young Harris." Tom was clearly very upset.

"Just what did he say, Tom?" I questioned.

Tom's hands were shaking. "He just blurted out 'you'd better watch your back!' It sounded as though he was trying to disguise his voice. Then after a short pause, he added 'and I ain't kiddin.' That's when I was sure it was Morey Harris. I was just ready to ask him when he hung up. Several times when I was talking with his father in the gardens, Morey was with him, and he constantly used the word *ain't*. The more I think about it, the more certain I am that it was him."

"Tom, Gordy and I will be around all evening. We'll sit in our car and watch closely for that rusty old Chrysler. As your security representative, I'll notify the troopers, if you'd like," I offered.

"I'd certainly appreciate that, Jason. I'm going to retire about 9:00. I have had a rough day and I'm all in. But if there is anything you fellows need, feel free to call my suite."

"I will, Tom." I looked at my friend and he looked tired. The situation was definitely taking its toll on him. I would be glad when this case was completed, but in the meantime, we'd have to exercise caution and be watchful.

I was just preparing to pay our check when Tom shook his head, taking the bill from my hand.

"Jason, as long as you are in my employ, and that goes for Gordy, too, your meals are part of our verbal contract. You will not pay for your meals or coffee. When you're here as a guest, that's different. Do we understand each other?" he said emphatically.

"Yes, Tom, we both appreciate that, but you know it isn't necessary," I countered.

"Young man, I'm the boss around here."

It was the tone of his voice that convinced me to drop the issue. Tom was a proud man from old money and indeed he was the boss, at the moment. My other boss was in Old Forge, and boy, she was the boss, too. But I enjoyed every minute of it.

The three of us sat at the table and sipped another cup of coffee. It was another half-hour before we left for our rooms. I told Tom to kindly inform the chef who prepared the roast pork that it was the very best I ever had.

"Remember, gentlemen, if there is anything you need during the night, call me. If you need something to eat, go to the kitchen, and the night cook, Leland, will prepare something for you. I had the day chef leave a note for him."

"Tom, Gordy and I appreciate your fine hospitality. We're going to our rooms now to see if we can get some rest. Around 10:00 tonight, we'll begin by checking the outer buildings, the lodge, and the grounds. There is no telling what Morey Harris is capable of at this juncture. As you know, an overt act is necessary before a legal action can take place," I reminded him.

"I appreciate what you fellows are doing. Maybe I should have taken another approach with regards to Morey's father at the time I discharged him."

"Let's face it, Tom, you gave the father a break. He could have gone to court and possibly served some jail time."

"That's true; he could have. Well, gentlemen, get some rest. Dress warm tonight; the temperature is going down into the teens."

Tom was a thoughtful person. We thanked him again and headed to our rooms.

"Gordy, I'll see you later. Right now, I've got to call my wife," I said.

"So have I. My wife isn't used to my being away."

When I got to my room I immediately called Patty. She had just returned from taking Ruben for a walk.

"Jason, I'll be happy when you're home with me. It's cold in bed at night without you, precious."

"I know, I know, hon. You'd better put another quilt on our bed tonight. The temperature is going to dip into the teens. Oh! By the way, Tom sends his regards to you. He keeps hoping I'll take over a security position at the Breakshire and wants you on his hostess staff. I told him that we'd possibly consider it in a couple of years. Remember I said possibly."

"Honey, it would be difficult for us to leave Old Forge. So many friends. We'd have to start all over again meeting new people. I just don't know...," she said hesitantly.

"I know. You're right. We both love our region so very much. Well, honey, I'm going to try and get some sleep before Gordy and I go on duty later tonight."

"You be careful. Love you, Jason."

"I will, dear. Love you, too. So long for now."

I heard the click of the phone as Patty cradled the receiver. My days were empty without her with me, and I would be glad when this matter was settled and I was back home with her.

Alone at night in my room at the lodge left me with time to reflect on my life. There were so many memories. How fortunate I had been to have worked so many years on a job that I so dearly loved. I missed my duty days with the troopers. There is not another organization that, when the going gets tough, can pull together like the troopers. During the training phase of rookie members, I had the privilege and honor to participate in their instruction, whereby a new recruit would be assigned to a senior trooper for about two months. I believe I trained ten to thirteen members during my career. Through the remaining years on the job, I followed their progress within the division. I'm proud to say that they did good, going up the promotional ladder. Yeah! They did good. Just about every one of them got promoted, except the trainer, me. Oh well, that's the breaks. I did it my way, and if I had it to do all over again, I would still do it my way.

I lay back on the bed. I heard the thermostat kick on, and the room started to warm up. My eyelids became heavy as I fell off to sleep.

CHAPTER TWENTY-SEVEN

At Hewitt Pond, southeast of Newcomb, Morey Harris was scheming to further harass Tom Huston. Harris's hatred for Huston was taking over his entire thought process. He decided that he would wait till the wee hours of the morning. He remembered the tool sheds at the edge of the Breakshire property. He had been with his father several times, watching him go into the sheds for tools, and taking the large lawnmower out for cutting the rolling lawns surrounding the lodge. It was his plan to break into the sheds for the purpose of stealing tools and whatever else of value he could locate. Harris wasn't aware of the two security people patrolling the grounds at Breakshire, nor did he visualize the possibility of getting caught in the act. His thinking process focused on one channel; to make life miserable for Tom Huston, the owner and proprietor, while making a profit for himself.

Harris loaded his 12-gauge shotgun and placed it in his car on the rear seat under an old blanket. He also placed a medium-sized crowbar and a flashlight under the blanket next to the shotgun. He decided he would wait until 10:30 p.m. before he headed to Lake Placid. He didn't know how long the money that he had in his pocket would last, but he knew that he could sell more tools in Utica if he could acquire them.

With several hours to wait, he added wood to the stove and lay down on the old worn couch, covering himself with a

217

makeshift blanket which consisted of sewn-together burlap bags. He missed his two pit bulls, which he had trained to take on any stranger that would appear on the property. Now they were buried out in back of the the house next to the outhouse. Harris never contacted the E-Con people about the huge bear he had towed into a clearing near his house. The last he had seen of the dead bear was two coy dogs tearing the meat from the carcass. Harris didn't care much for bear meat, preferring the taste of venison. The tenderloin was his favorite, especially fried in butter with diced garlic cloves. Morey was just about to fall off to sleep, when he heard a voice calling his name. He threw the burlap covering onto the floor, got up from the couch, and went to the door.

"Luther, is that you?" he asked.

"Yeah, Morey, it's me. How is your car running? Did that wire hold up on the resistor?" he asked.

"It's running okay," Morey answered.

"Where's your pit bulls? I haven't seen them lately."

"Oh! I got rid of them. I didn't want to get sued in case they bit someone." he lied.

"Well, I'll get going. Let me know if you have any more problems with the car."

"I will, Luther."

Harris closed the door and went back to the couch. He had about three hours to rest before he headed for Lake Placid.

CHAPTER TWENTY-EIGHT

I woke up from my nap at about 10:00 p.m. I called extension 109 and Gordy answered on the second ring.

"What time do you want to start, Jason?" he asked.

"I'll meet you in the lobby at 10:30," I advised him.

"Okay," he acknowledged.

"Not that we'll use them, but you'd better bring your pistol. Just in case." I would have preferred leaving them behind.

"I understand."

We hung up and I went into the bathroom and splashed some cold water into my face. It was refreshing. I then gave Patty a quick call.

"Honey, I hope I didn't wake you," I said, apologetically.

"No, sweetheart, I was waiting up for your call."

We talked for just a few minutes and I assured her that I'd be home as soon as this case was completed. I again told Patty how much I missed her and loved her.

At 10:30 I met Gordy in the lobby. We sat down. I went over to the night desk clerk, advising him that we were going to have a cup of coffee, and that we'd be on duty until daylight. When I went back to Gordy, he was admiring the carved bears that Wilt and I had presented to Tom.

"Jason, whoever carved these bears is certainly a master-carver. They look so real. The claws and eyes stand out. Do you know who the carver is?" he asked.

"His name is Wilton Chambers, from Boonville. He goes by the name of Wilt. We're close friends. He's a logger in that region. It was Wilt and me who donated the big bear to Tom. The small bears were donated to Tom by Wilt."

"God! They're beautiful! Some people have all the talent. I tried carving a mallard duck once and almost severed a finger. Do you think this Wilt would carve me a medium-sized black bear?" he asked.

"I'll give you his telephone number and you can call him sometime at your leisure. He's usually at his home on Turin Road in the evening."

"I'd appreciate that, Jason."

The coffee was nice and hot and it was fresh. I added a little cream to mine. Gordy drank his black. We discussed our plan for the night. Tom had furnished us with a couple of small radios that we could use to communicate with. We decided that we'd take different directions around the grounds. Gordy was used to this type of security work. He had been an air policeman in the US Air Force, stationed at the Plattsburgh AFB, which is now closed. He was a likeable fellow, about my age, and carried his weight well on his medium frame. He had been on the boxing team in the service and, according to some of my trooper contacts in the Plattsburgh area, Gordy could handle himself. I had met him when he was in the service and he had assisted me on a narcotics investigation at one time. I liked him and I trusted him.

I had been following a mid-level dealer of marijuana, and when I had neared the main gate to the base the dealer had pulled over into a parking area. He had gotten out of his car with a brown paper bag and had walked to another parked car. A redheaded, white male had been behind the wheel of an old Plymouth Cambridge. I'd observed the buy as the redhead handed the dealer some currency in plain view. I had driven over to where the two individuals had parked, pulling up in front of them so they couldn't take off in their vehicles. I had identified myself. The dealer had put his hands up in the air, surrendering. The freckled-faced redhead had jumped out of his old Plymouth and taken off running. The air policeman on the main gate had observed the actions of the fleeing druggie and run after him. I'd put the cuffs on the dealer and observed the airman execute a flying tackle, catching the wiry individual just above the knees. They'd crashed to the ground. The redhead had struck out at the airman, which was the wrong move on his part. The air policeman had landed a right cross square on the jaw of the redhead when the druggie had tried to grab the airman's pistol from its holster. That's how I had met Staff Sergeant Gordon Whigham.

A few days after the apprehension, I had sent a memo through channels commending Sergeant Whigham for his action on that day. We kept in touch ever since.

We were wearing heavy jackets made even more bulky by the bulletproof vests that I had brought along for our protection. Our hunting caps helped insulate us from the cold and crisp air. The night sky was filled with sparkling stars, and every so often when looking up, I could catch a glimpse of one falling. There were only about two inches of snow on the ground.

The security lights were shining brightly along each side of the lodge and the garages in the rear. There were two large tool sheds located near the garages. I had suggested to Tom that we should turn off the two security lights that covered the tool shed area. This was a bit of reverse psychology. A perpetrator might approach a darkened area faster than a well-lit area. It was just an experiment. Of course, Gordy and I would be so situated on the grounds that one of us would be able to observe any unusual activity near the sheds. Both the sheds had been entered in the past, and were always a good target for a would-be thief or thieves.

Occasionally in the past Tom had hired outside security people, especially if he had a diamond or art show scheduled at the lodge. However, with winter here, those activities would not be taking place. Tom always emphasized to his guests that people with ski equipment should take extra care in the security of their vehicles, especially if they kept that equipment locked up in there. The majority of his guests complied, but occasionally one would forget. Sure enough, often the skis were stolen, along with the harness and sometimes the boots.

The Lake Placid area draws visitors from all over the world, because of the fame garnered from being the site of two winter Olympics, in 1932 and 1980. Since the venues are all still intact, it serves as a magnet for skiers and ice-skaters to hone their skills.

The vast majority of Adirondackers are honest hard-working folks taking pride in all they do, whether in the working arena or their leisure time. Naturally, some of our visitors, a small percentage, had a bit of larceny in them, and it had been these folks who had caused problems. Sometimes the crime was drug-related and sometimes people were hurt or even had lost their precious lives. And, to be realistic, some of our natives committed various violations of the law. Let's face it: if it were a perfect world, there would be no need for armies, police, nor any other law-enforcement agencies, but as long as the word greed existed the word perfection was in a great deal of trouble. Nevertheless, with crime or without crime, the great Adirondack Region of this fine State of New York was the place to be, and it is my desire to remain there until my last day.

At about 11:30 p.m., Gordy was in the rear of the lodge property and I was walking near the front entrance. A New York State Police troop car pulled in near the entrance and parked. Two tall troopers exited the car and approached me.

"Are you Jason Black?" one asked.

"Yes, I am. What can I do for you fellows?" I queried.

"Lieutenant Jack Doyle wanted you to know that the fingerprints on the gas can at the arson attempt in Newcomb and those prints that were found at the recent burglaries of Mr. Huston's properties come back to one suspect."

"Is that so?" I asked, excitedly.

"Yes, sir. The suspect in all the cases is Morey Harris, age 29, of the Hewitt Pond area. The reason we stopped by is that when we were leaving on night patrol, the lieutenant had to rush to Massena on a case and he asked us if we'd mind stopping by to see you here at the lodge. He wanted you to have the information right away."

"I appreciate that very much. Kindly thank the lieutenant for me."

I talked with the two troopers and filled them in on what Gordy and I were doing at the lodge. They told me that they would be in the area if we needed them. I asked them if they'd like some coffee, but they declined, as they had a matter in Saranac Lake to take care of. I wished them well and they departed. Seeing that troop car brought a great many memories back to me. I knew the division of state police was in good hands with representatives like these two troopers. They were businesslike and polite, and to me those are key factors in being a law enforcement professional.

At 2:00 a.m., Gordy and I met for coffee in the lobby. The night clerk, Tom Sullivan, was busy on the computer. The night cook brought my partner and me some Danish pastry with cheese topping. It tasted good with the hot coffee. The cook, Bill Foster, had moved to Lake Placid from Saratoga Springs, where he had worked in several Saratoga restaurants. He refilled our cups with fresh coffee and then excused himself, as he had other duties to perform in the kitchen. He always came in early to prepare fresh pastries for the breakfast patrons.

After we finished our snack we went over to the desk and thanked Tom for arranging the coffee and pastry.

"Hope you fellows are dressed warm enough out there. It is cold outside," Tom said.

"A bit chilly, but we're bundled up," I replied.

We left by the main entrance. We decided that we'd walk together on our rounds. Everything seemed to be in order. But as we approached the rear parking area, we both saw that a car was parked by itself on the edge of the paved portion. The lights were out, and we assumed that it could be a couple of lovers. We walked toward the car. It was difficult to determine its make at the distance we were from it. We knew that it hadn't been there forty-five minutes before, as Gordy had checked that particular area.

We decided to walk over to inform the driver he must leave the parking area. As we approached, to my grim satisfaction I recognized the familiar rusty old 1986 Chrysler sedan belonging to Morey Harris. As it was driverless, I knew he must be somewhere on the grounds of the Breakshire Lodge. The location where the car was parked was dark. Our dilemma: should we start a search for the individual, or should we stay hidden near the vehicle and wait for his return? We decided to stay together to observe the vehicle for the time being.

Our main fear was that Morey Harris knew where Tom Huston's suite was located. Another factor to consider was whether or not Morey was armed with a weapon or a gas can containing gas to start a fire. We now had a full plate of possibilities. I remembered well how Harris's face had changed at the mention of Tom Huston's name.

"Gordy, we know this suspect, Morey Harris, can be considered dangerous, so we've got to exercise caution," I said in a low tone to my partner.

"I understand, Jason. I agree," he replied in a near-whisper.

The main purpose of having Gordy and me stay at the Breakshire Lodge was for security. It had been the alleged actions of Harris that had prompted Tom to hire us as a precautionary move. He wanted to prevent personal injury or damage to the employees of the Breakshire, as well as protect the safety of the guests and the lodge property itself.

Now, the eventuality had occurred. Morey Harris was somewhere on the grounds of the Breakshire Lodge, possibly armed, apparently set to act out his emotional, imagined grievance against the Huston establishment.

I immediately took some evasive action to prevent the rusty old Chrysler from leaving. The car was unlocked. Not wanting to damage the wiring on the vehicle, I sent Gordy to my Bronco for a log chain that I always carried in the rear compartment. I waited in the dark behind a tree until he returned. In a few minutes, he arrived carrying the heavy chain.

Fortunately for us, Harris had parked near a sturdy tree. I took the chain from Gordy, got down and reached under the car, and fastened the chain around the right rear spring. I attached it securely, taking the other end and wrapping it around the sturdy red maple tree.

Assured that the car was securely held in place, Gordy and I proceeded to Tom Huston's suite. With my key card, we were able to gain entrance through the north side door of the lodge. We didn't use the elevator, but instead quietly ascended the stairs to the second floor. No one was in the hallway. I radioed the desk clerk and apprised him of the situation at hand. I told him to call the troopers and to call Tom's suite, as Gordy and I were right outside his door. The clerk assured me that he would make the calls immediately.

Gordy and I heard the telephone ring in Tom's suite. He answered it on the fourth ring. We heard Tom's muffled voice through the door talking to the clerk.

"I'll get dressed right away. You say that Jason is right outside my door, as we speak?" We then heard him thank the desk clerk for notifying him.

In two or three minutes Tom took the security chain off his door and opened it. "Come in, fellows," he said.

We entered Tom's room and immediately gave him an update of the ongoing events, and how we had Harris's old Chrysler fastened to the red maple to prevent his escape.

"Jason, I've seen that old Chrysler before. I just remembered it last night. One time I even rode in it when Morey was here visiting his father one afternoon. I was out in the far garden area and needed to get to the office to answer a long-distance call. Morey was talking with his father and asked me if I'd like a ride to the office. I remember that Morey was stocky-built, probably in his mid-twenties at the time. He was there to pick up his weekly allowance from his father."

"That's right, Tom. Morey appears to be a little simple, but personally, I think he is as smart as a fox and cunning, too. I'm now certain he has an imagined grievance against you. He blames you for his not receiving that allowance any more."

"Is that what this is all about?" Tom's eyes opened wide with disbelief.

"I'm afraid it is, Tom. Morey Harris apparently can't handle the loss of his father together with the loss of his allowance emotionally. He could be dangerous at this moment in time. He's already going to possibly face some jail time with the burglaries he committed on your properties, but it even goes further, Tom. Your personal safety could be at stake," I cautioned, not wanting to over-alarm him.

"I understand what you're saying, Jason."

"Hopefully, we'll be able to apprehend him before he hurts someone. I'm not a shrink, Tom, but I've seen many cases like this, and he is being delusional, blaming you and blaming his father for the financial predicament he finds himself in. I have no idea what the criminal justice system will do with him at this juncture. We'll have to see, but right now we have got to locate him and apprehend him so we can get to the bottom of this situation. You can't afford to have this guy running loose, not knowing if you're going to be shot at or whether or not he'll burn your properties. At this moment, I'd consider him very dangerous."

"I understand, Jason. I trust your judgment. What should we do?"

"I've had your night clerk put in a call for the troopers. I want you to go to one of your lodge rooms. I believe that Morey knows the location of this suite and I don't want you here if he should decide to break in." I tried to keep from showing my deep concern to Tom.

"Good idea, Jason. I see your point. In fact, if it's all right with you I'll have you and Gordy escort me down to your room 108," he suggested.

"That's what we'll do. I have an extra radio, so I can stay in contact with you. Once we get you down to your room—I stress it—do not go out of the room until Harris is apprehended," I said emphatically.

"I won't. You can rest assured of that." His voice trembled.

Perhaps for the first time he realized the degree of his danger.

"After we get you secured, we'll fill in your night desk clerk. No telling what Harris will do. He might even try to commit a robbery," I said.

We locked Tom's suite. Gordy and I, one on either side of him, escorted Tom down the stairs to my room on the first floor, which was a considerable distance. As a precaution, Gordy and I removed our pistols from their holsters and held them high, expecting any second that Morey Harris could appear around a corner. Luckily, we delivered Tom to the room without any problem and had him lock the door. He turned his radio on, and we made a radio check to make certain we were in communication with each other.

After leaving Tom, we went directly to the lobby to check on the night clerk.

"Mr. Black, I called the troopers. It seems their night patrol is investigating an accident near Meachum Lake. Their radio dispatcher advised me that as soon as they're finished, they will come here. The Lake Placid PD is tied up on another matter. Winter roads, I guess," he informed us regretfully.

I did not like this news. "I want you to lock the front entrance and stay in the rear office. We don't know if the suspect has a weapon or not. Keep your radio on in case we have to get a hold of you." We were both concerned for the clerk's personal safety. We could tell he was growing nervous.

CHAPTER TWENTY-NINE

While Jason Black and Gordon Whigham were tightening the security at the Breakshire Lodge main building, Morey Harris had already broken into one of the tool sheds in the rear of the lodge property and stolen two chain saws, which he had placed in the trunk of the Chrysler. He was returning to the shed for two boxes that contained new saw blades that he had spied on a shelf. In his greedy haste he had failed to observe the heavy log chain attached to his vehicle when he was at the car loading the stolen property.

Harris was armed with his 12-gauge shotgun, which was slung over his shoulder. His plan was to break into the other shed after he deposited the saw blades in his car. When he had finished taking what he wanted out of the sheds, he would make a visit to Mr. Tom Huston. He knew that Huston had a fancy suite on the second floor of the lodge. And he knew its exact location.

CHAPTER THIRTY

I told Gordy that instead of looking for Morey Harris on the grounds, it made best sense to set up an observation point to keep an eye on the Chrysler. Some high shrubs located behind the car would make an excellent location. We took up a position where we had a full view of anyone approaching the immediate area. We waited in the cold dark. About twenty minutes had passed when we detected movement. It appeared to be someone in a crouched position, moving slowly in our direction. As the person approached, we could see that he was carrying something. The closer he came to the Chrysler, the more confident I was that it was Morey Harris.

I looked at Gordy in the dark and whispered to him, "It's Harris. Looks like he has a weapon slung over his left shoulder. Let's wait until he loads the items into his car. Let him get behind the steering wheel. He's not going anyplace. You take the passenger side and I'll take the driver's door."

Gordy nodded his approval. It wouldn't be long. Harris opened the trunk, placed what appeared to be two boxes inside, and then closed the lid. We watched him remove what appeared to be a rifle or a shotgun from his left shoulder and place it in the back, just behind the driver's seat. He closed the back door. We watched closely as he opened the driver's door and got in behind the steering wheel. He just sat there for a few minutes. He lit a match, apparently for a cigarette.

231

Harris then engaged the ignition and the old Chrysler started up. He put it in gear and started to move. We could hear the chain clank as it tightened. Then the car came to a complete stop and we heard Harris bellow, "What the hell!!"

Before he could make a move, Gordy was pulling open the front passenger side door and I yanked open the driver's door. It seemed we had a hold of a Bengal tiger instead of a pudgy twenty-nine-year-old male. With Gordy holding on to Harris's right arm, Harris came out of the driver's side pulling Gordy across the front seat and onto the ground. Harris drew a hunting knife from his belt and made slashing motions with his left arm. Gordy, to avoid being cut by the knife-wielding Harris, relaxed his grip. As fierce as a cornered raccoon, Harris slashed out with the knife and screamed at the top of his lungs, freeing himself.

We tried to reason with him, but it was to no avail. In the dark, it was impossible to see his face. Harris crouched down, holding the knife in his right hand now, and continued to make slashing motions toward us. He snarling, was almost yelping in his fear and anger.

"Huston, I'm coming after you!" he shouted maniacally.

I kept pleading with Harris to put the knife down, but he wouldn't comply. Gordy had been able to get around behind him. I looked directly at Harris as he moved toward me, threatening me with the knife, now in his left hand. He was about three feet from me when Gordy took him down with a powerful karate kick from behind. The knife flew out of Harris's hand and we both were on top of him. The struggle continued for another five minutes, until suddenly, unaccountably, Harris relaxed.

"Jay, is that you?" he asked in amazement. "What the hell...?"

"Yes, Morey, it's me," I answered grimly.

"What are you doing here?" Harris asked, incredulous.

"Waiting for you, Morey," I stated.

"But, I--I thought you were--were my friend. You gave me a push into the driveway that day." He lowered his head dejectedly as he began to realize some of the truth.

It was difficult to comprehend how Harris's emotional state had taken such a rapid turn. He appeared to have calmed down, to have completely relaxed, maybe in shock.

Gordy, with the help of his flashlight, located the knife on the ground and secured it. He then went over to the gurgling Chrysler and turned the ignition off. The struggle was over. We told Morey that we were security for the Breakshire Lodge and that we were making a citizen's arrest. We accompanied Harris into the lodge, where we awaited the arrival of the troopers.

I contacted Tom immediately, notifying him of our apprehension of Harris.

"Thank God," Tom simply said, breathing a sigh of extreme relief.

The Troop S night patrol arrived and we turned a subdued Harris over to them. After securing the stolen property from the rear of the car, the troopers made arrangements to have the vehicle towed to a nearby garage. We turned over the evidence in our possession: shotgun, deer slugs, and knife. The troopers checked the two tool sheds for any additional evidence.

The senior trooper, Tom Larkin, asked us each for a sworn statement relative to the events that had taken place. We submitted our statements to Trooper Larkin. Tom Huston came to his office and identified the property that was now under the control of the state troopers. Huston also gave Trooper Larkin his statement.

I asked Trooper Larkin if I could talk with Morey Harris before they took him to Troop S for processing. He permitted me to talk with the suspect.

Morey entered, staring at me with a blank look on his face. Perhaps in his own mind he had felt he was too clever to be apprehended, or just overwhelmed that he had been. He was completely devoid of any anger.

"Morey, you're in some trouble now. I'm not an attorney; however, I'd like to know something. What is this ill feeling that you harbor toward Mr. Huston?" I asked, trying to keep my voice sympathetic.

"Jay, I can't explain it. I just feel that Huston is part of my trouble. He fired my dad. I don't have an allowance anymore. I don't have any money." He looked sheepish and wouldn't look directly at me.

"Morey, I hope that this will be the end of your crime spree. It is the wrong path to take. All it will bring you is grief down the road. Mr. Huston is one of the kindest and most considerate persons I know. He feels badly about your predicament; however, you have committed several burglaries and you've attempted to burn his Newcomb house down. Don't you know that was the wrong thing to do?" I felt that I was talking to a child.

"Yes, I guess you're right, Jay," he said somewhat sheepishly.

"You're going to go now with Trooper Larkin and his partner to the Troop S Headquarters and you'll probably be interviewed by a BCI man. Just tell the truth and cooperate with them. They are fair people, but don't tell them any lies."

Morey nodded his head in childlike understanding. I explained that I was a former member of the troopers and now a private detective and that I had been hired by Mr. Huston to watch over the Breakshire Lodge. I wanted him to know just where I stood and what my involvement was.

Morey and I shook hands. His shoulders slumped. I believe he was beginning to realize the gravity of his predicament. I thanked Trooper Larkin for allowing me to speak with Harris. I didn't know if it would truly do any good, but I hoped it would. It appeared to me that he would need some type of counseling. Maybe the state could take that into consideration.

It was about 6:30 a.m. before Trooper Larkin and his partner left the Breakshire with Harris. The old Chrysler had been impounded. The evidence had been collected, including some fingerprints, a crowbar, and the recovered stolen goods. Tom Huston would receive his property after the court proceedings that would determine the outcome of the case. Gordy and I had done our part. We were happy that no one was hurt seriously, although Gordy had a sore arm from being dragged across the front seat of the Chrysler. I asked him where he had learned that type of kick movement.

"Jason, I learned that in a karate course I attended," he answered.

"Well, that kick surely toned Harris down a little."

"We could have wrestled with him for an hour. He's a strong man."

"You're right; he is. He spends a lot of time in the woods cutting up a lot of firewood. I imagine, though, that he'll be spending some time now in a correctional facility."

"You're right on that," he agreed.

Gordy and I met with Tom over a well-deserved breakfast. He thanked us for our participation in the apprehension of Morey Harris. He also suggested that before we headed back to our homes, we should feel free to return to our rooms and rest, as we had been up all night. He told us to pick up our pay envelopes at the front desk when we left, as he was flying to New York City on business.

"We'll do that, Tom. But that hurry wasn't necessary. You surely could have mailed our checks," I told him, reaching out to shake his extended hand.

I thanked Gordy for taking time out of his busy schedule to assist me in this troublesome matter. I would certainly keep him in mind for any further security work with which I needed assistance. Work for a private detective was not very plentiful in the Adirondack Park, and I was grateful for the bad-check cases that trickled into my mailbox and helped sustain my private investigation business.

We appreciated Tom's offer of our rooms for rest, but were anxious to return to our homes and our wives. I bid Gordy farewell. He smiled when he opened the envelope that Tom Huston had left for him at the desk. I, too, was pleased with the generous check that I found in mine. After Gordy had headed back to Plattsburgh and I had removed my baggage from my room to the Bronco, I reentered the lodge to thank the personnel for their cooperation over the previous few days. All were thankful that Morey Harris had not located their employer. Perhaps Harris would never have harmed Tom, but in his state of mind, anything could have happened. All in all, I was pleased with the outcome.

I had another cup of coffee at the lodge before I left. I didn't call Patty, as I knew she would be hard at work waiting on her customers at John's Diner. I also wanted to surprise her. I left the lodge for the parking area, the Bronco, and home.

It was cold and blustery outside and a light snow was beginning to fall. Before long the area would be blanketed with snow. The Bronco started up on the first engagement of the ignition switch. I left Lake Placid, deciding to stop by Troop S Headquarters to see my friend, Lieutenant Jack Doyle, before heading to Old Forge.

When I entered the front entrance of Troop S Headquarters, the lieutenant was standing by the receptionist desk.

"Jason Black! Well, it's about time you checked in with me. Come to my office and we'll go over a couple of matters."

I could tell that he really was glad that I had stopped by en route to Old Forge. I followed him down the hall to his office, and seated myself at a chair near his desk.

"Jason, I want to thank you and your assistant—Gordy, I believe his name is according to my night patrol people." He looked over at me with a pleased look on his face.

"Yes, it is Gordon Whigham from Plattsburgh. His nickname is Gordy."

"Well, we appreciate your citizen's arrest earlier this morning. You were darn lucky that it turned out the way it did. My night patrol, which I interviewed early this morning, informed me that Harris had a loaded shotgun in the rear seat of his car. We're all lucky that he didn't have a chance to use it," he said, shaking his head.

"Lieutenant, I believe that Morey Harris should have some type of counseling."

"Jason, I did interview Harris briefly. Possibly something can be arranged through the court. Of course, that will be up to the magistrate. He may even arrange for an evaluation of Harris."

"I hope, Jack, that something can be arranged along those lines. I kind of feel sorry for the guy. But that's just my opinion."

"Believe me, I'll look into it."

"I'd appreciate it. It would appear that Morey is quite disturbed. His father leaving him alone didn't help. Anyway, that's how I feel about the situation," I offered.

"You've always had compassion for people, Jason. You've got a heart," he said.

"Guess that's the way I was brought up."

"Jason, as long as you're here, I want to bring you up-to-date on another matter. It's the Bernard Draper case. I have some news for you. The feds took over and Draper's doing a life's sentence in a federal detention facility. He snitched on some other white-collar criminals in Arizona and therefore the government saw fit to strike a deal with him. His trucking operation is out of business," he went on.

"How did you obtain this information, Jack?" I was sharply curious. It was odd that my friend, Jack Flynn in Phoenix hadn't advised me of the news. I would have to give him a call.

"Captain Jay Silverstein of the Phoenix PD called me."

"How about the gift shop and warehouse between Cranberry Lake and Tupper Lake? What's happening there?" I queried.

"I heard that it is going to be auctioned off, as well as Draper's house in Tupper."

"Well, that's good news! We don't need the criminal element of our society fleecing the consumers here in the Adirondacks, or any other place for that matter."

"Jason, Silverstein indicated that several civil suits have been initiated against Draper's holdings."

Lieutenant Doyle completed our meeting and I thanked him for the information. He inquired how Tom Huston was doing now that this matter had been resolved. I informed Jack that Tom was very relieved by the apprehension of Morey Harris and that he was already off to New York City for a hotel owners' convention. We conversed for a few minutes longer, then said our farewells, and I resumed my journey home to Old Forge and Patty.

After I left the headquarters, I stopped at a station in Saranac Lake to gas up the Bronco. The snow was still falling and the highway was beginning to get slippery. I put the Bronco into four-wheel drive, just to be on the safe side.

The trip to Old Forge took me about two and a half hours. I was relieved when I pulled into my driveway. Smoke was lazily coming out of our fireplace chimney. I noticed that Ruben wasn't in his dog run. I tooted the horn, so as not to alarm Patty. As I pulled up and parked, the side door opened and Patty came running out without a jacket on. I got out of the Bronco and hurried to her.

"Oh, honey! I'm so glad you're home," she said with excitement. "I missed you so much."

"Darling, it is so good to see you." We embraced and kissed. Her lips were warm and moist. "I missed you, too. But go back inside! You'll catch cold without your jacket." She hurried back to the door.

Ruben came out and jumped up on me joyfully. I gave him a big hug, too, then unloaded the Bronco. I carefully placed my 9mm semi-automatic pistol in the locked cabinet, then locked the Bronco and went inside. The wind was whipping up and there was an accumulation of about three inches of fresh white snow.

"Why didn't you call me, honey? I would have started dinner," Patty admonished lovingly.

"Honey, I know I should have, but my cell phone won't work up in the higher peak region. Anyway, I wanted to surprise you. I hope you're not upset." I regretted now that I hadn't called her.

"No, I'm not upset, you big lug. I'm so happy that you're home. Tell me what happened at the Breaksire Lodge. I didn't think that you'd be back so soon. What about Tom? Is he okay?" Patty asked me excitedly.

"Honey, first of all, no one got hurt. Tom is feeling much better since we apprehended the burglar. It was the son of his former groundskeeper, just as we suspected," I said.

"Oh, I'm so glad that everything worked out for you. I haven't been able to sleep since you've been away. I was so worried about you. Please tell me more," she said with sincere interest.

"I had an acquaintance of mine, Gordy Whigham, a former U.S. Air Force Air Policeman, who is now a private detective in Plattsburgh. I'm sure I mentioned him before. He came down and assisted me. It was a darn good thing he did, too. The fellow we apprehended had a loaded shotgun, and if I had been alone, no telling what might have happened. Gordy used karate on him. Anyway, everything worked out. And, Tom generously compensated both Gordy and myself for our time and service. Before I headed home, I stopped at Troop S Headquarters and talked with Jack Doyle. Their department was involved in the case."

"How is the lieutenant, Jason?" she asked.

"He's doing well. He said to say hello to you."

"That was nice of him. He has a great deal of respect for you, Jason."

"Yes, he's a good man, Patty. Troop S is fortunate to have such a hard worker. He gets out into the field and works closely with his subordinates," I added.

While Patty prepared fried chicken for dinner, I went into my office. She had placed all my incoming mail on top of the desk. I checked the list of calls that she had written on a sheet of paper for me. There were several, most from business places. It was too late to contact them that night; I would wait until morning. I called my friends Wilt Chambers, Jack Falsey, Dale Rush, and Charlie Perkins. Luckily, all of them happened to be home. I told each that I wanted to thank him for watching over Patty while I was away, and asked each to meet me at John's Diner in the morning for some conversation and coffee. They all agreed to a meeting in the diner at 8:30, and said they were looking forward to it.

I continued to straighten my desk. Patty had placed the bills that needed to be paid in a separate pile so they would not be mixed in with my business mail. I began to review the envelopes, separating junk mail from legitimate letters.

As I was sitting at the desk, I began to sense the aroma of fried chicken as it wafted into the office.

I hollered out, "Is dinner ready, honey? It sure smells pretty good."

"Shortly, dear," she replied with a chuckle and added, "Are you famished?"

"Yes, I am. I've missed you and your cooking, honey," I replied.

"You're just saying that. Do you mean it, dearest?" She waited for my answer.

"I sincerely do mean it, sweet."

I closed the desk drawer and went toward the kitchen. Ruben was lying on his air mattress. The table was set with two lighted candles placed in the center.

Patty had just finished mashing potatoes and asked me to put the assorted relishes on the table, including one of my favorites, pickled beets with sliced onions. I noticed the orange carrots she had prepared as our vegetable. She smiled as she removed the hot dinner rolls from the oven.

I went to the sink and washed my hands before I sat down to eat. Everything looked especially wonderful.

"Patty, you work too hard. Your dinner looks superb," I said, admiring her efforts.

"I guess we're all set, darling," she acknowledged, as she set the platter of crispy fried chicken in front of me. I got up and went to her chair and seated her, giving her a warm kiss on the top of her head.

I said grace, thanking the good Lord for the gifts we were about to receive. I then passed the dishes of food to Patty, except the platter of fried chicken. For that I used a long-handled fork to place a crispy, fried breast of chicken on her plate.

We didn't speak very much during dinner. We were both busy passing the dishes back and forth to one another. The chicken was tender and moist, completely delicious. Patty had added sweet butter to the mashed potatoes, really enhancing their flavor.

While we were delighting in our meal, we noticed the snowflakes had increased. The wind seemed to have slackened off.

"If that snowfall keeps up, looks like we might be able to do some more snowmobiling tomorrow, Patty," I said, knowing that she'd like that.

"Lila asked me to come in tomorrow and work till noon. Do you mind?" she asked.

"No, honey. We can go out in the afternoon—that is, if you're not too tired," I offered.

"That sounds great! It'll be beautiful. And can we take a flask of blackberry brandy with us, of course for medicinal purposes only?" she asked playfully.

"Sure we can, sweetheart!" I sat back contentedly. "I want to thank you for the great dinner tonight. Everything was excellent."

"I'm glad you liked it. We both love crispy fried chicken. I certainly haven't cooked like this while you've been gone."

I helped Patty clear the table and told her to rest while I washed the dishes and cleaned the kitchen. I then fixed Ruben's food dish after I let him out for a quick run into the woods. I could tell he was glad I was back home.

After putting the dishes away, I went into the living room. Patty had placed some old seventy-eights on our antiquated record player. "Ebb Tide" was playing. The record finished, and dropped "In the Mood" next onto the turntable. This song will be forever popular in our hearts. Patty got up from the davenport and came toward me with her arms extended. We embraced and began to dance. Glenn Miller's orchestra played this song beautifully. I thought of how several generations had had the privilege of hearing the sound of this popular orchestra. As the music stopped and the record player sought the next song from the past, Patty and I pressed our lips close together in a long warm kiss. We turned the records over, and continued dancing until they had played to the end.

I informed her that I had to catch up on some office work if we were going to do some snowmobiling the next afternoon. She smiled and gave a me a peck on the cheek. Patty told me that while I was working on my reports she would continue to work on knitting her sweater. She hoped that she'd have it finished by Christmas time. Her knitting materials were on a small table in the living room. I went on into the office. I wasn't too surprised when Ruben followed me in and lay down in front of my wooden desk. I leaned over and petted his head.

"Did you miss me, boy?" I asked.

Ruben looked up at me for an instant and then placed his head between his two front paws. As I looked at him I smiled again, knowing that he was a loyal dog who loved us both. His coat showed how Patty had recently taken him to Lynn's kennel for grooming. She loved giving him his bath, and Ruben enjoyed it as well, as long as he didn't have to stay overnight. I noticed that the more he aged, the more he seemed to want to stay at home with us.

I typed several letters to individuals requesting that, before the initiation of criminal action, they take care of the insufficient-fund checks that they had passed. Such diplomacy often went a great deal further than a police officer at the door of their home or place of business with a warrant for their arrest.

With checks, whether there is an insufficiency, or whether they're forged and passed, there is always the possibility of criminal intent. Some of the large-scale check schemes can be intricate during the investigation process. In the last days of my trooper career as an investigator, I on occasion traveled to other parts of New York State on the trail of several perpetrators of numerous check scams.

One such plot occurred in a city in western New York. Two middle-aged Caucasian males checked into an up-scale hotel. They told the hotel clerk that they were plumbing contractors and were going to establish their business in that particular city. During the process of establishing their alleged business, they filed a dba (doing business as) certificate indicating their intention to operate a plumbing company. They next located an answering service and registered their plumbing company and a telephone number. After opening up a business account at a local bank with a thousand-dollar deposit, they ordered five hundred checks bearing the name of their firm. Then they ran an advertisement in the local paper under business services.

The perpetrators received their business checks at a mail drop, which was operated by the answering service. The answering service began to receive telephone calls for the plumbing service. The two alleged plumbers were busy, but not pursuing the work they had advertised. Instead they were keeping a check-writer busy making out phony payroll checks to two non-existent employees. Assured that they had a dba, a business checking and savings account in a well-known local bank, an address, and a telephone number, they set their scheme in motion. On a busy Friday evening around five o'clock, the two operators went to numerous supermarkets and cashed their large payroll checks, after purchasing just a few groceries. They were dressed in work-clothes, which displayed the plumbing company name. They even went so far as to soil their hands with pipe cement. The unsuspecting cashiers had no way of knowing that the two men posing as plumbers were in fact two scammers executing a fraudulent scheme.

This clever scheme netted the two would-be plumbers several thousand dollars, and they would have gotten away with it—except for a sharp cashier who, becoming suspicious, quickly followed the two men outside to the supermarket's parking lot, wrote down the New York State license plate number, and promptly called the local police, who in turn called the thruway authority. An alert thruway employee and one of New York's finest brought this scam to a halt. The check passers were turned over to me for further processing and arraignment before a magistrate. All monies were recovered and accounted for and held as evidence.

Further checking with agencies revealed that these two bad actors had been going from city to city in several states committing this lucrative crime. After the processing, the two men and all the evidence were turned over to the city detectives for further criminal action as many of the crimes had occurred in their jurisdiction.

All business people, especially where checks are cashed, should always be alert to this type of activity. Any employee who becomes suspicious while cashing checks for alleged customers should, when in doubt, consult their supervisor. I perceived that some of the bad checks on my desk probably could have been stopped if the employee had only asked some questions. All of us in this fast-moving, fast-talking society should take a moment when accepting a check from a stranger, to ask the question, "Is this a legitimate transaction?" There are proficient check-scammers out there amongst the rest of us in society. As a private detective I say, "Beware."

Having caught up on my bookwork, I cleaned off the top of my desk. It looked much neater. Patty had come into the office and told me she was going to bed early.

"Honey, as soon as I let Ruben out for his nightly run into the woods, I'll be right in to join you," I told her.

"I'll be waiting for you, Sherlock," she said coquettishly.

I slipped on a warm jacket and let the big fellow outside. While Ruben ran off to the woods, I shoveled some of the fresh snow from our small walkway. Patty's Jeep would be covered with the stuff in the morning, so I placed a good-sized piece of cardboard over the front windshield and the rear window. She had to be at the diner by 6:00 a.m. I had one piece of cardboard left, so I placed it over the driver's side of the windshield on the Bronco.

It was frigid outside, and Ruben's and my breath could clearly be seen. When my faithful K-9 returned from the woods, he ran around in front of me, rolling over and then standing, shaking the loose snow from his back. I patted him on his head. I then placed the shovel against the porch railing. I hoped that the snow would ease up a little overnight. If it doesn't, I realized I might have to call Dale Rush to plow us out. Even though Patty and I both had four-wheel-drive vehicles, keeping it plowed was easier on our older models.

Ruben and I went back inside. He went to the air mattress and lay down. I shook the snow off my jacket before I hung it up, then prepared for bed. When I entered the bedroom, Patty was on my side of the bed, sound asleep. Instead of waking her, I went to her side and slipped between the covers. I looked over at the alarm clock and saw it was set for 5:30 a.m. I reached up and turned off the reading lamps, realizing Patty must have been dead tired. While I had been away from the house overnight, she probably hadn't slept well.

CHAPTER THIRTY-ONE

When the alarm went off at 5:30 a.m., Patty reached over me to shut it off.

"I've got it, honey," I said.

We embraced for a few minutes.

"Wish I didn't have to work this morning, sweetheart," Patty said, still groggy.

"I know what you mean, my darling," I agreed.

We hugged and kissed for a few minutes until Patty pushed the blankets back to get up out of bed. The cold air from the room immediately sent a chill over me.

"Wow!" I shouted, "Patty, the air's cold."

"I'm sorry, Jason. I didn't mean to uncover you." She quickly covered me up and gave me a warm kiss.

I heard Patty start the Jeep, warming it up for five minutes or so before she left the yard. I lay in bed and rolled and tossed, trying to get back to sleep, but since sleep was not forthcoming, I finally climbed out of bed and got dressed. I decided that if we were going to do some snowmobiling that afternoon after Patty got out of work, I'd better clean the house and mop the floors. Before I started this project, I let Ruben outside, as he was standing by the side door, waiting. While he was out, I placed the coffeepot on the stove and took out two eggs, ham, onion, and green peppers from the refrigerator. I put two slices of Italian bread in the toaster, but didn't push it down.

I proceeded to dice the onions, along with the green peppers, braising them off in the heavy iron frying pan I had heating on the front burner of the stove. I beat the two eggs in a bowl, then mixed in the braised vegetables along with some of the diced ham. I whipped the mixture a little and then stirred it for a moment.

Ruben barked at the door, and I let him in. I filled his water and food dishes. Washing my hands and drying them on the hand towel, I went over to the cabinet and stirred the ingredients in the glass bowl. I poured a small amount of olive oil into the iron skillet and heated it. When it was hot, I poured the western omelet in. It sizzled as it hit the heated oil. I turned the burner down. When the eggs began to set, I turned the omelet over, adding a slice of American cheese. I pushed the toaster down and the electric coils heated up to a glowing red. The odor of the onions, peppers, cheese, and ham wafted throughout the kitchen. I wished that Patty could have joined me.

The toaster popped up. I removed the two slices, spread them with sweet butter, and placed them on a warmed plate: I then removed the tempting western omelet, one of my favorites—from the hot iron frying pan and placed it on one of the toasted slices. I covered it with the other.

The coffee I poured into my mug was very hot and the aroma blended well with the western. It must have gotten Ruben's attention, as he approached the table and sat on the floor. I pulled out the chair and seated myself. With a knife I cut the western egg in half. I picked up the slightly larger portion and tasted it. Great! I loved it. Maybe not so fine as Slim's Restaurant in Boonville, but it came in a close second. I glanced at my watch: 7:40. It suddenly dawned on me that I had arranged to meet the group at John's diner at 8:30 sharp! Because of my Lake Placid assignment and my lack of sleep, I evidently had had a senior moment. I realized though, that I still had time to meet them for coffee. My start on cleaning the log home would have to wait until I returned from John's and the post office.

After I finished my breakfast, I quickly washed the dishes, cleaned the stove, and went to the bathroom to shave. At 8:15, I changed my clothes, placing the ones I took off into the laundry hamper. I knew that Ruben would be all right until I returned. I donned a warm jacket and boots, picked up all the mail in my outgoing basket, and locked the house.

The snow stopped falling and we had about ten inches on the level. I went over to the Bronco, removed the cardboard from the windshield, unlocked the door, and climbed in. (Patty and I hadn't plugged in our block heaters overnight, but when the temperature dips below ten degrees, we definitely plug the heaters in.) I was happy to have the choke that Dr. Don had installed. I pulled it out and hit the ignition, which turned over and finally caught. After a slight backfire from the exhaust system, five minutes later it leveled off and ran smoothly.

I placed the vehicle in four-wheel-drive and backed up in a reverse Y, a maneuver we used in the troopers. I moved out of the drive and stopped at Route 28. A large semi-trailer outfit passed, heading toward Inlet. I made a right-hand turn and headed to John's Diner.

The minute I pulled into the parking lot I could see my friends were all there. Charlie Perkins' rig was at the far end of the lot, headed out toward Route 28. It appeared he had a full load of logs on for Vermont. Wilt Chambers' big white Dodge was parked next to Jack Falsey's maroon van, and Dale Rush's new SUV was next to Wilt's.

I parked the Bronco and got out. As I was walking toward the diner, I noticed the new entrance door that John had installed in an effort to keep the cold air from rushing in. I opened the door and entered. The first thing I heard was Wilt's booming voice from the far end of the dining area.

Patty was serving another table. Her tray looked heavy, laden with large plates of eggs, home fries, and ham. She smiled happily at me as I walked over toward my friends' table.

Sitting at the large table with Wilt were Charlie, Jack, Dale, and Jim Jenny, the new man at the O'Brien's marina. To my surprise, seated next to Wilt was Penny Younger from the WBRV radio station in Boonville. I extended my greetings to the group, apologizing for being late.

Wilt spoke up. "Jason, don't you stay home anymore? You've been away for almost a week. We all missed you."

"I've missed you guys, too," I quickly replied.

"You didn't have to worry about Patty, Jason. We watched over her every day at the diner. And we knew she was safe at night with Ruben on guard," Wilt continued.

"Well, fellows, it is my nature to worry, but with Ruben there, it does ease my mind. By the way, don't forget that Patty can handle her shotgun better than I can." I paused. "Speaking of that, I spotted a coy dog just before the Art Center entrance. I didn't think much of it at the time. He was after a wild turkey that had been in an overhanging tree."

"When did you see this, Jason?" Jack Falsey asked in concern.

"On the way down here. I couldn't believe it, but there they were," I responded.

"Sounds like that story that was going around about the cougar that was supposedly sighted crossing the South Shore Road a while back," Dale said. "Jason, I know you've met Jim Jenny before. He's going to be servicing some of the stored boats over the winter and is planning to handle some of the repair work that might be needed on snow sleds. I introduced Jim to J.R. Risley, and he's going to put skis on J.R.'s plane."

Jim Jenny smiled and looked over toward me.

"That's great, Jim. Sounds as though you're going to be a busy fellow," I said.

"Love to keep busy, Jason, and I hope to get a little flying in," he answered.

"You fellas talk about being busy. We're busy on the farm all the time. And with my western music show, you can imagine there aren't enough hours in the day." Penny finally joined in the conversation.

"I don't know how you do it, Penny, but we do enjoy your

show very much. You have many, many fans." I asserted.

"I enjoy doing the show and I enjoy people," he said.

We engaged in conversation for about an hour before Charlie Perkins excused himself, as he had to head for Vermont. Dale and Jim Jenny were next to leave, headed to Brewerton for parts for a cruiser.

Jack Falsey, Wilt, Penny, and I had refills on our coffee. Penny told us about a possible trip to Nashville and Branson with Ronnie Smith's group. He and his wife, Sharon, had made several trips with Ronnie over the years, either by bus or by air to their destination. They had even participated in several boat cruises, and found them all well planned and enjoyable.

I looked at my watch: 10:15 a.m. I excused myself, telling the fellows that we'd get together again in the future.

"It was great seeing you fellows, but I've got to get to the post office. Say hello to your families. See you later," I said as I made my way to the door.

I didn't disturb Patty, as she was very busy waiting on customers. I smiled playfully and nodded to her on my way out. Wilt wouldn't let me pay for my coffee, grabbing the check that was lying on the table.

I thanked him, promising that next time it would have to be my treat.

I noticed that it was getting cold outside. I started the Bronco and left the parking lot for the post office. Traffic had picked up. Dozens of vehicles towing snowmobile trailers were entering our hamlet from the south. Before I negotiated my left turn into the post office, I had to wait for a good five minutes until a kind citizen stopped his vehicle and motioned me to turn. I waved a thank-you to him as I entered the intersection.

My post office box contained several letters, which I rifled through before putting them into my briefcase. I ran into some of my acquaintances and, after a short conversation, proceeded on my way home. Even though our winter was in progress and snow covered the ground, everyone appeared to be in a cheery mood.

Before heading home, I drove down to Dr. Don's garage.

With the advent of winter, and the drop in the temperatures, I thought it would be a good idea to have him check my radiator to ensure that I had enough antifreeze.

When I arrived, I found he was busy under the hood of a car. He looked up at me as I approached.

"What can I do for you today, Jason?" he asked.

"I was just going to have you check my antifreeze and the heater hoses to see if I'm ready for the cold weather, but I can see you're busy. I'll come back some other time when you're not so busy," I offered.

"It's okay. You're here and the car's warmed up. I'll take a minute and do it now," he volunteered, getting out from under the hood.

He walked over to the Bronco, raised the hood, and released the radiator cap in order to test the temperature. He looked at the reading, and hollered over to me, "You're good for fifty below."

I thanked him and left for home. Don would normally carry on a conversation, but this morning he was surrounded by customers waiting anxiously for service on their cars and trucks.

When I was finally able to enter Route 28, I found myself behind a vehicle towing a trailer carrying four snowmobiles. The occupants appeared to be a family coming into our area for winter sport. They probably had already paid their fees for the snowmobile permits, which gave them access to the extensive trail system that had made this area so popular. They would soon be enjoying the pristine beauty of the winter season. Mother Nature has a way of spreading her natural beauty over this great region, and it was personally joyous to me, as a resident, to observe people having a wonderful time in a special place, the Old Forge region of the great Adirondacks. My only hope was that it would be here for years to come, to be enjoyed by the adults and children of future generations.

For hundreds of years our forefathers enjoyed these mountains and the wilderness they represent. Great pains were taken in 1894 when drafting legislation to ensure the area remain forever wild. I'm certain that the minds and hearts of people of that era, thought and felt as I do today: maintain and protect. It is my conviction that planners of today and tomorrow should take a moment at their drawing boards and their statistical data to consider future generations. Once the wilderness areas are gone, they are gone forever. Planners should do their planning, but temper it with reason and common sense, which I'm sorry to say is scarce today. It seems that the almighty dollar too often dominates the issues.

When I arrived home, I placed my mail on my desk. I then put Ruben out in his dog run. He immediately went into his doghouse. I went back inside and hurried to finish my cleaning project. The vacuum cleaner worked well, but I noticed that the cord was frayed and would have to be replaced in the near future.

After I finished my inside project, I put my warm jacket on and went outside to brush off the two snowmobiles. I took both sleds off the trailer and checked the fuel tanks. I started each machine. Patty's wouldn't start. When I checked the sparkplug, I noticed that the end of the plug had cracked. I replaced the plug, and the machine started up right away on the first pull of the cord.

About 12:45 p.m. the red Jeep pulled into the yard. I met Patty at the door. I noticed she had a covered dish in her hands.

"Jason, would you take this and set it on the stove. Lila had chili left over from lunch, and I thought we'd enjoy it for a quick snack before going out in the cold."

"That was thoughtful of her," I said.

I helped Patty off with her jacket and hung it in the closet. She washed her hands, then put the chili in a medium-sized pan. She heated it and placed some homemade bread in the toaster. After the toast popped up, she buttered it and added a touch of garlic salt. I set the table and poured us two glasses of ice water. When the chili was boiling hot she served it in two bowls and we sat down to eat. The chili tasted good, along with the garlic-flavored toast.

Patty and I discussed the location that we'd snowmobile to

and decided to travel on the trail system. While she got dressed, I took care of cleaning the table and washed the few dishes we had used for lunch. After I finished I got dressed. Our snowmobile suits, helmets, and boots fit well and were comfortable. I remembered to pour blackberry brandy into our flask. We were ready for the trails.

I locked the log house and we went over to the dog run to check on Ruben. The K-9 was smart. He was standing by the gate with his tail swishing back and forth.

"No, Ruben, you can't go with us." Ruben turned and put his back to us. "Be good, boy," I said.

I started both Ski-Doos. They sounded good and ready to hit the groomed trails. We cut through the woods and ended up on Rondaxe Road. There were several snowmobiles in the region. The drivers we met all waved. If they spoke, I wasn't able to hear what was said over the loud drone of the sleds. There was no doubt about it: the two sleds we owned were probably considered antiques by the rest of the sled lovers with their bright, shiny, new equipment. However, we were enjoying what we had and, as long as they ran well, they would serve our purpose.

On the trail, I took up the rear and let Patty take the lead. I had cautioned her about going too fast. From this position I could see ahead and to both sides. The majority of the riders on the trail were operating their sleds in a safe manner. Occasionally we'd observe an operator of a sled pass another sled on a hill, especially dangerous where the trail narrowed. One such incident was a near head-on. The operator of the oncoming sled made a split-second decision and fortunately was able to find a clearing between two large trees. The operator who had failed to use good judgment, guiltily sped up and went out of sight, obviously realizing he had almost caused a catastrophe. The operator who drove off into the woods between the two hardwoods brought his sled to a halt and shook his head in disbelief. Patty and I witnessed the incident and felt sorry for the fellow who had to leave the trail to avoid a collision.

Personally, I would have loved to talk with the operator who had caused this life-threatening moment. Maybe it was just as well that I didn't, especially for him. There are always reckless operators, not only on the trail, but also on the highways. One must always be vigilant.

We stayed on the trail system for about three hours, but not always in motion. We met a group of people who had their sleds pulled off the trail and were cooking hot dogs. One of the sleds was pulling another sizable sled loaded with several large thermos jugs and other supplies. We slowed down when we saw the activity. A very friendly guy, who evidently recognized Patty from the diner, came running over.

They exchanged greetings. It appeared that Patty had served the group a full breakfast that very morning.

"How'd you two like to join us for a hot dog? We've got plenty and we won't take no for an answer." He was wearing a big smile. I didn't know the people, but they were obviously sincere.

"Are you certain we won't be intruding?" I inquired.

"Not at all," he said.

I looked over at Patty. "Is it okay with you?" I asked, sensing she would like to.

"I'd love to join them," she acknowledged.

Patty and I drove our sleds over to where the others were all lined up and turned them off. I could see the people were a friendly group. There were six of them. We introduced ourselves all around and it wasn't long before we learned that the three men were brothers and two of their wives were sisters and the third wife was a cousin to the two sisters. They were from the Silver Creek region and all of them taught school.

We chatted about our mutual enjoyment of snowmobiling, and how much it helped pass the long winter season. I gleaned from the conversation that they all loved the Adirondack Park and enjoyed the sport. In addition, they all played tennis during their free times in the summer. All appeared to be in their forties. One of the couples had children, but had left them with their grandparents. We had an enjoyable afternoon, discussing our mutual love of the mountains, and our shared enjoyment in snowmobiling. We avoided any controversial subjects. To Patty and me, it was a fun afternoon with other wholesome American citizens, strangers to us a few hours ago, and now friends. We exchanged names, addresses, and phone numbers and expressed a desire to repeat our festivities.

By the time lunch was over, Patty had had two hot dogs with mustard topped with coleslaw, and a cup of hot chocolate to drink. I had had three hot dogs accompanied by a cup of coffee. There was plenty of food left over.

Patty and I thanked our gracious hosts and told them to contact us any time they came to Old Forge. We shook hands, promising each other that our paths would cross again. It had certainly been a pleasant, but unexpected afternoon. I found myself being grateful that there are many folks like these, warm, friendly, and generous.

The small fire that had been used to roast the hot dogs had not emitted a great amount of heat. Even though we had on our heavy snowmobile suits, we began to feel the chill. When we drove down the trail, I pulled off to the side and opened our flask. The brandy quickly seemed to warm our bones. I had noticed that each of the group we had left had carried a small flask, but I hadn't observed anyone open them.

Snow was coming down steadily as we pulled onto our property. The fresh air in our lungs felt good. Patty was handling her Ski-Doo like a pro. I was proud of her. We pulled both sleds to the rear of the trailer. I had blocked the trailer wheels so they wouldn't move. We drove our sleds onto the trailer, one at a time. I placed a block of wood at the rear of the sleds to elevate the track. We then covered the machines.

Both of us were tired and our faces were red from the cold air. Tired, but feeling refreshed, we removed our suits and dressed in jeans and sweatshirts. Patty proceeded to make us some hot chocolate with marshmallows to warm us up. Still full from the hot dogs, we decided that hotcakes would be on the menu for that night. Patty knew how much I loved hotcakes with plenty of butter and syrup. And it didn't take long to prepare the batter.

Patty went into the living room to work on her knitting and I went outside and did some shoveling. I liked to keep the walks clear instead of letting the snow and ice build up. When I was finished, I checked the sleds and tied down their covers. The wind whipped fiercely behind my log home, and I didn't want them to end up in the woods.

From his doghouse Ruben kept an eye on me. With my chores completed, I went over to his run. He came out and bounded toward me. I opened the gate and decided that a little walk would do us both good. I went to the side door and hollered in to Patty that I was taking Ruben for a walk.

"You two be careful," she answered.

"We will, darling."

Making our way to the wood line took longer than usual, as we encountered a couple of sizable snowdrifts. The snow was soft, not yet hardened at the base. Ruben plowed through the drifts with the snow up to his chest. Finally we entered the woods. Three or four large crows perched in the treetops, swaying back and forth. The wind had come up and the crows were apparently enjoying a free ride. I pulled my jacket collar up and buttoned the top button. The cold air seeped under the fabric. I hadn't brought my gloves with me, so I kept my hands deep in my jacket pockets.

The traffic on route 28 could be heard for some distance through the woods. I couldn't see through the trees and over the incline, but I knew that much of the traffic would be vehicles towing their snowmobiles into the region for a week or two of sledding and having a good time.

I was following behind Ruben a short way when a jackrabbit crossed the trail. My K-9's ears went up at attention and he stopped in his tracks momentarily. Suddenly he leaped forward and the chase was on. In a short while he came back to me, breathing hard. The rabbit had made its getaway.

The walk back to the house was slow. The wind had picked up even more, blowing the snow through the frigid air. By the time we reached the porch, we were both weary. I took my boots off and opened the door. Ruben pushed on me and we both squeezed through the door at the same time. He wasn't taking any chances on being left outside.

Patty came out from the living room to help me remove my jacket.

"Honey, is it really cold outside now?" she asked, seeing me shiver.

"Yes, dear. Very cold, and windy, too," I answered.

We embraced and kissed each other. Her soft warm lips felt good pressing against mine.

"Jason, after the lakes freeze, could we do some ice fishing?" she asked.

"Certainly. I'll have to pick up some tip-ups, but that's no problem. Just as soon the ice is safe to walk on, we'll try our luck. I know that Jack Falsey has an auger. I'm sure he'd let me borrow it," I added. "By the way, since when are you interested in ice fishing?"

"Well, some of the fellows at the diner were talking about it, and I thought it would be a good idea for us to try it. We're here for the winter. We might as well make the most of it."

"It's funny you brought it up. I was going to mention it to you. We must be on the same wave-length." I chuckled.

"Oh, we are, Jason," she answered.

About six o'clock, Patty whipped up some buckwheat pancakes and grilled some sausages. She made a fresh pot of coffee and warmed up some of the grade A maple syrup we had purchased from the farmer over on Route 12, out of Boonville.

While Patty was tending to the pancakes and sausage, I proceeded to set the table. The aroma wafting through the kitchen was tempting my taste buds. As usual, I enjoyed following up the pancakes with a glass of ice cold milk. She had made up six pancakes and two sausages apiece. We both sat down at the table and enjoyed our easy-to-prepare supper. Patty loved pancakes, too. No seconds tonight, not with what we had already consumed that day.

After dinner, I helped Patty do the dishes and clean up the

kitchen. When everything was put away, we sat down at the kitchen table to check the envelopes that we were using for our budget. We decided that we would forego the concept of budget envelopes and place our money in joint checking and saving accounts instead. That way we would be able to monitor our spending more accurately, and it would be far safer than having envelopes with money lying around the house. We calculated that by the time the necessary bills were paid, there wasn't a great deal left over for pleasure.

CHAPTER THIRTY-TWO

Tomorrow was Sunday, which we had designated as our time of rest. We had the day off together, so we decided that we would like to clean out our closet area, giving us some much-needed space. After attending church services, we tackled the task in order to take some of our clothes that we no longer wore and other odds and ends to the church for the needy. The church basement provided receptacles, clothes racks, and containers where one could deposit these used but serviceable items. I still recall my dad's words to me as a youngster: "If you ever have anything for the needy, such as clothes, shoes, boots, etcetera, give it to the church or the Salvation Army. There may be a family down on their luck that can put it to good use." I never forgot his advice. I believe dad had two suits when he passed away. One was for his burial, and mom gave the other one away to the needy.

The day passed as we sorted and weeded clothes. We loaded boxes with seldom-used cups, plates, and various duplicates that were crowding the cupboards. It was a long but productive day.

The evening found us in the living room. Patty was knitting and I was trying to clean up a few reports that had accumulated while I had been away. It was approaching 9:30 when the telephone rang.

"I'll get it, honey," I said, wondering who would be calling at this time.

I got up and went into my office to answer the phone.

"Hello, may I help you?" I answered.

"Jason, Chief Wilson here. How have you been?" he asked.

"Todd, so good to hear from you. We've been fine. Just finished a matter up at Lake Placid."

"Yeah! I heard you had something going on involving a Morey Harris."

"That's correct. Why, did you know him?" I asked with surprise.

"I had him as a suspect on some stolen tool cases a couple of years ago. He can be a bad actor, but it is his upbringing that influenced him. It wasn't good, Jason. In fact, it was downright sad. Anyway, that's not what I called you about. Are you sitting down?" he queried.

"Actually I am at my office desk. What's up, Todd?"

"What is the worst possible thing that could happen to our peaceful community?" His voice sounded troubled.

"I can think of several, but what is it?" I coaxed.

"Kenneth Olson, Patty's former husband, came into town today!" he announced.

"Wha…what?" I stammered. "You must be joking." I certainly hoped so.

"You heard me. Jason, we could have problems with this guy."

I knew he was serious from the tone in his voice.

"Where is he staying?" I asked, trying to regain my composure.

"I don't know that yet, but he was asking around town if you and Patty were married and where you lived."

"You've got to be kidding me."

"No, I'm dead serious. My informant told me Olson had booze on his breath and had a mean look on his face. You know how I feel about him. Oh! And he asked my informant who the police chief was. I wasn't happy to hear that, Jason."

Olson held grudges against several of the residents of our community mainly because at the time of his marital problems with Patty, they had quickly sided with her because of his drunken rages and the physical abuse that she had been subjected to during his rampages.

"What's he driving?" I asked.

"The informant tells me that it looks like a 1984 GMC black pickup truck with a small camper on it. It has Arkansas plates and he thinks the number is—let me check—yeah, 2603 KT. He may be staying in the camper, but I don't know. It's pretty cold to sleep in one of those small campers if you don't have proper heating," he added.

"Todd, that's all I need is this guy bothering Patty and myself or, for that matter, anyone else in town. I thought he had gotten himself squared away and had quit his drinking." I could feel myself getting all churned up inside, remembering the tremendous pain he had caused Patty when she was married to him.

"I had heard that, too. But he's here and I don't like it either. I wanted to be certain before I called you. I had one of my officers check around, and he spotted the vehicle in Thendara."

"I appreciate your letting me know. I don't know how Patty will take it, but I'll have to tell her." I did not look forward to informing her.

"Yes, you'll have to. If I were you, Jason, I'd let Lila and John know about it, so they can be prepared in the event he comes into the diner. We'll arrest him and put him in jail if he starts any trouble. He was spotted near the liquor store."

"Thanks for calling," I said sincerely before we hung up.

"I'll stay in touch, Jason."

I was stunned. I sat at my desk seeking answers as to why this miserable person would return to a place that did not appreciate his presence. I knew that I had to share the information with Patty. She'd be so upset! I wondered if he had brought a weapon along with him. Why would he even show his face in this town? I knew one thing: I would be there to protect Patty. She didn't deserve any hassle from Kenneth Olson, her ex-husband.

Working on my reports for the evening immediately ceased after I received Chief Wilson's telephone call. My stomach continued to churn. Olson hadn't returned to the Adirondacks to ski or snowmobile. I was certain that he had other intentions that undoubtedly had something to do with my wife, Patty. I remembered the fracas between Todd and Kenneth Olson at the time he was arrested almost three years ago. Olson had been violent and had kicked out the window on the police car as he was being transported to jail. It was going to be difficult for me to tell Patty, but she had to be aware.

I went back into the living room and sat down next to her. She looked up at me and smiled.

"Honey, I have something to tell you," I said, grasping her hand.

"What's that, Jason? Do you want to tell me you love me?" She looked at me coyly.

"Indeed, I do love you. But this is something else, and it's very important for you to know." My stomach was tight with tension.

"What? What is it, Jason? Tell me." She looked concerned.

"Kenneth Olson is back in town! That was Todd who called. He wanted to let us know." I looked into Patty's face. Tears began to trickle down her cheek.

"Oh, no! What is he doing back here? For what reason?" Patty's voice cracked and the tears kept running down her cheeks.

"I don't know. But we must take extra precautions. You know how he is when he's been drinking." I held her hands tightly.

"How did he get here? Is he alone?" she asked. Her shoulders began to shake.

"Todd said he's driving a black GMC pickup. It has an Arkansas plate and Todd gave me the number. Supposedly it has a small camper on the back. We don't know if he's staying in it. I don't know whether he's alone or not. I'll have to do some further checking." I tried to comfort her.

"Jason, he is dangerous! I'm afraid of him. He beat me up

so many times during his states of drunkenness while we were married. What are we going to do? He'll probably be causing us trouble all over town. He'll be telling everyone that it was all my fault. And what if he tries to see me?" She dried away her tears with a tissue from her pocket.

"We, my dear, will do what we do every day. I'm not too concerned for your safety at work. You know John will not allow intoxicated customers into the diner, but I'll be concerned about you when you drive back and forth to the diner. Patty, if you don't mind, I'll plan on taking you to work and picking you up, at least for a while. Or until we find out what he's up to." I tried to reassure her.

"I'll appreciate that, honey." She tried to smile, but continued to tear up.

"Tomorrow is Monday. I'll drop you off at the diner, and then I'll drive around town and see if I can spot him or his truck. I don't know of any place where he would be welcomed."

"Okay, honey. I'll try not to be so upset. I'm sorry. I know you'll watch out for me."

"Listen, you have a right to be concerned, and so do I. This guy isn't our friend. He doesn't have you to slave for him anymore. You don't have to be sorry, either. You are your own person and, I might say, a wonderful person, too." I reached out and drew her into my arms.

After we held each other for a while, Patty prepared for bed and I returned to my office to call Wilt Chambers to let him know about the return of Olson. Wilt shared my concern.

"Jason, do you want me to come over now? We'll go right out, look for him, and have a little talk with that fella!" I sensed Wilt was getting excited. He'd always watched over Patty like a big brother or a father.

"No, stay put, Wilt. I'm just letting you know, just in case. I have no idea why he's up here, unless it is to give Patty a rough time. I'm not concerned about handling him, but my concern is for Patty's safety." I tried to calm him down.

"I know what you mean. Jason, thanks for calling me. I'll

pass the word and, don't you worry, if he starts his shenanigans up here in the North Country, we'll set him straight. You know. You were in the business. You can't tell a drunk anything, especially when they're intoxicated," he said emphatically.

"True, you cannot. Take care, Wilt."

I looked at my watch and decided to give Dale Rush a quick call, too.

"Hello. Dale Rush speaking," he answered.

"Dale, this is Jason. Guess what? Kenneth Olson is back."

"I heard about it a half-hour ago. He's got a black GMC pickup with a camper on the back and the truck has an Arkansas plate. I knew the chief was going to call you."

"News travels fast, Dale, especially about that guy. I don't have any idea where he is staying. I was told that he was at the liquor store this afternoon," I informed him. "Well, I won't hold you up. Let me know if you hear anything about where he's staying. Thanks, Dale."

"Stay in touch, Jason. I'll talk with you later." He hung up.

I knew that I shouldn't worry so much. Patty had more friends in town than I did. I just didn't want anything to happen to her. I was thankful that we had fresh snow on the ground. If Olson or anyone else came around, there would be footprints. And Ruben would alert us if anybody approached. I looked down at the big fellow. He was lying not on his air mattress, but in the doorway of my office. He must have sensed that something was up. He was on guard. I got up and let him out for his last run of the night. Patty was already in bed.

When Ruben returned, he went directly to his mattress and lay down. I checked all the doors and went to the bathroom to brush my teeth. When I went by the bedroom door, I glanced in. My beautiful wife was sound asleep.

I was careful when I got into bed so as not to disturb her. Our stress levels would certainly be tested with the arrival of Kenneth Olson back to the Adirondack region. I couldn't sleep all night. I rolled and tossed, getting up two or three times. Ruben was restless as well. I finally fell off to sleep about four.

CHAPTER THIRTY-THREE

When I awoke, I sensed the smell of bacon in the air. I looked over to Patty's side of the bed and she wasn't there. She was out in the kitchen preparing breakfast. I pushed the covers back and groggily made my way to the bathroom. I dashed cold water onto my face, then hastily dressed and went out to the kitchen.

"I heard you moving around in the bathroom, Jason. How's my darling this morning?" She looked radiant standing there with a fork in her hand turning the bacon strips that sizzled in the iron frying pan. I had forgotten that she wasn't going in early because she had gone in Saturday morning. I looked at my watch: 7:50. It was great to have Patty at home at this time in the morning.

"That bacon sure smells good. Did you let Ruben out yet?" I asked.

"Yes, dear. He ran into the woods and back and stood by his dog run. So I went out and opened the gate and he went inside. If you'll look out the window, I'm sure you'll see him in the doghouse."

I walked over to the window. I could see his big head peering out of his house. His ears were standing up straight. I looked over at Patty as she cracked three eggs and put them into the iron frying pan. Just as she did, the toaster popped up. The four-slice toaster had been one of our wedding presents. I removed the toast and buttered it. We soon sat down at the table and drank our cold glasses of orange juice. Then we enjoyed our eggs, bacon, toast, and hot coffee. We didn't discuss Ken Olson at the breakfast table. I had no idea why he had come back to town. We discussed generalities, our snowmobiling adventure on Saturday, and the Sunday closet-cleaning project. We carefully avoided the subject of Patty's ex-husband. I got up from the table and refilled our coffee cups.

"Patty, why don't you get ready for work, and I'll do the dishes and clean up the kitchen?" I volunteered.

"Okay, honey. I'll just clear the table." She got up and began to bring the dirty dishes over to me.

I went to the sink and prepared to wash the dishes. I noticed that our liquid detergent was getting low, so added it to our grocery list for the next visit to the store. While Patty was getting dressed, I finished the dishes, put them away, and swept the floor. I quickly surveyed the area, went into the bathroom, and had a hasty shave. I then changed my clothes.

Patty had changed into her uniform. Her blond hair flowed down to her shoulders. She wore very little makeup. She went to the closet and got out our heavier coats. I had previously placed a bag of clothes for the church thrift store in the rear of the Bronco.

I splashed some shaving lotion on my face. I went over to Patty and embraced her, giving her a kiss on the cheek. We helped each other on with our coats and put our winter boots on. The snow on the ground measured about fourteen inches. Except for Ruben's tracks, the ground surrounding our log home was blanketed with untouched white snow. I was certain that there would be some deer tracks closer to the woods. Outside the brisk air felt refreshing to our faces. Ruben came out of his doghouse as I walked to his gate. I let him out and he bounded up onto the porch. I knew he wanted to accompany us, but it would have to be another time. I opened the side door and let him in. It was too cold for him to spend much time outside.

Opening the passenger side door of the Bronco, I helped Patty in. I closed her door and went to the driver's side. The door failed to open.

"Patty, will you push on the door? Apparently it's iced up," I said loudly.

Patty pushed hard from inside the Bronco, and with my pulling on the door from the outside, the door gave way to the combined pressure and opened. I noticed the ridge of ice that had formed along the top.

"Thanks, honey," I said as I entered.

I put the Bronco into four-wheel drive as we started, for the driveway was covered with snow. If it got much higher, I would call Dale to plow it for us. He'd kept my driveway open for years and refused to charge anything for it. But any time we had lunch together, I always tried to pick up his check. *We're fortunate to have him for a friend,* I thought.

The traffic was light going into town. We pulled into the church parking area and found a parking space near the rear door. I exited the vehicle, removing the bag of clothes. I entered the church, took the clothes down the stairs, and placed them on the appropriate table. Patty waited for me at the top of the stairs with a box she had carried in. I removed it from her hands and carried it down the stairs to add to the other contributions.

Back in the Bronco, I noticed that the exhaust system was loud.

"You've had it in the garage so much. Do you think we'll need a new muffler?" Patty asked.

"We'll purchase a new one if we have to," I replied.

We had not mentioned anything about Kenneth Olson since the previous evening. I asked Patty if she would like to drive around town to see if we could find out where he was staying, since she had time before she had to go to work. She agreed.

The year before we had heard that Kenneth was not drinking and was working in the Carolinas, but it now appeared that he was going back to his habit of imbibing alcohol, possibly to excess. I knew one thing: he wouldn't have

Patty to use as a punching bag anymore.

We were more than concerned to learn of his return to the Adirondacks. He had become a nightmare to Chief Wilson when he was drunk and disorderly in town, which had prompted his arrest.

Our search was about exhausted, when we finally spotted the black GMC bearing Arkansas registration parked in a space at one of our local campsites. We took a drive through the park and noticed that there was an electrical cord running from the small camper to an outlet. No one was outside the camper, and we assumed that he might be sleeping off a drinking episode. Patty had firsthand knowledge that when Kenneth imbibed he didn't stop with just one drink. Even as we passed by the camper we knew there was a good possibility that he was lying in there in an intoxicated condition.

There was nothing that Patty nor I could do, except to be cautious and keep our eyes open. Obviously, he knew that we had married. He had a few contacts in the Old Forge region and had been known to exchange letters with them. Rumors had long circulated around town that Olson stayed in touch with his drinking friends. It was fortunate that we had a good watchdog. I decided not to let Patty go anywhere without me for a while, just to be on the safe side. We drove by once more, then turned right out of the campsite and onto Route 28.

We could see snowmobiles moving on the trail system. From Route 28, our observations were somewhat hampered, as the trails went into the areas off the main highway. We went by some of our local motels and snowmobile trailers were in sight everywhere. Some had sleds on them and others were empty.

"Honey, would you care for some hot chocolate? We could stop at John's Diner before you go to work," I asked.

"Jason, I'd love some. But I'm so upset, I think I'll call Lila and tell her that I can't make it in today. She'll understand. Would you mind if we had our hot chocolate at home? I have a box in the pantry," she said. "You know I'm not going to feel secure while Kenneth is in our area. I have too many unpleasant memories from the times that he assaulted me," she said, tearing up.

I pulled the Bronco off the road and stopped. I placed my arm around her, holding her close.

"Don't worry, honey. He's never going to hurt you again, not while I'm alive." I blotted her tears with my handkerchief, and kissed her cheek.

Patty reached into her purse, took out her cell phone, and called Lila, explaining the situation to her. Lila told Patty not to worry, as she understood completely. She would contact one of her relief waitresses to come in.

We decided to stop at the store for the paper, marshmallows, and the liquid soap. Fortunately, there was one newspaper left. Patty and I went up and down the aisles and located the marshmallows, and then the soap. The marshmallows would go well with our hot chocolate. After speaking to a few friends who were doing some shopping, we went out to the Bronco and headed home. I noticed that Patty had composed herself and was more upbeat. We were determined not to let Olson cause us grief—but little did we know what was ahead of us.

When we pulled into the driveway, a large cottontail rabbit hopped out in front of our path. It was a good thing that our dog hadn't seen him. The floppy-eared rabbit stopped behind some brush near the edge of the woods. Seeing the rabbit reminded me of one of my friends in the BCI. He raised domestic ones, killed and skinned them when grown, and sold a few to his friends for food. I had had several of his rabbits. They were tender as chicken when cooked. I had placed them in a pan and covered them with mushroom soup right out of the can. They were delicious. Of course, that's history now, and that particular BCI member has passed away.

Ruben was glad to see us. I let him out and he raced into the woods. The small snowbanks didn't slow him down. When he returned, his coat was covered with crystals and all he wanted to do was frolic in the snow.

"Later, Ruben. Go inside," I said, holding the door open for him. He went directly to his air mattress and lay down. Patty hung her coat in the closet.

"Jason, if you don't mind, I'm going to sit down and knit for the rest of the afternoon. I find it relaxing, and I'd like to finish that sweater by Christmas." She was very dedicated to any undertaking that she pursued.

"That's fine with me, honey. I'll be in the office if you need me." As long as Patty was knitting, I would write some letters to several bad-check passers, offering them the opportunity to correct their mistakes in issuing checks without proper funds from their respective accounts.

I had been in the office less than a half-hour when the telephone rang. I picked up the receiver.

"Hello." No answer. "Hello," I repeated. All I heard was heavy breathing followed by a click.

Patty had heard the telephone ring and shouted in from the living room. "Was that for me, sweetheart?"

"No, it was a hang-up call. Perhaps someone calling the wrong number," I replied. I was suspicious of the call, but didn't want to alarm Patty.

"Oh, I see. Thanks, hon," she called back.

"How are you doing with the knitting?" I inquired.

"It's a slow process, but I'm gaining on it," she replied.

The telephone call hadn't upset me, as we had had several other hang-up calls during the past few months. I continued with my letter writing. I hadn't yet invested in a low-priced computer. I know it would be so much easier than typing on my antiquated typewriter, and we had decided if we budgeted our finances carefully, that would be one of our next purchases. In the meantime I continued to type my letters.

The afternoon passed by rapidly, and Patty told me that we'd have a supper of broiled pork chops, if that was all right with me.

"That sounds good to me, honey. Do you have everything you need?" I inquired.

"I think I do."

I asked Patty if there were anything I could do to assist her in the kitchen.

"You can set the table, dearest, if you like," she replied.

After finishing up filing a few reports, I went to the bathroom and washed my hands. When I came out, Patty had already spread the tablecloth. She had taken the plates out of the cupboard and placed them on the countertop. I picked them up, and set them on the table, along with the napkins, silverware, and coffee cups. Then I filled two tall glasses of ice water and set them by the plates.

Patty came over to me, putting her arms around my shoulders. We kissed.

"Thank you for setting the table," she said, looking up into my eyes.

"We are a team, Patty," I told her as she gently pulled away to return to the stove.

"You know, honey, these pork chops are so lean. I easily finished trimming the fat off," she said as she placed them on the broiler.

I noticed she had already put foil-wrapped potatoes, along with a couple of sweet potatoes, in the countertop toaster-oven to bake. Two salads were chilling in the refrigerator. She had been a busy girl.

While Patty was preparing our evening meal, I let Ruben out for a quick run into the woods. I noticed that when he returned, he was especially eager to come inside. Ruben was smart. His shortness of breath told me that he had traveled through some deep snow. The temperatures were dipping low. He immediately went to his air mattress and lay down.

Although I said nothing aloud, I wondered if the recent telephone hang-up calls were just mistakes in dialing or actually Ken Olson attempting to talk with Patty. The mystery of the heavy-breathing call made me wonder if Olson were on the other end of the phone line, possibly in an intoxicated stupor. I wondered if Patty were trying to hide her nervousness about that possibility.

I walked back into the kitchen as she was removing the broiled pork chops to a heated plate. She had already placed the white potatoes, the sweet potatoes, and the applesauce on the table along with the butter and sour cream. The smell of fresh-perked coffee permeated the room.

We thoroughly enjoyed our meal. I tried to limit myself to one chop, but they were so delicious, I had a second. Dinner, as usual, was a treat.

When we finished, I told Patty to go into the living room and rest for a while, as I would take care of the dishes and the cleaning of the kitchen.

"Oh, honey, I'll help you with the dishes," she offered.

"No, no. You rest. It won't take me long to do up a few dishes," I countered.

"Okay, if you insist," she retorted, kissing me on the cheek.

She disappeared into the living room. I knew she would take up her knitting again.

The kitchen was back in order in less than an hour. I put the dishes away and swept the floor, noting that soon I would have to wash and wax the tiles. We always tried to remove our shoes by the side door to avoid tracking dirt in. Of course, this rule didn't apply to Ruben. Occasionally, we would take a towel and wipe off his paws, especially if it were muddy outside.

Patty continued with her sweater and I went into my office to finish up my bookwork. There had been a considerable number of bad checks over the recent months. I was just beginning to make an entry into my casebook when the telephone rang. I picked up the receiver.

"Hello," I answered. Nothing. "Hello?" I repeated.

There was definitely someone on the other end of the line. I heard breathing as before, then the click. This time, I had no sooner hung up the receiver than it rang again. I decided to let it ring and have the caller leave a message on my answering machine. I listened intently. A clicking sound but no voice came on the machine. This annoyed me. If someone wanted something, they should have spoken. I couldn't help but feel that it was Kenneth Olson, back in Old Forge, endeavoring to talk with Patty.

CHAPTER THIRTY-FOUR

During the next few days, the telephone calls persisted, with several hang-ups on our answering machine. We contacted the telephone company and they advised that if the calls persisted, they would install a locking device on our line.

A week went by and the telephone calls received at our home tapered down to one hang-up call a day. Patty learned that Kenneth had been spotted in his GMC pickup parked on the street near the real estate office across the road from the diner. We both suspected that he was not coming into the diner because he didn't want to confront our police chief, Todd Wilson. To me, it appeared that Olson was stalking Patty. When I dropped her off for work and when I picked her up, we observed Olson several times sitting in his truck in the parking lot. Not knowing if Olson was intoxicated, I hesitated to approach him. In the meantime my telephone calls to Wilt, Dale, and Jack Falsey revealed there were several sightings of Olson in the vicinity of John's Diner.

I did learn from Chief Wilson that Olson had left the campsite south of Old Forge and was living in his small camper anywhere he could park it. We received information that he had made purchases at the grocery store. The chief also advised me that Olson had obtained a camping kerosene heater that he must be using when he wasn't hooked up to an electrical outlet.

From my experience as a former law enforcement officer, I was well aware that an overt act had to take place before a criminal action could be considered. Rumor had it that when Olson left Old Forge for the south he had had intentions of cleaning up his act and had joined Alcoholics Anonymous to combat his drinking problem. But it was apparent that he was back to his old tricks. When sober, he was a reasonable person, but under the influence of alcohol he had a complete personality change. Patty had frequently been the recipient of both his mental and physical abuse. Not knowing what his intentions were, naturally we were on edge. I stayed in touch with the police chief on a daily basis and continued to be with Patty as much as possible.

One afternoon after I picked her up, at the beginning of the second week of taking her to and from work, instead of going right home we decided to stop by Drew's Restaurant, north of Inlet, for one of chef Michael's famous cheeseburgers. We stayed there about an hour and a half. On the way out, we spoke to Mike. The bar was full of locals on their way home for dinner.

I helped Patty into the Bronco and, as I was going around to get in, I spotted the old black GMC pickup with the homemade camper on the back. I couldn't see who was driving, but felt it had to be Olson. The flapping Arkansas license plate was in plain view. He was driving slowly, headed in a northerly direction. He rounded the slight curve in front of Drew's. The GMC backfired. It sounded like a shotgun going off. I watched until he went out of sight, then went to the driver's door and got in behind the steering wheel.

"It was him, I'm sure, Patty, headed north in his old camper," I said. Her eyes began to tear up. "Don't cry, honey. Everything will be all right. I promise."

"Jason, I know I'll be okay as long as I'm with you. But for God's sake, what is he up to?" She dried her eyes with a tissue from the glove compartment.

"Maybe he just wants to talk to you. Or maybe he wants to harm you, or both of us, in some way. I don't think we should try to approach him until we determine what his intentions are. Who knows? I don't." I could feel my blood pressure rising. It was a situation where we just had to wait and see. I believed his presence was definitely a form of harassment. It was obvious that he was up to something or he wouldn't have returned to the region where he was widely disliked. Winter was no time to be living in a camper of that kind. He surely was roughing it.

It was beginning to snow lightly as we pulled into our driveway. Ruben was jumping up and down in his dog run. I noticed a set of tire tracks that had not been there when I'd left to pick up Patty. Our K-9 seemed unusually over-excited. I stopped the Bronco immediately and we got out. I told Patty that there was a possibility that Wilt Chambers had stopped by, but then I saw that the tracks weren't large enough to be Wilt's big Dodge truck.

"What the--!" Two tires on Patty's Jeep were flat, the left front and the right rear. I gave a closer look. There seemed to be cuts on each of the tires. I looked over at Patty. Her tears broke loose again. I went to her.

"Honey, don't cry." I held her close to my chest as she sobbed. I walked into the house and took her to the living room. She sat down on the couch, holding her head in her hands. My heart ached for her.

Obviously we had had a malicious visitor while we were out. Kenneth Olson immediately became the suspect at the top of my list. After I made sure that Patty was resting as comfortably as possible, I dialed the telephone for the police.

"Town of Webb Police Department. May I help you?" Todd Wilson answered the phone.

"Chief, could you come to the house? I believe we have a problem."

"I'll be right there."

Todd didn't ask me what the problem was. He knew I wouldn't call unless it was important.

In a matter of a few minutes, Todd's police car pulled into our yard. Ruben gave him a greeting with a couple of loud barks. I immediately put my jacket back on and went out to greet him.

The chief, a tall man with a keen perception of people, got out of his car and came toward me.

"What's up, Jason?' he asked.

"Todd, it would appear that we had a visitor while we were gone. Two tires on Patty's Jeep are flat. It looks to me like someone used a knife or an ice-pick." I pointed down to the flattened tires as I walked Todd over to the Jeep. He kneeled down to examine them.

"I can see where the cuts were made, Jason." He looked up at me.

Both of us were sure that the criminal mischief perpetrated on the Jeep's tires was undoubtedly Olson's, but to prove it in a court of law would be difficult. The chief spent considerable time looking at the undistinguishable tire tracks in the yard. Ruben was the only one that knew who the perpetrator was, and he couldn't tell us.

"Wish you could talk, Ruben," the chief said. Ruben barked hopefully.

"Chief, I appreciate your stopping by. I'm fuming over this. Patty's overwrought. And, of course tires are expensive." I shook my head in exasperation.

"I understand, Jason. But you know as well as I do that unless we have a witness or some other evidence, there is very little we can do. Possibly we might pick up some information, especially if the perpetrator shoots his mouth off in a bar. If the suspect is Olson and if he's intoxicated, I know from past dealings with him, that he'll be out in the bars telling everybody. I have a couple of snitches who frequent the local establishments. I'll put some feelers out and see what we can come up with," he reassured me.

"Thanks, chief. We'll be grateful." I was getting distraught over this incident.

Chief Wilson finished making out his report and told me that he would get back to us if any information was developed. Our hamlet of Old Forge is just small enough that it doesn't take long before gossip ferments—and not just Old Forge, but any small town where information between people is exchanged, whether it be at the laundromat, gas station, grocery store, beauty or a barber shop. This phenomenon can be good for a community. In the event suspicious individuals come around with bad intent, sometimes police departments can suppress the undesirable situation before the crime is actually committed.

I took Ruben into the house. "Patty, you and Ruben stay inside. I'm going to take a look around town just to see if I can spot Olson," I advised her.

"Honey, do you think that is wise? Chief Wilson is working on the case. I don't think you should." It was clear she feared for my safety.

"You've got a good point, Patty, but I'm just going to drive around town for a while. Maybe I'll cool off. I'm quite upset to think that someone would come on to our property and slit your tires." I was visibly upset.

"I know. I know, Jason. You're right, I'm upset myself. You be careful, dear," she cautioned.

"I will, sweetheart," I said, reaching over to kiss her on the cheek.

I made certain that Patty and Ruben were safely locked in the log home before I left, with all curtains drawn. It was no telling what Olson would do, especially if he learned that Patty was alone. Thank goodness for Ruben; Olson would never make it through the front door without confronting the big K-9.

The four-wheel drive on the Bronco worked well. The highway was becoming slippery from the dip in the temperatures. Supposedly it would be going down to the low twenties the next morning. As I drove into Old Forge, I wondered where Olson was. Checking streets and parking lots failed to reveal the older model GMC with the makeshift camper on top.

I swung over by O'Brien's Marina, which was open only for the portion that had been converted into snowmobile sales and service. I had heard that Dale Rush's betrothed had left to go to Boston to visit her brother concerning business. I was surprised to see several cars before me in the parking lot. There was Wilt's big white Dodge pickup, Charlie Perkins' Ford pickup, Jack Falsey's maroon van, Dale's SUV, and Jim Jenny's Ranchero pulled in beside Wilt's. I turned my engine off, got out, and walked to the entrance.

I hadn't seen much of my friends since I had told them about Olson being back in town. As I approached the door, I heard Wilt's voice. When I entered, they all looked up, surprised to see me standing there as they leant over a new snowmobile. Wilt spoke first.

"Jason, what the heck are you doing here? You mean to tell us that you left Patty alone? Is everything okay?" Wilt asked dubiously.

"Hi, fellas. Yes, Wilt. Patty let me out for a little while. But seriously, we have had an unwelcome guest come onto our property." They all anxiously waited for me to continue.

"What do you mean, Jason?" Charlie asked.

"Someone came on our property and slit two tires on Patty's Jeep." I looked at Wilt. I immediately observed his face turn crimson.

"What? Jason!" Wilt doubled up his fist. "Who was it, Jason?"

"We don't know for certain, but I believe it was Olson. Chief Wilson came over and took a report. The only thing we observed were the tire tracks. The right rear apparently had very little tread on it, and there were some oil spots on the white snow."

Wilt spoke. "That son-of-a -----! I've spotted him twice up by the high school. What are you going to do about it, Jason?" Wilt's face was contorted with anger.

"Nothing at this time. We really have nothing that we can go on," I said dejectedly. My friends circled around me in the workshop offering any assistance they could render. I continued, "Fellows, if you do see Olson around the area, make a note of where you saw him. If any of you hear any scuttlebutt about the two tires, let me or Chief Wilson know right away.

There's a good possibility that Olson may be driving while intoxicated at times, so we may be able to get him on a DWI charge. When he's imbibing, he's a real wild man. I have no idea if he has a firearm on him or secreted in his camper."

My friends listened carefully. They acknowledged that they would keep their eyes peeled for him.

I told them that I would have Doctor Don come down to the house with two good used tires to mount on the Jeep. Whoever did it had sliced the tires just below the top of the tread. They couldn't be repaired. In my heart, I knew it had to be Olson.

I learned from talking with them that Charlie Perkins was in the process of purchasing two used snowmobiles for his two oldest children and that all the fellows had volunteered to assist Dale and Jim Jenny in getting them in shape for the snowmobile trails. These were the first two sleds that Charlie had ever purchased. I was very happy that he was getting them for his kids. Of course, knowing Charlie as I did, I was certain he would have to test them out first before he let his offspring hit the trail system.

I gave Patty a quick telephone call so she wouldn't be worried. She was surprised to learn where I was. She told me that she had made a large pot of chili and if I wanted to invite the fellows over for a bowl, I could. I thanked her, told her that I loved her, and assured her that I would be home soon.

"Fellows, how would you like to join Patty and me for a cup of hot chili?"

A hush fell over the group. After a brief discussion, they agreed that they would love to join us if it wasn't too much of an inconvenience. I called Patty to let her know they had accepted her generous invitation.

Dale Rush and Jim Jenny finished adjusting the track on one of Charlie Perkins' sleds and then went over to the sink and washed their hands. Instead of all the fellows following me to the log home, I suggested that Wilt and Charlie drive Wilt's Dodge and Jim Jenny, Dale, and Jack Falsey could ride with me in the Bronco. I told Wilt that I'd be right along after I stopped at the grocery store to pick up several loaves of their delicious Italian bread.

We pulled into the parking lot of our supermarket. Dale and I went into the store. Fortunately there were five loaves of fresh Italian bread near the deli. Dale grabbed three of them and I picked up the remaining two. When we were walking toward the checkout counter, Dale pushed me aside and insisted that he was paying for the bread.

"Jason, it's only fair that I chip in," he said firmly.

Knowing how proud he was to have beaten me to the checkout counter, I didn't argue with his offer.

When we reached the log home, Wilt had already turned his big Dodge around and parked it near Patty's Jeep. Both Wilt and Charlie had gone inside. I parked next to the Dodge. We got out of the Bronco. Dale took all five loaves of bread into the house and we followed him. Inside, Wilt was helping Patty finish setting the table after they had put the two leaves in to give us plenty of room.

Each of our friends gave Patty a hug and thanked her for the invitation. The room was fragrant with the smell of the freshly prepared chili. Dale took the bread out of two of the paper sacks after washing his hands for cutting it with our only bread knife. To complement the chili, Patty had opened up a big bottle of red wine and had cooked up some hot dogs in the event someone would like to make a chilidog. She had also opened a large jar of dill pickles.

In about ten minutes, the seven of us were seated around our extended kitchen table enjoying Patty's hot chili. Jim Jenny and Jack Falsey made up a chilidog apiece. Patty offered them grilled hot dog rolls. The two men tried to bite into the chilidogs, but finally gave in to using a knife and fork. Some of the fellows had a glass of wine, while others preferred hot coffee or a cold beer. There was plenty of ice water in pitchers on each side of the table. Our conversation included everything from Charlie's newly purchased sleds to the unfortunate return of Ken Olson and the cutting of Patty's tires on her Jeep.

Jim Jenny related to us a recent event that involved J. R.

Risley assisting a snowmobiler who had fractured his leg while falling off his snowmobile. Someone in the group had had a cell phone and had called J.R. to see if he could fly into one of the remote lakes to transport the injured sled operator to Old Forge. Jim went on to say that J.R.'s airplane, a Cessna 172, had skis mounted on it. We all held our breath when Jim indicated that J.R.'s plane had momentarily stalled out, but that he had been able to restart the engine. I knew that if anyone could restart an engine, it would be J.R. Jim indicated that J.R. and his passenger were two lucky people. We were overjoyed to hear the rescue was successful. We all agreed that J.R. was a hero that day.

The conversation turned again to Olson's return to Old Forge, with assurance from the fellows at the table that they would keep an eye out for him. It was about ten o'clock when everybody thanked Patty for her hospitality and I took them back over to the marina to pick up their vehicles. Before Wilt and Charlie left, they helped clear the table and offered to do the dishes.

After I let my passengers out, I took a drive around town just to see if I could spot Olson or his camper. There was no sign of him at any of the drinking establishments. I knew we'd be hearing about Olson in the not too distant future. I wasn't the only one with that certainty. Chief Todd Wilson would be keeping a lookout, too, after his several unpleasant encounters with him in the past. Clearly the rehab that Olson had been involved with had been unsuccessful. Part of his return to the Adirondacks was to harass Patty and, of course, I was now in the equation. I knew that Chief Wilson was concerned for the safety of the entire community and especially for Patty, based on the prior encounters he had had with Kenneth Olson.

I continued taking Patty to work and picking her up at night. One Friday afternoon, Patty and I thought we saw Olson's GMC camper near the entrance to our driveway; however, it was snowing so hard that we couldn't be positive. I did call Chief Wilson to alert him of our suspicion.

I received a telephone call from Tom Huston early on

Saturday morning. He told me that Lieutenant Jack Doyle had stopped by the Breakshire Lodge with the news that the judge involved with the Morey Harris case had ordered psychological counseling for him and that, during the counseling period, he would be assigned to a group home under close supervision. Tom seemed pleased with the outcome. Our phone conversation ended when Tom told me he had another call waiting for him, but we agreed to get together in the near future to discuss the case further.

With Patty's work schedule at John's Diner and my pursuit of bad-check artists, we didn't find a great deal of free time to snowmobile. Patty did paint some scenes of mountains and trees in watercolor. She was pleased with her endeavors, and so was I. We learned she had had a hidden talent that now found its way out onto the canvas. One of her customers was a local artist, who willingly shared with her some valuable knowledge on how to brush the watercolors for the proper effect, especially when it came to the shading of the trees on the mountaintops.

Just before Christmas week we did find time to activate our snowmobiles. When I went to take the covers off the sleds, a medium-sized snowshoe hare jumped out from under the engine cowling, taking me by surprise. It hopped off toward the woods. Ruben would have given eager chase, but the gate on the dog run was closed.

I started both sleds with some effort and gave each a short run around the yard. Both were full of fuel. I went into the house and asked Patty if she were ready to go snowmobiling for a while.

"Honey, almost, but I'd like to finish this row on my knitting. I'll dress in a few minutes. Is that okay with you, Sherlock?" Her voice sounded gleeful over the prospect of sledding. She gave me a big smile.

"Okay, babe. I'll put on my suit and then go hook up the trailer," I told her.

When I finished dressing, I went outside and let Ruben go for a quick run into the woods. The wind had been active in the small field to the side of our property. I watched Ruben take the drifts one at a time. I was amazed at his agility as he leaped over an especially large wave of snow.

When he returned, I put him into the house. He went directly to his air mattress and lay down. The big K-9 was breathing heavily. His coat emitted a strong smell.

Patty had heard me come in.

"I'm just about ready, Jason!" she called out from the bedroom.

"I'll meet you outside. This suit is warm," I commented.

"You're always warm, Sherlock. Quit complaining!" she joshed.

In twenty minutes we had left our driveway and were headed to Eagle Bay. We had decided to meet some of the locals over on Big Moose Road. It didn't take too long to drive to the Hard Times Café parking lot. Lisa, the owner of the café, had given us permission to park in their lot anytime we wanted to. I pulled into the backside of the parking area and we both got out to unload the sleds. I proceeded to start Patty's sled. I could tell that she was eager to get on.

"Jason, do you mind if I start out?" she coaxed.

"No, not at all. Just be careful on the shoulder of the highway." Big Moose Road was not a very wide highway. I told her that I would catch up with her shortly. The parking area had several other sleds being taken off their trailers. I recognized some of the faces of the local snowmobile operators.

My sled started up and I prepared to climb onto it. I slid my goggles down over my eyes. Suddenly I was slammed to the ground with such force that I couldn't catch my breath. Then a kick struck my shoulder, just missing my face. The goggles twisted lopsided on my face, making it difficult for me to see out of the plastic lens.

A woman screamed out, "What are you doing to that man?" Then she shouted, "Get off that sled! That's not yours!"

I then heard what I believed to be my sled take off out of the parking lot. In my disorientation I felt the presence of several people gathering around to help me. My shoulder ached fiercely and my head was throbbing.

I heard the woman's voice again. "Are you all right?" she asked. "I saw this large man knock you down and then he jumped on your sled and rode away toward Big Moose road."

I ripped off my helmet and goggles and struggled to get up. Two men helped to assist me to my feet. One of them said, "Do you know the person that knocked you down? I was standing near my car and I saw him strike you from behind. Then I saw him kick you violently."

I could feel my senses returning. My shoulder felt almost dislocated. But my thoughts were all for Patty by herself out on the road. A sudden sure knowledge filled me: my assailant must have been Kenneth Olson! And now he was following Patty.

The lady I had heard in the beginning came toward me. "Sir, if you want, you can borrow my sled to go after that man. I saw the whole incident. My name is Lillian Baldwin," she offered. "Can you ride with that shoulder?"

I identified myself to the woman and thanked her, assuring her I felt capable of driving. I asked her to go inside and call the police. I told her I would gladly use the sled and take full responsibility. She told me she'd wait at the Hard Times for my return. I thanked her, and climbed onto her Arctic Cat, ignoring the burning pain in my shoulder. Time disappeared, as I accelerated the snowmobile. I pushed the sled to the limit. It was a fast sled.

My whole focus was Patty and her safety. I had always tried to keep a cool head during any time of turmoil or action, but now I could feel the agitation in my heart and soul. When I rounded a curve about a mile from Eagle Bay, I saw them: two sleds parked at the side of the road, with a man holding on to a woman near the shoulder of Big Moose Road. I knew even before I got closer that it was Patty and her former husband, Kenneth Olson. When I pulled up, next to me was my wife's helmet lying on the ground. She turned to me and all concern for my own injuries disappeared when I saw her swollen, discolored eye. My instinct said *kill,* but I fought to keep control of my emotions. In my capacity as a trooper I had responded to so many domestic-violence calls, always believing a man should never strike a woman, no matter what—and now here was my beloved wife, abused by a man right before my eyes!

I immediately slammed the sled to a stop, jumped off, and started toward Olson. I called upon my military training and that of the troopers. Patty in her turmoil finally realized it was me who had gotten off the strange sled. Deliberately keeping my voice calm and staring steadily at Olson, I told her to walk down the road and get away from this immediate area and try to summon help.

Olson had already started cursing me and menacing me physically. He was well built weighing about two hundred pounds. My adrenaline was running high and I was sharply alert. Olson appeared to be emotionally unhinged, possibly intoxicated.

He began to circle me, arms and fists poised. I knew I had to take some direct action. The stances of bullies were not new to me. This coward that had struck my wife would understand shortly that if I had anything to do with it, he would never assault anyone again.

Olson was wearing a heavy coat, blue denims, and a wool hat pulled down over his ears. For a moment I felt like a bullfighter. That's when I saw the shining blade of a hunting knife, which he held in his right hand. Olson finally made his move and lunged toward me with his arms straight out in a slashing motion. Although my shoulder was burning from his vicious kicks, I sidestepped hastily, turning sideways and giving his right leg a downward kick just above the knee. The knife flew out of his hand into a snow bank. His two hundred pounds went down. He howled like a wounded wolf, cursing me out.

"You broke my leg, you -----------!" he screamed out in pain.

While Olson was hollering as he lay crumpled on the

ground I rushed toward Patty, who had stayed nearby instead of going for help, not wanting to leave me.

"Honey, did he hurt you?" she asked. Her face was smeared with tears.

"I'm okay, sweetheart. It's you I'm worried about." As we embraced, I heard a siren. I was relieved to hear it. Who knows what else I might have done to Olson?

Our assailant must have heard it, too, I realized. I turned from Patty to look back at him. I couldn't believe what I saw. He had dragged himself to Patty's sled, which was still running and hauled himself up on to the Ski-Doo. As the Town of Webb PD cruiser pulled up, Olson took off through the woods.

As I held my beaten wife in my arms, I was glad to see Chief Wilson. He quickly exited his cruiser and rushed over to Patty and me.

"Patty, your eye is black. Did Olson do this to you?" Todd asked in a harsh voice.

I placed my arm around my wife's shoulder as she began to cry. Todd urged Patty to get into his car to keep warm. I opened the door for her to sit in the front passenger side. I immediately informed the chief how Olson had come toward me with a hunting knife, attempting to stab me. In our scuffle, somehow the knife had fallen into a snow bank. I pointed to the general vicinity where I felt it could have landed. The chief walked over to the area, and after a brief search, had located the knife, which he secured as evidence.

A crowd of snowmobilers from the area were gathering and several of the men asked if they could assist in any way. Todd knew two of the fellows and asked them to stand by the car with Patty. One of the wives rushed over to Patty, placing her arm around her shoulders and comforted her.

I assured Patty that the chief and I were going to take off after Olson on the remaining snowmobiles. Todd quickly opened his trunk, and took out a heavy parka, and put it on, along with a pair of leather gloves. He then radioed for backup. I had both of the sleds started. Before we started I went over to Patty to check on her. One of Todd's associates had thoughtfully poured her a cup of hot chocolate from a thermos. She seemed a bit calmer as she sat sipping it, but was still in a state of shock. I kissed her tenderly on the cheek and told her how much I loved her and returned to the snowmobile that I had borrowed, while Todd mounted my Ski-Doo. He led the way and I was right behind him. From the erratic trail I could see that Olson had no sense of direction. It did appear that he was vaguely headed toward Big Moose Lake.

Todd slowed down to permit a sled to pass by. He stopped and asked the operator if he had seen a Ski-Doo on the trail. The young man told Todd that he had observed a sled traveling too fast for the terrain. His description of the sled operator, especially with the detail that the fellow looked as though he were in pain or were ill, left no doubt that it was Kenneth Olson fleeing from the area. The chief thanked the young man and we continued toward the lake.

When we came to the south side of the lake we observed the snowmobile tracks leading onto its surface. Very clearly, Olson had thoughtlessly driven to an area where the ice was thin and broken through. His ratty wool hat lay on the ice, apparently jerked from his head by a shard. He and the sled had gone into the lake. There was no sign of life.

"Jason, will you stand by here while I go for assistance?" Todd asked grimly.

My emotions were a raging conflict, but I managed to say, "Yes, I will. But Todd, will you please be sure to have someone drive Patty to the medical center for a check-up right away? Oh, and when Olson stole my sled in Eagle Bay a Lillian Baldwin let me borrow hers to pursue him. Could you have one of your officers stop at the Hard Times to tell her what happened and that I will return the sled as soon as possible?"

"I'll take care of that, Jason. And I'll try to get back as soon as I can. I'll take the Baldwin snowmobile and return it to her, with your thanks," Todd offered.

"That's a good idea. Tell her I'll be in touch with her to thank her personally."

"Will do." Underneath our seemingly calm conversation I could tell that Todd, too, was feeling painful conflict over Olson's demise. We both knew his body must be in the lake, as there were no footprints in the snow or near the point of entry. It was strange to feel my shoulder still aching from the kicks he had administered to my arm and upper body.

This situation was troublesome for everybody concerned. Even with my intense animosity towards Olson for the way he'd treated Patty, I still felt saddened that he had ended his life this way. I've always been a firm believer that everyone has good in them. In his case, it probably was an addiction to alcohol that had so darkly affected his behavior. Patty had certainly suffered from it in the past and now again today. I was worried about her, but knew I could count on Todd to make certain she went to the medical center.

It was so cold near the lake that even in the snowmobile suit I felt frozen. I stayed there almost an hour, walking around for better blood circulation, before Todd returned with the coroner and several officers. One of the men was a diver already suited up to enter the frigid water. Todd approached me.

"Jason, there is really no reason for you to have to be here any more. I'll take a statement from you tomorrow. The sled has been returned to Lillian Baldwin and Patty is presently at the medical center. She's okay, but I bet she'd like you with her. I talked to a few people at the Hard Times who witnessed Olson's attack on you. They told me that he kicked you about three times. Before any of them could grab Olson, he took off on your sled."

I nodded. "That sounds about right to me. My shoulder does hurt. But you know I'll be glad to stay around, if you want me to," I said.

"No, you go ahead. You'd better get that shoulder looked at, too. We'll take care of Patty's sled; we have to impound it until my investigation is completed," he advised me.

"I understand," I replied. "And please keep in mind that I'm willing to talk to any second of kin, if necessary."

Chief Wilson and I were very much aware of the heartache that family members experience over the loss of a loved one, no matter what behavior patterns they had. I personally wasn't aware of any relatives of Olson. All I knew was that he had been wed to Patty and had physically assaulted her during their married years. However, I did feel sad that a fellow human had lost his life.

I had just mounted my Ski-Doo when I observed the diver being assisted by two other officers in the retrieval of Olson's body. I knew that Patty would feel sad over his death, for they had fallen in love when they were young. According to Patty, it had been a good marriage until Kenneth started to drink alcoholic beverages to excess. After only a few years, their marriage had ended in painful divorce. The chief and I knew firsthand how Patty had been treated by him.

When I got back out to Big Moose Road, cars were lined up on the shoulder along with dozens of snowmobiles. I stopped for a moment, and several people fired questions at me. I told them that Chief Wilson would be making a statement later on in the day. I continued on toward Eagle Bay.

When I got to the Hard Times parking area, I loaded my machine onto the trailer with help from some snowmobilers. They secured it for me. I went into the café and called the medical center. They told me that Patty was fine and would meet me in the waiting room. I didn't mention anything about the death of Olson. I wanted to tell Patty myself, so I'd be there to comfort her.

I talked briefly with the owner of the Hard Times. Lisa shared information with me about Lillian Baldwin and the concern that Lillian had shown about my being assaulted and kicked so brutally.

"Lisa, I'll heal. But it is difficult to understand why some people commit such violent acts." I shook my head in disbelief.

"Jason, you were in the law enforcement business and you've seen a lot, but I feel that society has taken a drastic change since our grandparents' era, or maybe even our own parents' era."

We lamented over the violence one can view on television any day of the week. Then I ended our discussion, for I knew that Patty would be anxiously awaiting my arrival. On the way to Old Forge, I stopped by our log home and unhooked the trailer. I let Ruben out of the house for a short run, then I put him back inside. While I was there I decided to quickly change my clothes as my snowmobile suit was wet and uncomfortable. Then I headed to the medical center. The ache in my shoulder was quite bothersome. I knew it must be deeply bruised.

The medical center was busy. I had to park the Bronco on the far side of the building. I got out and went inside. Patty and Harriet, her former landlady, were sitting just inside the doorway of the waiting area. Patty got up from her chair when I entered. I gave her a hug and a careful kiss on the cheek; I knew her face must still be tender. Anxious to know what had happened, she started to ask me some questions.

"Honey, I'll tell you all about it on the way home." I turned to Harriet. "Thank you so much for being here for Patty. We both appreciate it."

"No problem, Jason. I'm glad I could help. But I do have plans for dinner tonight, so I'd best be on my way now that you're here. Call me if you need any help in the future," she said, while warmly embracing Patty.

We said our goodbyes and she hurriedly left.

I seated Patty again, then went up to the nurse's station. People were waiting their turn to see one of the doctors, and several nodded to me. I told the nurse that I needed to have a doctor take a look at my shoulder. She handed me a paper to fill out. Patty motioned to me and indicated that she'd make out the sheet. When she had completed it, I looked it over, signed it, and returned it to the nurse.

We waited in the lobby until the nurse beckoned for me to go to the doctor's area. Patty accompanied me. It wasn't long before the doctor was ready to see us. I asked him if Patty could join me. He told us both to come into his office, then asked me what my complaint was.

"Doctor, I was jumped and pushed to the ground, then

kicked with a heavy boot two or three times. This occurred about two or three hours ago." I explained to the doctor where the pain was generating. I removed my shirt and the doctor examined the area on the shoulder and down the arm to the triceps muscle. He did indeed find a bad bruise. He had me lift my arm straight up. It was tender, but movable.

"Jason, you're lucky. You must have had a good jacket on or the damage would be more severe. Try to rest it. It wouldn't be a bad idea to use a sling on your arm for a while. I think you're going to survive just fine, Jason," he pronounced, jesting a little. I thanked the doctor and, after a short conversation regarding the details of the skirmish, Patty and I left the office.

I had avoided mentioning anything about the tragedy involving Olson to the doctor in front of Patty. The news would be around town fast enough.

I assisted my wife into the front passenger seat of the Bronco. On the drive home, I looked over at Patty and again told her how sorry I was that Olson had assaulted her. The black eye was puffy underneath and there was a slight laceration just above her cheekbone. I didn't go into detail on what happened prior to my arrival on Big Moose Road. She was suffering enough.

"Jason, were you and Todd able to catch Kenneth?" she asked in a low voice.

I thought carefully before speaking. "Yes, honey, we did find him. Remember how Todd and I took the snowmobiles and went into the woods after him? When we reached the southern end of the lake, we found an area where thin ice covering the lake had broken through. Kenneth's wool hat was lying on the ice that was still intact." I paused, choosing my words, "He's not with us any more, honey. He drowned when your sled broke through the ice and went into the lake. Probably that heavy coat and the boots he was wearing became waterlogged and he was unable to swim."

Patty began to sob. "Honey, I--I did--didn't love him anymore, but I didn't want to see any harm come to him. You know he was his own worst enemy." She pulled a tissue from her pocket to wipe away the tears that were flowing down her cheeks.

"Yes, dear. I know. I didn't either." We were both silent the rest of the way home.

When we arrived home I helped Patty out of the Bronco and we went inside. Ruben must have surmised that there was a problem. He came over and rubbed up against us. His tail wagged slowly back and forth. We patted his head to comfort him.

"It's all right, Ruben. Everything's all right." I continued to stroke his head.

After I rigged up a sling for my arm, it was time to call Lila at the diner to inform her of the sad events. Patty's black eye needed care, and she wouldn't be in to work for a few days. But when I reached Lila, it was clear that the news must have already gotten around town, for she seemed to know all about it.

"Jason, if there is anything John or I can do, please let us know. Just a few minutes ago I sent one of the local customers, Louis Holt, over to your place with a quart of potato soup. Patty knows him. He should be there any minute. Is she okay?" Lila sounded very concerned.

"Lila, she's got a bad shiner. Olson struck her in the eye," I said.

"All I heard, Jason, is that he went through the ice on Big Moose Lake. Is that right?" she asked hesitantly.

"You heard correctly. He's gone. I'll talk to you and John later to fill you in on all the details."

"Call us if you need anything, Jason," she offered. "I mean it."

"Thanks, Lila." I didn't tell Lila about my skirmish with Olson and what he had done to me. It was Patty I was most concerned about.

I had Patty go into the bedroom and lie down on the bed. I covered her with a blanket. I went out to the kitchen and made up an ice pack to apply to her swollen eye. I told her to let me know if she wanted an aspirin for the pain, but she said she would let me know if she felt the need. I lovingly kissed her on the cheek.

"I'll get supper tonight, sweetheart," I said. "You just take the day to rest."

"What will you fix, Jason? You'll have to take something out of the freezer."

"Don't worry, honey. I thought I told you, Lila's sending some soup."

Louis Holt arrived shortly after I had settled Patty in bed. He was a mature man with snow-white hair and deep-set blue eyes. Ruben let out a bark.

He introduced himself after I opened the door, then handed me the container of potato soup. I asked him if he would like to come in.

"No, sir. I have some errands to run. I hope Patty's all right. Give her my best," he responded.

"I certainly will, Mr. Holt. Thank you for bringing the soup to us. It is most appreciated." I extended my hand to shake his. He said goodbye and left the porch for his vehicle.

"Patty, would you like a bowl of Lila's potato soup? It looks great!" I called in.

"I'd love some. I'll be right out, dearest. I'll just wash my hands."

I went to the cupboard for two bowls and set them on the table. I lit the burner, poured the contents of the container into a pan, and heated it. I located some oyster crackers in our small pantry and placed them on the table, along with the silverware and napkins.

"Jason, you're a dear to wait on me like this," she said.

"How's your eye feeling?" I asked.

"It's sore, but hopefully it'll heal soon."

I seated Patty, then back at the stove removed the soup and ladled it into our two bowls. It was steaming hot.

"Lila sure knows how to make soup," Patty said after tasting a spoonful.

"Yes, it seems especially excellent," I agreed.

After having this special treat, I cleared the table. I had planned on fixing something more, but we both found the soup to be quite filling. Patty went into the living room to try to continue her knitting, while I cleaned up the kitchen. When I was done I joined Patty in the living room for a quiet night of television. We had had enough excitement for one day, and both went to bed very early.

CHAPTER THIRTY-FIVE

During the next few days, Patty rested mostly on the couch in the living room. My shoulder was improving. Chief Wilson called the house and asked me to stop by to give a statement concerning the incident in Eagle Bay and the subsequent drowning of Kenneth Olson. Everyone felt badly that Olson had lost his life. Patty and I especially felt the impact of the tragic event. Life is precious to all of us. Chief Wilson told us that Olson's cousin from Atlanta, Georgia, had flown into Syracuse, identified the body, and had made arrangements with a funeral director to have the body cremated. The ruling by the coroner had been accidental death by drowning.

During these same days I wrote business letters to financial institutions. I also wrote a letter to Lillian Baldwin, thanking her for the use of her snowmobile. She had been a courageous and cooperative citizen who had come to my aid. Her response to Olson's attack on me almost certainly saved me from further injury, and her generous loan of her snowmobile had allowed me to get to Patty before Olson harmed her further.

Soon Patty returned to her position at John's Diner. Her black eye had healed well and my shoulder was feeling better. About a week before Christmas, we and a group of our friends decided to meet at Drews Restaurant for a party to celebrate the forthcoming holidays. Michael, the owner, made arrangements to have Penny Younger and the Rhythm Riders put on a show. On the night of the gathering, Penny and the band were in the process of playing some of my favorite songs as all of us arrived.

Michael Drew and Paula acted as our hosts. There were assorted snacks, hors d'oeuvres, small sandwiches arranged on trays, and a large punch bowl filled with a colorful concoction. Most of our friends were there for the gala occasion.

Talk still touched upon the recent dramatic event. Wilt thought to mention Patty's water-soaked snowmobile, telling her not to worry. If the insurance did not cover its replacement, he said, he had one stored in one of his barns that he didn't use anymore, and she was more than welcome to ride it. Patty was very touched and thanked him for his generosity, giving him a hug.

Some of the group danced to the music of the Rhythm Riders while others conversed about their plans for the holidays. You could feel the Christmas spirit rising. Michael had to refill the punch bowl once and bring out more snacks for the trays.

Everybody had a good time. Before the party broke up around eleven, everyone made a special stop to see Patty to wish her well.

Wilt asked Penny Younger if he could use the microphone to make a quick announcement. Penny handed it to him. Wilt spoke directly into the mike.

"Folks, before you leave, I think we should give the Rhythm Riders a big hand." Everybody clapped loudly. Wilt continued, "I want everyone to be careful going home tonight. The highways are a little slippery with the temperatures dipping into the mid-twenties. We don't need any more mishaps," he cautioned.

A few of the people went to the bar to continue their conversations. Patty and I said our farewells to everyone and left for home. On the way out the door we thanked Michael for his hospitality and the Rhythm Riders for their fine performance.

Patty and I sat in the Bronco for a few minutes while it

warmed up. Wilt had been right; the cold air was frigid and we wished we had worn heavier jackets. When the needle on the heat gauge moved toward the center, we backed up and headed toward Inlet.

We pulled into the yard just as two snowmobiles cut across our property towards the woods. I drove the Bronco as close to our home as possible. I turned the engine off, got out, and walked over to the passenger side to open the door for Patty. We could hear Ruben barking inside.

As soon as we entered our home, Ruben welcomed us by rushing over and rubbing his head against our legs. He was ecstatic to see us. I walked over to open the door to let the big fellow out for his last walk of the night. He bounded off towards the woods.

I helped Patty off with her coat and hung both of our coats in the closet. We were happy, but tired. After Ruben returned, he went to his air mattress. Patty and I then retired to the bedroom, where we read for a while. Just before turning off our reading lamps, and kissing goodnight, we both agreed we had had an enjoyable evening at Drew's with all of our friends.

Before drifting off to sleep, my thoughts wandered to our limited winter budget. We had to watch our pennies closely, as the fuel expenses ate up much of our household funds. We burned our woodstove as often as possible to help defray the costs and keep the fuel bills down. My investigative business, as usual, was slowing down, except for a few check cases and serving the civil process for attorneys. Once in a while Lieutenant Jack Doyle would call or stop by to see me. If I had any important information relative to serious criminal matters throughout the Adirondacks, I would share it with him. Because of my service in Troop S for a number of years, especially in the backcountry, my informants always kept me abreast of activities inside the Blue Line. I had always, on the job and off, paid attention to the remote areas, where sometimes evil can lurk.

The alarm clock went off at about 5:30. Patty slid out from under the warm covers and put the thermostat up. The furnace went on and I could hear the noise of the pipes as the warm air circulated through them.

"Honey, put the teakettle on for coffee, please?" I asked Patty.

"Will do, dear," she replied, yawning.

I forced myself out from between the warm covers and went into the bathroom. While the coffee water was heating, I shaved hastily so Patty could get dressed. I had continued to drive Patty to work. Her eye was just about healed, but the incident and subsequent drowning of Olson had shaken her. We had been through a tremendous strain.

I finished dressing and went to the kitchen. The teakettle was whistling away. I took two cups out of the cupboard and placed a half-spoon of decaf in each. I then poured the hot water into the cups. In a few minutes my blond-haired beauty came into the kitchen all dressed for work. We sat down and sipped our coffee. Ruben came over to us and lay down at our feet.

When I finished my coffee I went out and started the Bronco to warm it up by the time we left. I opened the rear of the car and told Ruben to get in. The big K-9 jumped into the back of the vehicle. I then went back inside the house for Patty. She had removed the cups from the table and had already washed and rinsed them. I helped her on with her heavier coat as the temperatures were hovering around twenty degrees.

Our driveway was icy, causing the Bronco to slide a little. As we approached the highway a pickup truck passed us, headed into town. I turned onto the highway and followed the truck. We moved along the highway slowly. The sanders could be seen ahead of us on the road with their flashing lights. It wouldn't be long before the thin coat of ice would be melting.

There was a line of cars and pickup trucks parked at the diner. I drove into the parking area and let Patty out after giving her a hug.

"I'll pick you up around 3:00 this afternoon, unless I hear differently from you. Love you, Patty." I hated to see her leave.

"Love you, too, Jason. Be careful on the highway!"

I waited there until she went inside. Then I went to Charlie's for a newspaper.

Before I headed back home, I drove down to Doctor Don's garage to pay him for the two used tires that he had mounted on Patty's Jeep. The garage was already busy even though it wasn't officially opened yet. Doctor Don was at his desk when I entered the office.

He looked up over his glasses with a puzzled expression on his face.

"What the heck are you doing here so early, Jason? I heard that you got knocked on your butt up in Eagle Bay. Is that true?" he asked incredulously.

"You heard that right, Doc! Yes, I did. The attacker came from behind me, knocking me down. And while I was struggling to stand, I received several kicks to my shoulder."

"Holy cow! That must have caught you by surprise." He looked perplexed.

"Doc, I was in a few skirmishes in the Marine Corps, but this wasn't played by the rules of combat." I was still wincing that Olson had caught me off guard.

"How's your shoulder now?" he asked.

"It's healing, Doc."

"Well, what can I do for you today, Jason?" he inquired.

"I want to pay you for the tires you put on the Jeep. And, as long as I'm here, could you check my heat gauge on the dashboard?"

"Sure can. I'll just be a few more minutes here," he acknowledged.

I went over and sat down. Two customers that I didn't recognize were reading papers across the room. I assumed that they were passing through and had experienced problems. I didn't make any inquiries. But I was always curious when it came to strangers in town.

In a few minutes, Doc got up from his desk and went out to the Bronco. He drove it around to a side bay, opened the overhead doors, and drove the Bronco inside. Ruben didn't make a move. Doc knew the dog and they liked each other.

It wasn't long before Doctor Don appeared, wiping his hands with a paper towel.

"You're all set, Jason. It was just a loose wire. You should get a good reading on that gauge now, " he assured me.

"How much do I owe you?"

"Just for the tires, Jason. Here's the bill," he said as he handed it to me.

I paid the amount shown.

"Are you sure that's enough for the tires and mounting them?" I asked.

"That's just right."

I thanked Don and left. One of the strangers looked up from his paper and stared at me with a blank look. I had seen the type before. The look on his face made me feel uneasy. I couldn't put my finger on it, but something wasn't right. My sixth sense alerted me. Those two fellows didn't seem to fit the profile of legitimate customers. I left the garage as Don backed the Bronco out for me. Don didn't say anything, but went back into the bay and closed the large door.

I thought, *Is Doctor Don in some kind of trouble? How? What kind?*

I started down the road toward home, but felt more and more certain that something was amiss with the two strangers. I turned around and headed back toward Doctor Don's. This time, though, I drove right past the garage and pulled off onto a side street. I took Ruben's leash out of the glove compartment and snapped it onto his collar. I walked quietly back towards the garage, approaching the windows from the rear of the building. I looked through the glass pane. The two strangers were out of their chairs and it looked as though they were in the process of tying up Doctor Don's wrists. Doc wasn't wearing his glasses, and there was an oil-wiping cloth shoved into his mouth. The two strangers were angrily demanding money, and Doc kept shaking his head back and forth as if to say no.

I knew I had to act fast. My stomach started to knot up. My adrenaline began to pump. It was a little too early for our police patrols in the area, and the matter couldn't wait. I held the leash tightly and Ruben came close to me. Fortunately he remained quiet. I knew that there was a small door on the side of the garage. I quietly opened it and entered the working part of the garage. I hadn't seen any weapons displayed by the strangers. I looked around for a weapon and found a large wrench. Ruben was picking up my tension now. Armed with the wrench and trying to control my K-9, I edged my way along the hallway. I had noted that the two strangers were of medium build, one a little taller than the other. Ruben and I crept slowly towards the waiting room. Doctor Don's radio was playing western music from the Boonville station, and it was a blessing that it was, for it offered me a good opportunity to make my move. I didn't want to strike the taller one in the head, but decided that a good blow to the shoulder would put him out of action.

I could tell that Ruben was on alert. His ears were standing at attention. I knew he would obey my command and could still make the bite. I was close to the back of the taller man. I quickly raised the long-handled wrench and struck his right shoulder with sufficient force. He screamed in pain and went down to the floor.

"Ruben, attack!" I commanded.

With lightning speed, the K-9 charged the smaller man, connected with the upper calf of his right leg, and made the bite. The would-be thief went down on the ground in pain, calling me foul names that even I had never heard before. I moved fast to untie Doctor Don, gently grabbing the wiping cloth away from his mouth at the same time.

"Where in the hell did you come from, Jason?" he asked gratefully.

"Call the police, Doc! I'll watch them."

Doc dialed the telephone, as Ruben stood over the smaller man in a threatening mode. I coldly told the smaller man not to move or the dog would go for his throat. The man was holding his bitten leg, but didn't try to move. The taller man was still calling me names. He was writhing in pain on the floor of the office. I told him to shut up or I'd hit the other shoulder, too.

Both of the perps were out of commission. Doctor Don wasn't hurt, but he did tell me that the two intruders had threatened his life.

I went over to the men lying on the floor, wondering where they had come from. I told them who I was and that I was making a citizen's arrest. Just then Chief Todd Wilson came through the door.

"Hi, Doc. Hello, Jason," the chief said. "What's going on here?" His eyes quickly scanned the room.

I described to Chief Wilson what had transpired from the time I came into the garage to pay for my tires up to the present time. I told him that there had been no time to waste. I had had to take the immediate, appropriate action against the two strangers as they had threatened the life of Doctor Don. I told the chief that I had made a citizen's arrest and I was turning the two men over to him.

The chief nodded and thanked me. He told us the two men had to be treated for the dog bite and the smashed shoulder. He requested sworn statements from Doc and me.

The ambulance arrived at the scene as well as other Town of Webb police personnel. The police examined the scene of the crime, taking some photos. Before the chief accompanied the ambulance to the medical center, he asked me to meet him at the police station. I was about to leave the garage when Doc came over to me.

"Jason, I owe you. Thanks for being there for me." His face showed his heartfelt feeling.

"You don't owe me anything, Doc. I just had a bad feeling about those fellows."

"Your sixth sense worked well this morning. I didn't know you could move so fast." His glasses slipped down to the end of his nose.

"We were both lucky, Doc. It's a good thing that I decided to bring Ruben along this morning when I dropped Patty off at work. I couldn't be sure he would obey the attack command any more. I was hoping." I leaned down to pat my faithful K-9.

"Well, Jason, you know I'm not a man of a lot of words, but I want to thank you. I truly believe those people were going to do me harm. They pulled into the garage claiming they had engine trouble. Ha!"

I could tell that Doc was sincere. "You're a good man, and besides if they'd gotten you, who else would work on our vehicles?" I joked. "We all need you, Doctor Don."

Before I climbed into the Bronco to leave for the police station, I walked Ruben to the adjacent lot next to the garage, where I removed his leash. He ran off for a few minutes and returned shortly. He acted frisky, wanting to play.

"No time for play, Ruben," I told him. "But I'll have an extra biscuit for you later.

We went to the Bronco and I opened the rear gate. He jumped in. Several pickup trucks and cars were pulling into Doctor Don's garage for repairs. He would surely have a tale to tell his customers that morning. I knew that we had both been lucky.

When I arrived at the police station, Chief Wilson was just pulling in from the medical center. I parked the Bronco and followed him inside. The telephone was ringing. He answered it.

I sat down in the waiting area while the chief conversed on the telephone. I didn't listen to what he was actually saying, but I did notice a look of surprise come over his face. He finally finished talking and hung up the phone.

"Jason Black, you never cease to amaze me," Todd said with a grin.

"How's that, Chief?" I was definitely curious.

"Well, the two men that we have over to the medical center under guard are wanted in Beckley, West Virginia, for robbery and assault. They seriously injured a garage owner three days ago. The same M.O.: early in the morning when the garage owner was alone. They may be involved in other incidents in the State of Maryland and also southern Pennsylvania. You did a good job, Jason. You probably saved Doctor Don from being severely beaten. These two birds won't talk, choosing to remain mute for the time being. What I need from you is a sworn statement from you relative to the entire incident."

"You know I'll be glad to give you a statement, Chief," I responded.

Chief Wilson took my statement. He had secured the wrench that I had used and tagged it. The car they were driving was impounded and searched. Chief Wilson didn't disclose to me what evidence, if any, was found in the vehicle. The chief did indicate that the two men would not even give him their names. It was after the noon hour before I left the station for home. I knew the town would be buzzing with the story about Doctor Don. I was happy that the Doc didn't get hurt. We were both lucky, and I knew that Chief Wilson and his department had a lot of work ahead of them concerning this case.

When I arrived at our log-home, I put Ruben in his run. He immediately went into his doghouse and lay down. When I entered the house, the telephone was ringing. I answered it.

"Hello, Jason. What happened? I've been hearing all kinds of stories. Are you all right, honey? You're not hurt, are you?" Patty sounded nervous and upset.

"Sweetheart, settle down. No, I'm not hurt. I'll tell you all about it this afternoon when I pick you up. I didn't want to disturb you at work. I love you." I wanted to soothe her fears. Now I realized I should have contacted her.

"Okay, dearest, I'll see you about three this afternoon." She sounded more relaxed.

"Talk with you later, honey." I hung up the phone.

The rest of the afternoon I spent in the office working on some of my bad-check cases and tallying up the number of legal papers I had served for the attorneys.

Tom Huston called, and I was pleased to hear that he was feeling more like himself. He had returned from his trip, and wanted to share with me the news about the goods that had been taken from his properties. The troopers had been able to recover a substantial number of items that had been stolen. He again urged me to join his staff at Lake Placid. When I politely refused his generous offer, he told me that the position of

Security Director at the Breakshire would always be there for me if I should change my mind. I was honored, but knew that Patty and I both remained dedicated to the Old Forge region.

"Tom, I'll always be available to assist you in any matter that may develop in the future. You can be assured of that."

"Jason, I appreciate it. And you should also know that you have made it possible for me to feel at ease calling the troopers at Raybrook on any matter," he remarked.

"Tom, they're a good group of professionals, and Lieutenant Doyle has assured me that he and his able staff will respond to any event you deem important. They may be contacting you sometime in the near future regarding the holding of one of their retirement parties or retiree events at the lodge."

"I want them to know they're always welcome here at the lodge, Jason."

"I know that, Tom, and so do they. I'll be talking to you again, but I guess I'd better get going now. It was a pleasure to hear from you."

"The pleasure is all mine. So long for now."

I heard the click and I hung up the phone.

When I contacted Dale Rush by telephone, I was pleased to hear that a date had been set for their wedding in the autumn. I made a mental note to write it on our new calendar. He told me that Evelyn O'Brien was definitely the lady for him. I agreed.

My call to the Mountain Bank assured me that several of their customers' discrepancies had been taken care of. Some had claimed, of course, that it was an error in their checkbooks. I was pleased to hear that once again diplomacy had gone a long way in the retrieval of funds. I had employed it in my business dealings with several of the bank's customers.

When I finished with my office chores, I swept and mopped the kitchen floor. I then dusted the furniture and ran the cleaner. It was a continuing pleasure to me that both Patty and I liked to keep everything neat.

I looked out the window and saw that it had begun to snow. Large flakes spiraled as they fell to the ground. This fresh snow would be welcomed by the hundreds of snowmobile enthusiasts enjoying our trail system. Patty and I, too, would be out on the trails again soon. The snowmobile that Wilt was giving her to use was in excellent condition. We only awaited some free time. I looked at the clock. It was now two-thirty, and I had to pick Patty up at John's by three.

The snow was falling heavily when I pulled into the parking lot diner. Patty was on the porch waiting for me. I pulled close to the steps. Her blond hair was flowing on her shoulders below her blue knitted cap. I was a lucky guy.

I reached to my right and opened the door. She climbed in. I leaned over and kissed her on the cheek.

"Hi, honey. How was your day, sweetheart?"

She looked at me with loving eyes. I was waiting for her reply. She smiled more widely, hesitated, and then spoke:

"Jason, I think I may be pregnant."

(continued from back cover)

Born in Theresa, New York he moved to Syracuse during the late 1930's, then to Throopsville, New York, where he graduated from Port Byron Central School in 1948.

He served three years and three months with the 27th Infantry Division until 1950 when he entered the U.S. Air Force during the Korean War, serving in Keflavik, Iceland. In 1953 he became a member of the New York State Police where he served in Troop "D" and Troop "B" first in uniform and then as member of the Bureau of Criminal Investigation. After retiring he served in the banking sector for seven years. A life long learner he received his B.S. Degree from the State University of New York. He resides in the Adirondack Park of New York State. He is a published poet and writer of short stories.

John Briant describes the Adirondacks like a master painter. But then he zooms in to illuminate the corruption or heroism of the people who either defile or fight to preserve life in the midst of nature's abundance. We see all this through the hardened eyes of PI Jason Black who clearly loves these precious mountains. We are in good hands for the treacherous climb. –

Ed Dee, Retired NYPD Lieutenant
Author of *The Con Man's Daughter*

Private Investigator/retired cop Jason Black continues his quest for a life of peace and quiet in the idyllic Adirondack Mountains; however, crime, adventure and danger seem to confront him at every fork and turn in the road. Many good friends and his love for beautiful Patty Olson Black keep him on track as he strives to rid his beloved environment of crime. Adirondack Detective III continues the delightful saga that will establish Jason Black, ala, John Briant as an Adirondack hero and eventual legend.

Wayne E. Beyea

http://webpages.charter.net/web2106